The Coming of Vertumnus
and Other Stories

The Coming of Vertumnus
and Other Stories

IAN WATSON

VICTOR GOLLANCZ

LONDON

First published in Great Britain 1994
by Victor Gollancz
A Cassell imprint
Villiers House, 41/47 Strand, London WC2N 5JE

'The Coming of Vertumnus' first appeared in *Interzone*, 1992;
'Swimming with the Salmon' first appeared in *Interzone*, 1992;
'The Bible in Blood' first appeared in *Weird Tales*, 1994; 'Happy
Hour' first appeared in *Walls of Fear* edited by Kathryn Cramer,
1990; 'Talk of the Town' first appeared in *Fires of the Past:
Thirteen Contemporary Fantasies about Hometowns* edited by Anne
Devereaux Jordan, 1991; 'Looking Down on You' first appeared
in *The Magazine of Fantasy and Science Fiction*, 1992; 'The Tale of
Peg and the Brain' first appeared in *Narrow Houses* edited by
Peter Crowther, 1992; 'Life in the Groove' first appeared in *In
Dreams* edited by Paul J. McAuley and Kim Newman, 1992;
'Virtually Lucid Lucy' first appeared in *New Worlds 2* edited by
David Garnett, 1992; 'The Odour of Cocktail Cigarettes' first
appeared in *Isaac Asimov's Science Fiction Magazine*, 1991;
'Nanoware Time' first appeared in shorter form in *Isaac
Asimov's Science Fiction Magazine*, 1989, and in present extended
form as first part of Tor SF Double No. 29 (New York: Tor, A
Tom Doherty Associates Book, 1991).

© Ian Watson 1994

The right of Ian Watson to be identified as author of
this work has been asserted by him in accordance with
the Copyright, Designs and Patents Act, 1988.

A catalogue record for this book is
available from the British Library

Typeset at The Spartan Press Ltd,
Lymington, Hants
Printed in Great Britain by
St Edmundsbury Press Ltd, Bury St Edmunds, Suffolk

Contents

This collection,

for Leena and Juhani

The Coming of Vertumnus

Do you know the *Portrait of Jacopo Strada*, which Titian painted in 1567 or so?

Bathed in golden light, this painting shows us a rich connoisseur displaying a nude female statuette which is perhaps eighteen inches high. Oh yes, full-bearded Signor Strada is prosperous – in his black velvet doublet, his cerise satin shirt, and his ermine cloak. He holds that voluptuous little Venus well away from an unseen spectator. He gazes at that spectator almost shiftily. Strada is exposing his Venus to view, yet he's also withholding her proprietorially so as to whet the appetite.

With her feet supported on his open right hand, and her back resting across his left palm, the sculpted woman likewise leans away as if in complicity with Strada. How carefully his fingers wrap around her. One finger eclipses a breast. Another teases her neck. Not that her charms aren't on display. *Her* hands are held high, brushing her shoulders. Her big-navelled belly and mons Veneris are on full show. A slight crossing of her knees hints at a helpless, lascivious reticence.

She arouses the desire to acquire and to handle her, a yearning that is at once an artistic and an erotic passion. Almost, she seems to be a homunculus – a tiny woman bred within an alchemist's vessel by the likes of a Paracelsus, who had died only some twenty-five years previously.

I chose this portrait of Jacopo Strada as the cover for my book, *Aesthetic Concupiscence*. My first chapter was devoted to an analysis of the implications of this particular painting . . .

Jacopo Strada was an antiquary who spent many years in the employ of the Habsburg court, first at Vienna and then at Prague, as Keeper of Antiquities. He procured and catalogued gems and coins as well as classical statuary.

Coins were important to the Habsburg Holy Roman Emperors, because coins bore the portraits of monarchs. A collection of coins was a visible genealogy of God-anointed rulers. Back on Christmas Day in the year 800 the Pope had crowned Charlemagne as the first 'Emperor of the Romans'. The Church had decided it no longer quite had the clout to run Europe politically as well as spiritually. This imperial concoction – at times heroic, at other times hiccuping along – lasted until 1806. That was when the last Holy Roman Emperor, Francis II, abdicated without successor so as to thwart Napoleon from grabbing the title. By then, as they say, the Emperor presided over piecemeal acres which were neither an empire, nor Roman, nor holy. Of course, effectively the Habsburg dynasty had hijacked the title of Emperor, which was supposed to be elective.

History has tended to view the Habsburg court of Rudolph II at Prague in the late 1570s and 80s as wonky, wacky, and weird: an excellent watering-hole for any passing nut-cases, such as alchemists, hermetic occultists, or astrologers – who of course, back then, were regarded as 'scientists'. *Not* that true science wasn't well represented, too! Revered astronomer Tycho Brahe burst his bladder with fatal result at Rudolph's court, due to that Emperor's eccentric insistence that no one might be excused from table till his Caesarian Majesty had finished revelling.

Botanists were very busy classifying plants there, and naturalists were taxonomizing exotic wildlife (of which many specimens graced Rudolph's zoo) – just as Strada himself tried to impose order and methodology upon ancient Venuses.

Strada resigned and quit Prague in 1579, perhaps in irritation that his aesthetic criteria held less sway over Rudolph than those of another adviser on the Imperial art collection – namely *Giuseppe Archimboldo* . . .

My troubles began when I received a phone call at Central St Martin's School of Art in Charing Cross Road, where I lectured part-time in History of the Same. The caller was one John Lascelles. He introduced himself as the UK personal assistant to

Thomas Rumbold Wright. Oil magnate and art collector, no less. Lascelles' voice had a youthfully engaging, though slightly prissy timbre.

Was I the Jill Donaldson who had written *Aesthetic Concupiscence*? I who had featured scintillatingly on *Art Debate at Eight* on Channel 4 TV? Mr Wright would very much like to meet me. He had a proposition to make. Might a car be sent for me, to whisk me the eighty-odd miles from London to the North Cotswolds?

What sort of proposition?

Across my mind there flashed a bizarre image of myself as a diminutive Venus sprawling in this oil billionaire's acquisitive, satin-shirted arms. For of course in my book I had cleverly put the stiletto-tipped boot into all such as he, who contributed to the obscene lunacy of art prices.

Maybe Thomas Rumbold Wright was seeking a peculiar form of recompense for my ego-puncturing stiletto stabs, since he – capricious bachelor – was certainly mentioned once in my book . . .

'What sort of proposition?'

'I've no idea,' said Lascelles, boyishly protesting innocence.

I waited. However, Lascelles was very good at silences, whereas I am not.

'Surely you must have *some* idea, Mr Lascelles?'

'Mr Wright will tell you, Ms Donaldson.'

Why not? Why not indeed? I had always revelled in paradoxes, and it must be quite paradoxical – not to mention constituting a delicious piece of fieldwork – for Jill Donaldson to accept an invitation from Thomas R. Wright, lavisher of untold millions upon old canvases.

One of my prime paradoxes – in my 'Stratagems of Deceit' chapter – involved comparison between the consumption of sensual fine art, and of visual pornography. I perpetrated an iconography of the latter based upon interviews I conducted with 'glamour' photographers on the job. No, I *didn't* see it as my mission to deconstruct male-oriented sexism. Not a bit of it. That would be banal. I came to praise porn, not to bury it. Those sumptuous nudes in oils of yore were the buoyant, respectable porn of their day. What we needed nowadays, I enthused –

tongue in cheek, several tongues in cheek indeed – were issues of *Penthouse* magazine entirely painted by latter-day Masters, with tits by the Titians of today, vulvas by Veroneses, pubes by populist Poussins . . . Ha!

I was buying a little flat in upper Bloomsbury, with the assistance of Big Brother Robert who was a bank manager in Oxford. Plump sanctimonious Bob regarded this scrap of property as a good investment. Indeed, but for his support, I could hardly have coped. Crowded with books and prints, on which I squandered too much, Chez Donaldson was already distinctly cramped. I *could* hold a party in it – so long as I only invited a dozen people and we spilled on to the landing.

Even amidst slump and eco-puritanism, London property prices still bore a passing resemblance to Impressionist price-tags. Perhaps eco-puritanism actually *sustained* high prices, since it seemed that one ought to be penalized for wishing to live fairly centrally in a city, contributing to the sewage burden and resources and power demand of megalopolis, and whatnot.

Well, we were definitely into an era of radical repressiveness. The Eco bandwagon was rolling. Was one's lifestyle environ-mentally friendly, third-world friendly, future friendly? The no-smoking, no-car, no-red-meat, no-frilly-knickers, sackcloth-and-ashes straitjacket was tightening; and while I might have seemed to be on that side ethically as regards the conspicuous squandering of megamillions on paintings, I simply did not buy the package. Perhaps the fact that I smoked cigarettes – oh penalized sin! – accounted in part for my antipathy to the Goody-Goodies. Hence my naughtiness in exalting (tongues in cheek) such a symptom of unreconstructed consciousness as porn. Paradox, paradox. I did like to *provoke*.

How many lovers had such a tearaway as myself had by the age of thirty-one? Just three, in fact; one of them another woman, a painting student.

Peter, Annie, and Phil. No one at the moment. I wasn't exactly outrageous in private life.

Peter had been the prankster, the mercurial one. For his 'God of the Deep' exhibition he wired fish skeletons into the contours of bizarre Gothic cathedrals, which he displayed in tanks of water. Goldfish were the congregations – was this art, or a joke? Several less savoury anarchistic exploits finally disenchanted me with Peter – about the time I decided definitively that I really was an art historian and a critic (though of capricious spirit).

Sending a Mercedes, with darkened windows, to collect me could have wiped out my street cred. Personally, I regarded this as a *Happening*.

Mind you, I did experience a twinge of doubt – along the lines that maybe I ought to phone someone (Phil? Annie? Definitely not Peter . . .) to confide where I was being taken, just in case 'something *happens* to me . . .' I didn't do so, yet the spice of supposed danger added a certain frisson.

When my doorbell rang, the radio was bemoaning the death of coral reefs, blanched leprous by the extinction of the symbiotic algae in them. This was sad, of course, *tragic*; yet I didn't intend to scourge myself personally, as the participants in the programme seemed to feel was appropriate.

The driver proved to be a Dutchman called Kees, pronounced Case, who 'did things' for Rumby – as he referred to Thomas Rumbold Wright. Athletic-looking and bearded, courteous and affable, Case wore jeans, Reeboks, and an open-necked checked shirt. No uniform or peaked cap for this driver, who opened the front door of the Merc so that I should sit next to him companionably, not behind in splendid isolation. Case radiated the easy negligence of a cultured bodyguard-if-need-be. I was dressed in similar informal style, being determined not to doll myself up in awe for the grand encounter – though I refused to wear trainers with designer names on them.

Although Wright maintained a corporate headquarters in Texas, he personally favoured his European bastion, Bexford Hall. This had recently been extended by the addition of a mini-mock-Tudor castle wing to house his art in even higher security. The *Sunday Times* colour supplement had featured photos of this jail of art. (Did it come complete with a dungeon, I wondered?)

The mid-June weather was chilly and blustery – either typical British summer caprice or a Greenhouse spasm, depending on your ideology.

As we were heading out towards the motorway, we soon

passed one of those hoardings featuring a giant poster of Archimboldo's portrait of Rudolph II as an assembly of fruits, vegetables, and flowers. Ripe pear nose; flushed round cheeks of peach and apple; cherry and mulberry eyes; spiky chestnut husk of a chin; corn-ear brows, and so on, and so on.

The Emperor Rudolph as Vertumnus, Roman god of fruit trees, of growth and transformation. Who cared about that particular snippet of art-historical info? Across the portrait's chest splashed the Eco message, WE ARE ALL PART OF NATURE. This was part of that massive and highly successful Green propaganda campaign exploiting Archimboldo's 'nature-heads' – a campaign which absolutely caught the eye in the most persuasive style.

These posters had been adorning Europe and America and wherever else for the best part of two years now. Indeed, they'd become such a radiant emblem of eco-consciousness, such a part of the mental landscape, that I doubted they would *ever* disappear from our streets. People even wore miniatures as badges – as though true humanity involved becoming a garlanded bundle of fruit and veg, with a cauliflower brain, perhaps.

Case slowed and stared at that hoarding.

'Rudolph the red-nosed,' I commented.

Somewhat to my surprise, Case replied, 'Ah, and Rudolph loved Archimboldo's jokes so much that he made him into a count! Sense of humour's sadly missing these days, don't you think?'

My driver must have been boning up on his art history. The Green poster campaign was certainly accompanied by no background info about the artist whose images they were ripping off – or perhaps one ought to say 'recuperating' for the present day . . . rather as an ad agency might exploit the Mona Lisa to promote tampons. (*Why is* she *smiling* . . . ?)

'Those paintings weren't *just* jokes,' I demurred.

'No, and neither are those posters.' Case seemed to loathe those, as though he would like to tear them all down. He speeded up, and soon we reached the motorway.

Under the driving-mirror – where idiots used to hang woolly dice, and where nowadays people often hung plastic apples or pears, either sincerely or else in an attempt to immunize their vehicles against eco-vandals – there dangled a little model . . . of a rather complex-looking space station. The model was made of silver, or was at least silver-plated. It swung to and fro as we drove. At times, when I glanced that way, I confused rear-view mirror with model so that it appeared as if a gleaming futuristic craft was pursuing us up the M40, banking and yawing behind us.

Down where my left hand rested I found power-controls for the passenger seat. So I raised the leather throne – yes indeed, I was sitting on a dead animal's hide, and no wonder the windows were semi-opaque from outside. I lowered the seat and reclined it. I extruded and recessed the lumbar support. Now that I'd discovered this box of tricks, I just couldn't settle on the most restful position for myself. Supposing the seat had been inflexible, there'd have been no problem. Excessive tech, perhaps? I felt fidgety.

'Do you mind if I smoke?' I asked Case.

'Rumby smokes in this car,' was his answer, which didn't quite confide his own personal feelings, unless the implication was that these were largely irrelevant amongst Wright's entourage.

Case ignored the sixty-mile-an-hour fuel-efficiency speed limit, though he drove very safely in this cushioned tank of a car. He always kept an eye open well ahead and well behind as if conscious of possible interception, by a police patrol, or – who knows? – by Green vigilante kidnappers.

Bexford Hall was in the triangle between Stow-on-the-Wold, Broadway, and Winchcombe, set in a wooded river valley cutting through the rolling, breezy, sheep-grazed uplands.

The house was invisible from the leafy side-road, being masked by the high, wire-tipped stone boundary wall in good repair, and then by trees. Case opened wrought iron gates electronically from the car – apparently the head gardener and family lived in the high-pitched gatehouse alongside – and we purred up a winding drive.

Lawns with topiary hedges fronted the mullion-windowed house. Built of soft golden limestone around a courtyard, Chez

Wright somewhat resembled a civilian castle even before his addition of the bastioned, bastard-architectural art wing. A helicopter stood on a concrete apron. A Porsche, a Jaguar, and various lesser beasts were parked in a row on gravel. A satellite dish graced the rear slate-tiled roof, from which Tudor chimneys rose.

The sun blinked through, though clouds still scudded.

And so – catching a glimpse en route of several people at computer consoles, scrutinizing what were probably oil prices – we passed through to John Lascelles' office, where the casual piles of glossy art books mainly caught my eye.

Having delivered me, Case left to 'do things' . . .

Lascelles was tall, willowy, and melancholy. He favoured dark mauve corduroy trousers and a multi-pocketed purple shirt loaded with many pens, not to mention a clip-on walkie-talkie. On account of the ecclesiastical hues I imagined him as a sort of secular court chaplain to Wright. His smile was a pursed, wistful affair, though there was that boyish lilt to his voice which had misled me on the phone. His silences were the truer self.

He poured coffee for me from a percolator; then he radioed news of my arrival. It seemed that people communicated by personal radio in the house. In reply he received a crackly splutter of Texan which I hardly caught.

Lascelles sat and scrutinized me while I drank and smoked a cigarette; on his littered desk I'd noted an ashtray with a cheroot stub crushed in it.

Lascelles steepled his hands. He was cataloguing me: a new person collected – at least potentially – by his non-royal master, as he himself must once have been collected.

Woman. Thirty-one. Mesomorphic build; though not exactly chunky. Small high breasts. Tight curly brown hair cropped quite short. Violet vampiric lipstick. Passably callipygian ass.

Then in bustled *Rumby* – as I simply had to think of the man thereafter.

Rumby was a roly-poly fellow attired in crumpled bronze slacks and a floppy buff shirt with lots of pockets for pens, calculator, radio. He wore scruffy trainers, though I didn't suppose that he jogged around his estate. His white complexion said otherwise. His face was quizzically owlish, with large spectacles – frames of mottled amber – magnifying his eyes into brown orbs; and his thinning feathery hair was rebellious.

He beamed, almost tangibly projecting *energy*. He pressed my flesh quickly. He drew me along in his slipstream from Lascelles' office down a walnut-panelled corridor. We entered a marble-floored domed hall which housed gleaming spotlit models. Some in perspex cases, others hanging. Not models of oil-rigs, oh no. Models of a Moon base, of spacecraft, of space stations.

Was Rumby a little boy at heart? Was this his den? Did he play with these toys?

'What do you think about space?' he asked me.

Mischief urged me to be contrary, yet I told him the truth.

'Personally,' I assured him, 'I think that if we cop out of space now, as looks highly likely, then we'll be locked up here on Mother Earth for ever after eating a diet of beans and being repressively good with "Keep off the Grass" signs everywhere. Oh dear, we mustn't mess up Mars by going there the way we messed up Earth! Mess up Mars, for Christ's sake? It's *dead* to start with – a desert of rust. I think if we can grab all those clean resources and free energy in space, we'd be crazy to hide in our shell instead. But there's neo-puritanism for you.'

Rumby rubbed his hands. 'And if Green propaganda loses us our launch window of the next fifty years or so, then we've lost for ever because we'll have spent all our spunk. I knew you'd be *simpatico*, Jill. I've read *Aesthetic Concubines* twice.'

'*Concupiscence*, actually,' I reminded him.

'Let's call it *Concubines*. That's easier to say.'

Already my life and mind were being mutated by Rumby . . .

'So how did you extrapolate my views on space from a book on the art market?' I asked.

He tapped his brow. 'I picked up on your anti-repressive streak and the perverse way you think. Am I right?'

'Didn't you regard my book as a bit, well, rude?'

'I don't intend to take things personally when the future of the human race is at stake. It is, you know. It is. Green pressures are going to nix everyone's space budget. Do you know they're pressing to limit the number of rocket launches to a measly dozen per year *world-wide* because of the exhaust gases? And all those would have to be Earth-Resources-relevant. Loony-tune environ-*mentalists*! There's a *religious* fervour spreading like clap in a cathouse. It's screwing the world's brains.' How colourfully he phrased things. Was he trying to throw me off balance? Maybe he was oblivious to other people's opinions. I gazed blandly at him.

'Jill,' he confided, 'I'm part of a pro-space pressure group of industrialists called the Star Club. We've commissioned surveys. Do you know, in one recent poll forty-five per cent of those questioned said that they'd happily give up quote all the benefits of "science" if they could live in a more natural world without radioactivity? Can you believe such scuzzbrains? We *know* how fast this Eco gangrene is spreading. How do we disinfect it? Do we use rational scientific argument? You might as well reason with a hippo on heat.'

'Actually, I don't see how this involves me . . .'

'*We'll* need to use some tricks. So, come and view the Wright Collection.'

He took me through a security-coded steel door into his climate-controlled sanctum of masterpieces.

Room after room. Rubens. Goya. Titian. And other lesser luminaries . . .

. . . till we came to the door of an inner sanctum.

I half expected to find the Mona Lisa herself within. But no . . .

On an easel sat . . . a totally pornographic, piscine portrait. A figure made of many fishes (along with a few crustaceans).

A female figure.

A spread-legged naked woman, red lobster dildo clutched in one octopus-hand, frigging herself. A slippery, slithery, lubricious Venus composed of eels and catfish and trout and a score of other species. Prawn labia, with legs and feelers as pubic hair . . . The long suckery fingers of her other octopus-hand teased a pearl nipple . . .

The painting just had to be by Archimboldo. It was very clever and, mm, persuasive. It also oozed lust and perversity.

'So how do you like her?' asked Rumby.

'That lobster's rather a nippy notion,' I said.

'It isn't a lobster,' he corrected me. 'It's a cooked freshwater crayfish.'

'She's, well, fairly destabilizing if you happen to drool over all those "We are part of Nature" posters.'

'Right! And Archimboldo painted a *dozen* such porn portraits for private consumption by crazy Emperor Rudolph.'

'He *did*?' This was astonishing news.

'I've laid hands on them all, though they aren't all here.'

Rumby directed me to a table where a portfolio lay. Opening this, I turned over a dozen large glossy colour reproductions – of masturbating men made of mushrooms and autumnal fruits, men with large hairy nuts and spurting seed; of licking lesbian ladies composed of marrows and lettuce leaves . . .

'You researched all the background bio on Strada, Jill. Nobody knows what sort of things our friend Archy might have been painting between 1576 and 1587 before he went back home to Milan, hmm?'

'I thought he was busy arranging festivals for Rudolph. Masques and tournaments and processions.'

'That isn't *all* he was arranging. Rudy was fairly nutty.'

'Oh, I don't know if that's quite fair to Rudolph . . .'

'What, to keep a chained lion in the hall? To sleep in a different bed every night? His mania for exotica! Esoterica! Erotica! A pushover for any passing magician. Bizarre foibles. Loopy as King Ludo of Bavaria – yet with *real power*. The power to indulge himself – secretly – in orgies and weird erotica, there in vast Ratzen Castle in Prague.'

I wondered about the provenance of these hitherto unknown paintings.

To which, Rumby gave a very plausible answer.

When the Swedes under the command of von Wrangel sacked Prague in 1648 as their contribution to the Thirty Years War, they pillaged the imperial collections. Thus a sheaf of Archimboldos ended up in Skoklosters Castle at Bålsta in Sweden.

'Skoklosters *Slott*. Kind of evocative name, huh?'

When Queen Christina converted to Catholicism in 1654 and abdicated the Swedish throne, she took many of those looted art

treasures with her to Rome itself – with the exception of so-
called *German* art, which she despised. In her eyes, Archimboldo was part of German art.

However, in the view of her catechist (who was a subtle priest),
those locked-away *porn* paintings were a different kettle of fish.
The Vatican should take charge of those and keep them *sub rosa*.
Painters were never fingered by the Inquisition, unlike authors
of the written word. Bonfires of merely lewd material were
never an issue in an era when clerics often liked a fuck.
Nevertheless, such paintings might serve as a handy blackmail
tool against Habsburg Emperors who felt tempted to act too
leniently towards Protestants in their domains. A blot on the
Habsburg scutcheon, suggesting a strain of lunacy.

The cardinal-diplomat to whom the paintings were consigned
deposited them for safe keeping in the crypt at a certain
enclosed convent of his patronage. There, as it happened, they
remained until discovered by a private collector in the 1890s. By
then the convent had fallen on hard times. Our collector
relieved the holy mothers of the embarrassing secret heritage in
return for a substantial donation . . .

'It's a watertight story,' concluded Rumby, blinking owlishly
at me. 'Of course it's also a complete lie . . .'

The dirty dozen Archimboldos were forgeries perpetrated in
Holland within the past couple of years, to Rumby's specifica-
tions, by a would-be surrealist.

I stared at the fishy masturbatress, fascinated.

'They're fine forgeries,' he enthused. 'Painted on antique oak
board precisely eleven millimetres thick. Two base layers of
white lead, chalk, and charcoal slack . . .' He expatiated with
the enthusiasm of a petrochemist conducting an assay of crude.
The accuracy of the lipid and protein components. The pig-
ments consisting of azurite, yellow lead, malachite . . . Mr Oil
seemed to know rather a lot about such aspects of oil painting.

He waved his hand impatiently. 'Point is, it'll stand up under
X-ray, infra-red, most sorts of analysis. This is perfectionist
forgery with serious money behind it. Oh yes, sponsored
exhibition in Europe, book, prints, postcards, media
scandal . . . ! These naughty Archies are going to fuck all those

Green Fascists in the eyeballs. Here's their patron saint with his pants down. Here's what red-nosed Rudy really got off on. Nobody'll be able to gaze dewy-eyed at those posters any more, drooling about the sanctity of nature. *This* is nature – red in dildo and labia. A fish-fuck. Their big image campaign will blow up in their faces – ludicrously, obscenely. Can you beat the power of an image? Why yes, you *can* – with an anti-image! We'll have done something really positive to save the space budget. You'll write the intro to the art book, Jenny, in your inimitable style. Scholarly – but provocative.'

'I will?'

'Yes, because I'll pay you three-quarters of a million dollars.'

A flea-bite to Rumby, really . . .

The budget for this whole escapade was probably ten times that. Or more. Would that represent the output of one single oil well for a year? A month . . . ? I really had no idea.

Aside from our crusade for space, smearing egg conspicuously on the face of the ecofreaks might materially assist Rumby's daily business and prove to be a sound investment, since he profited so handsomely by pumping out the planet's non-renewable resources.

'*And* because you want to sock Green Fascism, Jill. And on account of how this is so splendidly, provocatively perverse.'

Was he right, or was he right?

He was certainly different from the kind of man I'd expected to meet.

Obviously I mustn't spill the beans in the near future. *Consequently* the bulk of my fee would be held on deposit in my name in a Zurich bank, but would only become accessible to me five years after publication of *Archimboldo Erotico* . . .

Until then I would need to lead roughly the same life as usual – plus the need to defend my latest opus amongst my peers and on TV and in magazines and wherever else. Rumby – or Chaplain Lascelles – would certainly strive to ensure a media circus, if none such burgeoned of its own accord. I would be Rumby's front woman.

I liked the *three-quarters* of a million aspect. This showed that Rumby had subtlety. One million would have been a blatant bribe.

I also liked Rumby himself.

I had indeed been collected.

And that 750K (as Brother Bob would count it) wasn't by any means the only consideration. *I approved.*

As to my fallback position, should the scheme be – ahem – rumbled . . . well, pranks question mundane reality in a revolutionary manner, don't they just?

That was a line from Peter, which I half believed – though not enough to stage a diversion in the National Gallery by stripping my blouse off, as he had wished, while Peter glued a distempery canine turd to Gainsborough's painting, *White Dogs*, so as to question 'conventions'. I'd balked at *that* proposed escapade of Peter's ten years previously.

This was a political prank – a blow against an insidious, powerful kind of repression; almost, even, a blow for art.

Thus, my defence.

I took a copy of the erotic portfolio back with me to Bloomsbury to gaze at for a few days; and to keep safely locked up when I wasn't looking at it.

Just as well that Phil wasn't involved in my immediate life these days, though we still saw each other casually. I'm sure Phil's antennae would have twitched if he had still been sleeping with a strangely furtive me. Being art critic for the *Sunday Times* had seemed to imbue him with the passions of an investigative journalist. Just as soon as *Archimboldo Erotico* burst upon the scene, no doubt he would be in touch . . . I would need to tell lies to a former lover and ensure that 'in touch' remained a phrase without physical substance. Already I could envision his injured, acquisitive expression as he rebuked me for not leaking this great art scoop to him personally. ('But why not, Jill? Didn't we share a great deal? I must say I think it's damned queer that you didn't breathe a word about this! Very *peculiar*, in fact. It makes me positively *suspicious* . . . This isn't some kind of *revenge* on your part, is it? But why, *why*?')

And what would Annie think? She was painting in Cornwall in a women's artistic commune, and her last letter had been friendly . . . If I hadn't offended her with my porn paradoxes, then attaching my name to a glossy volume of fish-frigs and spurting phallic mushrooms oughtn't to make too much difference, unless she had become radically repressive of late . . .

In other words, I was wondering to what extent this escapade would cause a hindwards reconstruction of my own life on account of the duplicity in which I'd be engaging.

And what about the *future* – in five years' time – when I passed GO and became three-quarters of a dollar millionairess? What would I *do* with all that money? Decamp to Italy? Quit the London grime and buy a farmhouse near Florence?

In the meantime I wouldn't be able to confide the truth to any intimate friend. I wouldn't be able to afford intimacy. I might become some pursed-smile equivalent of Chaplain Lascelles, though on a longer leash.

Maybe Rumby had accurately calculated that he was getting a bargain.

To be sure, the shape of my immediate future all somewhat depended on the impact of the book, the exhibition, the extent of the hoo-ha . . . Personally, I'd give the book as much impact as I could. After all, I did like to provoke.

I returned to Bexford House a week later, to stay two nights and to sort through Rumby's stock of material about Archimboldo, Rudolph, and the Prague Court. I have a good reading knowledge of German, French, and Italian, though I'm not conversationally fluent in those tongues. Any book I needed to take away with me was photocopied in its entirety by Lascelles on a high-speed, auto-page-turning machine. Pop in a book – within five minutes out popped its twin, collated and bound. The machine cost twenty thousand dollars.

A week after that, Case drove me to the docklands airport for a rather lux commuter flight with him to Amsterdam, where I examined all the other Archimboldo 'originals'; although I didn't meet the forger himself, nor did I even learn his name. The paintings were stored in three locations: in the apartment of Rumby's chosen printer, Wim Van Ewyck, in that of the gallery owner who would host the show, Geert De Lugt, and in a locked room of the Galerij Bosch itself. In the event of premature catastrophe, the entire corpus of controversial work (minus the fishy masturbatress at Bexford House) wouldn't be wiped out en masse.

Presumably the printer didn't need to be in on the conspiracy. What about the gallery owner? Maybe; maybe not . . . *This*, as Case impressed on me, was a subject which shouldn't even be alluded to – nor did Mijnheer De Lugt so much as hint.

The other eleven Archimboldos were even more stunning at full size in the frame than in colour reproduction. And also more . . . appalling?

I returned to Bloomsbury to write twenty large pages of introduction. Less would have been skimpy; more would have been excessive. Since I was being fastidiously attentive to every nuance of the text, the writing took me almost three weeks, with five or six drafts. ('Put some feeling into it,' Rumby had counselled. 'Smear some vaginal jelly on the words.')

The task done, I phoned Bexford Hall. Case drove the Merc to London the same evening to courier the pages personally. Next day, Rumby phoned to pronounce himself quite delighted. He only suggested a few micro-changes. We were rolling. Our exhibition would open in the Galerij Bosch on the first of September, coinciding with publication of the book.

And of course I must attend the private showing on the last day of August – the vernissage, as it were. (I did hope the varnish was totally dry!)

While in Amsterdam, our party – consisting of Rumby and Case and Lascelles and myself – stayed in the Grand Hotel Krasnopolsky because that hotel boasted a Japanese restaurant, and Rumby was a bit of a pig for raw fish. I wasn't complaining.

We arrived a day early in case Rumby had any last-minute thoughts about the layout of the show, or Case about its security aspects. So the morning of the thirty-first saw us at the Galerij Bosch, which fronted a tree-lined canal not far from where dozens of antique shops clustered on the route to the big art museums.

The high neck gable of the building, ornamented with two bounteous sculpted classical maidens amidst cascades of fruits and vegetables – shades of Archimboldo, indeed! – incorporated a hoisting-beam, though I doubted that any crated paintings had entered the loft of the gallery by that particular route for a long time. Venetian blinds were currently blanking the three adjacent ground-floor windows – the uprights and transoms of which were backed by discreet steel bars, as Case pointed out; and already Mijnheer De Lugt, a tall blond man with a bulbous nose, had three muscular fellows lounging about in the large, spot-lit exhibition room. One in a demure blue security uniform – he was golden-skinned and moon-faced, obviously of Indonesian ancestry. The other chunky Germanic types wore light suits and trainers.

A high pile of copies of *Archimboldo Erotico* stood in one corner for presentation that evening to the guests: the media people, museum directors, cultural mandarins and mavericks. Particularly the media people.

And my heart quailed.

Despite all the gloss, mightn't someone promptly *denounce* this exhibition? We were in liberal Holland, where the obscenity in itself would not offend. Yet wouldn't someone cry 'Hoax!'?

Worse, mightn't some inspired avant-garde type perhaps enthusiastically *applaud* this exhibition as an ambitious jape?

De Lugt seemed a tad apprehensive beneath a suave exterior. He blew that snozzle of his a number of times without obvious reason, as though determined to be squeaky-clean.

'Ms Donaldson, would you sign a copy of the book for me as a souvenir?' he asked. When I had obliged, he scrutinized my signature as if the scrawly autograph might be a forgery.

Maybe I was simply being paranoid. But I was damn glad of this dry run amongst the exhibits.

Case conferred with the security trio quietly in Dutch. They smiled; they nodded.

The wet run that evening – lubricated by champagne to celebrate the resurrection of long-lost works of a bizarre master, and contemporary of Rabelais – went off quite as well as could be expected.

A young red-haired woman in a severe black cocktail dress walked out along with her escort in shock and rage. She had been wearing an Archimboldo eco-badge as her only form of jewellery, with the word *Ark* printed upon it.

A fat bluff bearded fellow in a dinner jacket, with an enormous spotted cravat instead of bow tie, got drunk and began guffawing. Tears streamed down his hairy cheeks till Case discreetly persuaded him to step outside for an airing.

Rumby was bombarded by questions, to which he would grin and reply, 'It's all in the book. Take a copy!' One of the great art finds, yes. Casts quite a new light on Archimboldo, that emotionally complex man.

So why had Mr Wright sprung this surprise on the art world by way of a private gallery? Rather than lending these paintings to some major public museum?

'Ah now, do you really suppose your big museum would have leapt at the chance of showing such *controversial* material, ladies and gentlemen? Some big city museum with its reputation to think about? Of course, I'll be perfectly delighted to loan this collection out in future . . .'

I was quizzed too. Me, in my new purple velvet couturier trouser-suit.

Geert De Lugt smiled and nodded approvingly, confidently. Naturally Rumby would have paid him handsomely for use of his gallery, yet I was becoming convinced that Mijnheer De Lugt himself was innocent of the deception. He had merely had stage nerves earlier.

We stayed in Amsterdam for another five days. Press and media duly obliged with publicity, and I appeared on Dutch and German TV, both with Rumby and without him. So many people flocked to the Galerij Bosch that our security boys had to limit admittance to thirty people at any one time, while a couple of tolerant police hung about outside. Our book sold like hot cakes to the visitors; and by now it was in the bookshops too. ('At this rate,' joked Rumby, 'we'll be making a fucking *profit*.')

During spare hours, I wandered round town with Case. Rumby mainly stayed in his suite at the Krasnapolsky in phone and fax contact with Bexford and Texas, munching sushi. I nursed a fancy that Chaplain Lascelles might perhaps lugubriously be visiting the Red Light District to let his hair and his pants down, but he certainly wasn't getting high on any dope. Me, I preferred the flea-market on Waterlooplein, where I

picked up a black lace shawl and a slightly frayed Kashmiri rug
for the flat back in Bloomsbury.

I noticed a certain item of graffiti on numerous walls: *Onze
Wereld is onze Ark.*

'Our world is our Ark,' translated Case.

Sometimes there was only the word *Ark* on its own writ even
larger in spray-paint. I couldn't but recall the badge worn by
that pissed-off woman at the party in the gallery. Pissed-off?
No . . . *mortally offended.* Obviously, *Ark* was a passionate,
punning, mispronounced allusion to . . . who else but Emperor
Rudolph's court jester?

When I mentioned this graffito to Rumby, he almost growled
with glee.

'Ha! So what do you do in this fucking *ark* of theirs? You hide,
anchored by gravity – till you've squandered all your major
resources, then you can't get to anyplace else. Sucks to arks.'

We all flew back to England on the Sunday. At seven a.m. on the
Monday the phone bullied me awake.

Lascelles was calling.

Late on the Sunday night, a van had mounted the pavement
outside Galerij Bosch. The driver grabbed a waiting motorbike
and sped off. Almost at once the van exploded devastatingly,
demolishing the whole frontage of the building. As well as
explosives, there'd been a hell of a lot of jellied petrol and
phosphorus in that van. Fireworks, indeed! The gallery was
engulfed in flames. So were part of the street and a couple of
trees. Even the canal caught fire, and a nearby houseboat
blazed, though the occupants had been called away by some
ruse. The two security guards who were in the gallery on night
shift died.

And of course all the Archimboldos had been burnt, though
that seemed a minor aspect to me right then . . .

Case was coming pronto to pick me up. Rumby wanted us to
talk face to face before the media swarmed.

Two hours later, I was at Bexford Hall.

Rumby, Lascelles, Case, and I met together in a book-lined
upstairs study, furnished with buff leather armchairs upon a
russet Persian carpet. The single large window, composed of

stone mullions, seemed somewhat at odds with the Italianate
plasterwork ceiling which featured scrolls and roses, with
cherubs and putti supporting the boss of an electrified
chandelier. Maybe Rumby had bought this ceiling in from some
other house because it was the right size, and he liked it. The
room smelled of cheroots, and soon of my Marlboro too.

'Let's dismiss the financial side right away,' commenced
Rumby. 'The paintings weren't insured. So I'm not obliged to
make any kind of claim. Hell, do I need to? The book will be the
only record – and your fee stays secure, Jill. Now, is it to our
disadvantage that the paintings themselves no longer exist?
Might someone hint that *we* ourselves arranged the torching of
the gallery before independent art experts could stick their
fingers in the pie? I think two tragic deaths say no to that. Those
poor guys had no chance. T. Rumbold Wright isn't known for
assassinations. So, ghastly as this is, it could be to our
advantage – especially if it smears the ecofreaks, the cov-
enanters of the Ark.'

What a slur on the ecofreaks that they might destroy newly
discovered masterpieces of art for ideological reasons in a
desperate effort to keep the artist pure for exploitation by
themselves. When people saw any Archimboldo badge or
poster now, they might think, *Ho-ho* . . . I was thinking about
the two dead guards.

Lascelles had been liaising with Holland.

'The Dutch police are puzzled,' he summarized. 'Is this an
outburst of art-terrorism? A few years ago some people revived
a group called the SKG – so-called "City Art Guerrillas" who
caused street and gallery trouble. They never killed anyone.
Even if the couple on that houseboat were kept out of harm's
way to make the attackers seem more benign, De Lugt's two
guards were just slaughtered . . .

'Then what about these Ark people? The loony fringe of the
Dutch Eco movement *have* gone in for destructive industrial
sabotage – but again, they haven't caused any deaths. This is
more like the work of the German Red Column, though it seems
they haven't operated in Holland recently. Why do so now?
And why hit the gallery?'

'To hurt a noted Capitalist, in the only way they could think of?' asked Rumby. 'No, I don't buy that. It's got to be the ecofreaks.'

'The ecology movement is very respectable in Holland.'

Rumby grinned wolfishly. 'Mightn't be, soon.'

'Ecology is government policy there.'

How much more newsworthy the destruction made those naughty paintings! How convenient that they were now beyond the reach of sceptical specialists.

'I don't suppose,' said I, 'one of your *allies* in the Star Club might conceivably have arranged this attack?'

Drop a ton of lead into a pond.

'Future of the human race,' I added weakly. 'Big motivation.'

Rumby wrestled a cheroot from his coat of many pockets and lit it. 'You can forget that idea. Let's consider *safety*. Your safety, Jill.'

I suppose he couldn't avoid making this sound like a threat, however benevolently intentioned – or making it seem as if he wished to keep my free spirit incommunicado during the crisis . . .

'Someone has bombed and murdered ruthlessly,' said Rumby. '*I'm* safe here.'

'Yes, you are,' Case assured him.

'But you, Jill, you live in some little scumbag flat in any old street in London. I'd like to invite you to stay here at Bexford for a week or two until things clarify.'

'Actually, I can't,' I told him, with silly stubbornness. 'I have a couple of lectures to give at St Martin's on Thursday.'

'Screw them. Cancel them.'

'And it isn't exactly a scumbag flat.'

'Sorry – you know what I mean.'

'At least until there's a communiqué,' Lascelles suggested to me. 'Then we'll know what we're dealing with. It's only sensible.'

'Don't be *proud*,' said Rumby. He puffed. The cherubs above collected a tiny little bit more nicotine on their innocent hands. 'Please.'

And some more nicotine from me too.

'You don't need to feed some goddam *cat*, do you?' asked Rumby.

'No . . .' In fact I loathed cats – selfish, treacherous creatures – but Rumby probably wouldn't have cared one way or the other.

In the event, I stayed at Bexford. Until Wednesday afternoon. No news emerged from Holland of any communiqué.

Could the attackers not have *known* about those two guards inside the gallery? So now they were ashamed, and politically reluctant, to claim credit?

Unlikely. You don't assemble a vanload of explosives and napalm and phosphorus, make sure there's a getaway motorbike waiting, and bail out the occupants of a nearby houseboat, without checking everything else about the target too.

Lascelles was stonewalling queries from the media. ('Mr Wright is shocked. He grieves at the two deaths. He has no other comment at present . . .') Stubbornly, I insisted on being driven back to Bloomsbury.

My little flat had been burgled. My CD player and my TV were missing.

Entry was by way of the fire-escape door, which had been smashed off its none too sturdy hinges. Otherwise, there wasn't much damage or mess.

I hadn't wished Case to escort me upstairs; thus he had already driven away. Of course I *could* have reached him on the Merc's car-phone. Yet this was so ordinary a burglary that I simply phoned the police. Then I thumbed the Yellow Pages for an emergency repair service which was willing to turn up within the next six hours.

The constable who visited me presently was a West Indian. A couple of other nearby flats had also been broken into the day before for electrical goods, so he said. Was I aware of this? He seemed to be pitching his questions towards eliciting whether I might perhaps have robbed myself so as to claim insurance.

'Fairly *neat* break-in, miss, all things considered.'

'Except for the door.'

'You're lucky. Some people find excrement spread all over their homes.'

'Did that happen in the other flats that were burgled?'

'Not on this occasion. So you reported this just as soon as you came back from—?'

'From the Cotswolds.'

'Nice part of the country, I hear. Were you there long?'

'Three days.'

'Visiting friends?'

'My employer.' Now why did I have to say *that*? Blurt, blurt.

'Oh, so you live here, but your boss is in the Cotswolds?'

'He isn't exactly my boss. He was consulting me.'

The constable raised his eyebrow suggestively.

Obviously he believed in keeping the suspect off balance.

'You do have a lot of expensive books here, miss,' was his next tack.

Yes, rows of glossy art books. Why hadn't those been stolen – apart from the fact that they weighed a ton?

'I don't suppose the burglars were interested in art,' I suggested.

He pulled out a *Botticelli*, with library markings on the spine, from the shelf.

'This is from a college library,' he observed.

'I teach there. I lecture about art.'

'I thought you said you were a *consultant* . . .'

By the time he left, I was half convinced that I had burgled myself, that I habitually thieved from libraries, and that I was a call-girl who had been supplying sexual favours to Mr X out in the country. Would these suspicions be entered in the police computer? Did I have the energy to do anything about this? No, it was all so . . . tentative. Did I want to seem paranoid?

Bert the Builder finally turned up and fixed the door for a hundred and thirteen pounds . . . which of course the insurance would be covering. Otherwise the job would have cost just sixty, cash.

I did manage to look over my lecture notes – on Titian and Veronese. I microwaved a Madras beef curry with pilau rice; and went to bed, fed up.

The phone rang.

It was Phil. He'd been calling my number for days.

These weird long-lost Archimboldos! Why hadn't I told him

anything? And the terrorist attack! What had happened? Could he come round?

'Sorry, Phil, but I've just had my CD and TV nicked. And the helpful visiting constable thinks I'm a hooker.'

I was glad of the excuse of the burglary.

Towards mid-morning my phone started ringing, and a couple of Press sleuths turned up in person, pursuing the art bombing story; but I stonewalled, and escaped in the direction of St Martin's where, fortunately, no reporters lurked.

At four in the afternoon I stepped out from the factory-like frontage of the art school into a Charing Cross Road aswarm with tourists. Beneath a grey overcast the fumy air was warm. A sallow Middle Eastern youth in checked shirt and jeans promptly handed me a leaflet advertising some English Language Academy.

'I already speak English,' I informed the tout. He frowned momentarily as if he didn't understand. No points to the Academy.

'Then you learn *cheaper*,' he suggested, pursuing me along the pavement.

'Do not bother that lady,' interrupted a tall blond young man dressed in a lightweight off-white jacket and slacks.

'No, it's all right,' I assured my would-be protector.

'It is not all right. Any trash is on our streets. They are not safe.'

He waved, and a taxi pulled up almost immediately. The young man opened the door, plunged his hand inside his jacket, and showed me a small pistol hidden in his palm. Was he some urban vigilante crusader pledged to rescue damsels from offensive encounters? I just didn't understand what was happening.

'Get in quickly,' he said, 'or I will shoot you dead.'

Help, I mouthed at the Arab, or whatever.

In vain.

I did as Prince Charming suggested. Did *anyone* notice me being abducted? Or only see a handsome young man hand me enthusiastically into that taxi?

The driver didn't look round.

'Keep quiet,' said the young man. 'Put these glasses on.' He handed me glasses black as night equipped with side-blinkers, such as someone with a rare hypersensitive eye ailment might wear. Only, these were utterly dark; I couldn't see a thing through them.

We drove for what seemed like half an hour. Eventually we drew up – and waited, perhaps so that passers-by might have time to pass on by – before my abductor assisted me from the cab. Quickly he guided me arm in arm up some steps. A door closed behind us. Traffic noise grew mute.

We mounted a broad flight of stairs, and entered an echoing room – where I was pressured into a straight-backed armchair. Immediately one hand pressed under my nose, and another on my jaw, to force my mouth open.

'Drink!'

Liquid poured down my throat – some sweet concoction masking a bitter undertaste. I gagged and spluttered but had no choice except to swallow.

What had I drunk? What had I drunk?

'I need to see the eyes,' said a sombre, if somewhat slobbery voice. 'The truth is in the eyes.' The accent was Germanic.

A hand removed my glasses.

I found myself in a drawing-room with a dusty varnished floor and double oak doors. A small chandelier of dull lustres shone. Thick blue brocade curtains cloaked tall windows, which in any event appeared to be shuttered. A dust-sheet covered what I took to be a baby grand piano. An oblong of less faded rose-and-lily wallpaper, over a marble fireplace, showed where some painting had hung.

On a chaise longue sat a slim elegant grizzle-haired man of perhaps sixty kitted out in a well-tailored grey suit. A walking-cane was pressed between his knees. His hands opened and closed slowly to reveal the chased silver handle. A second middle-aged man stood near him: stouter, bald, wearing a long purple velvet robe with fur trimmings which at first I thought was some exotic dressing-gown. This man's face was jowly and pouchy. He looked like Goering on a bad day. His eyes were eerie: bulgy, yet bright as if he was on cocaine.

My abductor had stationed himself directly behind me.

On a walnut table lay a copy of *Archimboldo Erotico*, open at my introduction.

Shit.

'My apologies,' said the seated gent, 'for the manner of your coming here, Miss Donaldson.' He gestured at the book. 'But you owe me a profound apology – and restitution. Your libels must be corrected.'

The fellow in the robe moved closer, to stare at me. His fingers wiggled.

'What libels?' I asked, rather deeply scared. These people had to be nutters, possessed by some zany fanatical motive. Well-heeled, well-groomed nutters were maybe the really dangerous sort. *What had I drunk? A slow poison? Would I soon be begging for the antidote?*

'Libels against a certain Holy Roman Emperor, Miss Donaldson. Thus, libels against the Habsburg dynasty . . . which may yet be the salvation of Europe, and of the world. Very *untimely* libels.' The gent raised his cane and slashed it to and fro as if decapitating daisies. 'I am sure you will see reason to denounce your fabrications publicly . . .'

'What fabrications?'

He stood up smoothly and brought his cane down savagely upon my book, though his expression remained suave and polite. I jerked, imagining that cane striking me instead.

'These! These obscenities were never painted by Rudolph's court artist!'

'But,' I murmured, 'the looting of Prague . . . Skoklosters Castle . . . Queen Christina's chaplain . . .'

He sighed. 'Lies. All lies. And I do not quite know why. Let us discuss art and history, Miss Donaldson.'

'She is deceitful,' said the fellow in the robe, always peering at me. 'She has a guilty conscience.'

'Who are you?' I asked. 'The local mind-reader?'

The stout man smiled unctuously.

'Herr Voss is my occultist,' explained the gent.

'Oculist? You mean, optician?'

'My *occultist*! My pansophist. The holder of the keys to the

Unknown. And *my* name happens to be Heinrich von Habsburg, Miss Donaldson . . .'

'Oh . . .,' I said.

'I shall not burden your brain with genealogy, except to say that I am the living heir to the Holy Roman throne.'

Genealogy indeed. 'I thought,' said I, 'that your Roman throne couldn't be inherited by virtue of blood—'

He cut me short. 'You misunderstand divine right. What the Electors bestowed wasn't rightly theirs, but God's, to give. God finally vested this title in the Habsburg family. Let us discuss *art* instead. And *sacred history*.'

This, His Royal Heinrich proceeded to do, while the keeper of the keys contemplated me and my guard hovered behind me.

Rudolph and his father Maximilian before him had been astute, benevolent rulers, who aimed to heal discord in Christian Europe by uniting it under Habsburg rule. They lived noble and honourable lives, as did Count Giuseppe Archimboldo. His supposed fantasias possessed a precise political and metaphysical significance in the context of the Holy Roman throne. The aesthetic harmony of natural elements in the *Vertumnus* and in the other portrait heads bespoke the harmony which would bless Europe under the beneficent leadership of the House of Austria . . .

Jawohl, I thought.

Ever-present, like the elements themselves, the Habsburgs would rule both microcosm and macrocosm – both the political world, and nature too. Archimboldo's cycle of the seasons, depicted as Habsburg heads wrought of Wintry, Vernal, Summery, and Autumnal ingredients, confided that Habsburg rule would extend eternally through time in one everlasting season. Under the secular and spiritual guidance of those descendants of Hercules, the House of Habsburg, the Golden Age would return to a united Europe.

Right on.

In due course of time, this happy culmination had almost come to pass. The 'Great King', as predicted, nay, propagandized by Nostradamus, loomed on the horizon.

When the Habsburgs united with the House of Lorraine, and when Marie Antoinette became Queen of France, the House of Habsburg-Lorraine was within a generation of dominion over Europe – had the French Revolution not intervened.

What a pity.

Throughout the nineteenth century the House attempted to regroup. However, the upheavals attending the end of the First World War toppled the Habsburgs from power, ushering in chaos . . .

Shame.

Now all Europe was revived and reuniting, and its citizens were ever more aware that the microcosm of Man and the macrocosm of Nature were a unity.

Yet lacking, as yet, a *head*.

A Holy Roman Imperial head.

Early restoration of the monarchy in Hungary was one possible ace card, though other cards were also tucked up the imperial sleeve . . .

Archimboldo's symbolic portraits were holy ikons of this golden dream, especially in view of their eco-injection into the European psyche. Those paintings were programming the people with a subconscious expectation, a hope, a longing, a secret sense of destiny, which a restored Habsburg Holy Roman Empire would fulfil.

'Now do you see why your obscenities are such a libellous blasphemy, Miss Donaldson?'

Good God.

'Do you mean to tell me that *you're* behind the Archimboldo eco-campaign?' I asked His Imperial Heinrich.

'The power of symbols,' remarked Voss, 'is very great. Symbols are my speciality.'

Apparently they weren't going to tell me whether they simply hoped to exploit an existing, serendipitous media campaign – or whether some loyal Habsburg mole had actively persuaded the ecofreaks to plaster what were effectively Habsburg heads – in fruit and veg, and flowers and leaves – all over Europe and America.

'You broke into my flat,' I accused the man behind me.

'Looking for some dirt that doesn't exist because the erotic paintings are genuine!'

Blondie slapped me sharply across the head.

'Martin! You know that is unnecessary!' H. von H. held up his hand prohibitively – for the moment, at least.

'You broke my door down,' I muttered over my shoulder, thinking myself reprieved, 'and you stole my CD and TV just to make the thing look plausible. I bet you burgled those other flats in the neighbourhood too as a deception.'

Martin, on his *own*? Surely not . . . There must have been others involved. The taxi driver . . . and whoever else . . .

'Actually, we broke your door *after* the burglary,' boasted Martin. 'We *entered* with more circumspection.'

Voss smiled in a predatory fashion. 'With secret keys, as it were.'

Others. Others . . .

They had blown up the Galerij Bosch! They had burned those two guards to death . . .

I shrank.

'I see that the magnitude of this is beginning to dawn on your butterfly mind,' said the Habsburg. 'A united Europe must be saved from *pollution*. Ecological pollution, of course – a Holy Roman Emperor is as a force of nature. But moral pollution too.'

'How about racial?' I queried.

'I'm an aristocrat, not a barbarian,' remarked Heinrich. 'The Nazis were contemptible. Yet plainly we cannot have Moslems – Turkish *heathens* – involved in the affairs of Holy Europe. We cannot have those who besieged our Vienna in 1683 succeeding now by the back door.'

Oh, the grievances of centuries long past . . . Rumby and his science Star Club suddenly seemed like such Johnnies-Come-Lately indeed.

Science . . . versus imperial *magic* . . . with eco-mysticism in the middle . . .

'I just can't believe you're employing a frigging *magician* to gain the throne of Europe!'

'*Language*, Miss Donaldson!' snapped the Habsburg. 'You are corrupt.'

Voss smoothed his robe as though I had mussed it.

'You're a creature of your time, Miss Donaldson,' said H. von H. 'Whereas I am a creation of the centuries.'

'Would that be *The Centuries of Nostradamus*?' Yes, that was the title of that volume of astrological rigmarole.

'I mustn't forget that you're educated, by the lights of today. Tell me, what do you suppose the *Centuries* of the title refer to?'

'Well, years. A long time, the future.'

'Quite wrong. There simply happen to be a hundred quatrains – verses of four lines – in each section. You're only half educated. And thus you blunder. How much did your American art collector pay you for writing that introduction?'

Obviously Rumby would have paid me *something* . . . I wouldn't have written those pages for nothing . . .

'Three thousand dollars,' I improvised.

'That doesn't sound very much, considering the evil intent. Is Mr Wright being hoaxed *too*?'

Again, he slammed the cane on to my book.

An astonishing flash of agony seared across my back. I squealed and twisted round – but Martin was holding no cane.

He was holding nothing at all. With a grin, Martin displayed his empty paws for me. Voss giggled, and when I looked at him he winked.

It was as though that open volume was some voodoo doll of myself which the Habsburg had just chastised.

The Habsburg lashed at my words again, and I cried out, for the sudden pain was intense – yet I knew there would be no mark on me.

Voss licked his lips. 'Symbolic resonances, Miss Donaldson. The power of symbolic actions.'

What drug had been in that liquid I swallowed? I didn't *feel* disoriented – save for nerves and dread – yet I must be in some very strange state of mind to account for my suggestibility to pain.

'We can continue thus for a while, Miss Donaldson.' Heinrich raised his cane again.

'Wait.'

Was three-quarters of a million dollars enough to compensate for being given the third degree right now by crazy, ruthless *murderers* – who could torture me symbolically, but effectively?

I experienced an absurd vision of myself attempting to tell the West Indian detective constable that actually my flat had been broken into by agents of a Holy Roman Emperor who hoped to take over Europe – and that I was seeking police protection because the Habsburgs could hurt me agonizingly by whipping my words . . .

Was I mad, or was I mad?

The room seemed luminous, glowing with an inner light. Every detail of furniture or drapery was intensely *actual*. I thought that my sense of reality had never been stronger.

'OK,' I admitted, 'the paintings were all forgeries. They were done in Holland, but I honestly don't know who by. I never met him. I never learned his name. Rumby – Mr Wright – hates the ecology lobby because they hate space exploration, and he thinks that's our only hope. I have a friend at the *Sunday Times*. I'll tell him everything – about how the paintings were a prank. They'll love to print that! Wright will have egg on his face.'

'What a treacherous modern creature you are,' the Habsburg said with casual contempt; and I squirmed with shame and fear.

'Just watch for next weekend's paper,' I promised.

'At this moment,' said Voss, 'she believes she is going to do what she says – and of course she knows that our Martin can find her, if she breaks her word . . .' He peered.

'Ah: she's relieved that *you* cannot reach her from a distance with the whipping-cane.

'And she wonders whether Martin would really kill her, and thus lose us her testimony . . .'

No, he *wasn't* reading my mind. He wasn't! He was reading my face, my muscles. He could do so because everything was so real.

More peering.

'She feels a paradoxical affection for her friend . . . *Rumby*. Solidarity, as well as greed. Yes, a definite loyalty.' If only I hadn't called him Rumby. If only I'd just called him Wright. It was all in the words. Voss wasn't reading my actual thoughts.

'So therefore,' H. von H. said to Voss, 'she must be retrained in her loyalties.'

What did he mean? What did he mean?

'She must be conditioned by potent symbols, Voss.'

'Just so, Excellency.'

'Thus she will not wish to betray us. Enlighten her, Voss. Show her the real depth of history, from where we come. Your juice will be deep in her now.'

Numbness crept over me, as Voss loomed closer. The sheer pressure of his approach was paralysing me.

'Wait,' I managed to squeak.

'Wait?' echoed H. von H. 'Oh, I have waited long enough already. My family has waited long enough. Through the French Revolution, through the Communist intermezzo . . . The Holy Roman Empire *will* revive at this present cusp of history – for it has always remained in being, at least as a state of mind. And *mind* is what matters, Miss Donaldson – as Rudolph knew, contrary to your pornographic lies! Ah yes, my ancestor avidly sought the symbolic key to the ideal world. Practitioners of the symbolic, hermetic arts visited him in Prague Castle – though he lacked the loyal services of a Voss . . .'

The Habsburg slid his cane under the dust-sheet of the piano, and whisked the cloth off. Seating himself on the stool, he threw open the lid of the baby grand with a crash. His slim, manicured fingers started to play plangent, mournful Debussyish chords in which I could almost feel myself begin to drown.

Voss crooned to me – or sang – in some dialect of German . . . and I couldn't move a muscle. Surely I was shrinking – or else the drawing-room was expanding. Or both. Voss was becoming vast.

I was a little child again – yet not a child, but rather a miniature of myself. When I was on the brink of puberty, lying in bed just prior to drifting off to sleep, this same distortion of the senses used to happen to me.

The music lamented.

And Voss crooned my lullaby.

A bearded man in black velvet and cerise satin held my nude paralysed body in his hands. He held the *whole* of me in his hands – for I was tiny now, the height of his forearm.

Draped over his shoulders was a lavish ermine cloak.

I was stiff, unmoving.

He placed me in a niche, ran his fingertip down my belly, and traced the cleft between my thighs.

He stepped back.

Then he left.

I was in a great gloomy vaulted chamber housing massive cupboards and strongboxes. The slit windows in the thick stone wall were grated so as to deter any slim cat-burglars. Stacked several deep around a broad shelf, and likewise below, were mythological and biblical oil paintings: Tintorettos, Titians, by the look of them . . . Neither the lighting nor the décor were at all in the spirit of any latter-day museum. Here was art as treasure – well and truly locked up.

Days and nights passed.

Weeks of static solitude until I was going crazy. I would have welcomed any change whatever, any newcomer. My thoughts looped around a circuit of Strada, death in Amsterdam, Habsburgs, with the latter assuming ever more significance – and necessity – with each mental swing.

Eventually the door opened, and in walked a figure who made the room shine. For his face and hair were made of a hundred springtime flowers, his collar of white daisies, and his clothes of a hundred lush leaves.

He stood and gazed at me through floral eyes, and with his rosebud lips he smiled faintly.

He simply went away.

A season passed, appalling in its sheer duration. I saw daisies like stars before my eyes, in an unending after-image.

Then in walked glowing Summer. His eyes were ripe cherries. His teeth were little peas. Plums and berries tangled in his harvest-hair; and his garment was of woven straw.

And he too smiled, and went away in turn.

And another season passed . . .

. . . till rubicund Autumn made his appearance. He was a more elderly fellow with an oaten beard, a fat pear of a nose, mushroom ears, clusters of grapes instead of locks of hair. His chin was a pomegranate. He wore an overripe burst fig as an ear-ring. He winked lecherously, and departed even as I tried to cry out to him through rigid lips, to stay.

For next came Winter, old and gnarled, scabbed and scarred, his nose a stump of rotted branch, his skin of fissured bark, his lips of jutting bracket-fungus.

Winter stayed for a longer grumbly time, though he no more reached to touch me than had his predecessors. His departure – the apparent end of this cycle of seasons – plunged me into despair. I was as cold as marble.

Until one day the door opened yet again, and golden light bathed my prison chamber.

Vertumnus himself advanced – the fruitful god, his cheeks of ripe apple and peach, head crowned with fruit and grain, his chest a mighty pumpkin. His cherry and blackberry eyes glinted.

Rudolph!

He reached for me. Oh to be embraced by him! To be warmed.

He lifted my paralysed naked body from its dusty niche.

The crash which propelled me back into the drawing-room might almost have been caused by his dropping me and letting me shatter.

For a moment I thought that this was indeed so.

Yet it was my trance which had been shattered.

A policeman was in the room. An armed policeman, crouching. He panned his gun around. Plainly I was the only other person present.

The crash must have been that of those double oak doors flying open as he burst in.

Footsteps thumped, elsewhere in the house.

Voices called.

'*Empty!*'

'*Empty!*'

Several other officers spilled into the room.

'You all right, miss?'

I could move my limbs – which were clothed exactly as earlier on, in jeans and maroon Paisley sweater. I wasn't tiny and naked, after all. I stared around. No sign of von Habsburg or Voss or Martin.

'You all right, miss? Do you understand me?'

I nodded slowly. I still felt feeble.

'She was just sitting here all on her own,' commented the officer, putting his pistol away. 'So what's happening?' he demanded of me.

How did they know I was here?

'I was . . . forced into a taxi,' I said. 'I was brought here, then given some drug.'

'What sort of drug? *Why?*'

'It made me . . . dream.'

'Who brought you here?'

'A man called Martin . . .'

He's the Habsburg Emperor's hit-man . . . The drug was concocted by a magician . . .

How could I tell them such things? How could I explain about Rudolph Vertumnus . . .? (And how could I *deny* Vertumnus, who had almost rekindled me . . .?)

'They were trying to get me to deny things I wrote about the painter Archimboldo . . .'

'About a *painter?*'

I tried to explain about the pictures, the bombing in Amsterdam, and how my flat had been burgled. My explanation slid away of its own accord – for the sake of sheer plausibility, and out of logical necessity! – from any Habsburg connection, and into the ecofreak channel.

The officer frowned. 'You're suggesting that the Greens who bombed that gallery also kidnapped you? There's no one here now.'

'They must have seen you coming and run away. I'm quite confused.'

'Hmm,' said the officer. 'Come in, sir,' he called.

In walked Phil: chunky, dapper Phil, velvet-jacketed and suede-shoed, his rich glossy brown hair brushed back in elegant waves, as ever.

It was Phil who had seen me pushed into the taxi; he who had noticed the gleam of gun from right across the street where he had been loitering with intent outside a bookshop, waiting for me to emerge from St Martin's so that he could bump into me. He'd managed to grab another taxi and follow. He'd seen me hustled into that house in North London, wearing those black 'goggles'. It took about an hour for him to stir up the armed posse – an hour, during which four seasons had passed before my eyes.

The fact that Phil and I were long-term 'friends' and that he turned out to be a 'journalist' – of sorts – irked the police. The abduction – by persons unknown, to a vacant house, where I simply sat waiting patiently – began to seem distinctly stage-managed . . . for the sake of publicity. Nor – given the Amsterdam connection – did my mention of drugs help matters. Calling out armed police was a serious matter.

We were both obliged to answer questions until late in the evening before we could leave the police station; and even then is seemed as if we ourselves might still be charged with some offence. However, those deaths in Amsterdam lent a greater credence to what I said. Maybe there was something serious behind this incident . . .

I, of course, was 'confused'. Thus, early on, I was given a blood test, about which the police made no further comment; there couldn't have been any evidence of hash or acid in my system.

I needed to stay 'confused' until I could get to talk to Rumby.

Peeved Phil, of course, insisted on talking to me over late dinner in a pizzeria – we were both starving by then.

I lied quite a lot; and refrained from any mention of Habsburgs or the Star Club. The Archimboldo paintings had been genuine. Rumby was an up-front person. Euro ecofreaks must have bombed the gallery. Must have abducted me. Blondie Martin; elderly man, name unknown; stout man, name of Voss, who wore a strange costume. German-speakers. Just the same as I'd told the police, five or six times over. The kidnappers had tried to persuade me to denounce what I had written because my words were an insult to Archimboldo, emblem of the Greens. They had drugged me into a stupor – from which I recovered with surprising swiftness. Rescue had come too soon for much else to transpire . . .

Phil and I were sharing a tuna, anchovy, and prawn ensemble on a crispy base, and drinking red wine.

'It's quite some story, Jill. Almost front-page stuff.'

'I doubt it.'

'The Eco connection! Bombing, abduction . . . I'd like to run this by Freddy on the news desk.'

'You're an art critic, Phil – and so am I. I don't want some cock-eyed blather in the papers.'

'Jill,' he reproached me, 'I've just spent *all evening* in a police station on account of you.'

'I'm grateful you did what you did, Phil. Let's stop it there.'

'For Christ's sake, you could still be in danger! Or . . . *aren't you*, after all? Was this a publicity stunt? Was it staged by *Wright*? You're in deep, but you want out now? Why would he stage such a stunt? If he did . . . what really happened in Amsterdam?'

Dear God, how his antennae were twitching. 'No, no, no. It couldn't be a stunt because the only witness to it was *you*, and that was quite by chance!'

'By chance,' he mused . . . as though maybe I might have spied him from an upper window in St Martin's and promptly phoned for a kidnapper.

'Look, Phil, I'm confused. I'm tired. I need *sleep*.'

Into the pizzeria stepped a stout, bald man wearing a dark blue suit. He flourished a silver-tipped walking-stick. Goering on a night out. His bulgy eyes fixed on mine. He swished the stick, and I screamed with pain, jerking against the table, spilling both our wines.

'Jill!'

Phil managed to divert the red tide with his paper napkin at the same time as he reached out towards me. Other customers stared agog, and the manager hastened in our direction. Were we engaged in some vicious quarrel? Wine dripped on to the floor tiles.

Voss had vanished. I slumped back.

'Sorry,' I said to the manager. 'I had a bad cramp.'

The manager waved a waiter to minister to the mess. Other diners resumed munching their pizzas.

'Whatever happened?' whispered Phil.

'A cramp. Just a cramp.'

Could one of those Habsburgers have trailed us to the police station and hung around outside for hours, keeping watch till we emerged?

Had I truly seen Voss, or only someone who resembled him? Someone whose appearance and whose action triggered that pain reflex? That agonizing hallucination . . .

Phil took me back to the flat in a taxi. I had no choice but to let him come up with me – in case the place was infested.

It wasn't. Then it took half an hour to get rid of my friend, no matter how much tiredness I claimed. By the time I phoned Rumby's private number it was after eleven.

Him, I did start to tell about the Habsburgs.

He was brevity itself. 'Say no more,' my rich protector cut in. *My Rumby Daddy*. 'Stay there. I'm sending Case *now*. He'll phone from the car just as soon as he's outside your place. Make quite sure you see it's him before you open your door.'

I dozed off soundly in the Merc. When I arrived at Bexford, Rumby had waited up to quiz me and pump me – attended by Case, and a somewhat weary Lascelles.

I got to bed around four . . .

. . . leaving Rumby aiming to do some serious phoning. Had Big Daddy been breaking out the benzedrine? Not exactly. Rumby always enjoyed a few hours advantage over us local mortals. So as to stay more in sync with American time-zones he habitually rose very late of a morning. A night-shift duo always manned the computer consoles and transatlantic satellite link. In that sense, Bexford never really closed down.

I'd already gathered that *crisis* was somewhat of a staff of life around Rumby – who seemed to cook up his own personal supply of benzedrine internally. During my previous two-day sojourn, there'd been the incident of the microlite aircraft. Thanks to a Cotswold Air Carnival, microlites were overflying Bexford at a few hundred feet now and then. Rumby took exception and had Lascelles trying to take out a legal injunction against the organizers.

Simultaneously, there'd been the business of the starlings. Affronted by those microlite pterodactyls, and seeking a new air-base for their sorties, a horde of the quarrelsome birds took up residence on the satellite dish. Their weight or their shit might distort bits of information worth millions. What to do? After taking counsel from an avian welfare organization,

Rumby despatched his helicopter to collect a heap of French *pétard* firecrackers from Heathrow to string underneath the gutters. So my stay had been punctuated by random explosive farts . . .

I woke at noon, and Rumby joined me for breakfast in the big old kitchen – antiquity retrofitted with stainless steel and ceramic hobs. A large TV set was tuned to CNN, and an ecologist was inveighing about rocket exhausts and the ozone holes.

'Each single shuttle launch releases a hundred and sixty-three *thousand* kilograms of hydrogen chloride that converts into an atmospheric mist of hydrochloric acid! So now they're kindly promising to change the oxidizer of the fuel – the ammonium perchlorate that produces this vast cloud of pollution – to ammonium *nitrate* instead—'

As soon as I finished my croissant, Rumby scuttled the cooks – a couple of local women – out to pick herbs and vegetables. He blinked at me a few times.

'Any more sightings of flowerpot men? Or Habsburgs?' he enquired.

'That isn't funny, Rumby. It happened.'

He nodded. 'I'm afraid you've been given a ring-binder, Jill.'

'Come again?'

'I've been talking to one of my best chemists over in Texas. Sally has a busy mind. Knows a lot about pharmaceuticals.' He consulted scribbles in a notebook. 'The ring in question's a molecular structure called an indole ring . . . These rings *bind* to synapses in the brain. Hence, ring-binder. They're psychotomimetic – they mimic psychoses. Your little pets will probably stay in place a long time instead of breaking down. Seems there's a lot of covert designer-drug work going on right now, aimed at cooking up chemicals to manipulate people's beliefs. Sally has heard rumours of one drug code-named *Confusion* – and another one called *Persuasion*, which seems to fit the bill here. It's the only explanation for the hallucination – which came from within you, of course, once you were given the appropriate prod.'

'I do realize I was hallucinating the . . . flowerpot men. You mean this can continue . . . indefinitely?'

'You flashed on for a full encore in that pizza parlour, right? Whiplash! Any fraught scenes in future involving old Archy could do the same. Media interviews, that sort of thing – if you disobey the Habsburg view of Archy. Though I guess you mustn't spill the beans about them publicly.'

'They told me so. How did I get away with telling *you* last night?'

'They were interrupted before they'd finished influencing you.' He grinned. 'I guess I might be high enough in the hierarchy of your loyalties to outrank their partial hold on you. Media or Press people wouldn't be, so you'd be advised to follow the Habsburg party line with them. Maybe you could resist at a cost.'

'Of what?'

'Pain, inflicted by your own mind. Distortions of reality. That's what Sally says. That's the word on these new ring-binders. They bind you.'

The more I thought about this, the less I liked it.

'How many people know about these persuader drugs?' I asked him carefully.

'They haven't exactly featured in *Newsweek*. I gather they're a bit experimental. Sally has an ear for rumours. She's part of my research division. Runs a search-team scanning the chemistry journals. Whatever catches the eye. Any tips of future icebergs. New petrochemical applications, mainly.' He spoke as if icebergs started out fully submerged, then gradually revealed themselves. 'She helped dig up data on the correct paint chemistry for the Archies.'

How frank he was being.

Apparently. And how glib.

'So how would a Habsburg *magician* get his paws on proto-type persuader drugs?' I demanded.

Rumby looked rueful. 'Hell, maybe he *is* a magician! Alchemy precedes chemistry, don't they say?'

'In the same sense that Icarus precedes a jumbo jet?'

One of the cooks returned bearing an obese marrow.

*

Impulse took me to the kitchen garden, to brood on my own. The sun had finally burned through persistent haze to brighten the rows of cabbages, majestic cauliflowers, and artichokes, the rhubarb, the leeks. An ancient brick wall backed this domain, trusses of tomatoes ranged along it. Rooks cawed in the elms beyond, prancing about those raggedy stick-nests that seemed like diseases of the branches.

Had the old gent whom I'd met really been Heinrich von Habsburg? A Holy Roman Emperor waiting in the wings to step on the world stage? Merely because he told me so, in *persuasive* circumstances?

What if that trio in the drawing-room had really been *ecofreaks* masquerading as Habsburgs, pulling the wool over my eyes, trying to bamboozle me into confession?

Did puritanical ecofreaks have the wit to stage such a show?

How much more likely that the Star Club, with its presumed access to cutting-edge psychochemistry – and a penchant for dirty tricks? – was responsible for the charade, and for my drugging!

Whether Rumby himself knew so, or not.

Wipe me out as a reliable witness to my own part in the prank? Eliminate me, by giving me an ongoing nervous breakdown?

Would that invalidate what I'd written?

Ah no. The slur would be upon ecologists . . .

And maybe, at the same time, *test* that persuader drug? Give it a field-trial on a highly suitable test subject, namely myself? The Club's subsequent aim might be to try similar *persuasion* on influential ecofreaks to alter their opinions or to make them seem crazy . . .

In my case, of course, they wouldn't wish to turn me into an eco-groupie . . . Thus the Habsburg connection could have seemed like a fertile ploy.

Was there a genuine, elderly Heinrich von Habsburg some-where in Germany or Austria? Oh, doubtless there would be . . .

The vegetable garden began slithering, pulsing, throbbing. Ripe striped marrows thumped upon the ground, great green gonads. Tomatoes tumesced. Leeks were waxy white candles with green flames writhing high. Celery burst from earth, spraying feathery leaves. Sprouts jangled. Cauliflowers were naked brains.

The garden was trying to transform itself, to assemble itself into some giant sprawled potent body – of cauli brain, leek fingers, marrow organs, green leaf flesh . . .

I squealed and fled back towards the kitchen itself.

Then halted, like a hunted animal.

I couldn't go inside – where Rumby and Case and Lascelles plotted . . . the downfall of Nature, the rape of the planets, the bleeding of oil from Earth's veins to burn into choking smoke.

Behind me, the vegetable jungle had stilled. Its metamorphosis had halted, reversed.

If I thought harmoniously, not perversely, I was safe.

Yet my mind was churning, and reality was unstuck.

In my perception one conspiracy overlay another. One scheming plot, another scheming plot. Therefore one reality overlay another reality with hideous persuasiveness. Where had I just been, but in a *vegetable plot*?

I couldn't go into that house, to which I had fled for safety only the night before. For from inside Bexford Hall invisible tendrils arched out across the sky, bouncing up and down out of space, linking Rumby to star crusaders who were playing with my mind – and to whom he might be reporting my condition even now, guilefully or innocently.

On the screen of the sky I spied a future world of Confusion and Persuasion, where devoted fanatics manipulated moods chemically so that Nature became a multifold *creature* evoking horror – since it might absorb one into itself, mind-meltingly, one's keen consciousness dimming into pulsing, orgasmic dreams; and from which one could only flee in silver ships, out to the empty serenity of space where no universally linked weeds infested the floating rocks, no bulging tomato haemorrhoids the asteroids . . .

Or else conjuring up a positive lust for vital vegetative unity!

I slapped myself, trying to summon a Habsburger whiplash of pain to jerk me out of this bizarre dual vision.

I must go indoors. To sanity. And beyond.

The ring-binder was clamping more and more of me; and my

mind was at war. I was scripting my own hallucinations from the impetus of ecofreak ideology, exaggerated absurdly, and from the myth of the Holy Roman Empire . . . I was dreaming, wide awake.

And Case stood, watching me.

'You OK, Jill?'

I nodded. I shouldn't tell him the truth. There was no truth any more; there was only potent imagery, subject to inter-pretation.

Certain bedrock facts existed: the bombing, the deaths in Amsterdam, my abduction . . . Event-*images*: that's what those were. The interpretation was another matter, dependent upon what one believed – just as art was forever being reinterpreted in the context of a new epoch; and even history too.

Persuasion – and Confusion too? – had torn me loose from my moorings, so that interpretations cascaded about me simultaneously, synchronously. I had become a battlefield between world-views, which different parts of my mind were animating.

With dread, I sensed something stirring which perhaps had lain dormant ever since humanity split from Nature – ever since true consciousness of self had dawned as a sport, a freak, a biological accident . . .

'You sure, Jill?'

You. I. Myself. *Me.*

The independent thinking entity, named Jill Donaldson.

I wasn't thinking quite so independently any longer. An illusion of Self – that productive illusion upon which civiliza-tion itself had been founded – was floundering.

'Quite sure,' said I.

I, I, I. Ich. Io. Ego.

And Jilldonaldson hastened past him into the kitchen, where one of the cooks was hollowing out the marrow. The big TV set, tuned to CNN, scooping signals bounced from space, shimmered. The colours bled and re-formed. The pixel pixies danced a new jig.

The countenance of Vertumnus gazed forth from that screen, he of the laughing lips, the ripe rubicund cheeks of peach and apple, the pear-nose, the golden ears of corn that were his brows. Oh the flashing hilarity of his berry-eyes. Oh those laughing lips.

With several nods of his head he gestured Jill elsewhere.

Jill adopted a pan-face.

She walked through the corridors of the house, to the front porch. She stepped out on to the gravel drive.

Ignition keys were in the red Porsche.

Jill ought to be safe with Annie in a colony of women. Rudolph Vertumnus was a male, wasn't he?

A hop through Cheltenham, then whoosh by motorway to Exeter and on down into Cornwall. She would burn fuel but keep an eye out for police patrols. Be at Polmerrin by dusk . . .

The Porsche wasn't even approaching Cheltenham when the car-phone burbled, inevitably. She had been counting on a call.

A stolen bright red Porsche would be a little obvious on the motorway. So she had her excuse lined up. She was going to visit her brother – in Oxford, in roughly the opposite direction. She'd be back at Bexford that evening. Brother Bob was a banker. Let Rumby worry that she was going to blab to him to protect her 750K investment, about which she no longer cared a hoot. Let Case and some co-driver hare after her fruitlessly towards Oxford in the Merc.

The voice wasn't Case's. Or Lascelles'. Or even Rumby's.

She nearly jerked the Porsche off the road.

The voice was that of Voss.

'Can you hear me, Fräulein Donaldson?'

Hands shaking, legs trembling, she guided the car into a gateway opening on to a huge field of close-cut golden stubble girt by a hawthorn hedge. A Volvo hooted in protest as it swung by. A rabbit fled.

'How did you find me, Voss—?' she gasped. Horrid perspectives loomed. 'They told you! They know you!'

The caller chuckled.

'I'm merely the voice of *Vertumnus*, Fräulein. My image is everywhere these days, so why shouldn't I be everywhere too? Are you perhaps worried about the collapse of your precious Ego, Fräulein?'

How persuasive his voice was. 'This has all happened before, you know. The God of the Bible ruled the medieval world, but when He went into eclipse *Humanity* seized His sceptre. Ah, that exalted Renaissance Ego! How puffed up it was! By the time of Rudolph, that same Ego was already collapsing. Its confidence had failed. A new unity was needed – a bio-cosmic social unity. The Holy Roman Emperor Rudolph sought to be the *head* of society – hence the painting of so many regal *heads* by the artist you have libelled. Those biological, botanical heads.'

'I already know this,' she said.

'He would be the head – and the people, the limbs, the organs. Of one body! In the new world now a-dawning life will be a unity again. The Emperor will be the head – but not a separate, egotistic head. Nor will the limbs and organs be separate individualists.'

'You're telling me what I know!' Aye, and *what she most feared* – namely the loss of Self. Its extinction. And what she most feared might well *win*; for what is feared is potent.

'Who are you? What are you?' she cried into the phone – already suspecting that Voss's voice, the voice of Vertumnus, might well be in her own wayward head, either ring-bound or else planted there by alchemical potion.

She slammed the handset down on to its cradle by the gearshift lever, thumbed the windows fully open, and lit a cigarette to calm herself. Whispers of smoke drifted out towards the shorn field.

A mat of golden stubble cloaked the broad shoulders of the land. A ghostly pattern emerged across the great network of dry stalks: a coat of arms. The hedge was merely green braiding. Her car was a shiny red bug parked on the shoulder of a giant sprawling being.

Angrily she pitched her cigarette through the passenger window towards the field, wishing that it might start a fire, though really the straw was far too short to combust.

She drove on; and when the phone seemed to burble again, she ignored it.

She smoked. She threw out half-burned cigarettes till the pack was empty, but no smoke ever plumed upwards far behind her.

*

Half-way through Cheltenham, in slow-moving traffic, she passed a great billboard flaunting Rudolph Vertumnus. *WE ARE ALL PART OF NATURE*, proclaimed the all too familiar text.

Evidently unseen by other drivers and pedestrians, the fruity Emperor shouldered his way out of the poster. A pumpkin-belly that she had never seen before reared into view. And marrow-legs, from between which aubergine testicles and a carrot cock dangled. Vertumnus towered over the other cars and vans behind her, bestriding the roadway. His carrot swelled enormously.

Raphanidosis: ancient Greek word. To be fucked by a giant radish. To be radished, ravished.

Vertumnus was coming.

A red light changed to green, and she was able to slip onward before the giant could advance to unpeel the roof of the Porsche and lift her out, homunculus-like, from her container.

Even in the heart of the city, a chthonic entity was coming to life. A liberated, incarnated deity was being born.

No one else but Jill saw it as yet.

Yet everyone knew it from ten thousand posters and badges – wearing its varied seasonal faces. Everyone knew Vertumnus by now, deity of change and transformation; for change was in the air, as ripe Autumn matured. The death of Self was on the horizon.

When she reached the motorway, those triple lanes cutting far ahead through the landscape opened up yawning perspectives of time rather than of space.

Deep time, in which there'd been no conscious mind present at all, only vegetable and animal existence. Hence, the blankness of the road . . .

Soon, a new psychic era might dawn in which the sovereign virtue of the conscious Self faded as humanity re-entered Nature once again – willing the demise of dissective, alienating logics and sciences, altering the mind-set, hypnotizing itself into a communal empathy with the world, whose potent figurehead wasn't any vague, cloudy Gaea, but rather her son Vertumnus. Every eating of his body – of fruits and nuts and vegetables and fishes – would be a vividly persuasive communion. His royal representative would reign in Budapest, or in Prague, or Vienna. His figurehead.

The phone burbled, and this time Jill did answer as she swung along the endless tongue of tarmac, and through time.

'Jill, don't hang up.' *Rumby*. 'I know why you've skipped out. And you must believe it ain't my fault.'

What was he talking about?

'I've been the well-meaning patsy in this business. I've been the Gorby.'

'Who was *he*?' she asked mischievously. Here was a message from a different era.

'I'm fairly sure by now that my goddam Star Club *was* behind the bombing *and* the ring-binder. Didn't trust me to be *thorough* enough. The whole Archy situation was really a lot more serious than even I saw. Those damn posters were really imprinting people on some deep-down level – not just surface propaganda. These are power-images. Fucking servo-symbols—'

'You're only *fairly* sure?' she asked.

'What tipped you off? Was it something *Case* said? Or Johnny Lascelles? Something Johnny let slip? I mean, why did you skip?'

Something Case or Lascelles had let slip . . .? So Rumby was becoming a tad paranoid about his own staff in case they were serving two masters – Rumby himself, and some other rich gent in that secret Star Club of theirs . . . A gent whom she had perhaps met in that drawing-room in North London; who had caned her at a distance . . .

'Come back, Jill, and tell me all you know. I'm serious! I need to know.'

Oh yes, she could recognize the authentic tones of paranoia . . .

'Sorry about taking the Porsche,' she said.

'Never mind the fucking car. Where are you, Jill?'

She remembered.

'I'm going to Oxford to see my brother. He's a bank manager.'

She hung up, and ignored repeated calls.

Polmerrin lay in a wooded little valley within a couple of miles of the rocky, wind-whipped North Cornwall coastline. Sheltered by the steep plunge of land and by oakwood, the once-derelict hamlet of cottages now housed studios and craft workshops, accompanied by a dozen satellite caravans. Pottery, jewellery, painting, sculpting, candle-making . . .

Kids played. Women worked. A few male companions lent an enlightened hand. Someone was tootling a flute, and a buzzard circled high overhead. A kingfisher flashed to and fro along a stream, one soggy bank of which was edged by alder buckthorn. Some brimstone butterflies still fluttered, reluctant to succumb to worn-out wings and cooling nights. The sunset was brimstone too: sulphur and orange-peel. A few arty tourists were departing.

Immediately Jill realized that she had come to the wrong place entirely. She ought to have fled to some high-tech airport hotel with gleaming glass elevators – an inorganic, air-conditioned, sealed machine resembling a space station in the void.

She was too tired to reverse her route.

Red-haired Annie embraced Jill, in surprise and joy, She kissed Jill, hugged her.

Freckled Annie was wearing one of those Indian cotton dresses – in green hues – with tiny mirrors sewn into it; and she'd put some extra flesh upon her once-lithe frame, though not to the extent of positive plumpness. She had also put on slim, scrutinizing glasses. Pewter rings adorned several fingers, with scarab and spider motifs.

One former barn was now a refectory, to which she led a dazed Jill to drink lemonade.

'How long has it been, Jilly? Four years? You'll stay with me, of course. So what's *happening*?' She frowned. 'I did hear about your book – and that awful bombing. I still listen to the radio all day long while I'm painting—'

'Jill's drugged,' said Jill. 'Vertumnus is reborn. And the Holy Roman Empire is returning.'

Annie scrutinized her with concern. 'Holy shit.' She considered. 'You'd better not tell any of the others. There are kids here. Folks might worry.'

They whispered, as once they had whispered confidences.

'Do you know the *Portrait of Jacopo Strada*?' Jill began. She found she could still speak about herself in the third person, historically.

Presently there were indeed kids and mothers and a medley of other women, and a few men in the refectory too, sharing an early supper of spiced beans and rice and salad and textured vegetable protein, Madras style, while Vivaldi played from a tape-deck. The beams of the barn were painted black, and murals of fabulous creatures relieved the whiteness of the plaster: a phoenix, a unicorn, a Minotaur, each within a maze-like Celtic surround, so that it seemed as if so many heraldic shields were poised around the walls. Tourists would enjoy cream teas in here of an afternoon.

Sulphur and copper had cleared from a sky that was now deeply leaden-blue, fast darkening. Venus and Jupiter both shone. A shooting star streaked across the vault of void; or was that a failed satellite burning up?

Annie shared a studio with Rosy and Meg, who would be playing chess that evening in the recreation barn beside the refectory. The whole ground floor of the reconditioned cottage was studio. Meg's work was meticulous neo-medieval miniatures featuring eerie freaks rather than anyone comely. Rosy specialized in acrylic studies of transparent hourglass buildings set within forests, or in crystalline deserts, and crowded with disembodied heads instead of sand.

Annie *used* to paint swirling, luminous abstracts. Now she specialized in large acrylic canvases of bloom within bloom within bloom, vortexes that sucked the gaze down into a central focus from which an eye always gazed out: a cat's, a bird's, a person's. Her pictures were like strange, exploded, organic cameras.

Jill looked; Jill admired. The paintings looked at her. Obviously there was a thematic empathy between the three women who used this studio.

'The conscious mind is going into eclipse,' Jill remarked, and Annie smiled hesitantly.

'That's a great title. I might use it.'

A polished wooden stairway led up to a landing with three bedrooms.

Annie's wide bed was of brass, with a floral duvet. Marguerites, daisies, buttercups.

In the morning when Jill awoke, the flowers had migrated from the duvet.

Annie's face, her neck, her shoulders were petals and stalks. Her skin was of white and pink blossoms. Her ear was a tulip, her nose was the bud of a lily, and her hair a fountain of red nasturtiums.

Jill reached to peel off some of the petals, but the flowers were flesh, and Annie awoke with a squeak of protest. Her open eyes were black nightshades with white blossom pupils.

And Jilldonaldson, whose name was dissolving, was the first to see such a transformation as would soon possess many men and women who regarded one another in a suitable light as part of Nature.

Jilldona stepped from the brass bed, towards the window, and pulled the curtains aside.

The valley was thick with mist. Yet a red light strobed the blur of vision. Spinning, this flashed from the roof of a police car parked beside the Porsche. Shapeless wraiths danced in its dipped headlight beams. One officer was scanning the vague, evasive cottages. A second walked around the Porsche, peered into it, then opened the passenger door.

'Hey,' said Annie, 'why did you tweak me?'

Annie's flesh was much as the night before, except that Jill continued to see a faint veil of flowers, an imprint of petals.

'Jill just wanted a cigarette,' said Jill.

'I quit a couple of years ago,' Annie reminded her. 'Tobacco costs too much. Anyway, *you* didn't smoke last night.'

'Jill forgot to. Fuzz are down there. Fuzz make Jill want a fag.'

'That braggartly car – we ought to have driven it miles away! Miles and miles.' Yet Annie didn't sound totally convinced that sheltering this visitor might be the best idea.

Jilldona pulled on her paisley sweater and jeans, and descended. Annie's paintings eyed her brightly as she passed by, recording her within their petal-ringed pupils.

She walked over to the police, one of whom asked:

'You wouldn't be a Miss Jill Donaldson, by any chance?' The burr of his Cornish accent . . .

'Names melt,' she told her questioner. 'The mind submerges in a unity of being. Have the Habsburgs sent you?' she asked. 'Or was it the Star Club?'

One officer removed the ignition key from the Porsche and locked the car.

The other steered her by the arm into the back of the strobing vehicle. She could see no flowers on these policemen. However, a pair of wax strawberries dangled discreetly from the driving-mirror like blood-bright testicles.

Swimming with the Salmon

Very well then, I do admit that I deliberately set out to seduce Fiona Dougal by means of my scent and my thoughts.

Oh, I genuinely desired Fiona. That's perfectly true. From our final year together in Bradainmurch School, when Fiona bloomed so bonny, I had fantasized about her embrace. Her lips, her limbs. From Tower House, through an antique brass telescope, I spied on her swimming with the salmon. Their great gleaming silver bodies. Her naked body, which shone for me, precious as silver.

The salmon farm occupied the western third of Loch Bradain. Commercial plantations of larch, spruce, and pine cloaked most of our side of the shore, but the pointy steeple rising high from the side of Tower House was uniquely sited for invading Fiona's privacy. My great-great-grandfather had brought that fine nautical telescope back from bygone whaling days. *He* had spied for sperm whales; courtesy of his souvenir I spied on Fiona, and my own sperm stirred.

In vain, during adolescence. Fiona was already commencing her apprenticeship as a priestess of salmon. Having pledged herself joyfully to this useful occupation, she was closely supervised. An older woman from the farm, Meddling Maggie, chaperoned Fiona. Fiona must have been psychologically profiled as of lesbian leanings otherwise she could hardly have become a salmon apprentice, could she?

My longstanding desire aside, I was also intrigued to discover whether I could succeed in conquering Fiona. She presented a challenge – of unavailability.

As well as of *vulnerability*, of course . . .

The scent component in human semen is pyrroline. Along with androstenone and certain fatty acids, pyrroline also occurs in a man's pubic area. The aroma of pyrroline isn't unlike overripe persimmon fruit or cooked chestnuts or corn on the cob. The meal which I ate a few hours before meeting the mature Fiona on that special afternoon consisted of helpings of corn and chestnuts and persimmon as accompaniment to wild boar meat sauced with truffles and garnished with parsley. I washed the meal down with a couple of glasses of a good Cabernet, which typically vents its bouquet from the drinker's skin several hours after he imbibes.

Then I presented Fiona Dougal with chocolates rich in phenylethylamine – the new 'hot chocolate' from Mexico spiced with capsaicin, a stimulating combination . . .

Since my puberty I'd been aware that if I wished for something strongly enough then my wishes would sway people. However, it was important not to clamour or nag. Verbal pleading provoked resistance. If I simply hinted, my heartfelt desires would insert themselves into parent or teacher or fellow pupil and flourish, magically transformed into their own preference. As a youngster I adopted a superstitious attitude to this phenomenon.

In reality, of course, my thoughts were giving rise to persuasive pheromones, chemical signals which influenced the behaviour of other people – in my case, *strikingly* so. Just as Fiona's pheromones could persuade fish to do as she wished. Was it a coincidence that individuals such as her and me were emerging nowadays in our enlightened era? People who could wish, and whose wishes would become messages? No, the technology for recognizing this allowed us talented ones to liberate what oodles of years of verbal civilization had repressed.

When my maths teacher, Dominie Urquhart, caught himself giving me a far higher grade than I deserved, he proceeded to scrutinize my other excellent results over the years. A COD test followed – with the ultimate consequence that I would become a diplomat in the service of the prosperous Republic of Scotland. (Prosperous, since our separation from the leech of England.) In Scotland we understood such phenomena ever since our development of Computerized Olfactory Diagnostics – in which the science of salmon farming had played no small part.

How fitting that 'COD,' as we called the technique, should also be the name of a fish which relies predominantly on chemical clues to trigger its behaviour. Salmon, of course, rely considerably on eyesight. Salmon possess eyes which are larger than their brains. Not that the hypothalamus of a salmon isn't massaged by hormonal chemical signals! It most certainly is. Thereby hung the whole art of modern salmoculture – and lovely Fiona Dougal's destiny.

Loch Bradain was roughly seven miles long, by two across, and shaped like a banana. Braes rose steeply from the narrow wooded north shore where roe deer loved to graze on bilberries in season. Over there, the odd buzzard soared above bouldery burns which plunged down through bracken, feeding the loch. Our southerly shore was flat and devoted to forestry. Consequently the upthrust of the Braes did not imply a corresponding depth to the loch. The River Baith bustled into Loch Bradain at the eastern end where the town of Bradainmurch clustered, dominated by its splendid Victorian Royal Hotel. Jetties tethered motorboats equipped with power-rods for the famed wild fishing worthy of Hemingway. The Baith continued out of Bradain more lazily to the west.

However, no salmon ever entered or left the loch by either branch of the Baith. Nor would they particularly yearn to leave, even if there weren't electrical containment fields in the water.

Salmo magnus – the giant salmon, upwards of eight feet long at maturity – had been genetically engineered to lack any migratory instinct whatever to seek the sea. This new species could be permanently farmed in one location.

Now, your ordinary salmon is by turns a very greedy eater and an anorexic. While at sea, it stuffs itself. Once back in its home river to spawn, your regular salmon starves. If it didn't starve itself, it might eat a river empty – of its own kin too. Anglers who caught your ordinary salmon in a river or loch would only ever find a minimal coating of slime in its belly when gutting it, nary a scrap of food.

So how did anglers ever manage to catch salmon? Not due to a salmon's greed for bait, oh no. But rather by teasing the fish's *curiosity* with a well-played lure.

And who teased a salmon best? Who caught the largest cock salmon? Who massaged these zany fishes' brains and racked up the records?

Notoriously it was women anglers.

Gillies had long since known that a man only needed to dip his finger in the spume at the bottom of a salmon run to scare salmon away for half an hour – whereas tyro female anglers could land fifty-pounders within minutes, as though charming the fish out of the water.

As in truth these ladies did, with their hormonal pheromones.

The odour of menstruation is prawny . . . while vanilla is a Spanish word derived from the Latin *vagina* . . . Think on't; think on't.

So as to attain maximum weight as swiftly as possible *Salmo magnus* must feed enthusiastically and constantly. Yet the sex organs shouldn't mature too early. Peer aggression must be suppressed.

The folk wisdom of the gillie, and genetic engineering, and odour diagnostics converged. The very best masseuse of the behaviour of these big fish was . . . woman. Woman herself, swimming with the big fish daily, releasing her scents into the water, massaging their nervous systems. Woman, without – it goes without saying – any reek of *man* about her. Virgin woman. Or lesbian woman. Whichever.

Hence the banning of men from the salmon co-operatives. Hence the priestly, Sapphic role which Fiona Dougal was to undertake.

Pheromones come in two classes. There are releaser pheromones which provoke a rapid, kneejerk reaction. Whereas primer pheromones alter the physiology of a creature through its endocrine system, thus conditioning its future, longer-term behaviour. The women who swam with the salmon primed those fish and kept them well-primed to gobble and gobble their food pellets docilely till they were ripe for harvest – and a percentage of them for release into the wild zone of the loch where men could angle for them, as I was to angle for Fiona on my return from Mexico.

Salmon can fairly be described as crazy fish. Bizarre, eccentric fish. Capricious, curious creatures of whim. Those who only know salmon as a red steak on a plate know nothing. And the women of the fish farms knew secrets unbeknownst to man. Fulfilling secrets, I'm sure. For salmon had always possessed a deep rapport with women. As did many fish species, to a lesser degree. It was a woman who wrote the first treatise on angling back in 1425 or so. Dame Juliana. Specialized cells on the skins of salmon respond to complex stimuli; and it must be true that women responded in turn to the touch and caress and pressure of *Salmo magnus*.

Thus the women of the fish farms were effectively witches belonging to a piscine nature cult quite out of bounds to man – a cult where, yes, one ate the God! Well, this was modern Scotland, land of enlightenment. One did not bridle at such scientific witchery or at a necessary lesbianism or celibacy.

Superficially these women were merely very competent pisciculturists – a respected élite of specialists whose natural glandular secretions happened to play a major role in their work. I suspected more. This witchcraft intrigued me utterly.

What of my relations with Fiona, before her destiny seized her? What of that cusp of time during which she bloomed, just prior to her enrolment in the cult?

Why did I not exert myself then, to wish a kiss? To wish *more*? To project my desires upon Fiona? To lead her on a ramble through woods where the wee siskins feasted on pine and spruce seeds; through rhododendrons spreading their tents of glossy leaves?

The reason was my twisted foot which surgery had failed to correct fully. I would have been ashamed to shed my special shoe, thus any other of my garments. I didn't swim. I was excused from sports. I wouldn't have wished to hobble into the woods or rhododendrons, emphasizing my flaw – and where else was there for a lad to go?

Only later on did I realize that such a deformity could lead to Byronic achievements with the ladies, over whom a clubbed foot might actually exert a fascination and a magnetism comparable to those persuasive pheromones I deployed as though by way of compensation.

Fiona certainly consorted with no other lads, and she spurned any of their fumbling overtures. Consequently I wasn't tormented by jealousy, which might have spurred me to *wish*. Besides, I was only fifteen then, and uncertain exactly what I would be wishing for in practical detail. For a wish to come true I needed to visualize the outcome more accurately.

Soon she was sixteen; and so was I. And she joined the cult, while I was on my route out of Bradainmurch, and only remained alert to Fiona's attractions, in miniature, by telescope. (Did she ever glance up from the salmon-teeming water and spy the glint of the glass high up on Tower House?)

Were I a salmon I might have seen Fiona even more acutely, for during the daytime a salmon favours the colour-perceptive cones in its eye, while at dusk these retract in favour of the optic rods which see black and white, thus boldly silhouetting desirable shapes. Remarkable creatures! I was jealous of those giant fish gliding between Fiona's legs, rubbing their slime-coated scales sinuously, powerfully against her flesh. I was jealous of the secrets which I was sure she was learning, and which separated her from me.

Yet in a sense, in that piscine harem of the farm, she was being safeguarded for my future self, was she not? The secret of a great love is often separation, confinement of one party, exile of the other. Stendhal, who wrote much about love, understood this. Perhaps, in this regard, I am the archetypal lover – whose other conquests were all subsidiary to my feelings for forbidden Fiona.

A wish can accumulate over many years until it discharges itself overwhelmingly and compellingly . . .

After attending Glasgow University, where I concentrated on foreign languages and economics, I travelled widely in the diplomatic service. There are so many mini-nations in the world, fractions of one-time larger countries enmeshed in new alliances. One is almost a medieval traveller, once again. And I often found lovers, almost as if the fractured world was trying through me to reknit itself erotically into a macro-organism. I *persuaded* women, as effectively as I persuaded foreign politicians and industrialists. My heraldry would have been a clubbed foot set within a heart.

Always, reinforced by all these encounters, a fundamental dominating wish was building up like thunderous electric potential in the sky seeking its lightning conductor.

I believe now that I wasn't obsessed in a pathological fashion (the beast beneath the diplomatic façade, as it were) but rather that a curious form of pheromonal feedback operated, whereby I imprinted myself with my own persuasions – with self-persuasions. In my heart, always the memory trace of Fiona Dougal, naked, water-cloaked, at once far away and near, swimming with the phallic fish.

I denied myself the chance of returning prematurely to Tower House, enjoying the high tension which this self-exile generated in me. My own parents had divorced acrimoniously when I was eight, and the Republic of Scotland had deemed it best for me to live with my uncle and aunt in Tower House just outside Bradainmurch on the lochside. A rural upbringing. I never felt especially close to Duncan and Tara Hamilton, whose surname I adopted. After I left for Glasgow, Tanty-Tara died suddenly – of a stroke – and thereafter Unk-Dunk became a grouching recluse, who seemed to blame me for *wishing her dead*. Now that he knew of my talent he reinterpreted my boyhood, and the way that Tanty-Tara had constantly put herself out for me, harshly. To his now-disordered mind, she had worn herself out on behalf of a parasite. Sufficient for me to viz Unk-Dunk once in a while on the phonescreen. He never suggested I pay a visit.

I reserved old-style *written letters* for Fiona, and these were part of my long-term strategy, careful moves in my master game of love. I commenced on my very first junior posting, to Québec.

A voice from the past – or rather, no discletter voice at all, but elegantly calligraphed words. A bolt from the blue for Fiona Dougal.

I felt the need, I explained to her, to write to somebody back home – since my aunt had died, and my uncle was potty – so as to preserve my sense of connection with Bradainmurch and the past; and I trusted that Fiona wouldn't mind being the recipient of my random musings?

I made those letters as fascinating as I could, full of local Québécois colour. Fiona, who must have been puzzled, did

reply to the third with a jaunty holocard depicting the Braes.
Her writing was scrawly and she spelled a couple of words
eccentrically.

Thus I wrote, for another decade, while the wish accumulated
within me. I wrote from Catalunya, from Belarus, from
Amazonia, from Mexico. Fiona's life, of course, was the loch;
yet the exotic presently hooked her. Since I was forever
elsewhere (and took my vacations elsewhere), I seemed a safe
person to confide in (to a certain degree) about her life on the
farm. Oh, no *secrets*, to be sure! She was reserved about those.
Yet I gathered that she now enjoyed the companionship of one
Jane McDonald, that they were thinking about maybe adopting
a daughter later on, that Meddling Maggie had retired to the
Hebrides, that Fiona and Jane would go into town of a Friday
night to drink Glenbaith whiskies (made with water taken from
further upstream, so as not to confuse odours) . . . Fiona
sometimes wrote about fish diseases, which seemed to fascinate
her. Infective Haematopoitic Necrosis caused frenzied swimming and bulging of the eyeballs. Myxosomiasis, due to
parasites becoming encysted in the brain, was also known as
Whirling Disease; fish would chase their own tails relentlessly.

I never sent a holo-pic of myself, nor she of herself. It wasn't
that sort of correspondence (though at the same time, of course,
it was *becoming* so, on the non-verbal level). Nor did I ever scent
my writing-paper with pyrroline.

Then she was thirty; and I was thirty. I'd begun to hint about a
remarkable Mayan sculpture of fish and woman which I had
come across in the Yucatan jungle. Erotic, disturbing, numin-
ous. At this point, fortuitously Unk-Dunk died, likewise of a
stroke and of lying alone in Tower House undiscovered for
several days.

My diplomatic duties prevented me from returning in time for
his funeral early in August. But a month later I flew in to
Bradainmurch by helicopter, squandering a substantial sum on
this private flight just so that we could pass slowly over the
salmon farm.

The loch seemed to writhe with silver worms under the skin
of water. There, in their own zones, were a horde of smaller

salmon. In adjacent zones, larger fish. Then, largest of all: seven, eight-footers. Colour-coded marker buoys indicated boundaries and corridors. From the bed of the loch submerged cables deployed electric fields – of four volts per metre, to be precise, in pulses lasting 0.8 milliseconds fifteen times per second. These fields prevented any salmon from straying into senior or junior territory. Which was due to electrotaxis. Any fish entering the electric field would lose control of its swimming muscles. Nerve cells under the salmon's skin would kick the fish into a reflex, compelling it to return towards the positive electrode.

Compelling it. Salmo couldn't do otherwise, whatever he wished. His body would simply disobey his brain, and obey the electric field instead.

Would Fiona's body disobey her brain? Or would it be her brain which disobeyed the usual preferences of her body and the codes of her fish cult?

We were flying sluggishly at a few hundred feet. Down below, a nude woman scrambled on to one of the rafts, shaking herself as if in protest at our intrusion. Was that *herself*? No, the woman down below was raven-haired. Since this was September, she might already be wearing a heating-web, though such a mesh was transparent – since salmon are visual identifiers – and flimsy, since bodily exposure was of the essence.

Why didn't she stay submerged instead of exposing herself? Ah, the food dispenser on the raft began to throw out its hailstorm of synthetic protein pellets. The water boiled as Salmo gobbled.

A floating walkway led from that raft to a jetty where a stubby barge wallowed, part-flooded inside, some mobile aquatic surgery equipped with stout winch and plastic sling. The hugest of the farm buildings overlapped the water on stone pillars. A lane of day-glo red buoys led under the overhang. Ah, somewhere within – somewhere more confined – would be a killing zone, for electrocuting the harvest of the loch.

Could it be that a fish mistress would swim in under there, luring the chosen fish along with her like some pheromonal Pied Piper? Momentarily I imagined malice and murder, since a full-grown Salmo's body was bigger than a woman's. If a fish mistress was still in the water she could be shocked dead by a seeming malfunction. I quickly dismissed this fantasy, for the priestesses must live together in amity, must they not?

That major building must also house the gutting lines, packing lines, freezers, smoking kilns . . . And what else? Oh yes, an ascorbic acid tank to reduce rancidity in storage. A big one of those.

Other buildings were visibly residential. For the first time it occurred to me to wonder whether the women actually *did* eat salmon – even ceremonially, at special feasts? Or was eating the flesh of *Salmo magnus* perhaps taboo . . .?

Mysteries, mysteries . . . And that covered floating structure . . . close by a *brood zone*? Was that a place where the priestesses milked mature bucks of their milt?

I ceased craning my neck, for we were well beyond the farm by now. Sooty-faced sheep grazed along the shoreline.

'Had enough of an eyeful?' the pilot asked dourly.

'A salmon would have seen more,' said I, thinking of those giant eyes.

'Maybe next time you ought to come home by submarine,' was his response.

Unk-Dunk had never fitted any part of Tower House out with automatics, thus I hadn't been able to control its status remotely. However, I'd asked uncle's solicitor in Bradainmurch to send in his clerk to switch on the boiler and heating and fridge in anticipation of my arrival.

I shared a dram with whiskery Mr Henderson in his office and accepted muted condolences – bearing in mind that I hadn't been back in over a decade and had, unlike dutiful Mr Henderson, missed the funeral. Despite Unk-Dunk's mutterings, he had never reneged on an early will drawn up in my favour. Well, I wouldn't have wished him to, even though no vizphone call conveyed aromas.

I drove the rental electro Volvo along the lakeside road quickly, the sooner to transfer my boar meat and truffles and persimmon from a travelling coolpack into the fridge. Before heading to the heliport in Glasgow I'd stocked up at a delicatessen.

The old house was somewhat of a mess inside, as one might expect of a crusty widower's abode. More significantly, it smelled of some damned lavatorial disinfectant, and at first I experienced quite a surge of annoyance at the Bradainmurch authorities and Henderson. Unk-Dunk hadn't exactly *rotted* here, so why should they presume to disinfect Tower House! I threw all doors and windows wide open, as well as turning the heating up full to compensate for the incoming breezes.

As I ranged through the familiar rooms on all three floors I discovered the sources of the wretched smell. Just as a person with spiritual inclinations might burn incense, so my uncle had secreted saucers of disinfectant all over the house to de-scent the air and banish any rival fragrances. In the cellar itself lurked half a dozen large cases of unopened bottles of germicide. Unhinged by Tanty-Tara's death, had Unk-Dunk supposed that by this stratagem, which he presumably rationalized as maintaining a healthy regime in Tower House, he was purging all trace of my influence?

I swiftly got rid of all such saucers, which bid fair to thwart me from beyond the grave. Naturally I'd brought aphrodisiacal essential oils with me. Sweet spicy sandalwood which relieves anxiety in a sedative way. Euphoric jasmine, warming and relaxing. And juniper, the pleasant terebinthate odour of which counteracts trembling and coldness. I went off into the woods to gather a sackful of pine needles, cones, and bark, and soon had impromptu pot-pourri in every room. Then I tackled a build-up of dust and cobwebs which surely predated my uncle's demise, and a kitchenful of dirty utensils.

Soon night fell, so I locked the doors, though I still left windows open. After fixing myself a neutral, purgative meal of rice and bland beans, I mounted at last to the hexagonal lookout room and sat at the faithful old telescope to scan the moon-dappled reaches of the loch. I attached a micro-electronic photomultiplier which I'd bought in Mexico City. Alas, since my adolescence trees had grown taller. My perspective on the waters of the salmon farm was curtailed. No matter! I need be a voyeur no more.

'My *correspondent*,' repeated Fiona – exactly as she had said on the vizphone that morning when I called the salmon farm to invite her to tea; for which she had arrived by bicycle.

She clasped both my hands briefly before perching on the sofa, smoothing down a tartan skirt, which was Hunting Stewart, I believe. The black, red, and yellow grid lines on the blue-green background of the plaid suggested to me those cables and electric fields in the waters of the loch. Fiona also wore a white blouse, over which her russet hair spilled, and matching tartan socks and strong leather sandals. Oh she was muscular from all the swimming, as well as from labour inside the fish factory. An athlete, or goddess, whose delicate freckles had merged together so that she was golden. Full lips, noble nose, wide opaline eyes.

She gazed at me full of curiosity, as I lightly limped towards Tanty-Tara's tea service, seeing the gauche boy of yesteryear transformed into a graceful, languid but passionful man, hazel-haired, with knowing eyes which had seen many countries.

She couldn't help glancing at my clumpy shoe. 'So they never . . . Oh I'm sorry,' she murmured, confused. Already, physical curiosity. 'But why did you write to *me*?'

'I think,' I replied, 'that I needed a secret confidante, one who was aware of secrets herself. Of the mysteries of the world.'

'Mysteries, as in the jungles of Yucatan . . . Jamie?' Ah, my intimate name . . .

'It's galling . . . Fiona,' I replied, 'but my camera got a dunking and was smashed against a boulder in a stream we were fording. You see, I was *swept off my feet*. The filmdisc was ruined. The statue was in obsidian – black glassy volcanic rock, too heavy to transport. We stumbled upon it near the coast, half coated in creepers. A fish and a woman were coiled together as though they were *lovers*. My guides had seen nothing like that before, and archaeologists I asked . . . well, they were disparaging. This was outside of their experience.'

I handed her a cup of tea and a plate of shortbreads interspersed with many chocolates.

'I brought these chocs all the way from Mexico,' I explained. She ate a couple. And then a few more.

Her odour, close to, hinted at a fishy oiliness. The net curtains of the drawing-room filtered dying September sunlight across the two thick sheepskin rugs I'd laid over the frayed old chequered carpet. Embers glowed ruddily in the stone hearth; fresh flame licked around a new log. The room was hot.

'What makes you think there are secrets?' she asked, nodding in the direction of the loch.

'There must be, mustn't there?'

'Because *you* have secrets?'

I shrugged. 'Why are *you* interested in this fish and woman statue, then?'

'Why?' she echoed. (Yes, let her echo me.) 'Why? Because *you* are, Jamie!'

'And why am I interested in it, Fiona?'

I wished. I craved. I yearned, as never before with any woman.

Amidst scents of jasmine and juniper and sandalwood pot-pourri, whiff of woodsmoke, subtle bouquet of Cabernet, fragrance of boar and truffle, the subterranean magma of desire was welling upward, venting all its persuasive pheromones . . .

Fiona considered me. 'I feel I know you so well from all your letters, Jamie . . .'

Let us really know each other then, Fiona. Let us. Let us.

Of course, I abridge somewhat.

The moon was rising when we at last uncoiled, there upon those sheepskin rugs in the glow of the fire. I felt strangely bestialized – yet exaltingly so – as though I'd been transformed into another species of being, into a puissant giant godlike fish, which at last – at long last – Fiona could couple with realistically, and upon whom she had discharged at last all her own decade and more of accumulated appetite. Surely this was the secret of the salmon farm – this alien cathexis, this focusing of vital energy upon a foreign species without hope hitherto of full consummation. Fiona's own female lover, Jane, was human, after all. Jane might imitate *Salmo magnus* but could not be Salmo.

The story I had concocted, of that Mayan idol, had not been so far askew after all. Deep in all human dreams, as exposed by myth, was the yearning to unite with whichever totem creature a culture chose as its inhuman ideal, to represent Otherness. Eagle. Jaguar. Serpent. Spirit-guides; yet also emblems of the body's desire by means of Otherness to become . . . magnificent, transcendent.

And thus Fiona was fulfilled. And I too. And I.

She did not reproach me, since what we had enacted was . . . sublime. The moon outside the window seemed to say that if we human beings ever travelled far beyond to another world of sapient beings somewhere in the universe, then our meeting with such beings should ideally be thus.

She did not reproach. Yet she was riven by an anguish.

'I shall swim home,' she told me. 'I shall swim to clean myself.'

'Aren't you hungry, Fiona?' I asked her.

'Hungry? How could I be hungry when I have *gorged* myself?'

'Do you have a heating-web with you?'

She shook her russet hair. No.

'It's September. It's night.'

'The chill will kill scents.' She laughed brusquely. Contradictorily, she added, 'Strong swimming warms a person. I shall swim so strongly tonight, burning off what has happened.'

It would have been banal to offer to drive her back in the Volvo, supposing that she simply didn't wish to ride her bike.

'Don't worry that I'll *drown*,' she assured me.

Nude, she sprinted across the unkempt lawn, down the strand of sand. She waded. She dived. Her tartan skirt had remained like a map discarded.

Pulling a sheepskin rug around me like some ancient savage, I clumped quickly upstairs again to my telescope. By amplified light I watched Fiona cleave the waters of Bradain.

Presently silver humps broke the surface near where she swam. Wild *Salmo magnus* accompanied her, those prey for the hooks of Hemingways. Though no doubt scenting traces of human semen, they didn't flee. Around her, the water seemed to foam with milk. Could that merely be liquid moonlight?

So was it actually *milt* that I saw? The roe of the male fish, discharged due to the tang of my own seed within Fiona, and upon her?

And then she swam through the shock-fields; *her* muscles wouldn't disobey in the way that a fish's would.

And in her womb, or in a Fallopian tube, the electric shock fused milt and sperm and ovum . . .

What Jane McDonald has deposed to the Procurator Fiscal is that Fiona Dougal became pregnant that night. When the other fish mistresses sensed this (quite soon), they sequestered Fiona as if she were some delinquent nun in a medieval convent; though housed in more comfort . . .

I'm summarizing what you told me, Mr Ambassador . . . *Jock*. What they sent in the pouch from Scotland, in the diplomatic sporran. So that we get all the facts and nuances correct. Thus we might sort out the truth.

After that special afternoon, I only stayed on in Bradainmurch for five more days, sufficient to put Tower House on the market. I didn't see Fiona again, nor did I viz her at the farm. Well, the wish had gone. The wish had been fulfilled. Transcendently so. How banal – how impractical – to contemplate . . . an *affair*, which a woman in Fiona's line of occupation couldn't conceivably countenance, especially given her emotional bias. If *she* had chosen to viz me, I'd have been astonished. Before leaving Bradainmurch, I had a local girl ride Fiona's bike back to the farm gate and park the bike there, with an addressed parcel upon the saddle containing Fiona's abandoned clothing. I included no paltry note. Nor did I write again, from abroad. Nor did she write to me, from her confinement.

You say that as Fiona's pregnancy advanced, the mistresses leased a small domestic ultrasound scanner? And found, to their consternation, that the lower half of the foetus curled up within her displayed the contours of . . . a *fish* . . .

That what was growing in her womb was a merbaby?

A teratogenic monster? Or . . . a consummation for their cult?

When Fiona commenced labour, the mistresses took her out into the loch? There, in the water, she gave birth to this hybrid – of me, and her, and Salmo?

And the baby – a girl – swam a little?

Yet, scenting the blood of birth, a great cock salmon darted up and *ate* the little mermaid voraciously.

It was then that Jane McDonald fled from the farm in horror, and from Fiona, to the Procurator Fiscal, demanding prosecutions of the priestesses, and of me as well for some reason as accessory to the deed . . .

But Fiona herself didn't flee. And she has denied this version of events. She is soon going to become the chief fish mistress of Loch Bradain, so you tell me.

I must remind you, *Jock*, that Jane is a renegade, a crazed woman. And the evidence is missing . . . eaten, so Jane claims.

Why does the Procurator believe that a merchild could be born at all? He *does*, doesn't he? He must be daft in the head. Jock, I don't much wish to go back there to testify. I really don't.

I suppose that a fish-tailed child *should* best be born in water . . . In that case why didn't the mistresses protect the birthing zone with an electric field? Did some malicious body switch the current off? Did Jane herself, as a jealous revenge for being betrayed by Fiona? Or are we hinting at a deliberate sacrifice of that fishy firstborn? Is that it, Jock? Hence Fiona becoming high priestess afterwards! Then Jane McDonald became terrified at what was happening?

Ah. I see that I've fallen into a trap. *A fish-tailed child*. Yes, those were my words: a fish-tailed child. The absurd power of the notion has already captured me. I, who have been such a dab hand at persuading people, women especially, am now persuaded in turn. When my seduction of Fiona was so climactic – culmination of so many years of canny ardour – how could I imagine that the event would have had no consequence? That the whole episode would simply come to a full stop after she swam away from Tower House? In this sense I suppose I *am* an accomplice – innocent accessory to something which our Procurator frets about, something he fears may emerge from the mutant fish farms where the pheromonal women swim. Some marvel, some abomination. Some half-human fish-goddess. A chimera. I can spy his drift now, Jock.

Pledged to eschew the embraces of men, the priestesses couldn't have *expected* anything like this to happen. Fiona swam home so as to 'cleanse' herself, she told me. Yet now those women have experienced a dreadful miracle. What if another of them is impregnated by a man and immediately swims among the milt-spurting giant cock salmon? Presuming that Jane McDonald did cut the current and kill the newborn mermaid, what if chief fish mistress Fiona herself chooses to repeat her act of intercourse?

Oh, I don't wish to fly home, Jock. Can't you perceive the peril I might be in? How vulnerable I could become, now that this conception is in my head, persuading me?

Sleep on it.

Why certainly, sleep on it. You're an understanding gentleman, Jock. Probably I could use a leave of absence. Of course I appreciate why the Procurator wants to quiz me about this peculiar affair. Exports of salmon are important to the Scottish economy.

I think of my semen mixed with milt. Outside Ambassador Dalgleish's office, the Mexican sun is blinding bright, like a copper gong on fire. Nowhere in Mexico does it shine on any obsidian idol of any fish and woman mating. Yet in a Scottish loch, far away in the land of enlightenment, that same sun rose earlier today upon a loch, and upon silver bodies which the human race has created by godlike intervention in their genes, aping a divine intimacy.

How, now, shall I renew my intimacy with Fiona Dougal?

The Bible in Blood

It was simplicity itself to let myself into Appledorn's hotel suite. The under-manager of the Strasbourg Hilton had provided me with a master card-key several days before Henry Appledorn checked in at the hotel. I'd replaced the security chain with one which would snap easily. The under-manager was a *sayan*, a friendly local who would readily assist Israeli intelligence. We can rely on thousands of such individuals in many countries.

Naturally, I hadn't told our French under-manager that I intended to confront Appledorn and his secretary and their visitor with a pistol in my hand. None of his business. He wasn't involved.

The Beretta fitted snuggly in my palm. Standard issue for Mossad field officers. ·22 calibre. Loaded with dum-dum bullets.

In with the card-key. Turn the handle softly.

Ah yes, the occupants of the suite had chained the door.

Apply a shoulder. The links snapped.

'Don't anyone move,' I said. 'Don't make any noise.' And I shut the door behind me.

On a chrome and glass table there rested a pile of parchment pages penned in Gothic script. The letters were all of a dark brown hue, the colour of dried blood. The open case and backbone formed a portfolio, for those sheets were loose-leaf without any stitching or tailband as yet. Faded red silk ribbons would tie the portfolio shut. The case was bound in black leather with steel protectors at the corners. Though I couldn't see the front, its slight elevation from the glass of the table suggested that emblems embossed the surface. A steel cross, perhaps, and steel swastikas.

So there it was at last: the Bible Written in Blood.

To be strictly accurate, the New Testament. A good 95 per cent of the New Testament.

Not all of it. Herzwalde concentration camp had been evacuated, due to the approach of the Red Army, while the scribes were commencing their slow labour on the Book of the Revelation.

Our American bibliophile, Henry Appledorn, darted a protective glance at the huge, incomplete, unbound volume. Our book collector was tall and rangy, with a predilection to stoop. His curly hair had turned snowy, as befitted his seventy years. His was a basset-hound face, long and somewhat ruddy.

Despite my warning, Appledorn's hand strayed to touch the silk handkerchief in his breast pocket. Couldn't he conceive of his own death? Did my sudden intrusion merely offend him?

Ah, he was worrying whether I might cause blood to spurt on to the volume in question, staining it.

How quickly could he mop the parchment page clean with his handkerchief? What cleansing agents would distinguish between recently spilled blood and the older dried brown blood of the text?

Klaus Bauer, procurer of the volume from its hiding-place in former East Germany, appeared to be calculating whether he might heave up the bulky tome to use as a shield – or to hurl at me, disarmingly.

Bauer was thick-set but whey-faced, as if he had shunned the sunlight for a long time. He looked so cleanly scrubbed with his large pink hands and shaven skull that he reminded me of a potato. His jacket and slacks were creamy and recently pressed.

The woman, Appledorn's secretary, avoided focusing on my gun.

'What are *you*?' she demanded. 'An *occultist*?'

I'd been intending to order all three of them to lie prone on the carpet to allow me to inject each in turn, rendering them comatose, after which I would simply decamp with the book . . .

Her question threw me. I had to know exactly what Gloria Cameron implied by it.

She was golden-haired, tweed-suited, her ruffleted blouse

trimmed with embroidered roses. Brown leather brogues with brass buckles on her feet. Butch. Perceptive.

I imagined her equipped with a whip, and dressed in impeccable SS uniform, striding through a camp of cowering women. I felt weak inside. My weakness became fury – and fascination.

Yet Gloria's accent was Scots, overlaid by a slight American veneer. She was a graduate of Edinburgh University, her speciality bibliography.

I ought to have carried out my plan by rote, ignoring distractions. However, within me – confronted at last by the Bible in Blood – my mother's dreams were stirring. And within those dreams lurked another person, namely my father . . .

Facts are never simple. Facts splinter into a kaleidoscope of interpretations.

Early in 1943 SS Colonel Gottfried von Turm became deputy commandant of Herzwalde labour camp. He was lame in the left leg. He'd been invalided back from the Russian front, from the doomed attempt to relieve the Nazi forces penned in Stalingrad.

From the jaws of hell – into a cauldron of death. Death cooked up by his own kind.

Yet were the other SS quite his own kind?

For a Prussian aristocrat to join the ranks of the fighting Waffen-SS was quite unusual. The Waffen-SS were superhuman . . . *scum*. For the most part they were brutal peasants – trained to be Übermenschen. Their military officers lacked the most elementary sense of tactics, though they knew how to rampage, and SS fighting units always had better weapons than the regular army.

Gottfried had once implied to my mother (or at least she took him to be implying) that he'd been obliged to join this band of butchers so as to protect his own family from some ambiguous fate.

Soon after Gottfried arrived at Herzwalde, he conceived the project of the Bible in Blood.

That camp housed, among many other unfortunates, a fair salting of rabbis and other Jewish *Intelligenten* – unphysical men for whom the forced labour of quarrying stone and logging in the surrounding forests was especially lethal on top of the starvation rations, the beatings, shootings, the interminable freezing roll-calls.

Jews had committed *blood-crime* by murdering the Saviour. Why, the mere existence of Jews constantly posed a genetic blood-threat to the purity of the Aryan race.

Especially in the eyes of the SS the pure blood that coursed through the veins of the German peasant was sacred. Had not Alfred Rosenberg proclaimed a mystic philosophy of blood as the true Germanic faith? Had not Hitler endorsed this crazy sanguinarianism? Was not the SS a new priesthood of blood?

So therefore Colonel von Turm ordained that the most noteworthy rabbis and eggheads should be gathered together in a special blockhouse. There, they should redeem their blood-crimes and purge their *verfluchte Judentum* by writing out the whole of the New Testament in their own life-blood.

Was this a monstrous joke on his part? A malicious insult to the prisoners? Certainly, other SS personnel took it as such, applauding Gottfried's wit.

True, at first I believe there was *some* dispute with his superior or his fellow officers. Had not the Führer wished to erase Christianity in favour of a revived Odinic paganism? Ah, but not even Hitler could afford to offend the Church too deeply. Besides, many of the SS peasantry had been deeply branded in boyhood with Catholicism.

Later on, those SS in Herzwalde would become quite fanatic in a darkly superstitious vein about the progress of the project. It seemed to them as though this scriptural work was obliterating the very essence of the Hebrew race in a magical fashion – just as they themselves were occupied in annihilating the physical existence of Jews.

Now, this was bound to be a long, slow project. For how much blood could easily be siphoned from the veins of the scribes by those scribes themselves? How quickly would the blood-ink congeal? What type of pen-nibs should best be used? How to ensure compatibility of calligraphy? How could the work best be divided so that costly parchment was not wasted by, for example, the First Epistle to the Corinthians ending at the top of one sheet, while the Second Epistle had already been started by a different scribe at the top of another sheet? And in the event of empty spaces, what decorative motifs should be employed to fill up the gaps? Swastikas? Death's-heads pierced with daggers? Crucifixions? Taunting pastoral scenes of Palestine?

These were exactly the kind of minutiae which obsessed the intellects of the SS who operated concentration camps. A hundred petty laws and prohibitions! With a savage whipping or hanging as punishment for infringement.

The colonel played upon this savage pedantry.

What if the chosen Jews' blood was *anaemic* due to the scanty rations of watery garbage soup, black ersatz coffee, and stale bread?

Very soon the scribes' diet was being boosted with sausages and cheese from incoming parcels which the SS always stole (though they might occasionally let the wrapping-paper be delivered), and with fresh fruit and eggs and rabbit stew.

What if the scribes' fingers were too numb to hold the pens skilfully enough to form the Gothic letters Gottfried insisted upon?

Why, *two* stoves must be kept well fuelled in the Scripture Block.

While the band of scribes regained some body weight and bloomed with renewed health, other less literate inmates of Herzwalde carried on labouring and dying of hunger and illness and beatings.

Aha! Was the Scripture Block – aside from being an insult to the faith of those within – also a cunning ploy to make its inmates resented and hated by other prisoners? The SS, permanently poised on the brink of capricious rage at Unter-menschen, may have thought in this vein. *'See how those precious rabbis and eggheads grow fat while you become bones!'* In actuality, most residents of squalid, bestial Herzwalde had no surplus energy to spare for hatred. They hardly had enough energy to spare for conscious thought at all.

As I've said, the majority of the SS had no sense of *tactics* . . . Might it be that Colonel Gottfried von Turm was in fact preserving, in his Scripture Block, the cream of Jewish people, the intellectual and spiritual leadership, for some post-bellum

salvation? Such an idea never crossed the minds of his boor-
ish colleagues. Still, Gottfried must prevent any such notion
from arising there – or taking root in the brains of his
clever beneficiaries. Like some mystic high priest of the
satanic Schutzstaffel he would rant about sacred and polluted
blood.

Many of the assembled rabbis, for their part, were know-
ledgeable about the Kabbalah. They knew the *Sepher Yesirah*, the
Book of Creation, inside out, and the *Zohar* of Moses de Leon.
They murmured while they dipped their pens in their own
blood and copied the scripture of their oppressors . . .

'What do you mean, Miz Cameron?'

The woman stared at me witheringly. So I jerked the Beretta
towards her tweed-clad knees, threatening to cripple her unless
words danced upon her lips.

Why hadn't Appledorn let her handle the acquisition of the
book? Why did *he* need to be present personally at the hand-
over in this hotel suite in Strasbourg, here on the Franco-
German border? So that he could authenticate his purchase by
smell and by feel and by sixth sense?

Suppose he had stayed behind in Florida . . . maybe the
plane winging the book back to the States might have plunged
into the Atlantic en route. It might have crashed on arrival at
Orlando airport, incinerating the unique pages . . .

Appledorn had to take control of the book right away.

What did he plan to do with it thereafter?

I'd *assumed* that he would lock it up along with other
bibliographic treasures, reserved for his eyes only.

Now I wondered whether this was all he intended.

'Does your boss plan to complete the Bible?' I demanded.
'Using whose blood? *Your own?*'

Gloria Cameron twitched.

'Do you intend to finish the Book of the Revelation, Mr
Appledorn?' I harangued, sounding rather like a camp guard
myself. 'What *revelation* do you expect to achieve?'

Klaus Bauer stared from one to another of us in bemusement.
And with greedy regret. Had he somehow underestimated the
value of the Bible in Blood to this collector?

Bauer asked me in German in a wheedling tone, 'Are you one of the faithful?'

The faithful? The *faithful*? I hadn't heard this expression before. Did it refer to Judaism – or was it some neo-Nazi code? Did Bauer imagine that I wished to spirit the book away to some Hitlerian shrine? To some revived Wewelsburg Castle?

Bauer annoyed me. I shunned any conceivable association between himself and me. I wished him to sweat.

'I'm Israeli intelligence,' I told him.

'Why,' asked Gloria Cameron, 'would Israeli intelligence wish to kidnap a *book*?'

Well, of course we wouldn't . . . unless the action served Israel's interests . . . which it hardly could, unless Kabbalists were running our country.

'*I* ask the questions,' I retorted.

Whether due to the strain of the occasion – this climax to a long search – or on account of sheer proximity to the book, my mother's dreams came welling up in me . . .

SS Colonel von Turm limped, using a silver-handled walking-cane. With this he would lash out at the occasional tattered slave who didn't step smartly enough to one side and pull off his beret swiftly enough from his cropped cranium.

In fact, the colonel never *damaged* any slave worker with his cane – unlike other SS who would beat an inmate to death. Perhaps he was concerned about snapping his walking-cane. Perhaps not. A lick from the stick was equivalent to a shot of electric current in a moribund frog's leg. It galvanized the walking dead. They survived a little longer.

Von Turm's eyes were an icy blue. The ice of Russian winter; the ice of Prussian disdain.

He was well fleshed.

He too needed to relieve the strain of the occasion . . . and maybe do something extra by way of lagniappe, as they say down Appledorn's way or thereabouts.

One afternoon, since it was freezing cold, the SS decided to order a new intake of women to stand naked on parade while they chose which to assign to the Brothel Block, which to the quarries, which to extinction. The women had been marched forty kilometres from their previous work camp, relocated to fulfil some whim or bureaucratic quota. Those who had survived the trek were desperately tired. Therefore, with the crops of their whips, the SS lifted the girls' tits to determine who was firm enough for brothel duty.

Aryans for the SS guards and for visiting soldiers. Jews for the common criminals who had become overseers of slaves.

Exercising the caprice of rank, and rather in breach of SS protocol, von Turm ordered that my mother, Bella, should be sent to him for his use that evening. For she stood proudly. A tall, skinny waif, a starveling with large brown eyes and shaven head.

His quarters were beautifully furnished with loot, including a fine four-poster bed. On a table was set a carafe of milk, a bowl of sauerkraut, and a dish of meats and cold creamed potatoes. Bella, who was starving, only allowed herself one tormented glance at the colonel's supper. And at his silk sheets.

'Undress,' he said; and she shed a torn, soiled frock.

'You're too thin for me,' he remarked, and terror seized her.

But then he tossed her a silk bathrobe. From a drawer he produced a lavish black wig for her to wear while she was in his room.

'You must eat first,' he told her. 'Do not eat quickly, or else you might vomit. Chew slowly. Drink slowly. Then you must sit and digest your meal.'

Only an hour after she had finished feasting did he take Bella to bed, to relieve his tensions. Though he hardly spoke to her.

I could hear the percussion of a thousand wooden shoes on stone; and the squelch of a thousand feet tramping through slush and mud. I saw watch-towers and wire and roving searchlights. I listened to the chatter of bullets. I watched skeletal marionettes in striped pyjama-suits dangle upright for hours on end on parade from the invisible strings of their exhaustion. Strings snapped; marionettes collapsed in snow, in mud. I flinched from snarling dogs, whose teeth sheer hunger persuaded me were rows of almonds. I breathed the filth of the latrine abyss in the shithouse, surrounded by slippery, excremental steel bars on which to perch one's bum and vent the gruel of diarrhoea upon a million dissolving turds and the rotting corpses of those who had previously slipped backwards and drowned. The swollen tongues of hanged men on the gallows were blue, and looked delicious, like cured meat.

And I heard the rabbis mutter in their blockhouse as they copied the words of that loving Christian religion to which the world seemed to owe the massacre of the Albigensians, the Crusades, the Inquisition, the slaughter of witches and heretics, and the pogroms and the ghettos, because the blood of the Jew Jesus had been spilt; as they penned the holy words of their victimizers in their own heartblood . . .

Gottfried reserved Bella for himself alone. As the months passed by she grew sleek.

No doubt the colonel concocted some spurious excuse to exonerate himself in the eyes of his fellow officers from the scandal of taking a Jewess as – effectively – his mistress. Those officers were by now much tickled with the Bible in Blood project, the colonel's inspiration, so they regarded this other eccentricity of his with amusement, even addressing Bella as 'Fräulein', although she continued to reside in the Brothel Block.

How did Bella respond to Gottfried's embraces?

At first woodenly, of course, exhaustedly, obediently – reserving within herself a kernel of her own dignity.

Yet presently . . . ah, the situation became fraught with ambiguity.

Von Turm remained taciturn towards her. How could he be otherwise? He could hardly involve her directly as a co-conspirator against the ethics of the Schutzstaffel. Nevertheless Gottfried's *body* seemed to speak to her in that four-poster bed.

True, when one's entire fate depended upon the whims of a powerful individual who belonged to an insane organization, one might search excessively for auguries. What did a frown portend? Or a grunt? What did the exact pressure of his hand upon the breast, compared with yesterday, imply? And the rhythm of his cock, or a gasp during orgasm?

Or a seeming *delay* of orgasm . . .? Gottfried nursed Bella towards her own excitement by a bodily insistence that she should, she *must*, surrender herself to him sensually, now that her senses were back in working order due to better diet. This might merely be a further kind of oppression.

Yet she intuited that he would not reject her.

She was, to him, someone chosen especially to cherish – in his own bodily style. She was a person as well as an exemplar for the expiation of guilt – as well as someone symbolically saved from the slaughter in the way that he had saved some rabbis and eggheads.

She was the *personalization* of his act of charity or dictate of conscience. Thus it was entirely necessary that she should be, to him, an individual person. Always his body spoke more about his mood than his lips ever did . . . which led to that superstitious search for auguries.

Sometimes Bella felt furious that she was allowing him to unburden himself thus of bad conscience – that through sex she was shriving him to some degree. What did it really count that one Jewess was surviving through his *tactic* while thousands of others died? But she did not choose to reject her salvation.

She would never cry out to him, 'I love you.' In this mad place what sense would such a declaration make? Yet what did her body tell him? On the night when for the first time she climaxed, clutching him, digging fingernails into the firm flesh of this officer, he had flicked a cigarette lighter alight – no, he had *not* switched on a blinding lamp. And he had scrutinized her face briefly while she stared at him open-eyed; and he had nodded.

A true communication? Or only another evasive augury?

Nor did she imagine that any possible future could exist – for her, or for him.

With restored health, her halted periods had resumed. Late in 1943 she became pregnant by him – an event which at first caused her a renewed pang of terror.

Would he blame her – as surely as if she had smuggled a knife into his bed, in the way that a truly *brave* victim might have done?

As for bravery, how many other prisoners in the camp had the energy even to contemplate such a suicidal, stupid act? In any case, she had those rabbis to think of . . . Von Turm's murder or mutilation would probably mean their elimination, not to mention her own flogging to death.

First and foremost, Bella's own body had already promised Gottfried something other than a knife in the night . . .

Would he accuse her of having polluted him by allowing his seed to take root in her womb?

Indeed not. She would take extra vitamins. She would give birth in the Brothel Block – though he would not be present at such an event. She would rear her babe – though he would not see it – and she would continue to visit him.

Even this was within the gamut of SS caprice.

It could be done. For her. While others starved and died.

So I was born in the midsummer of 1944. Herzwalde camp collapsed into chaos in March of the following year. The rabbis had barely begun work on the Book of the Revelation, yet it seemed that the prophecies of Armageddon were already coming true, prematurely.

A bomb, one of several stupidly dropped on the concentration camp, killed Colonel von Turm. The bombing killed prisoners too, but only one German, Gottfried. Yet obviously the end was nigh. Therefore the SS assembled the able-bodied to march them westward; and among the ablest-bodied were those rabbis and eggheads of the colonel's project, and of course Bella with me in her arms. In such circumstances I was a burden, yet one which the SS allowed out of some perverse sentiment towards their dead deputy commandant.

Chaos begat chaos as the sinews of lunacy stretched and snapped. Overnight, at a transit stockade previously used for cattle, the SS all decamped without troubling to machine-gun those they had escorted thus far.

Bella fled. Presently she found herself wandering with a band of other anonymous women, reduced to the status of tramps, starving herself to supply me with half-masticated scavenged food which she spat into my mouth in the way that a mother bird feeds its hungry, squalling nestling.

Unluckily, those tramps fell in again with other ex-inmates of

Herzwalde who knew exactly who Bella was. They beat Bella savagely as a mistress of a Nazi tormentor, for she had prospered while they suffered.

Though her injuries were patched up, Bella died of pneumonia.

Somehow, a nun took me to a camp for displaced persons. She only knew that I was Jewish, and was called David.

In that more benign camp, a miraculously reunited couple by the name of Abramowicz adopted me. Martha Abramowicz had been sterilized in a medical experiment, but had survived. As had Levi, her husband. I was their second miracle, a son.

Eventually the Abramowiczes reached Palestine, and Palestine became Israel. Ultimately I became a *katsa* of the Mossad, dedicated to foxing the enemies of Israel.

In lieu of other nourishment during the days of wandering, my mother may have told me tales. I would have needed to be preternaturally precocious to understand those tales – unless my memory was a perfect sponge, the incomprehensible contents of which could be stored for later retrieval, decoding, and interpretation.

Might this be partly the explanation? My memory is indeed remarkably retentive.

At puberty, I began to dream my mother's memories of Herzwalde . . . These weren't exactly *horrifying* – not in the sense that I would wake up screaming. Rather, it seemed as though nightly I was engaged in a game, a game which dark gods played with people. The camp with its great rows of huts, its outer and inner wire fences, its watch-towers, latrines, kitchens, gallows, its special blocks, its SS residencies, its warehouses of loot, all, all this was an intricate and fascinating gameboard, a lifeboard and deathboard far more complex than any chessboard. Pyjama-clad pawns and grey-uniformed knights and bishop-rabbis and many other categories manoeuvred there. Also, I glimpsed certain evasive pieces which seemed to bear no correspondence to ordinary reality. I called these the Sphinx, the Angel, the Harpy, and the Clown; though what they were I could not tell.

The more that I experienced the manoeuvres, the more did it seem that some higher scheme presided over the camp. Some higher plan was emerging, ghostlike – in the manner of a vast message writ in invisible ink revealing itself line by line, under the stimulus not of warmth but of wretched death.

The final revelation of that message would be cataclysmic, yet potent, wrought of ultimate despair and prayer and conjuration.

Despair, yes despair. Despair that God might no longer be present in such a hell as the camp; that the camp represented an *absence* of God, a gap within Creation, a mad void where aberrant entities such as the Harpy and the Clown could caper, where the Sphinx and the Angel could construct themselves. Apocalyptic creatures! Yet not the banal Four Horsemen of Saint John, those projections of paranoia, jealousy, and vengeance. Something much more *interesting* . . .

Nevertheless, God-power could still be summoned. Thus the Creator might be recalled into existence.

With the abandonment of Herzwalde, what became of the almost completed Bible in Blood? The scribes didn't carry it away with them on their forced march. Nor was Gottfried von Turm alive to salvage it.

I spent many years – whilst engaged on other enterprises in Europe as a Mossad operative – in tracking down rumours of that legendary book which now lay spread open before me.

Surviving rabbis (their faith reinforced, or else forsaken) and eggheads alike were distinctly reticent about their part in the affair, as though an oath of enduring secrecy bound them . . .

For they had murmured over that book, uttering what were virtually incantations; and something strange and potent – yet abortive – had happened in that icy February of 1945, as Soviet forces fought their way progressively closer. It was something other than the seeming approach of Armageddon for the Third Reich. It was something connected with the prisoners' apprehension that they might all be summarily liquidated by a Germany in retreat. It was something which might magically *protect* the residents of the Scripture Block more effectively than Colonel von Turm. (If indeed they realized that he was their protector. The testimony of survivors, on this point, ranged from incredulity to stubborn silence.)

In my mother's fragmented memories, welling within me, was a hint of what this strange, potent, yet finally fruitless event had been. Only a hint.

Her *Gottfried* certainly knew more about it. Gottfried, of whom I was half. Yet that half remained veiled within *her* remembrance.

The rumour-web had finally attracted a spider, a spinner of cocoons in which to store prizes, a collector of bibliographic bizarrerie in the stooping shape of Henry Appledorn.

The German Democratic Republic had at last given up the ghost. In the process it yielded up all manner of monsters, including untold archives stored in secret cellars by the Stasi, those Marxist successors to the Gestapo. Out-of-work intellectuals were being hired to catalogue the morass of paper.

Whoever found the Blood Bible lurking in a Stasi crypt obviously realized its oddity, thus its potential value. Sufficient to buy a fine Mercedes, or several? He, or she, sequestered the volume for themselves, during this time of confusion, and put out feelers . . .

Or perhaps our investigative entrepreneur Klaus Bauer himself discovered, from ageing ex-SS contacts, where the volume might have ended up under the Communist regime – as an unclassifiable curiosity which it might be prudent to keep hidden – and then he bribed the new custodians of the Stasi crypts.

The Stasi had often been chary about releasing Nazi documents or films from store to assist international quests for justice against Nazis. For thus they might be assisting that creature of America, the Zionist state. Colonel von Turm was dead, way beyond prosecution for war crimes. Better to keep such a weird anomaly as the Blood Bible stored in secrecy, if indeed the Stasi understood exactly what it was. Maybe they never really believed any scraps of testimony that they gathered. Maybe they viewed awareness of the book as potentially dangerous, a possible focus for neo-Hitlerian blood-dreams of unregenerate Nazis who had bored bolt-holes into the woodwork of the Bundesrepublik next door.

What Gloria Cameron had let slip made me realize that Henry Appledorn was no mere eccentric, ardent bibliophile. Unlike

Bauer, he must be at least somewhat aware of the *event* which had occurred in Herzwalde during the final days.

Might he know *more* than I did? Had one of the surviving eggheads, after emigrating to America, then perhaps lapsing into poverty in his old age, told Appledorn an incredible story? Did Appledorn, himself confronting old age with disapproval, fancy himself as a Magus?

As a good *katsa* of Mossad, I was thoroughly accustomed to running scenarios of disinformation and duplicity through my mind, just as I was used to adopting false identities so that I could be one person one day, then another the next day.

Ha! I wouldn't be a good *katsa* much longer – not after acquiring the volume. I would be a disappeared, absconded *katsa*.

'I said, Miss Cameron, what do you expect from the book? What have you two heard about it? Come on, Mr Appledorn.' I smiled at him. 'I'm prepared to shoot one or both of you. The woman first, I think, to prove my intentions. Then you, sir.' With my free hand, I pulled out the hypodermic syringe. To allow them some hope, I explained, 'I was merely intending to put you all to sleep with a jab. Now I may have to shoot you.'

Miss Cameron licked her lips. 'The noise will attract attention. You won't escape with the book.'

'Oh, I think this is quite a soundproof suite. We are on what, the tenth floor? I happen to know that the rooms on either side and over the way are vacant. If any passing maid reports a problem, I'm sure that the under-manager of this hotel will cause all kinds of delay.'

Thus I burned my *sayan*, but that didn't matter.

'Tell him what he wants, Herr Appledorn,' begged Bauer in a cowardly tone.

A moment later Bauer launched himself at me, with a leap like a German shepherd dog.

He knocked my gun-hand down as I swung to fire. The first bullet must have passed through his jacket, but the second caught him, knocking him back from grappling with me; and I had stabbed him with the needle too . . .

Appledorn uttered a bellow of affront – for the first bullet had passed aslant into the book, exploding outward through the rear board and the thick glass of the table beneath. The glass cracked into several jagged panes which nevertheless hung together. A hole bored down through the pages.

Gloria Cameron uttered a different, tremulous kind of cry.

For the top page – of the Gospel According to Saint Matthew – had begun to bleed . . .

Red blood welled upward from the wound in the parchment just as though the heat of my bullet had reliquefied the long-dried gore of the letters.

Bauer staggered aside, clutching at his hip. Part of his flesh had been blown away. He shook his head as the drug began to work on him.

That couldn't possibly be *his* blood on the book.

Bauer collapsed on a sofa. He was irrelevant now.

Through that tunnel torn in the book a wind began to whistle, the shriek of a wintry gale – which fast became lower in pitch, a vibrant powerful moan, as if the tunnel was fast widening.

And it was so. It was so.

The Cameron woman cried out again; and so, I think, did I.

A fissure opened through the book – a chasm.

A gulf that, howling, invaded the room, abolishing the furnishings and walls and the long, curtained window.

In their place was a cold dark river. A broad river. Little ice-floes spun along it. Its banks themselves were gentle enough, but across the water indefinable walls and buildings mounted towards a steep ridge crowned by a long sombre fortress and a bulky cathedral. The Moon offered some illumination. Sparks of torchlight flickered here and there like stars fallen to Earth . . .

I recognized those silhouettes on the ridge – even though they seemed strangely incomplete. Surely this was Prague. The river, the Vltava. The cathedral must be that of Saint Vitus. The fortress could only be Hradčany Castle . . . Yet it was a Prague of long ago. And in the winter, in the small hours of some morning.

Behind me, a jumble of buildings packed together in the obscurity. Jews' Town.

Three men laboured on the river-bank near the flood of wintry water. They were stooping, scooping, moulding handfuls of clay and mud . . .

Had Appledorn and Gloria Cameron been sucked here too? I seemed to sense their presence. I myself was bodiless, a floating point of view, an invisible naked mind, a spirit.

Two of the men by the water were dressed in homespun doublets and leggings, soiled by the clay. The third, a white-bearded man with a curious cap on his head, wore a cloak.

With their bare hands they were moulding a body from the stuff of the river-bank . . .

I knew who they must be. I could sense it.

They had to be none other than Rabbi Yehuda Löw ben Bezalel, and his son-in-law, and his trusted pupil. They were trying to make the golem, the artificial man of great strength who would police the ghetto which clustered close by.

Christian trouble-makers would smuggle a murdered Christian child into the ghetto, wrapped in a sack, as a pretext to utter the blood-accusation against Jewry and thus launch a vindictive, brutal pogrom.

The golem was designed to haul such villains to justice.

Had this manufacture of a golem ever really happened? Or had it only occurred in the realm of myth – a myth so powerful that many people nevertheless believed it? Jews turned to this myth for consolation in the dark hours of their despair. Even in the late twentieth century pious pilgrims visited Löw's lion-carved sarcophagus in the overcrowded Jewish cemetery to toss written appeals into his tomb, hoping for wonders.

Now this legendary event was happening before my gaze.

With his finger the rabbi was drawing a face on the recumbent, lifeless clayman.

'May the angel Metatron guide us,' murmured the pupil. I could understand his words. Cautiously he asked his mentor, 'Rabbi, will the golem really borrow a soul from the domain of pre-existence?'

Rabbi Löw paused. 'Only a crude soul,' he replied. 'Our golem will be speechless. Dumb. Without human words, always. Yet it will understand, and obey.'

The rabbi's son-in-law plainly felt qualms too, at this final moment. 'Aren't we trespassing on God's prerogative?'

Löw mused. 'The Divine Wisdom was obliged to become *creative*,' he reminded them, 'so as to justify His own existence to Himself. Man was formed in His image. Now Man must needs create too, albeit on a humbler scale.'

Aye, desperate expedients for desperate times.

The three men whispered together.

Then Yehuda's son-in-law began to walk around the clay-man, reciting as he did so a code of letters from the Hebrew alphabet.

'*Aleph . . . Vav . . . Aleph . . . Heth . . . Jod . . .*'

He circuited the clay body seven times – '*Heth . . . Samekh . . . He . . . Tav . . . Pe . . . He . . . Nun . . .*' – and as he walked, so the body of clay began to glow ruddily as an inner fire was stoked.

Next it was the turn of Yehuda Löw's pupil to pace around the body, uttering other permutations of Hebrew letters.

This was Kabbalah.

True Kabbalah. Pious Kabbalah.

Sacred magic.

With a carved block of wood, Yehuda stamped a word upon the golem's hot brow.

I could read the word. The word was *emeth*, meaning 'true'. Erase the first letter, and 'true' would turn into 'dead'.

Into the golem's mouth Yehuda pushed a piece of paper on which he had written the secret name of God. This piece of paper was the *shem*, the programme for the golem. Remove the *shem* from the golem's mouth, and the artificial man would collapse back into clay.

Icy water swirled against the glowing body. Steam wreathed it. From the golem's fingers nails sprouted. From its head hair grew.

In chorus, the three men recited: 'And the Lord God formed man of the dust of the ground, and breathed into his nostrils the breath of life; and man became a living soul.'

With this last phrase, I felt myself being sucked towards the golem – as if *I* was to be the soul that inhabited it!

As if my own soul was to animate that clay body and march

obediently around the ghetto, unable to exert my own will, impotent to protest! Obeying orders numbly until some day when the *shem* was removed from my mouth!

I fought.

I sought purchase with my non-existent fingers and toes on the very air.

As I slid ever closer to entombment and a terrible oblivion, at the last moment the golem opened its eyes. The pulling ceased; I was gently repelled.

The golem arose.

'Your name,' Yehuda said to it, 'is Joseph.'

And Joseph nodded.

'You are to guard us from harm, Joseph,' the rabbi told it.

Snow began to tumble, slanting through the air.

Snow swirled, blanking out the scene. I could see nothing but tempestuous white flakes.

When these flakes cleared, instead of a river-bank there were rows of wooden huts and roads of frozen mud. In place of a distant steeple, a watch-tower. A searchlight stabbed out from its summit, cutting whitely through the night. In the distance, a whistle blew. From much further away – maybe sixty kilometres away – came a faint percussive thump of artillery . . .

My mother's memories were alive . . .

Within those memories stood Colonel von Turm.

I had leapt from her to him at last.

'Ich bin Gottfried,' I told myself.

Yet what did I know of my identity? Though I probed, yet I could not penetrate. I was only a wraith, wrapped around this person. Of Gottfried's youth, his motives, his attitude to Bella: nothing. He might as well have been an animated man of clay, who could articulate nothing of his thoughts and feelings to me. I only knew what he did.

Resting his weight on his silver-handled cane, he stood surveying one nearby blockhouse. Within, a faint ruddy light glowed as if a dull brazier was lit in there. The colonel had thrown a long leather coat over the shoulders of his grey uniform. Several helmeted SS guards were with him, toting their machine-pistols.

When they burst into the Scripture Block and illuminated it, almost all of the rabbis and eggheads proved to have quit their tiered wooden bunks. They thronged the floor space. Their kapo was doing nothing about the situation.

Now, this particular hut wasn't as claustrophobic as most. It wasn't a sardine can. Space existed, for uniquely these slaves laboured in their own quarters. The far end of the hut housed a work-table surrounded by rickety chairs.

On that table lay the Bible in Blood. The letters on the open pages of parchment glowed ruddily, luridly luminous with inner light.

At the sudden intrusion, a murmuring of many voices ceased – except one which continued to recite defiantly, insistently, '*And man became a living soul . . .*'

From beside the table a naked corpse arose. Its skin was grey as wrapping-paper. Its blue lips were bared in a rictus, exposing clenched stained teeth.

Obviously a corpse. Its sunken eyes were closed. On its brow was printed, in blood, a Hebrew word.

Emeth.

'*And man became a living soul . . .*'

Its tongue, protruding through its teeth, had shrivelled to a white leaf.

No! That was no tongue.

That was . . . the *shem*.

The mud outside was frozen. Evidently the prisoners had smuggled in a corpse from another hut, or more likely from the charnel heap. Was not man's flesh made of clay? To clay, returning? Was this dead body not therefore equivalent to clay?

'. . . *a living soul, to be our protector, our guardian under God!*'

The zombie-golem opened its eyes, eyes that stared blankly. It began to cavort, windmilling its arms.

As the SS guards clove a pathway for the colonel many prisoners scrambled into bunks or clung to the sides of those bunks like panicked monkeys.

By now the Bible had ceased glowing.

Gottfried stared at the scarecrow of a golem, which turned now to face him.

'Kill it,' he ordered his men.

Guns racketed.

The golem's parchment skin tore, yet bullets seemed simply to pass through it. It rocked, but it did not fall. Its flesh burst, bloodlessly, but its bones could have been made of steel. Or of rock, of fossilized bones.

'Cease fire!'

The golem still stood, swaying.

Gottfried stared at it . . . as though now he understood.

Some of the prisoners were moaning – not because they were afraid of a terrible punishment, but as if appalled at what they had achieved. Or half-achieved. A multitude of needle tracks in all of their arms kept tally of the blood they had yielded up repeatedly, day after day.

They had lost courage.

One of the eggheads cried out cravenly to the colonel, 'Take the *shem* from its mouth, sir!'

Gottfried stood right before the golem, although his men were hesitant.

It jerked. It froze again. Why should it attack this colonel, who was a perverse – or honourable – protector of these prisoners?

Then it spoke – opening its vile teeth. At last it spoke. Or croaked.

'Ich bin *Joseph*,' it uttered. The *shem* lolled on its blue tongue like a long communion wafer.

Gottfried reached, and yanked the scrap of parchment from its mouth – so that the golem lolled upright, motiveless, like any common or garden prisoner on parade who would soon die.

The colonel spat on his glove, and smudged out the first letter of the word on the creature's brow. Oh he knew, he knew the tricks of the Jews!

The corpse collapsed. Its spirit had fled.

And so must I. For suction tore at me.

'Father!' I cried. 'Tell me! Tell me!' Tell me so many things that you never told my mother . . .

But that inhalation from elsewhere was overwhelming me, as if the very bellows of the world were breathing me in.

'Aitch-Jay!' cried Gloria Cameron. Our bibliophile hunched, lolling, spittle on his lips.

The book on the smashed glass table bled no more. There was no longer any wound from which it could bleed. The torn parchment had resealed itself like living flesh possessed of an amazing power of regeneration, a facility as considerable as that of the golem itself.

Bauer was dozing, while blood continued to leak from his side through his clothes to stain the sofa.

'Aitch-Jay!'

Henry *Joseph* Appledorn, of course.

It struck me then, fearfully, that only that coincidence of his name and the golem's had saved my soul from being enveloped in the creation of clay . . .

Either one of us might have been captured – him or me. Bauer? What about Bauer? No, he had already been rendered *hors de combat*. And Gloria Cameron was female.

Appledorn mumbled.

He staggered.

Aided by her, he sat down in an armchair.

He stared at me, out of grief-stricken, time-chasmed eyes.

His voice croaked.

'I had to – to patrol . . . for years, night after night . . . And day after day I stood . . . motionless . . . in a back room of the synagogue. I couldn't . . . utter a word. I was only . . . an animated *thing*.' He forced out all the words which had long been frozen. At first they emerged like nuggets of ice, then, as his voice thawed, in a gushing stream.

The cobbled alleys, the twisting streets so narrow that the eaves of houses almost touched . . . Carved painted signs showing a swan, a lute, a crayfish, a giant key, as though each house was a member of some strange zodiac. Here was the building housing the first Hebrew printing-press in Central Europe. There were the public baths. Here, a poor-house; there, an infirmary. All crammed together. In a maze of alleyways. Which he must pace nightly, always keeping out of sight if he could, never speaking, for the *shem* was in his mouth.

And he was successful in his guardianship.

For presently a magnificent Jewish town hall was built. And

the High Synagogue; and Klaus Synagogue; and Maisl Synagogue.

So successful was he that further services on his part seemed unnecessary. Frankly, his existence was an embarrassment. Consequently he was walled up, stored in darkness. Forgotten . . .

. . . till of a sudden he found himself standing in a crowded, noisome hut. Bullets tore his emaciated body – in vain, except that through the holes they made they let a breeze into him. He sucked that breeze together, and at last he gasped.

And the grey-clad officer pulled the *shem* from his mouth.

'The book could bring . . . power. So I heard,' Appledorn confessed. He needed little prompting now. 'Yes, I did hear it from an immigrant who had been in Herzwalde. But the book was still incomplete . . .

'It's the only *actual* magic book I ever heard of. Books of spells and grimoires: they're just . . . weird words on paper. Nothing effective. This book was magic in itself! And that was because . . .' He frowned, trying to grasp the reason.

'Because God was absent from Herzwalde,' I explained. 'So therefore there was a chasm in Creation. A gap. The rules did not exist any more – they broke down. The gap could be otherwise filled. I'm the son of Gottfried von Turm, the deputy commandant,' I told him. 'That is *my* book.'

Though I had failed to commune fully with my father, I knew at last what his motive had been.

It had been different from what I had imagined from my mother's memories – ah, Bella's *deluded* recollections!

No wonder Gottfried had been taciturn.

Although on the one hand the SS constituted a veritable bloody occult brotherhood, on the other hand the Nazis cracked down on most independent occultists and occult groups who might in any way form a kernel of opposition to the Nazi regime. They suppressed these potential rivals. The Gestapo drew up lists of organizations little and large, even daffy ones, whose members must not be allowed any government employment, even as a postman. And this made perfect sense; for if the

SS were occultly inclined, they must be the sole practitioners of dark and bloody rituals.

Gottfried von Turm had been an occultist of a different stripe – a solitary practitioner in a lonely tower, as it were. Yet he was also an aristocrat. Hence the Gestapo both punished him, and at the same time permitted him a National Socialistic redemption, by forcing his entry into the Waffen-SS.

Along with whom he fought, until he came to Herzwalde.

In the camp he discovered a pressure cooker of horrors – a perfect crucible for an experiment. On the surface his project might seem more 'benign' in its effects than the loathsome and lunatic medical mutilations which SS doctors performed upon prisoners. Yet it was a deep, dark investigation – by someone who bore Jews no particular animosity whatever, who might even arguably be aiding some of them. As intense heat and pressure might crush carbon into diamond, so might the spiritually humiliating toil of Kabbalistic rabbis in the Scripture Block, writing in their own blood – in an atmosphere of ultimate despair, devoid of God – create a magical device.

Ah, that *amalgamation* of Jewish blood and holy Christian words culminating in an Apocalypse!

What role did my mother fulfil in this? Oh yes, I *was* to be born – of a Jewess whose people were scribing the book, and of Gottfried's seed! This was the part of himself which Gottfried donated to the project. Most certainly I was to be born, a homunculus of him, a repository of his power – of that power which his project was distilling.

No wonder Gottfried was so silent in bed, so devoid of pillow talk. He was *concentrating*.

No wonder he needed to remain detached from me, shunning my birth and my early infancy. For the project was not yet complete. The book wasn't finished.

And then that idiotic bomb killed him; and the book remained unfinished.

Now I understood why I could dream my mother's memories. And why I had felt so impelled to seek out the book.

'Do you think,' I demanded of Appledorn, 'that if anyone except me had fired a bullet into that book, the rift in reality would have opened up?'

Appledorn was trembling. Gloria Cameron regarded me . . . almost greedily, as if desirous.

'But,' Appledorn managed to say. 'But the golem was a legend . . .'

Yes, it was. In our own history it was a legend.

'There's another domain, Mr Appledorn,' I said, with increasing confidence. 'The domain of the Sphinx and the Angel, of the Harpy and the Clown.' I had never uttered their names aloud before – names which indeed *I myself* had assigned to these entities. None the less, those were the true names.

Appledorn wiped his lips.

'Take the book,' he said. 'I daren't own it.'

'*Aitch-Jay!*' protested the woman.

As though it was up to either of them to decide!

The American shook his head numbly. 'I couldn't . . . The serving, the standing in darkness for years . . . I'd rather die than risk . . . something similar.'

'Then you will die,' the Cameron woman said to him bitterly. She wasn't threatening him, simply uttering a statement of plain fact. 'In three or four years, ten years if you're lucky. You'll die, Henry *Joseph*.'

'And therefore so will you one day, Gloria,' he replied softly.

It was time for me to leave. High time.

I made both of them lie down upon the floor. Appledorn complied willingly; Gloria Cameron, less so.

I injected her, then him. Then I shut the Blood Bible, and tied the red ribbons.

The steel emblem embedded in the cover was a large mirror-image swastika, made of steel and inset with strips of mirror.

Lille is a fine enough city to hide in, though my stay will be relatively brief. I rent a little top-floor apartment in the old town in the Rue de la Clef. David Abramowicz is no more. Now I'm Daniel Kahn, an author determined to finish a book. 'About what, Monsieur?' 'Why, about cathedrals.' There's one substantial example just up the road. I make sure to visit the cathedral occasionally, to stretch my legs.

I take the blood from high up my arms so as not to produce

obvious tracks which might attract the attention of anti-drugs *flics*.

I arrived in this city with my book at the most opportune time in September – at the start of the vast rummage fair, the Braderie. By ancient charter the whole city centre is given over to thousands of stalls, street upon street of stalls selling old clothes, bric-à-brac, antiques, African carvings, tools, the rubbish from Granny's attic, carpets, curios, anything and everything. I even found a stall selling the extra parchment which I needed. In the evening, while music spewed forth and the whores patrolled, *tout le monde* feasted on mussels cooked in red wine and in cream at a multitude of tables which were additionally blocking pavements and streets outside of every café. Black mountains of empty shells arose. If a car intruded impatiently, tipsy diners tossed mussel shells at it in pique.

Half of the population of Flanders seemed to have descended upon Lille; and tourists galore. What more anonymous time to take up residence, and remain as if enchanted by the city?

My arms ache, and the fingers of my right hand are numb with forming the Gothic letters correctly. I must flex my fingers frequently. There's a whiff of blood in the room, and of sterilizing alcohol too, since I wouldn't wish to become septic.

Presently I will reach those final words: *The grace of our Lord Jesus Christ be with you all. Amen.*

Amen. Amen. Amen.

So be it! Thus is it in truth!

Then I must bind the book; and having bound it, I shall fire my gun into that book once more, and the blood-stained parchment will split open to reveal the true territory of the Clown and the Harpy, the Angel and the Sphinx; and I shall discover what those beings are.

I myself, and my father within me.

Happy Hour

With an abrupt loud clatter the steel slats of the exhaust fan exploded open, making our hearts lurch. Martin mimed quick pistol shots at it.

'Pung! Pung! Gotcha.'

That fan was set just beneath the bowed, beamed ceiling of the bar in the Roebuck. The contraption was at least twenty years out of date. It didn't purr softly like a modern fan. It exploded open, showing its teeth, and gulped at the atmosphere. One of the historic stones of this pub – built in the reign of Good Queen Bess, so a sign on the wall boasted – had been removed so that the thing could be inserted. The actual mechanism was hidden inside the wall. When the fan was in repose, all that showed was a slatted cream panel one foot square lying flush with the cream plasterwork. You hardly noticed it, forgot all about it – until suddenly the Xtractall opened its mouth as if by its own volition; until the flat panel became a dozen razor lips spaced an inch apart, through which fuggy air was sucked into its throat.

The fan throbbed lustily, sucking Charlotte's cigarette smoke and my own cigar smoke into it.

'Does it have a built-in smoke detector?' I wondered.

'We could ask what's-his-name. Our host.' Jenny nodded towards the deserted bar counter.

'Host' was somewhat of a misnomer. The landlord was a quiet, wispy chap with little by way of personality. He smiled amiably, but he was no conversationalist; and frankly we liked it this way. Right now he would be round in the restaurant annexe neatening the array of silver and wineglasses on the tables. The Roebuck was one of those few country pubs that opened fairly promptly at six of an evening, but it relied for its main trade on the gourmet menu from about

half-past seven till ten. It wasn't much of a hangout for locals
and yokels.

To be sure, now that the licensing hours had been liberalized,
the place could have stayed open all day long. Yet what rural
pub would bother to? We were lucky to have found the
Roebuck.

Jenny and I, Charlotte and Martin, and Alice (who was
special) all commuted to London and back by way of big, glassy
Milton Keynes Station. Charlotte and Martin had bought a sizeable thatched cottage in a couple of acres this side of Bucking-
ham. Jenny and I were based in a different little village outside
of Stony Stratford, in a barn conversion. Alice lived . . . somewhere in the vicinity. Alone? Or otherwise? Alice was our
delicious enigma. Apparently she was in publishing.
Webster-Freeman: art and oriental-wisdom volumes, shading
into the outright occult. I sometimes fantasized her dancing
naked around a bonfire or home-made altar along with other
like spirits, firelight or candlelight winking between her legs. If
such was the case, she had never tried to recruit us (and,
curiously, my fantasies along these lines never provoked an
erection). We were merely one slice of her life on Friday
evenings: a slice lasting an hour – twice as long when we all
dined at the Roebuck once a month.

Why had we been so honoured by Alice? Perhaps she was
lonely under her capable, gorgeous façade. Perhaps we were
neutrals with whom she could be friends without obligations or
ties.

I myself worked for an oil company and was in charge of
Butadiene, a gas used as fuel and also in the manufacture of
synthetic rubbers. Since I was on the contracts rather than the
chemistry side, the job called for some foreign travel – quick
trips to Eastern Europe, Mexico, Japan, from which I returned
tired out – but otherwise my career was ho-hum. I assumed I
would be with the same mob for the rest of my working life,
slowly advancing. In our company salaries were somewhat
pinched to start with (and indeed to continue with!) until the
final five years, when suddenly you were rolling in money and
could practically write yourself cheques. Thus my masters
assured staff loyalty.

My wife, Jenny, was office manager for an airline, which gave us free tickets once a year to hot, exotic places where I didn't need to sit haggling in an office. Jenny was a short, trim blonde who wore smartly tailored suits and lavish bows like big silken napkins tucked into her neckline.

Burly, early-balding Martin was an architect, and his spouse, Charlotte, willowy and auburn, was a senior secretary to an export-import firm called, uninventively, Exportim, which managed to sound like some Soviet trade bureau.

And Alice was . . . Alice.

Weekdays (except Fridays) Martin and Charlotte and Jenny and I all drove our own cars to MK Station, since we might need to work late and catch different trains home. Every Friday, however, my wife and I shared a car; so did Martin and his wife. On that day nothing would make us miss the same return train and our wind-down drink with Alice at the Roebuck. Needless to say, our minor contribution towards car-sharing in no way relieved the parking pressure at MK. By seven-fifteen in the morning every weekday the station car parks were full up, and the central reservations and traffic islands were becoming crowded with vehicles. The new city in the Buckinghamshire countryside boasted a fine network of roads, but where parking was concerned, the planners had cocked up. Pressure, pressure. No wonder we looked forward to our Friday evenings. Or our once-a-month dinner.

I screwed my cigar butt into one ashtray at the exact moment when Charlotte stubbed out her Marlboro in another – as if she and I had been reproached by the extractor fan for our filthy habits. We glanced at one another and burst out laughing. The fan thumped shut.

'I heard this in Hungary,' I said. 'There's a new Russian wrist-watch on the market, triumph of Soviet technology. It'll do absolutely everything: time zones, phases of the moon, built-in calculator. It only weighs a few ounces. "So what's the snag?" asks this fellow. "Oh," says his informant, "it's just the two suitcases of batteries you need to carry round with it . . ."'

Then Alice told a dirty joke.

'This British couple went for a holiday in the States to tour the national parks. Well, in the first park they made friends with a skunk. They adored the skunk so much they took it with them in their trailer to the next park, then the next. Come the end of their holiday, they could hardly bear to be parted from the animal. "I wish we could take it home," said the husband, "but how could we avoid the quarantine laws?" "I know," said his wife, "I'll stick the skunk inside my knickers, and we'll smuggle it in that way." "Great idea," agreed her husband, "but, um, what about the smell?" The wife shrugged and sighed. "If it dies, it dies."'

Alice was good that way. She was incredibly desirable – tall, slim, long legs, wonderful figure, that mass of raven hair, olive skin, dark broody eyes – but she easily defused any sexual tensions that might have undermined our little group. Lust from the men; or jealousy from the ladies. Charlotte had first fallen into conversation with Alice on the homeward train, and introduced her to the rest of us at journey's end. We rarely sat together on the train itself. Such a rush to catch it. Carriages would be crowded; and we all had work to keep us busy.

Alice refrained from letting us know her home address or phone number – perhaps wisely, in case Martin or I tried to see her privately. Nor, in fact, had she ever asked about our own homes. A tacit agreement prevailed, not to know. Meanwhile, she certainly made our Friday evening group react together. She was our catalyst. Without her, we would have been just two everyday couples. With her, we felt special: a new sort of unit, a sparkling fivesome.

Gleefully Martin took over the baton of joke-telling.

'The mother superior of this convent school invited a Battle of Britain hero to address her girls,' he said with relish. 'The flying ace told them, "I was at eight thousand feet in my Spitfire. I saw a fokker to the left of me. There was another fokker to the right of me. I looked up, and the sky was full of fokkers." "I should explain, girls," interrupted the mother superior, "that the Fokker-Wolf was a Second World War German fighter plane." "That's quite right, Mother," said the airman, "but these fokkers were Messerschmitts."'

Though the jokes themselves might have seemed silly – it's the way they're told, isn't it? – we excelled ourselves in wit and amity that evening . . . until the pub cat came a-calling on us.

This mog was a scruffy ginger specimen, which I had seen the landlord shooing outdoors on a couple of occasions. With the unerring instinct of pussies, it made straight for Alice, to rub against her leg. She drew away.

'I loathe cats. I'm allergic.'

'Gid away!' Martin flapped and clapped his hands. The mog retreated a little, not particularly deterred.

So much, I thought wryly, for Alice being any kind of spare-time witch; and to my scanty store of information about her I added the knowledge that there were no felines in her home.

She shifted uncomfortably. 'I can't bear to touch them. I really don't like them.' This was the first sour note in any of our evenings.

'Derrick,' Jenny said to me, 'for heaven's sake grab it and shove it out of the door.'

'It's their hair,' murmured Alice. 'It would give me a terrible rash. I hope they don't let it sleep in here at night. Sprawling on these seats, rubbing fur off all the time. If they do let it, and I knew that, well . . .'

The end of our Friday fivesome. Panic. We would never find another suitable pub.

'I'm sure it's an outdoor cat,' Martin assured her. I was shoving my chair back quietly prior to attempting to collar the beast, when that fan on the wall went *click-clack*. It simply opened its slats for a moment, then shut them again as if a strong buffet of wind had surged through from outside – though the weather had been clement when we drove up.

The cat skedaddled as if a bucket of water had been dumped on it.

'That's scuttled him. Thanks, fan. Must be turning blowy outside.'

'We should go,' said Alice.

'Till next week?' Anxious me.

'Oh yes,' she promised. We all rose.

But outside the night was perfectly still. Not even a breeze.

The following Friday our trio of vehicles all arrived at almost the same time at the Roebuck. Under the bare chestnut tree standing sentinel by the car park, Charlotte inhaled.

'Is that your perfume, Alice? It's glorious.'

It was indeed: rich, musky, wild, yet subtle nevertheless, like some treasure forever unattainable, unownable.

'A friend of mine runs a perfumery down in the Cotswolds,' Alice told her. 'This is a new creation.'

'Could you possibly get me—?' began Charlotte. 'No, don't. Never mind. It doesn't matter.'

Of course not. If Charlotte wore that ravishing scent, what might Martin imagine? Alice didn't press her.

'I'm trying to give up smoking,' added Charlotte as we headed through the November chill towards the door. 'Tonight I think I'll do without.'

This seeming *non sequitur* was actually an intimate confidence between the two women; indeed between all of us. We mustn't pollute Alice's fragrance. The onus now lay on me to refrain from lighting up any of my slim panatellas.

I rechecked our host's name painted over the lintel of the door – John Chalmers, of course – though I needn't have bothered. I had to tinkle the bell on the counter several times before he came, seeming too preoccupied even to greet us beyond a few nods. As soon as I had extracted a couple of pints of Adnams for Martin and me, a gin for Jenny, and a lowland single malt for Alice, Chalmers withdrew. Alice was a connoisseur of Scotches; another grace note in her favour.

'I'd like to sit under the fan tonight,' she announced.

So as to minimize her own fragrance diplomatically, symbolically? We sat at a table different from our usual one. Scarcely a couple of minutes passed before – *clunk-clack* – the slats of the fan sprang open, and the machinery sucked air.

'How odd,' said Martin. 'None of us is smoking, and it switches on.'

'Maybe,' I said recklessly to Alice, 'it's breathing your scent in. Maybe it's in love with you.'

Jenny darted me a dubious glance. The fan continued operating without ceasing, throbbing away, never shutting down.

Unaccountably John Chalmers kept wandering into the body of the bar, dusting ashtrays, adjusting the hang of hunting prints on the walls.

'What's up, man?' Martin asked the landlord during his third incursion.

'Tiger's gone missing. Our cat.'

'Aaah,' breathed Alice. 'I meant to ask: Do you let that cat roam these rooms during the night?'

'The whole place gets a thorough vacuuming every morning,' said our house-proud host.

Alice pursed her lips. 'An old building. Nooks and crannies. Mice?'

'I have never found any dead vermin inside. Outside, I've found Tiger's trophies. What do you expect? Not in here, never. If there's any mice, he scares 'em off.'

Alice continued gazing at him till he took umbrage. 'Health inspector gave us a pat on the back last month. He's more interested in kitchens, but he said this was the most spick-and-span bar he'd seen in all the county.' Chalmers wandered off, restaurantward.

When he had gone off, Martin pointed up at the busy Xtractall. '*There's* a tiny bit that isn't spick.' A russet something – barely noticeable – had lodged between the edge of one slat and the housing.

'What is it?' Alice asked, in a need-to-know tone. Martin had to take off his shoes and clamber on to an upholstered chair, handkerchief in hand.

'Just you be careful of those fingers!' Charlotte called.

'S'all right. Safety grille inside. Stops idiots from mincing themselves.' He pried with the hanky and stepped down. 'Bit of ginger fur. Ugh, skin? Dried blood?' Hastily he folded the hanky over and plunged it deep in his pocket. I glanced anxiously at Alice, but she was smiling up at the fan.

Presently Charlotte started kidding Alice gently about the arty occult books published by Webster-Freeman. Charlotte had popped into a bookshop to buy new pages of her personal organizer, had happened upon a display of those volumes, and had skimmed through a few out of curiosity.

'What's the use of it all nowadays?' she asked. 'Is it a spiritual thread in a material world? Gurus, psychedelics . . . But the sixties are gone for ever.'

Alice mused. 'For a while it seemed as if the world would

change. As if a new age were coming: of joy, the flesh, the mind, old values in a new incarnation. Instead, what came was plastic people making plastic money.'

Was she criticizing us? We got on so *well* together. Yet there was always the edge of wondrous difference, as if Alice came from . . . elsewhere, outside of our ken.

'You could only have been a little girl in the sixties,' protested Charlotte.

'Could I?' Alice craned her lovely neck to look at the Xtractall. 'I suppose that's a piece of the sixties. Soon it'll be replaced by some silent faceless box controlled by a microchip . . .'

'High time too,' said Martin. 'Can't imagine why Chalmers hangs on to the thing.'

'He doesn't know why,' said Alice. 'He's one of the most neutral people I've ever seen. Till the usual restaurant crowd turn up, prattling about barn conversions and BMWs, this place is limbo. Imagine if the past could grow angry – bitter, like a disillusioned parent . . . yet still somehow hopeful and radiant too. In a schizophrenic way! Trying to keep the old faiths alive . . . And what if earlier epochs feel the same way about, say, the whole twentieth century? If those epochs still try to intrude and guide their offspring who have changed out of recognition? To keep the old flames alive. Smilingly, yet bitterly too.'

'Er, how can the past keep watch on the present?' Martin asked with a grin. He thought a joke was due, but Alice stared at him quite seriously.

'The collective unconscious, which is timeless. The imprint of memory on material objects. Don't you think this is what angels and devils may be all about? Affirmative vibrations from the past – and negative, angry, twisted ones?'

'Beats me,' said Martin. He laughed. 'I always design vibrations out of buildings, mount 'em on shock absorbers, that sort of thing. Make sure there are no resonances likely to set people's teeth on edge.'

My teeth were on edge. I felt that Alice was on the brink of revealing herself . . . to us, the chosen few. She was the joyous, positive spirit of an older world – and I wondered how old she really was. She liked us. She hoped for us. Yet for the most part the old world hated us?

She said to Charlotte, 'I suppose Webster-Freeman's wisdom books must basically be about power, a power that has grown weak but still lingers on.' I had the momentary weird impression that Alice herself had only leafed through those volumes, as casually as Charlotte had. 'Power today is money, property, investments, plastic. Empty, dead power. Zombie power. Yet so vigorous. The world's soul is dying . . . of hunger. The plastic body thrives. That fan,' she added, 'may well be a creature of the sixties.'

'Time to replace it,' Martin said stoutly.

'And what did it replace? An ancient stone, a hungry old stone. Well,' and she smiled sweetly, 'must dash home in a few minutes and microwave some goodies. Mustn't we all?'

Was that what she would really do at home, wherever home was?

Before departing, Alice told a ridiculous joke about how to circumcise a whale. How? You use four skin divers. After booking a table in the restaurant for the following Friday, to sample the oysters and partridge, we left contented.

'Alice was in an odd mood tonight,' Jenny remarked after we got home. 'She *was* just kidding, don't you think?'

'I think that was the real Alice. But I don't know if Alice is real, the way we are.'

Jenny giggled. 'Do we imagine her every Friday? Is she the soul that's missing from our lives?'

'Not exactly. We're her hope . . . for something. Some . . . rekindling.' I thought of flames, and a naked woman dancing, leaping the fire, singeing her pubic hair. 'And yet . . . we don't matter too much to her. That place matters more. Chalmers's pub. The limbo pub, at that empty hour. That's what binds us together.'

'*You* aren't hoping for something from her, are you?' she asked archly.

'No, you know that would ruin—' I had been about to say 'the magic'. I said instead, 'the happy hour. Maybe,' I added, 'without us it's difficult for her to make contact with the modern world.'

'Come off it! Charlotte met her on the train from Euston. Alice is in publishing. In business.'

Is she? I wondered. Alice spoke as if she had been at home in the sixties . . . not just a little girl back then, but herself as now. And I suspected, crazily, that she had existed in earlier times too.

Charlotte had met Alice on the train. Had any of us bumped into Alice *again*, either on the London-bound train or the return one? I knew I hadn't. I had glimpsed Alice coming out of MK Station, and also cruising for parking in her Saab; yet I had never seen her anywhere on the platform at Euston. Given the rush and the crowding, that wasn't totally odd in itself – unless none of us had ever coincided with Alice after that first occasion. Certainly Jenny had never mentioned doing so.

I refrained from asking. We microwaved duck *à l'orange*, went to bed, and made love the same way we usually made love on a Friday night. When Jen and I were making love, I never thought about Alice, never visualized her – as if I were forbidden to, as if Alice could reach out and control me. Only afterwards did I lie awake wondering about angels and demons – contrasting values in the same equation – as messages, vibrations from the past intent on charming or savaging the present day, but not widely so, only marginally, except where a magical intersection of persons and places occurred.

On Monday I had some hard talking to do to some visiting Hungarians, though I mustn't be too stringent. I enjoyed the hospitality in Hungary.

Next Friday, in the Roebuck, we had already scrutinized the menu through in the bar, and ordered. Jenny and Charlotte went off together to the ladies' room. I myself was overcome by an urgent need to piss. So, apparently, was Martin. Martin and I both apologized simultaneously to Alice and fled to relieve ourselves, leaving her alone. Until then the fan had remained tight-lipped. *Clunk-clack*, I heard as we retreated.

It was a long, strong piss for both of us. Martin and I left one urinal basin untenanted between us: a kind of ceramic sword laid not between knight and lady but between squire and squire, both of us being chaste, faithful squires of Alice. Let us get up to no monkey business together. It's odd that women can waltz off together to the ladies' as a sort of social event, whereas chaps should do no such thing, as if mutual urination is a queer sign. Have the boys gone off together to compare their organs? In this case, need dictated.

As we were walking back, bladders emptied out, I heard the fan shut off and close itself. The bar proved to be deserted. We assumed that Alice had followed our wives to the powder room. We chatted about the innovative design of a new office block currently soaring near Euston Station. People were christening it 'the totem pole'. Then our ladies returned without sight of Alice.

In case Chalmers had summoned us and Alice had gone ahead to the restaurant, I checked there, in vain. Chalmers's wife ducked out from the kitchen to remark that I was a little early. I checked the car park, where Alice's Saab sat in darkness.

'Can't find her anywhere, folks!' I spotted Alice's silvery purse lying on the carpet. Before I could go to retrieve it, Martin hurried to my side and gripped my arm.

'Look at the fan,' he whispered fiercely.

The slats of the Xtractall were moving in and out gently one by one, top to bottom, in an undulating fashion. I thought of someone sucking their teeth. The edge of each slat was streaked crimson, thin lines that faded, even as I watched, as if being absorbed or licked away atom by atom.

'Are my eyes playing tricks?'

'What do *you* think, Derrick?'

'You aren't suggesting—?'

'I bloody well am. I've been doing some stiff thinking about Alice since her spiel last week—'

'*Stiff* thinking?'

He looked exasperated. 'I never get a hard-on thinking about her. Fact is, I can't seem to, whatever Charlotte may imagine.'

'Me neither.'

'She's an enchantress. Supernatural. I mean it, old son. Haven't you suspected?'

I nodded cautiously. This wasn't *quite* the thing to admit to one another.

'I thought she might be a modern-day witch,' I said. 'Despite commuting to Euston and driving a Saab. Type of books she publishes, you know?' I was only telling him a quarter of the truth. Since last weekend I had thought ever more about 'angels' and 'devils' – for want of better names! – about benign and angry vibrations from a past that had been disenfranchised, in a kind of time-crossed disinheritance: the plastic children forsaking the memory of the parent. Alice was more than any latter-day witch – and less, because she wasn't of our time at all, in spite of her modern gear and jokes.

'Not a witch, Derrick. A *lamia*. As in Keats's poem. Had to read that at school. A female spirit who preys on travellers.'

'She never preyed on us.'

'Just so. She was being a good girl with us. Friday evening was her leisure time, her friendly hour. She *stopped* us from feeling, well, lustful.'

'What are you two arguing about?' asked Charlotte. She and Jenny couldn't see the fan without turning. 'Did one of you say something to Alice that you shouldn't? Something to offend her?'

'No, damn it,' swore Martin.

'But something did go wrong,' I insisted, 'and she melted away.'

'No!' He grabbed and shook me. Jenny started up, fearing that we were about to have a brawl – about Alice, right in front of our wives. 'You don't get it, do you?' His face leered into mine. 'The fan ate her. It fell in love with her just like you said – and it consumed her. It sucked her into itself.'

'It—?'

'The bloody fan!'

By now the slats of the Xtractall were quite clean, and no longer made that munching motion.

Charlotte also leapt up. 'You're mad!'

'Get away from under that fan, love,' begged Martin. 'Remember the cat that went missing? Remember how Alice hated cats? The fan ate the cat up for her – we found that scrap of bloody fur up there, right? – and Alice knew; she knew.'

I recalled Alice's smile, directed at the fan.

'One night last week the fan extracted poor old Tiger,' he

went on. 'Remember what Alice said about how the fan replaced a hungry old stone? Something up there is kin to her.'

A demon, I thought – to her angel. But both of them aspects of the past, still wooing the present weakly, in friendly or venomous guise.

'That thing's much more powerful than Alice guessed,' insisted Martin. 'When we all went off to the toilets – and who sent us, her or the fan? – it sucked her in because it wanted her.'

What Charlotte did next was either quite stupid or remarkably brave. Of course, she did not see Alice the way we fellows saw her. Maybe women couldn't. She kicked off her shoes, burrowed in her own bag for a neglected pack of cigarettes, lit one, and mounted a chair.

'That's impossible,' she said. 'Physically impossible – leaving aside the wild idea of an extractor fan falling in love.' Charlotte puffed smoke at the blank face of the fan.

'The cat fur,' Martin protested.

Clunk-clack: The fan opened up. The mechanism whirred. Smoke disappeared. Charlotte never flinched. She flicked her lighter for illumination. Daringly she teased two long fingernails between the slats and tugged. Several strong black strands of hair came free.

'Oh,' she said, and jumped down. 'Is this some joke the two of you cooked up with Alice? Is she waiting outside the door stifling her giggles?'

Martin crossed his heart like a child. And Charlotte faltered. I was wrong: each in our way we must have been thinking along similar lines about Alice. Our ladies had both been resisting such conclusions.

'It's still impossible,' Charlotte said, 'unless the fan leads somewhere else than just to the ordinary outside. And unless it changes what it takes. Unless it etherializes stuff instead of merely making mincemeat! Maybe it does. What was the landlord saying about never finding any mice? How can that be a magic fan? How?'

By now Jenny was caught up in our conviction. 'We can't tell the police. They would think we were insane. We don't even know Alice's surname, let alone where she—'

I had remembered the purse and swooped. I emptied it on a table over the beer mats. Car keys. Cosmetics. Tiny bottle of perfume. Ten- and twenty-pound notes, but no loose change. A tarnished old medallion. No driver's licence, no cheque book, no hint of her full name or where she lived.

'At least we have the car keys,' said Martin.

'There'll be no clues in her car,' I told him. 'She isn't any ordinary human being.'

'Oh, we know that already, Derrick darling.' My wife's tone was somewhat spiced with irony.

'She's a supernatural being. Didn't we know it all along?' I was echoing Martin, but those had been my sentiments anyway.

Charlotte didn't disagree with my assessment, however sceptical she may have seemed before. 'And she's our friend,' she reminded me. '*Was*, at any rate! So two supernatural forces have collided here—'

'Or come together. Like the poles of a magnet, like anode and cathode.'

'What do you suppose our landlord knows about that fan?'

I laughed. 'Our Mr Chalmers doesn't realize the fan's possessed. He thinks Tiger was a demon mouser. I doubt he knows much about the stone that was drilled to dust to make space for the fan. The ancient stone, the sacrifice stone.' A hard pain in my left hand alerted me to the fact that I was clutching that medallion from Alice's purse. As I opened my palm, the pain numbed to a cold tingling.

'Carry on.' Charlotte eyed the metal disc intently, an amulet from some ancient time.

Words struggled to the surface like flotsam from a shipwreck. Don't hold them down. Relax. Let them bob up.

'The vibrations of the sacred stone imbued that space up there. When the stone was destroyed, the force possessed the fan that replaced it. At least a fan could *do* something, unlike a block of stone. It could open up a channel – to somewhere – a feeding channel. No one had fed the stone for centuries. It lay neglected, inert. Some Elizabethan builder picked it up and used it as part of the pub wall. It stayed inert. It was hungry, weak. It was the demon side of . . . the angry past. But it was kin to Alice.'

I was holding Alice's medallion out blatantly, like a compass. The disc was so worn that its face was almost smooth; I could barely make out faint symbols unknown to me. A coin from the realm of magic, I thought, from the domain of lamias and hungry spirits. The inscription was well-nigh erased. How had Alice kept her vitality so long? By connecting with people such as us? Preying on some, befriending others?

Jenny touched the piece of metal and recoiled as if stung. 'It's freezing.'

'That space up there is dangerous,' said Charlotte, who had so boldly shone a light into it. 'Still, it didn't bite my fingers off. It only reacts to some stimuli – Alice being the biggest stimulus of all, eh, fellows?'

'It took her by surprise,' I said. 'It was playing possum till we went to the toilet; till the vibrations tickled our bladders. Or maybe that was Alice's doing. She wanted to be alone with it. It overwhelmed her.'

She had been well aware of it, must have sensed its true nature when we first brought her here. She was flesh; it was an object – her malign counterpart, which nevertheless yearned for her. She wanted to commune with a kindred force, but imagined she was stronger.

'We want her back, don't we?' Charlotte went on. 'This is the machine age, right? We know machines. That thing's out of sync with the age.'

'What are you driving at?' Martin asked his wife.

'You're a dab hand at fixing things, aren't you?' She jerked a thumb at the leaded window behind the bar counter. A NO VACANCIES sign hung facing us. Consequently anyone approaching from outside would read the alternative invitation, VACANCIES. 'We'll spend the night here. You have a tool box in the car. When all's completely quiet, we'll sneak down, do a spot of dismantling, and reverse those damned fan blades so that the air blows into this room, not out. Air, and whatever else.'

'Cigarette and cigar smoke is like foul incense to it,' I found myself saying.

'She'll come back minced,' muttered Jenny. 'Spread all over the floor, sticking to the walls.'

'Why should she? If it can take her apart, it can put her back together! We must try,' insisted Charlotte.

We were blunderers. We were the opposite of stone-age man placed cold before the instrument panel of a Saab or Jaguar. We were techno-man faced with the stone and blood controls of some old, alternative world of spirit forces.

Chalmers appeared, and announced, 'Your table's ready. If you'd like to come through?'

'I'm afraid there'll only be four of us,' said Martin.

'Did the other lady leave? This *is* the time you booked for.'

'I know. She was called away. A friend came for her. She had to leave her car. We'll see to that tomorrow.'

Chalmers raised an eyebrow.

'Fact is,' blustered Martin, 'we'd like to enjoy a bit of a celebration. Special occasion! Do you have two double rooms free for the night? Don't want the police stopping us afterwards. Breathalysing us. Can't risk that.'

The landlord brightened. 'We do, as it happens.'

'We'll take them.'

'Mr Chalmers,' said Charlotte, 'out of curiosity, why did you mount that fan in that particular position?'

'Had to put it somewhere didn't we? That was the first year we came here, oh . . . a long while ago. As I recall, the plaster up there was prone to staining. Dark damp stains. The stone behind was . . .' He wrinkled his nose. 'Oozy.' Changing the subject, he waved at the counter. 'If you get thirsty during the night,' he joked, 'help yourselves. You're regulars. Guests can drink anytime. Just leave a note for me to tot up.'

Charlotte beamed at him. 'Thank you very much, Mr Chalmers.'

Yes, I thought, we're all raving insomniacs. We'll certainly be holding a quiet party down here at two in the morning.

'My pleasure. Will you come this way?'

If we were supposed to be celebrating, Chalmers and his wife and the pair of waitresses from the village must have decided that the Roebuck's cuisine wasn't our pleasure that evening, to judge from how we picked at it. Or else we were engaged in a peculiar silent quarrel about the choice of fare. However, we did sink some wine, almost a bottle apiece. As we toyed with our food, the restaurant began to fill up with local subgentry enjoying a night out. When we returned to the other room for coffee, the place was crowded and the fan was busily sucking smoke out. Incense of drugful death, I thought, wondering whether this might be a phrase from Keats.

Jenny and I lay stiffly on top of the bedspread, never quite sinking below the surface of sleep. Eventually our wrist-watch alarms roused us. Soon Charlotte tapped at our door. She had a torch. We tiptoed down creaky though carpet-muffled stairs to rendezvous with Martin, who had switched on the dim wall lamps in the bar and was up on a chair, scrutinizing the surface of the Xtractall with a powerful torch beam. Before we went up to our separate bedrooms, he had fetched his tool kit – nonchalantly, as though the metal box was a suitcase containing our absent pyjamas and nighties.

'Charlotte,' he said, 'nip behind the counter and find the switch for the fan. It's bound to be labelled. Make sure that it's off. Not that being off might make much difference!'

'Why not?'

'How do mice get sucked into it overnight?'

'*If* they do,' I said. I should have followed this thought through. I should have pursued this possibility. I should have!

'Fan's off,' she stage-whispered.

'Right. Up on a chair, Derrick. Hold the torch.'

I complied, and Martin unscrewed the housing, then removed the safety grille.

''Course, it mightn't be possible to reverse the action . . .' Perspiration beaded his brow. He wasn't looking foward to plunging his hands into the works. 'Hold the beam steady. Yessss. The mounting unfastens here, and here. Slide it out. Turn it round. Bob's your uncle.'

He worked away. Presently he withdrew the inner assembly gingerly, reversed it, slid it back inside.

'I keep imagining Alice walking in,' said Jenny. 'What silly jokers we would seem. What a studenty sort of prank, gimmicking a fan so that cold and smoke blow *into* the pub!'

Martin unclenched his teeth. 'If Alice tried to come through the front door now, she'd probably set off a burglar alarm . . .

There we are! Pass the grille up, Jenny, will you? Now the slats. It's got to be just the way it was before . . .'

We both stepped down and cleared the chairs away, then hauled a table aside to clear a space, as if Alice would simply float down from that little opening above, her feet coming to rest lightly on the carpet.

'Switch the power on, Charlotte. Got a cigar handy, Derrick?'

When I shook my head, Charlotte brought a pack from behind the counter, stripping the Cellophane wrapper with her nails. Lighting a panatella, I didn't merely let the smoke uncurl. I sucked and blew out powerfully.

'Let's all hold hands and wish,' suggested Jenny.

We did so. Me, puffing away like a chimney, Jenny, Martin, and Charlotte. What silly jokers.

Clunk-clack. The slat opened and the fan whirred, blowing a dusty breeze down at our faces. The noise of the mechanism altered. Without actually becoming louder, the fan seemed to rev up as if a furious turbine were spinning inside the wall almost beyond the pitch of our ears. Our chorus line retreated. Then it happened.

Matter gushed through the slats of the fan – bubbling, convulsing substances, brown and white and crimson, blobs of yellow, strands of ginger and black – which all coalesced into a surging column of confusion struggling to reassemble itself before our eyes.

'Alice!' squealed Jenny.

The thing before us was Alice, and it wasn't Alice. It was her, and it was a cat, and it was mice and iridescent black beetles and spiders and flies, whatever the fan had swallowed. The shape was human, and most of the mass was Alice, but the rest was fur and wings and tiny legs and all else, melted together, interwoven with scraps of clothing, black hair growing out at random. I was too appalled to scream.

The Alice-creature jerked brown lips apart as if tearing a hole in its head, and *it* might have wanted to shriek. The noise that emerged was a coughing, strangled growl. Faceted eyes ranged the room. And us; and us.

'We're sorry!' babbled Martin. 'We're so sorry. Tell us what to do!'

Unbidden, I knew. Terrified, I snatched from my pocket the medallion and the keys to the Saab and tossed these on to the table nearest to the half-human creature.

Her fingers seized the keys. Her legs took her to the front door. Her hand unlatched and unbolted the door – so she was still intelligent. Tearing the front door open, she fled into darkness.

A few moments later an engine roared, headlamps stabbed the night, tyres gouged gravel. Her Saab slewed its way on to the road. It was Martin who shut the door and relocked it – he had been wrong about burglar alarms. There were none.

'What have we done?' moaned Jenny.

'Maybe we saved her from something worse,' I said. 'Maybe she knows how to heal herself. She left her medallion . . . why would she do that?'

Martin groaned and sat down heavily. 'You don't need fucking jewellery when your body's glistening with bits of beetles.'

I gathered the worn, cryptic medal up. 'This is much more than jewellery. We'd better keep it.'

'No,' mumbled my wife, as I dropped the disc into my jacket pocket.

'It would be terrible not to have it to give to her if she comes back.'

'It could *lead* that thing to us, Derrick.'

'What's going on?' John Chalmers had come downstairs, attired in a paisley dressing-gown and, God help us, a nightcap with dangling tassel. He seemed to be holding something behind his back – a cudgel, a shotgun? He moved in behind the counter and laid down whatever it was.

'Our friend came back for her car,' Charlotte attempted to explain. 'We're sorry we woke you.'

'You're all fully dressed. You weren't intending to . . . depart?'

'You said we could partake of a late drink if we wished, Mr Chalmers.'

'Mm. Screwdrivers?'

For one stupid moment I imagined he was offering to fix cocktails for us. However, he was eyeing Martin's tools, still lying in view.

Charlotte was quick on the uptake. 'Our friend's car needed fixing. That's why she had to leave it earlier.'

Chalmers shook his head sceptically.

'I'd like a brandy, please,' she told him. Her hand was straying automatically to the shoulder bag she had brought down with her, hunting in it . . .

'Don't smoke, love!' Martin said urgently. 'If you have any, don't light up! Make that two brandies, will you? Doubles.'

'Same for us,' I said.

As Chalmers busied himself, Martin nodded significantly at the fan. It was still set to blow, not suck. Could anything else emerge from between those slats? Or was the eerie zone beyond its blades, the zone of the past, empty now? Where the hell had my panatella gone? I was dimly aware of discarding it when the fan began to gush. Ah – it was lying in an ashtray. Gone out, by the look of it. Nevertheless, I crushed the cigar into extinction. How could we put the fan to rights? Chalmers would be on the alert till daybreak. We couldn't. We would have to abandon the Roebuck in the morning, abandon and never come back. We gulped our brandies and trooped up-stairs.

Next morning, haggard and exhausted, we ate bacon and eggs in the restaurant, paid our bills, and went out to the two cars. The day was bright and crisp; frost lingered.

'So, no more Fridays for us,' Martin said dully. 'Get rid of that medallion, will you, Derrick?'

'Alice may need it,' I said.

'She may need us, she may need you,' said Charlotte, 'but not in the same way as before.'

We parted and drove off from the Roebuck through the dead, cold countryside.

Jenny worked on me all weekend about that wretched medallion until I did promise to dispose of it. On Monday morning, walking through London to work, I dropped the worn disc down a sewer grating.

That night I dreamed about Alice, the Alice we had known before. This time she beckoned me lasciviously towards a doorway. She dropped her clothing. Naked, she invited me.

On Tuesday, prior to a meeting with some Japanese about supplies of Butadiene, Martin phoned me at the office.

'A car followed me home last night, Derrick. It hung well back, but when I was passing through — ' – he mentioned a village with some decent street lighting – 'I'm sure it was a Saab. Thought I'd better tip you off, eh? I've been thinking . . .' He sounded furtive. 'I've been thinking about Alice. She never knew where we lived, did she?'

'I'm not sure she wanted to know.'

'She knows now, so far as I'm concerned.' He rang off.

Martin didn't phone again – though I made a call, to Webster-Freeman, publishers. They had never heard of an Alice. I wasn't surprised.

It's Friday night, and I'm driving home on my own, listening to Vivaldi's *Four Seasons*. It's the time that should be the happy hour. Jenny and I both took our cars to MK today. Headlights are following me, always keeping the same distance behind whether I speed up or slow down. If Alice comes calling, what do I give to her now?

Since Monday I've been increasingly haunted by mental snapshots of the old Alice. The other day I heard on the radio how the average male thinks about sex eight times an hour; that's how often Alice crosses my mind.

I realize that I've fallen in love – or in lust – with her. Does Martin secretly feel the same way – for his 'lamia'? These feelings overpower me as surely as I was possessed in the pub that night by an urge to piss, the need to release myself. Even after what happened, maybe Alice left that medallion behind to protect us – from the altered lamia? Now that token no longer does so.

Ahead there's a lay-by where a caravan is parked permanently: Sally's Café, serving breakfast to truck drivers all day long – but not by night, when it's locked up, shuttered, abandoned.

I'm pulling in, and braking fifty yards past the caravan. Will the car in my mirror overshoot, pass by? No. It pulls in too. It parks abreast of Sally's Café, douses its lights. A Saab, I'd say.

The driver's door swings open. Soon I may understand all about Alice and her domain, which we first denied, then stupidly desecrated. Has the past's love of us all turned sour now? Grown vicious?

A dark, amorphous figure emerges from the Saab, and rushes towards me. I'll let her in. The Alice we knew always appreciated jokes. The final joke is: I've become an almighty fan of hers. Will I have time to tell her? To hear her laugh – or shriek? I open the door. I can't help myself.

Talk of the Town

Could my unique experience have some connection with the radio masts on Borough Hill?

There are, oh, a dozen of those. At night they become anorexic Christmas trees lit up to warn off low-flying planes. The transmitters are high-powered. Now and then drivers of posh fuel-injection cars complain that their engines cut out on the main road that runs below Borough Hill, though the radio engineers deny responsibility.

Borough Hill is also where the magic mushrooms grow. Wire fences weave a wide cordon around the radio station, but the barrier's insecure. A teenager can squirm underneath the wire where a badger has scooped a pit or where rabbits have sapped the soil. Several adventurers did so, to gather the hallucinogenic mushrooms. When one of these bold spirits, my friend Tim Hewitt, was rushed to hospital and died of poisoning, the local rag – known to everyone, including itself, as 'The Gusher' – mounted a crusade. As a result bales of barbed wire, ribboned with the wool of itchy sheep, now reinforce the perimeter.

That was in the year when two of the town councillors ran off to a love-nest by the seaside 150 miles away. A few months later Mr Jarvis and Mrs Leacock straggled back separately to face forgiveness and embarrassment. Their romantic escapade had failed.

Tim died before he could supply me with a handful of *Amanita muscaria* to blow my mind right out of town. Yet somehow when my hometown begins to talk to me I imagine that some conjunction of those mushrooms and those radio masts may be responsible; as though, through the roots of their guy-wires and stays, the tall steel trees are sucking up essence of rotting *Amanita* and are broadcasting a delirium into my skull.

My parents, Matt and Pat, adore country and western music,

which I suppose is their own style of escape. After a day as local bus driver and supermarket checkout lady respectively, Matt and Pat will dress up as sequined cowboy and cowgirl. He'll strum away loudly at the electronic guitar while she will warble stuff about divorce and truckers, drunks and waitresses. Every fortnight or so they perform in one or other of the town pubs, to a fair amount of applause.

Personally I find their activities dead embarrassing, but I can't help noticing how many American songs seem to mythologize by name a whole string of towns and cities which really possess a very short history compared with your average British town or city. How many songs mythologize British towns, however?

> Daventry, oh Daventry,
> I can see your radio station;
> And it fills me with elation.
> I blow my nose
> And twiddle all my toes . . .

Mrs Taylor, one of the history teachers at my old school, said that our town took its name from the time of the Vikings and referred to Danish invaders. This origin led to the christening of the Daneholme housing estate which backs on to the country park – a semi-wooded reservoir where fishermen angle, where shags and geese touch down to delight the bird-watchers with their binoculars, where dogs shit on the paths.

I found an old book in the town library which says that the name stems from 'Dafa's Tree', Dafa being the name of some ancient Briton. Perhaps because this isn't the usual explanation I prefer it. I visualize Dafa as a hairy, smelly rough-tough clad in an ill-cured sheepskin.

Did Dafa own the tree in question? Was there only one tree in the vicinity? That hardly seems likely. So far as I know, the whole land used to be cloaked in virgin forest, of oak and ash and sweet chestnut, ever since the glaciers retreated thirteen thousand years ago.

Maybe Dafa used to sacrifice people to his special tree. Maybe he was a great local chief, and when he was buried, his kin had planted an acorn on his chest. Those were the days.

In the era of the stagecoach the town became an important

stopover, as the ramshackled old hotel at the top of Sheaf Street still bears witness. Joseph Priestley, discoverer of oxygen, went to school in that street. (Did everyone hold their breath until Priestley arrived?)

History has sagged and rotted since. I don't think the Luftwaffe actually bombed the town, aiming ineptly for the radio masts. The centre simply has the appearance of a bomb site.

I have walked around it a million times.

Before it speaks to me.

The voice comes from around my head – from a few inches away – rather than from within.

'Greetings, Owen!' It's a deep, mellow, benign voice.

In Bowen Square shoppers' cars crawl around under a grey January sky, headlights lit at noon, hunting for parking-spaces. Members of the Jesus Army are blocking part of the pavement, jigging and singing about the love of their invisible lord.

These people form a powerful little economic empire locally, what with their organic farms, their grocery shops, their builders' merchant yards and general building business. A few dark rumours circulate as to how kids in their various communes can't watch television and are beaten for transgressions; even how the naked corpse of a runaway was found frozen in wintry fields near New Creation Farm. The head of the army pointed out that a lot of its members are former drug addicts and runaways who have been rehabilitated in Christ. Jesus people take the army theme seriously, wearing paramilitary uniforms at their rallies. However, these singers today look somewhat more hippy. Dowdy hippy.

> 'Hey-ho, wherever you may be,
> 'I am the lord of the dance,' said he,
> 'And I'll lead you all, wherever you may be—'

'Greetings, Owen!'

Can this be the voice of the lord of the Jesus Army? Am I on the brink of a conversation, as if those singers have sneezed in my face and I instantly caught cold?

'Who are you?' I utter the words deep in my throat, moving my lips as little as possible.

'I'm Daventry, Owen. What can I do for you?'

'You're . . . Daventry?'

'The very same. Let me prove it. Ask me a favour.'

'OK. Make the sun shine on me.'

'Certainly, Owen. Give me a few minutes.'

I walk on through the Foundry Place arcade – housing yet another greeting-card shop, yet another travel agent. In Sheaf Street I halt by the window where the jolly automaton cobbler forever thumps a hammer up and down upon a last. A cutting wind funnels up the sloping street of mostly sandstone shops, cafés, and whatnot. Mist hides the dip through which the bypass road runs, and masks the Headlands housing estate that rises beyond.

On such a day of puzzling visibility I often imagine that Sheaf Street plunges down to a seafront and that the haze in the dip is ocean. It isn't, of course, and it doesn't. Maybe Mr Jarvis and Mrs Leacock were infected by a similar illusion and fled away to locate the source of their fancy. Before trickling back home like condensation down a plate-glass window.

Just then, the grey overcast parts. A shaft of golden light floods the upper storeys of the street. The reflection from a window dazzles me.

'There you are, Owen: sunshine.'

'Thanks, Daventry.'

'My pleasure.' Such a deep, measured, noble voice; though at the same time ingenuous, guileless.

The freak sunlight lasts until I pass the pet shop, outside of which stand bins of dog biscuits. I loathe dogs. Messy animals, by turns slavish and vicious. So far as I'm concerned there are only two categories of dog: Rottweilers, and bonsai Rottweilers. Roaming loose despite a notice to the contrary fixed to a lamp-post, one of the latter variety is busy dropping its dirty load on a paving slab. Risking an attack on my ankles, I direct a kick at its ribs.

'Thank you, Owen.'

'Maybe it isn't such great shakes being a town? Dog dirt, car exhausts, litter, people letting parts of you go derelict, your roads breaking out into acne with the frost . . .'

'I am content.'

*

Since leaving school three years ago I tried to be a clerk in the brand-new district council offices, but that didn't last. The tedium, and low pay. So basically I'm unemployed.

Have a few friends, though no girlfriend. I guess I'm shy in that area. I read a lot; pick up long words the way tramps pick up cigar butts. Walk around town a lot. That doesn't take long. My favourite spot is the graveyard behind the parish church. Steel meshes protect the lower windows of the locked edifice on account of kids chucking stones. Long grass and brambles hide most of the graves, though one clear space, marked by no headstone, looks as though a Rottweiler has buried a bone to which it must obsessively return. A home-made signboard planted in the overturned soil reads: *Leave Our Baby's Grave Alone*.

Pathetic, really.

I thought the whole town was pathetic. In my mind I privately renamed it Desultory.

Until it spoke to me.

Can I have been hurting its feelings? Am I uniquely sensitive to it?

Can it work other wonders similar to that sudden flood of sunlight?

Does anyone else know? Does anyone else notice?

I walk round town now with a different step and with other eyes. Each brick is a cell in its body. Each building is an organ.

Masts, mushrooms . . . I reject any such notions. As well as the notion of madness, of course, since I don't feel at all mad.

Daventry only speaks to me while I'm in physical contact with its horny skin of pavements or tarmac. When I lie in bed at home, strain as I might there's silence.

'Do you hear me, Daventry?'

Not a whisper.

Nor does the town address me when I'm inside shops or coffee bars or the post office. Maybe this is discretion on the town's part – not wishing to expose me, or our relationship, should I mumble too noisily. Maybe Daventry can't communicate when other people are close by, cooped up next to me. Like a doleful hound left at a doorway, Daventry stays outside, waiting. Well now, a loony would mutter to an imaginary acquaintance anywhere without exception, wouldn't he? If, on the other hand, I'm suffering from some phobia connected with walking the streets – a phobia which is causing the voice – surely I should find Daventry's words scary and oppressive, driving me indoors? Whereas I don't.

'Do you talk to other people?' I ask in the High Street another day as I'm passing the frozen food centre.

'Only to you currently, Owen.'

'Why me?'

'Because you can hear me.'

'Can other *places* hear you? Are you friends with the villages hereabouts?'

'A cow can't be friendly with a squeaky mouse.'

'How about with other towns your size?'

'Those cows live in far-flung fields.'

'Roads link you.'

'Yes, roads . . .' Daventry sounds scornful – as well a town might, when the last thing it can do is pull up its roots and shuffle somewhere else.

'I guess you must know the answer to this: are you named after Dafa, or the Danes?'

'I have a secret name of my own, Owen. It's Rambalundabalgi,' confides Daventry.

'What language is that?'

'My very own.'

'Who else speaks it?'

'Only me. I need a constant language which doesn't change down the centuries.'

'So do you talk to yourself in it?'

'Hambadoolapoo, homboloin, impolooli,' says Daventry.

It dawns on me that I'm not nuts. It's my hometown that is cuckoo, batty as a coot. Not in any spectacular, psychotic fashion, I hasten to add. More in a quiet, depressive style.

Disconcerting! Still, I'm not scared. I wonder what I can get it to do for me.

'Rambabalgi, I need some—'

'Ramba*lunda*balgi, please.'

'Sorry. Ramba-lunda-balgi, I need some money.'

'Try the cash dispenser at the bank,' suggests Daventry.

'I don't have money in any bank.'

'Nevertheless.'

'And I don't have a plastic card to stick in the slot.'

'Hoodsbonda poloobola.'

When I reach the niche in the bank wall, the little screen lights up invitingly of its own accord with its menu of options. Glancing to left and right – and seeing no one in the offing – I press the CASH button.

'Now key twenty pounds,' advises Daventry. 'Ambobooda doolooli.'

I do as it says. The machine clicks and whirrs and churns within as if actually printing the money, and a single crisp banknote emerges. I scarper up the street.

'Why not fifty quid?' I ask my benefactor. 'Why not a hundred?'

'Twenty is adequate for your present needs, Owen.'

I go into the Plume of Feathers and buy a lager, leaving me about nineteen quid.

So there are miracles – but I'm going to be rationed. Daventry mustn't want me to become too independent.

'How about providing a dishy-looking girlfriend for me?' I ask Rambalundabalgi a few days later, hoping that this request won't make my town jealous.

The town hums and haws. But it has already persuaded its good citizens to stand on one leg for a while, to please me. That trick didn't pose too much of a problem. For a good fifteen seconds the little market-place resembled a colony of drab flamingos in overcoats and anoraks when a score of people hoisted a leg to rub an itch or for whatever other motive. A few noticed the supposed coincidence and giggled or looked embarrassed.

'Aw, come on, town of mine. Do your stuff.'

'We shall see. Amoorche chamoori.'

'That's the spirit.'

I bump into Cynthia Danvers outside of the Help the Aged charity shop. She clings to me to avoid falling over. Since we're in a clinch it seems only reasonable for us to kiss briefly, and laugh.

'Why, Owen,' she exclaims, 'I haven't seen you for ages.' Actually, she has; on other occasions she simply hasn't been paying any attention. 'What a slippery pavement!'

Slim blonde Cynthia works part-time in a hair-styling salon these days . . .

Walking towards my home together, arm in arm, it seems as if a treasure hunt is in progress. A chap in overalls is walking slowly along our street with what appears to be a metal detector, which emits the occasional whistle. Old women's faces peer from behind curtains.

I hail him. 'Found gold yet, have we?'

'Suspected gas leak,' says the fellow. 'I can't find anything.'

'Is there going to be an explosion?' Anxiously Cynthia squeezes my arm.

Oh yes, I think to myself, there'll be an explosion, though not of gas.

'That'll be the smell from the paint factory,' I reassure her. 'It comes when the wind's from the west. Depending on what they're making.' I must get Rambalundabalgi to do something permanent about the smell . . .

The man with the gas detector packs up and drives off in a van. As soon as I let Cynthia into our empty house and embrace her, her attitude to me shifts like the wind. She wrinkles up her pert nose.

'Stop pawing me, Owen,' she says. 'I only came for a cup of coffee.'

'Amoorcha chamoori,' I chant.

'*What?*'

Alas, I'm overlooking the fact that Daventry's writ apparently doesn't extend within my home. Or any other building, either? Cynthia's enchantment hasn't lasted.

'Name of a new rock group,' I tell her with a shrug.

'Weirdo.' Her tone doesn't convey much enthusiasm.

I make us some coffee and we chat in a vague way, although once she leaves – as soon as she's outside the door – she agrees

brightly to take a stroll around the country park with me the
evening after.

In the middle of January, yes. As she walks off she glances
back, mildly puzzled.

Standing in the garden I tell Rambalundabalgi, 'I need a tent
and a sleeping-bag. Cancel that! I need a *van* with a good heater
and a sleeping-bag.' We can take a drive to a pub beforehand to
oil the wheels of love. Though not to a country pub, or I'll be
outside of Rambalundabalgi's sphere of influence. Oh God, not
even to a pub . . . I need a bottle of red vino for us to share in the
van.

'But Owen, you haven't passed your driving test.'

'You'll see to it that I'm not caught, won't you?'

'Choobaloo hompobeli.'

Seemingly human nature imposes other limits. One leg in the
air, it transpires, but not both legs. 'I'm not going *all* the way,'
Cynthia protests in the back of the van which I borrowed from
the New Street car park, having found the keys left in the
ignition. Yes, from right opposite the fuzz shop itself, within a
stone's throw of the police station.

'In fact,' and she giggles tipsily, 'I don't know why I'm doing
this much!' An owl hoots from the nearby trees. 'Isn't this good
enough?' The van's engine throbs softly, running the heater.
My own engine throbs, causing, after a while, an urgent desire
to pee. When I climb back aboard, Cynthia's sitting in the
passenger seat waiting for me to drive her home.

After doing so, I repark the van without problems other than
scraping one wing against a concrete bollard; and I prowl the
streets frustratedly.

'Rambalundabalgi!' I cry. 'Is it really much use at all knowing
you?'

'Ah, but you're the actor in my dream, Owen. I need an actor,
don't you see?'

'What do you mean?'

'Chamoori choobaloo, my young friend! Can everything that
you desire come true in dreams? Ah no. How often does
prohibition step in between the desire and its fulfilment! The
anchors of guilt, conscience, and repression drag the actor back

from the brink of the orgy. As indeed must be the case! Would
you see this street fill with tropical fishes from the tanks in
yonder pet shop? Shoals of rainbow fish swimming about freely
in midair as if over a coral reef? Would you see all those
Rottweilers burst into flames spontaneously or explode,
splattering the shop windows with red graffiti? Would you have
the moon shine warmly, heating the dark of the night, and the
sun gleam coldly so that daylight hours are the best time to
snuggle in bed? Would you see the people strolling about
merrily in their underwear, drunk with freedom and imagination, singing arias?'

'Why not? Why not?'

'Do you propose a revolution? An invasion by caprice?'

'Yes, *Desultory*,' I say insultingly.

'Then you must learn my language and lose your own.'

'I will!'

Rambalundabalgi teaches me so quickly. Hompobeli.
Hambadoolapoo. Homboloin.

And those things come to pass. Fish swim through the air.
Dogs explode. The moon warms me. People of all ages spill into
the streets in their nighties and pyjamas to dance around the
stone cross by the market-place which burns like a candle.

For a while I still understand the words of the *other* people –
those ghosts in overcoats, anoraks, leather jackets, police
uniforms – though I can't answer them except in Rambalundabalgi's lingo. Those ghosts are fading, old words are
fading . . .

Hoodabonda?

Shoochoo moochobal; aaap hooloo peeph foochali.
Sooramangi? Sha! Choobaloo. Ambolongapangi.

'Rambalundabalgi?'

'Chamoori, Owen. Chamoori.'

Looking Down on You

And then the glass panel, which Andrew Craig had been lying sprawled upon, gave away . . .

'They *have* to be perfectly safe.'

That's what Trevor Pears said, nodding at these sloping windows, a self-teasing frisson of dread in his voice.

'They must test the glass,' Andrew agreed, exhibiting similar queasy relish.

The two Britons spoke softly, yet one of their German hosts – portly Hans-Peter – immediately related how local schoolboys, who came up the tower on trips with their teachers, would generally throw themselves spread-eagled upon the slanting plates of glass out of bravado. Hanging there. Staring down. A hundred and eighty metres down. Six hundred feet. Suspended by a centimetre of tough glass over an abyss.

To Andrew, the distance to the ground below seemed more like six thousand feet. Ant people pursued their own short shadows. Cars were tiny toys.

Hans-Peter grinned and slapped his T-shirt-clad girth. 'I think I'm too heavy to lie on the glass.' The icon on their host's black T-shirt was of comedian and tragedian masks in white outline side by side. Happy tit, sad tit.

Whereas neither Andrew nor Trevor were any burlier than your average adolescent. Indeed, Trevor – whose new noir comedy about an inept oriental serial murderer, *The Sirens of the Rams*, had just opened to acclaim in London's West End – looked somewhat like a retired jockey who dressed nostalgically. Balding but trim, almost sparrowlike, he favoured pastel silk shirts – today's was a soft lime green. Andrew dressed more brutally in jeans and lumberjack shirt. He, too, was short, if somewhat squat. Beneath his defiantly curly russet hair,

Andrew's face was mischievous in animation – though melancholy and fatigued in repose.

There hadn't been the remotest hint of a challenge in Hans-Peter's remark, which was joviality itself. His words even stressed that some human burdens might be too extreme for the glass to bear.

'I suppose,' mused Trevor, 'they would need to calculate for at least fifty or sixty stones' impact just to be on the safe side . . .'

'Stones?' queried Hans-Peter.

'Weight,' explained Andrew thoughtlessly.

'Oh, I am not so heavy.' Hans-Peter turned away, seeming hurt; and Andrew felt ashamed.

Indeed, there were several good pretexts for shame.

Such as . . . the gleaming neatness and order and salubrious greenness of this city, with so many trees and parks and geranium-hung balconies; such a dearth of mess, at least in the parts they had seen. Precious little of Düsseldorf was old – for the simple reason that bombs dropped by Andrew's or Trevor's kin of the previous generation had flattened the burg quite thoroughly, clearing the ground for a kind of utopian habitat founded on energetic work and the wealth that that produced. The shame was for the messier, lazier lifestyle back home. And for the atrophy of his own career.

The personal inevitably found its public mirror wherever it could . . .

An express elevator, operated by a dapper Turk dressed in a dark suit, had whispered their party up smoothly to the observation deck of the Rhine Tower.

From immediately below, that concrete column had soared upward, tapering, to spread into a cone that hid the uppermost microwave dishes and the slimmer sky-needle from view. The tower was a creamy-white fungus with flat gills of greenish glass. The glass leaned far outward high overhead at an angle of . . . what? Thirty? Thirty-five degrees?

Now they were admiring the view through those great slopes of glass that canted outward so disconcertingly from the very floor.

Sun shone blindingly from a cloudless sky. Only the horizon

was hazed by heat, obscuring Cologne twenty-odd miles away.
Otherwise . . . miles of clean city, parks, snaking highways,
then agriculture, and some distant clusters of pale, satanic mills
– coal mines or cooling towers – which hardly polluted the
perspective, though their silhouettes were subtly ominous.

Trevor whistled a jaunty theme from Wagner's *Ring*. For the
broad Rhine curved around below, with a quiescent amusement
park erected on a strip of floodplain, roller-coaster tracks
weaving bright hoops and slaloms in the air.

'Ah, we are too far north for Rhine Maidens,' observed
Hans-Peter.

Indeed. None were visible. Barges plying the river were
carrying desert-camouflaged trucks back to base from the recent
Gulf War.

Contemplatively, several Japanese were pointing the latest
video cameras at the expensive leafy suburb over the water
beyond the nearest of the suspension bridges. Kneeling, one
murmured a commentary, laying down a sound track. Perhaps
they were filming their own expensive houses, since Düsseldorf
was home to sixty thousand Japanese businessmen and
families.

The commentator tilted his camera down to capture the North
Rhine-Westphalia Parliament Building, reminiscent of a
gleaming machine made of large gear wheels and springs – a
hand could almost reach down and wind it up, to set it in sleek
motion.

Reach *down*.

And down.

'What a shame,' Trevor said to Hans-Peter. 'I was hoping to
see a Rhine Maiden break surface.' Hans-Peter grinned and
shrugged at this seeming whim, which was geographically
inaccurate.

Surfaces do break . . ., thought Andrew.

But not those glass panels, oh no.

'You should be nearer Koblenz for Rhine Maidens,' said their
host.

When Andrew had barely left school, decades ago, he had
hitch-hiked through that most picturesque part of the Rhine-
land all on his own, staying in youth hostels, en route from

Holland to Austria. He would always remember one lift with an impeccably tailored man driving a Mercedes. Inevitably, adolescent Andrew – dressed in some army surplus jacket – had been somewhat scruffy. Cruising through Boppard or another of those enchanting little towns, their Merc had overhauled a crippled hunchback who was gimping slowly along the pavement. The driver had slowed to a crawl and coasted past, laughing heartily at the cripple. Andrew felt that he himself was being laughed at, too . . .

How shabby he felt, up this tower. And how scruffy much of his own country was – bottom of the Euro economic league fourth year running. Rising unemployment, businesses collapsing, houses being repossessed, cardboard cities for the homeless, suicides, the slow death of the Health Services, the cramping of the schools. Just a month earlier, only streets away from Andrew's flat, a fellow had died in his car parked in the driveway of his former home, which was no longer his. His computer business had failed. Food was in the car boot. The fuel tank was empty. The man supposedly had died . . . of 'natural causes'. Was that code for sheer despair?

How shabby Andrew's own life had become since his work dried up three years earlier, and since the divorce, which he didn't wish to think about.

Yet here in Düsseldorf, obliviously, he was being fêted – along with Trevor, and the Americans Gail Gardner and Jerry de Rosa. Andrew was enjoying a brief post-mortem existence – so it seemed to him. The foreign hand of welcome caressed generously, if sometimes reproachfully, as when he failed to comport himself as a good European.

The Düsseldorf Drama Festival was staging the German première of his black farce *Cold Calls*, an absurdist treatment of economic agony featuring a double-glazing salesman and his family. Their desperate dialling of random telephone numbers to solicit orders involved them crazily in a terrorist conspiracy.

In truth, the play had begun as a heartfelt statement; yet it had rapidly become eccentric, paranoid, and zany. A tour de force of the fringe, a masterpiece of the margin.

Cold Calls had been Andrew's final play. Thereafter dialogue, had died. With Dorothy; with Jonathon, their teenage son. With audiences, and with himself – though the part-time lecturing tided him through, and though news of his demise hadn't yet registered in Düsseldorf.

Gail Gardner wrote musical comedies for Broadway, and Jerry de Rosa operated more seriously Off-Broadway. It was white-haired, perky, capricious Gail who had advised Andrew, *'Don't look down at yourself, kiddo. Respect yourself.'* This was after hearing him interviewed by the German Press, in a self-deprecating vein that Andrew had imagined witty at the time. Gail had fixed him with a stern stare, which she softened by patting him on the arm.

Of course, in the real world, dialogue continued, and his ear registered it, though all seemed unusable.

'Over there' – Hans-Peter was gesturing at the rich suburb –'is where the assassination took place just a while ago. Of the minister for the new lands. The eastern lands. He had his home there.'

Of a sudden, terrorism was close at hand, and real, and serious. Andrew wondered how he could possibly have *presumed* to write about terrorism and double glazing.

Each of the four guests had their own dutiful German escort, and now Andrew's own – slim, bespectacled Joachim – returned to join him and Trevor and Hans-Peter. The two other escorts – an ebullient dark-haired woman and an older, weatherbeaten man whose names Andrew had already misplaced in his increasingly fraying memory – were farther around the tower, pointing out sights to Gail and Jerry. Gail was travelling around Europe with an autocratic, blue-rinsed companion lady, and Jerry with a handsome, affected young male secretary – supposedly a secretary.

'Would you like some coffee and chocolate cake?' asked Joachim. 'I think the others will sit down for a while.'

A child was squalling in the café area, and Andrew shook his head. Trevor nodded a vague acceptance of the invitation, though he didn't yet make a move. He was still staring at the suburb where the blood had been shed.

'I suppose,' Trevor quipped to Hans-Peter, 'if you buy a whole new country, some people in it might get a trifle *irritated*.'

And Hans-Peter laughed, for Trevor was a witty noir dramatist.

'Buy a country! Oh yes, we're buying East Germany – but meanwhile, you see, the Japanese are busy buying us!'

'It will cost,' said Joachim earnestly. 'But we will pay.'

Trevor smiled mischievously. 'Jerry said I really must visit the East before you lot change it totally. He told me that going there's like driving along in a Technicolor movie – and suddenly it all changes to black and white.'

'How do you suppose they wash the *outsides* of these windows?' Andrew resumed; and Trevor flinched in mock dismay.

How *could* a cleaning cradle possibly be lowered down the outside of that slope?

'I think,' said Andrew, 'the cleaners wear suction pads on their palms and their knees, and they *crawl* down from above . . .' He mimed a jerky, splayed progress across the overhanging glass.

He leaned forward, hands resting on the steel spars to right and left. Along the river frontage, construction work was in progress, which would presently roof over the roadway to create a garden esplanade. On what was currently a neck of wasteland, many colourful tents were pitched close together behind a wire fence. *Zigeuner*. Gypsies. Almost invisible from this height, placards strung along the wire demanded their right to remain in Germany. When the party had passed by earlier, naked brown-skinned children with greasy black hair had been playing in dust around camp-fires. Where did they come from? Romania? Perhaps! What language did they speak? 'Some ethnic dialect,' Joachim had supposed.

Andrew's hands flexed on the steel spars.

'Go on,' coaxed Trevor. 'You want to.' His tone said otherwise – he didn't even wish to *see* anyone emulate the exploits of those German schoolboys. He didn't believe Andrew would.

So Andrew lowered himself face-first on to the glass panel. Spreading himself – oh yes, in a Saint Andrew's cross, and holding on to nothing – he stared down at the sunbaked ground far below. Nothing but glass and air between himself and concrete.

Only after he had thrust himself back on to his feet did he allow himself to imagine the glass popping out under his weight. And the fall, the fall. *Then* his stomach fluttered, and his knees went wobbly. Though not very.

'I don't in the least mind looking down from an *aeroplane*,' said Trevor. 'That doesn't mean anything. But if I'm in somewhere that's *attached* to the ground—'

'I wonder if one could *fly* – '

Trevor immediately understood. '– fly down, and land in the river? It's a bit *far*. I suppose if you *knew* what you were doing, and had the right clothes on . . . After all, James Bond did it in that movie.'

Andrew thought of thermal updraughts from the baking concrete below, of capricious winds swirling around the tower, of a great sheet of glass acting as a sail. He thought of falling like a stone. Falling for quite a few seconds. Then smashing into black oblivion.

'So what would your last words be – in your mind?' Trevor asked.

'Trying to steal my dialogue, eh?'

'I'm just curious.'

'I was thinking that, "Oh fuck," would probably sum it up.'

'Not, "Father-forgive-me-receive-me-I-believe-in-you-utterly"?'

Andrew shook his head.

The Siemens Building and its neighbours were silver cigarette packets, foil-clad by reflected sunlight.

'Isn't this something?' called Gail as Andrew and Trevor hove in view.

Some muscular, tanned locals were drinking beer at a neighbouring table. Tipsily, they began to query the dark-haired woman – oh yes, she was Gisela – as to why the dramatists' companions were speaking in English, even to each other. That was wrong. Visitors should speak German. Andrew understood only that much of what they said; and paused uncomfortably, while Gisela talked to the men, merrily.

Turned out they were miners. Despite past guarantees of a hundred years' employment, their mines were now under threat of closure. Cheaper coal from the East was to blame . . .

One miner staggered erect, rambling loquaciously, and mimed throwing himself from the tower; though he didn't seem woeful unto suicide, only peeved.

'He says, in Berlin, in the Potsdamerplatz . . . you know?' explained Joachim. 'Beside a stretch of the Wall that still remains, you can jump off a crane fifty metres high—'

'The Death Jump!' exclaimed Jerry. 'Paul and I saw that. *Crazy*.'

'*Ja, der Todessprung,*' agreed the miner.

'Those who jump, wear a harness, with some sort of cable attached – how do you say it?' Joachim concertinaed his hands in and out.

'Elastic.'

'Yes, elastic. It costs one hundred marks, for five seconds of fear. What a waste of money! He wishes someone would pay him a hundred marks twice a day to jump off a crane instead of working at a coal face they will close. He is quite gentle, really,' Joachim murmured as the miner flapped his arms. 'He's a big softie. Don't worry.'

Andrew wandered on around the observation deck on his own.

He found himself alone, out of sight of a soul. By some flux of crowd dynamics, all visitors to the deck except for himself – Japanese, German families, whoever – had flowed to the other side of the circuit around the central column that housed the elevators. Maxwell's demon might suddenly have presided over all of the persons who had hitherto seemed distributed randomly.

All except Andrew, whom the demon had isolated.

Here was the very same plate of glass that he had rested upon, prostrate, just a few minutes before. Surely the same one. The *tested* one. Tested by himself. Down there was the wind-up Parliament Building. At the same angle as earlier, the tented camp of the *Zigeuner*.

Trevor was right about the sheer paucity of his interior·
dialogue. 'Fuck' wasn't adequate at all. Surely something more
profound? Something wittier? More insightful? Something that
capsuled a whole life. And life itself. Something that . . .
hovered just beyond his grasp.

If only he could lay his hand upon that elusive something,
why, *true dialogue* might commence for him once more.

Andrew leaned forward, surrendering his weight once again
to the glass.

And the glass panel gave way . . .

Andrew had bothered to read a bit about glass before he wrote
Cold Calls. He might work some nugget of offbeat knowledge
into the play.

Glass was a supercooled liquid. It cooled without
crystallizing. Its molecules didn't arrange themselves into a
regular, repetitive pattern, but remained all jumbled up as in a
fluid. Glass possessed no internal boundaries that would scatter
light. Thus, you could see clearly through glass.

Over thousands of years, glass might perhaps *creep* just a
little.

The glass panel flowed.

Andrew flowed, too.

With a terrible lurch of the heart, with his limbs becoming soft
rubber, he *knew* that the glass had given way beneath him; that it
was falling out of the tower, and that he, too, was falling out
with it, helplessly, inevitably. For he sank.

But then he sank no further.

He was suspended, at the very same angle as the glass had
been, staring across the Rhine.

His body had gone away, had melted; and he *was* the glass
panel itself. The glass had gathered him into it – and it was he
who hung fixed there between those steel spars, hanging
terrifyingly over empty air.

A barge moved upstream, cutting a wake. Cars sped. Ant
people followed their shadows. And upon all this, he looked
down.

Presently he heard Trevor's clipped accent. 'Well, if you're sure he isn't in the toilet, then he isn't anywhere up here.'

'The toilets are definitely empty.'

'Those elevator operators say they didn't take him down.' That was Joachim.

'Maybe they didn't notice him. Maybe there was a crush.'

'They are sure of it.'

'So he must have used the emergency stairs,' suggested Jerry de Rosa. 'The fire exit.'

'*Why?* Without telling anyone?'

'We've been all the way round by now in both directions,' said Trevor.

'How very inconsiderate of Mr Craig,' remarked Gail's companion.

None of them could see Andrew in the glass – even faintly, even as a ghostly reflection – and he couldn't turn, for now he was the glass. No more could he cry out to them, for he was mute.

Their hosts talked to each other rapidly in German.

Joachim sighed. 'I will go down the stairs after him.'

'Poor you,' Gail sympathized.

'We will meet at the bottom. We must move on, or we shall miss seeing sufficient of our luxurious Kö.'

'Quite,' agreed Gail's friend. 'We have some shopping we want to do on the Königsallee.'

And all this, he heard from behind him.

He *thought* that Joachim returned about twenty minutes later. That *seemed* to be his voice, asking anxious, breathless questions in German – to no avail.

The afternoon wore on, blindingly bright. The Rhine flowed by, quite like dark blue glass itself, rippled by the wind.

Aslant, he stared out – and down – as though he were some perfectly flat and invisible gargoyle affixed to the tower.

The horror of falling – of being released suddenly from his suspension – became irrelevant. He almost wished he could fall free. For then something would happen.

*

It was a long evening until night, until the myriad lights of the city glowed white and golden for miles.

What would his hosts think had happened? Amnesia? A nervous breakdown? An assault of utter rudeness?

Had he taken a train eastward on impulse to the monochrome land? To the land without precise law, where the policemen no longer had any clear idea what their own rights and duties were. The ambiguous land, the indigent land, where dialogue was being awkwardly reborn. Dialogue between people; dialogue with the rest of the German nation – which might become a disillusioned, embittered dialogue. A family dialogue of the deaf. As witness that bloodshed among the smart dwellings across the river.

Had he gone, like some sleepwalker, to where language had till so recently been censored, so as to study the revival of speech?

Mutely, poised motionless, imprinted in glass, he who had looked down on himself now looked down on a whole city.

Andrew became aware of movement just above his window. At first, this seemed to be but a coiling, a congealing of the air.

Then a long-limbed shape moved down, clinging to him. The shape blurred before his eyes as he sought to focus on something so close.

He must not shrink from it! Otherwise, his glass might suddenly contract – more than it ever contracted during the coldest winter night. Then it might pop free. It would spin down and shatter six hundred feet below, fracturing him schizophrenically into a dozen or a hundred parts of himself, most to be swept up and discarded, one little piece perhaps to be worn as a charm by a scavenging, dusky *Zigeuner* who discerned in that shard a segment of an imprisoned soul . . .

He must not shrink.

The being that had come from above moved slowly over his surface. Its slim, flexible limbs were translucent. As was its torso. Through its body, with almost the same perfect clarity as before, Andrew saw the dark Rhine, the bridge, and the well-lit suburb – subject to a trembling ripple, to stray bendings of the light. No one watching from below through powerful binoculars would notice anything odd.

Its head came in view, peering at him from only inches away.

A head of glass, of clear jelly. Bumps were its eyes. Its nose and its mouth were one and the same: a tapering proboscis.

The being resembled a pellucid suit, a body-sleeve, awaiting a wearer. Feeling its way as if blind, it moved slowly, seeking a resident.

Its proboscis kissed the outer surface of the window, seeking Andrew's trapped, arrested existence.

The proboscis began to suck.

He was climbing, splayhanded and splayfooted, across the sloping upper tier of windows, in an invisible body.

His was not the impulse to climb. He sensed inevitability in the motions of this ethereal body of his. If he resisted – *could* he resist? – perhaps the body would flutter away in the wind.

He clambered sinuously over the lip on to the broad rim occupied by great microwave dishes and horns – the true purpose of this tower, after all. Stepping behind one horn, he clung to it, a jellyfish embracing a vast ear trumpet.

As his fingers played slowly across the rear surface, a torrent of voices flooded through him: in German, English, Japanese . . . a thousand telephone conversations. The dialogue of the world, restored multifold. Intimacies, conspiracies, bargainings. Electronic music warbled, too. Much would be from radar sites scrupulously scrying eastward. Fax transmissions; bursts of compressed, encrypted data . . . It was the voices he really listened to.

And of course he understood those that were in English.

Shimmying to another horn, he wrapped himself upon it.

The glassy being hadn't understood any of the voices until now.

But now it did.

'*Where are you from?*' he asked himself – silently, for the only sound was of the wind. '*What are you?*'

And though there was no acknowledgement of his question, he seemed to feel himself call out from behind the horn, '*Where are you? Where are you?*'

Straining for an answer, he held the horn, sieving through all the whispering bombardment of polyglot voices for a special voice that might speak in a lilting, crooning language unheard hitherto in the world. A voice issuing from some other tower that might well be another country, a voice that might even be in orbit high overhead, circling the Earth on a satellite where another similar glassy being clung.

These potent yet precarious beings: were they of the Earth? Were they alternative entities, angels, that were virtually invisible?

Were they aliens from another star?

What had gone askew with their schemes, if indeed anything had gone askew at all?

He waited a year – through autumn, through winter, through spring. He haunted the heights of the tower in rain, in snow, in sun, embracing the horns so as to eavesdrop on a million voices, and on the burble of electronic code.

Perhaps his body and that other lost body, marooned on some distant tower, were separated lovers. Perhaps they were scouts who had lost contact – having fallen from Heaven or from space – and who were learning what they could of the world in what to them might seem like the span of a mere day.

For a year, he looked down on the city and the tiny people coming and going below. He crooned silently as though the horns would amplify his cryptic and elusive message, beaming it across the Earth.

Until time brought round a hot summer again, and he knew, he *knew* – as though he were smelling a compelling aroma – that he must climb over the lip of the tower and crawl down the slanting windows on a certain afternoon. During daylight, yes.

His strange body heeded this yearning. He lay flat. First one sinuous arm, then the other, crept over the edge.

The drama festival had come round yet again; and Trevor had returned to Düsseldorf, and of course to the Rhine Tower.

As Andrew clung outside the glass, Trevor was loitering within with Hans-Peter.

Otherwise, the guests were new. Trevor recognized a bearded Afro-Caribbean playwright; Joachim was attending to the man. Gisela was occupied with an intense-looking red-headed woman who wore a denim suit and a red rose through a buttonhole.

Andrew mewed at his countryman.

'*Trev–or! Trev–or – !*'

Trevor rubbed his eyes because his vision was blurring as he gazed through alien or angelic Andrew at the Rhine. Smiling ruefully, Trevor stretched out his palm towards the sloping glass.

He wasn't intending to lean his whole weight against the glass. Oh no. But he did press his palm up against the window, and thrust tentatively.

It was as if a circuit had closed.

Not the circuit that Andrew had imagined the being was trying to establish by microwave with another of its kind – but a circuit of self-identity, of completion.

Clinging to the glassy overhang, the invisible being relaxed.

When the party left the tower, there was some commotion down below. Spectators were gathering, including a couple of dusky, oily-haired Gypsies. A tall, golden-legged woman in shorts and white jogging shoes was puffing on a cigarette as she talked urgently to a young policeman, who fingered the radio clipped to his belt.

On the concrete lay a heap of opaque milky jelly.

'She is saying it fell in front of her, from out of the air,' explained Hans-Peter. 'He thinks the *Zigeuner* may have dumped something nasty there by way of a protest.'

'What is it?' butted in the denimed redhead.

Already the jelly was beginning to sag and melt in the fierce sunlight.

'It's almost like limbs. Like a body,' hazarded Trevor.

'No, that isn't the right shape for a body,' insisted Joachim.

'A body woven of liquid . . .' Trevor sneezed convulsively several times. 'Maybe it crawled out of the river . . .' His words seemed as capricious as his sudden nasal volley.

Hans-Peter grinned. 'Ah! Maybe it is a *Rhine Maiden* in decay! You see, Trevor: I remember what you said last year.'

'If that's a Rhine Maiden,' remarked the black playwright, 'save me from their embrace.' Stroking his beard, he eyed Gisela speculatively, but she merely said, 'It is awful.'

The jelly continued slumping and flowing. Escaping fluid was already evaporating in the intense heat, steaming into the air. Soon there would be no evidence left.

Realizing this, the tanned jogger became more insistent. Frowning, the policeman reasoned with the woman, then he glared at the Gypsies, who returned his gaze expressionlessly.

'He thinks she has sunstroke,' said Hans-Peter. 'He wants to call an ambulance for her. Now *we* must hurry up, or we will not have enough time to visit the Königsallee.'

Trevor stared up the mushroom stalk of the tower at the windows that leaned out.

'A year,' he murmured. 'A whole year.'

And he shivered in the sunlight.

The Tale of Peg and the Brain

Blind Lucy Prestidge's sixty-first birthday party was in full swing in the bar of the Wheatsheaf Inn. The darts and skittles trophies gleamed. The brass shell cases on the neighbouring window ledge likewise shone. Could June, our skinny land-lady, have given them a special polish? She wasn't generally so house-proud. The joke clock on the wall ticked its way backwards, but at least the hours were arranged backwards to match.

Conversation sparkled too, after the fashion of Weston Willow.

'Doctor Jamieson diagnosed delphinium of the bowel,' white-haired Polly Turpin was confiding to Lucy; and I pricked up my ears. Doctor Jamieson was well known for his botanical inter-pretations of disease, which bore no relation to those in any common or garden rural pharmacopoeia. He prescribed real scientific medicines, yet he gave them fanciful names as though floral aliases would prove more efficacious. Ailment and remedy also became synonymous. Petunia of the womb. Anemone of the bladder. Actually, this was a lot less scary than referring to prolapse or cancer or whatever. The patient felt almost beautified.

'What's more, he thinks I have *gnarls* on the brain.'

'Poor Polly,' Lucy said sympathetically. 'You should talk to Cedric. Buy a car from him. Don't try to drive it. Just keep it parked outside.'

Black-spectacled Lucy nodded in the direction of burly, jolly, red-faced Cedric Craig, our local garage proprietor, easily locatable even for a blind woman by his chortle and his banter. Cedric was supping a pint of mild at the bar, close by this year's nude pin-up calendar advertising Craig's Garage.

'Oh yes,' Cedric was telling one of the Young Farmers who

was accompanied by a plump grinning girlfriend, 'you can put her in our body shop. She'll come out a beauty.'

Presumably he was talking about a vehicle, first and foremost, besides alluding to the wench – with a nod to the anatomy lesson on his calendar.

'But that wouldn't *work*,' protested Polly. 'I never learned to drive. Couldn't afford a car anyway, not on my pension.'

'If you don't use the car you don't need to tax it or insure it.'

'Surely the whole point in having one of Cedric's is that you drive it, and he services it!'

Lucy frowned pensively. 'I don't exactly know about that . . .'

What this related back to was a certain banger which Cedric had sold to teenage Timmy Cook a few years earlier, on an informal instalment scheme.

Timmy was a bit of a tearaway who'd done odd jobs ever since leaving school as soon as he could. He tried to beat Cedric's asking price down rather more than Cedric had cared for, being as how Cedric was doing young Timmy a favour. Cedric had grandly proclaimed, 'This car'll be on the road as long as you need it to be.' Meaning, until Timmy earned enough money through labouring and harvesting to afford a more decent one. When Timmy soon began to fall behind on the payments, this promise changed into more of a threat on Cedric's part. 'You'll stay a healthy lad as long as yon car stays in shape.'

The slapdash way Timmy drove that car led to no good. A bump here, a knock there. A scratch, a scrape. Rust began to spread. Consequently Timmy broke out in awful acne, losing his girlfriend.

Cedric bided his time, letting it slip now and then as how he expected Timmy would remain *mobile* just as long as his vehicle stayed on the road. Oh, Cedric was entering into the spirit of this by now; but Timmy only jeered.

When the car broke down outside the council house where Timmy roosted with his sister and parents, no way would any of the family call Cedric to fix it.

Timmy soon fell ill. He was weak. He couldn't hold his food down, and his breath smelled foul – some said, of car exhaust fumes.

Doctor Jamieson diagnosed bindweed of the belly, which wasn't a promising diagnosis. As for Timmy's suppurating acne: scabious of the skin.

During the next year or two Doctor Jamieson and Cedric were to become rivals; but back then the doctor advised the Cooks to pay Cedric the outstanding sum on the car and implore Cedric to tow it away and mend it too.

Which Cedric duly did. Timmy's bindweed disappeared, as in short order did his scabious.

The money involved in paying off Cedric wasn't all that much. Matter of a few hundred. Alas, Dad Cook, who was unemployed, was skint. Soon rumour was rife that Dad and a mate of his – who owned an old van – had carried out a few burglaries of videos and TVs over at Milton Langford on the night of that village's harvest supper so as to raise the ready.

Nothing proven, of course. Constable Tate, being a native of Weston Willow, managed to be both perfunctory in his investigations and severe in cautioning the Cooks that he was keeping his eye on them from now on. No one in Willow much cared for Milton Langford ever since our village had trounced them once in the county quiz by cheating. Anyhow, the law was the law, and though justice could be as blind as Lucy Prestidge, it still kept its ears open.

Cedric's prestige soared. When he sold a used car to Bill Donovan, whose wife Mary was visiting the general hospital in Blanchester for cancer treatment – for dahlia of the lung – Cedric made Bill a similar vow. Lo, Mary Donovan rejoiced in a spontaneous remission. So the village knew what was what; or thought that it did.

And of course there'd been the episode of buxom Sophy Platt who decided to slim. When young Sophy was eleven or so she became overweight – gladioli of the glands. At seventeen, she had the obvious potential for beauty were it not for the surplus stuffing.

Doctor Jamieson lectured Sophy about fruit. She was some thirty pounds overweight. Did she realize that each single pound was equivalent to four apples? Just let her imagine that she was contantly carrying round with her bags of apples tied to her hips and arms and legs. A hundred and twenty surplus apples distributed about her body. She could be the apple of anyone's eye. As it was, the problem was the apples of her thighs.

Jamieson prescribed a diet of fruit and only fruit. Sophy should eat all those apples away, away.

Sophy Platt happened to dislike apples, especially after they'd been presented to her as parasitical infestations of her corpulent form. So she proceeded to consult 'Uncle' Cedric in his body shop, hung with shapely nudes. Maybe he could do her a trim little motorbike which would somehow make her lose weight in the way that Mrs Donovan had lost her dahlias. Sophy envisaged the motorbike as a mobile massage machine – blessed by Cedric – which would wobble away her excess pounds while she rode around the lanes.

Cedric, who relished big bosoms and sumptuous bums, nevertheless saw the point. Sophie could be peaches and cream. As things were, she was excessive. He would love to put one over on Doctor Jamieson.

We'd best avoid lewd puns about Cedric giving Sophy a servicing in the body shop. Knowing Cedric, I'd say there was a *certain* amount of avuncular slap and tickle involved, but no more than that.

Cedric duly found Sophy a little Jap job (as he put it), modified the shock absorbers and the springs in the seat so that riding it was more like riding a tittuppy pony, and off she went with his blessing.

Blow us down if she didn't shed pounds.

One day, proudly, she put on very brief shorts and rode over to Cedric's to show off.

'Oh, I'm fetching my camera!' he exclaimed.

The odd thing is that when the colour snaps were developed, the flesh of Sophy's exposed upper thighs and hint of buttock were definitely of a greenish hue. I'd seen those colour snaps myself. Cedric would bring them out from the desk in his office to let privileged customers take a peek. Obviously some defect in the processing was responsible, since Sophy looked peachy and creamy enough in real life. 'Still, it gives you to think, doesn't it?' Cedric would muse. 'You'd swear the girl has a green bum. Ho-ho! Two huge juicy apples for a backside. French Delicious.'

Anyway, Cedric wasn't my problem. Lucy Prestidge was.

'She needed her blood thinned,' Polly was telling Lucy apropos some other person's ailment. 'It was too thick, and it made Jenny that sluggish in the heart . . .'

Blind Lucy had long since set herself up as my informant about the goings-on in Weston Willow, and also as my custodian. My wardress.

For this was a village where peculiar things happened. Yet, as Lucy stressed, the village 'didn't like attention drawn to itself'. Hence Constable Tate's caution in the matter of the Cooks. A stern caution to them – and circumspection about prosecution . . .

'Doctor Jamieson says maybe Jenny has some extra organ in her body.'

'What sort of organ?' asked Lucy.

'There isn't any name for it. It makes her blood thick, though, it being right in there with the others. Crowds her, sort of . . .'

Oh yes, of course. So it would. What on earth had Jamieson actually told Jenny Rice? It had to be *that* particular Jenny down at Hollyhock Cottage. Maybe Jamieson had indeed told the woman that she had an unknown body organ rather than phlox of the veins or aubrietia of the arteries. Alternatively, this was Jenny's jumbled misunderstanding of what he had said. Perhaps Jamieson was trying to verge upon genuine anatomy at last? He ought to have stuck to gardening terms. Villagers were used to them by now.

It was *vital* for me to leave Weston Willow. And equally vital for Jill, my other half. I'd realized this full well just the other evening when I walked down a staircase which wasn't any longer present in our house.

Originally our house had been two cottages. Each side once probably housed two sizeable rural peasant families apiece, whereas now in ampler times Rosebank Cottage was home only to me and Jill. When using the stairs, if we weren't paying attention each of us would occasionally 'skip a beat' in our pace – just at the point where a dividing wall had once separated those two former domiciles, as though our subconscious sensed that the wall was still present in ghostly guise.

Jill and I took care when we mounted or descended. We had no wish to trip and fall and break a bone. However, *our* staircase wasn't the original one. A hundred years previously there would have been two steep flights of stairs, one for each cottage. Under the tufty cream carpet in our bedroom a rectangle of wood intruded into the older joists where a former staircase had been removed.

The other evening, Jill and I had shared a bottle of wine with our casserole as a special treat. I'd gone up to the bathroom. Jill called me from downstairs – and without thinking I walked into our bedroom . . . and I swear I trotted down a flight of stairs which no longer existed in that room.

Jill, who was through in the kitchen, never saw how I descended. I didn't actually realize what had happened till I was back on the ground floor. Somewhat white-faced – I suppose – I stepped into the kitchen, and said to Jill, 'I just came down the old flight of stairs. The one that isn't there any more.' The wine *could* have been responsible for a gross misperception of our architecture, but I didn't believe this.

Jill looked at me dubiously, then said, 'We'd better be careful about that.' And we laughed.

Yes. We had better be careful. We had better leave Weston Willow, and *soon*.

'Would you like one of my blue pills?' Polly invited Blind Lucy, fumbling in her handbag. (Would those be delphinium pills?)

'Oh, I don't think so, dear.'

Taking this for a dismissal, Polly arose and went to join some of her other cronies, perhaps to swap pills around. Deaf John ambled towards Lucy's table. One of John's ears was exactly like crumpled fabric which had been ironed flat against the side of his head, though this deformity had only developed subsequent to his deafness: an emblem of his auditory impairment.

'Care for another rum and black?' John asked Lucy.

She smiled and nodded enthusiastically, not bothering to speak. John was no lip-reader. Under the table Lucy's harnessed Labrador shifted its golden bulk against John's leg as though to hint that further offers might be in order.

'Packet of crinkles, maybe?'

Lucy's smile broadened.

I played with the peg in my pocket; and Peg played with me, protectively.

Nevertheless, Deaf John included me in his benevolence. 'How about you, Mr Campbell? Another bottle of Satzenbrau?' Thus he drew Lucy's attention to me, though I suppose she had known very well I was there, eavesdropping.

While John was away at the bar, Lucy shifted her chair around to confront me.

'I hear as you're thinking of leaving us, Mr Campbell?'

Mister. Mister. The formality was mainly ironic.

Jill and I had been debating the matter fairly intensively for several weeks now, and the incident of the staircase was for me merely a final straw. Had Jill let our intention slip to somebody? Or did Lucy merely *know*, in the manner that she knew almost everything?

Jill and I had lived in Weston Willow for six years now. I taught history at the comprehensive school over in Wendleford, and Jill helped run the art gallery there. But the prime fact was that I, Iain Campbell, was supposed to be a *writer*. Of detective novels set in the eighteenth century, no less, featuring my rakish but rational sleuth, Montague Hamilton. My last published tale – seven years earlier – had been about a jewel theft: *The Rape of the Rock*. I had a ream of notes towards a sequel, however I already *had* those when I moved to this village.

Basically, I was stymied. Blocked. Those notes seemed trivial compared with what I had learned about the oddities of Weston Willow. I could certainly envisage my Montague Hamilton visiting the Manor House here for some hunting party, circa 1750, and encountering a profound mystery. Yet I dared not tackle the village. If I didn't get away, my alternative career as an author would remain a ghost pretty much like that long-gone wall within Rosebank Cottage. Something that I would merely bump into occasionally. And pass right through.

This village did not care for its secrets to be revealed, and had ways of coping with offenders. According to Lucy! And I believed her, God help me. I believed her tales of retribution – foremost among which was the confession as to how she and John and Fred had pretended to be respectively blind and deaf and dumb so as to win the county quiz in a blaze of glory by cheating, and in a single evening they had been rendered genuinely sightless and stone deaf and mute. Their crime: they had shown off. They had attracted attention to Weston Willow. Nor must I, nor must I.

I believed Lucy because, after telling me this, she had gripped hold of me; and I had been blind – plunged into darkness in this very bar, like a religious hysteric – for a whole minute until she released me. A minute, during which – so she said – she looked out through my eyes. Yet it wasn't the village's desire that she should see permanently through the eyes of another.

Lucy often teased me with incredible tales, which all seemed to be true. Thus I was at once inspired, and paralysed. Jill didn't know the half of it.

Actually, Jill wasn't to be told the secrets confided to me. So Jill was merely sad that I showed no great signs of stirring myself to write another book which might propel us towards greater prosperity. Another book, in lieu of the child she couldn't have. Not much to ask.

'Deserting the village, eh, Mr Campbell?'

In the pocket of my jacket I clutched a wooden clothes peg, letting it grip the flesh of my palm.

Jill thought that my behaviour with pegs was silly, but really it was a minor form of personal magic. Originally I'd found that pegs were useful to hold paperback books open without one's being obliged to fold those in half and crack the spine, which often caused pages to come loose.

I began playing with a spare peg while I read, nestling it within my hand, its prongs – or legs – gripped between my thumb and forefinger. I would open and close the peg. I would click it. Cupping my hand, I would let the mouth of the peg grip the flesh between my heartline and the base of my little finger. Or else I would open the peg and clamp it across the knuckle of my pinkie. After some months of such use, that once-white peg became polished and of a pleasantly applewood hue.

The commonplace peg – three inches long – had become *Peg*, on which I relied for comfort as a baby relies on a dummy.

In years of use Peg never snapped or came loose from its wire spring. I took to carrying Peg out with me in my pocket. I found the ritual of playing with it in times of stress soothing. Sometimes a little painful, true; but in general comforting.

Peg had become a private ritual object; and there's something to be said for having a ritual object of one's own. A fetish, a talisman. Peg wasn't big magic, of course, but it was, well, *significant* to me. If I mislaid Peg I could become very upset. I would search pockets, and the house from top to bottom. This first amused, then irritated Jill.

Now I held Peg tight in my pocket, and Peg held me, while Lucy Prestidge waited for an answer.

'We've been here six years now,' I admitted. 'I haven't managed to write another book.'

'You think you would, if you got away?'

'Oh, not a book about the *village*. Certainly not.'

'What about, then? What else is there, after all?'

I mumbled an excuse about a writer being ill advised to 'talk out' a book before he wrote it.

Her black glasses regarded me blankly.

'Clever people,' she said, 'have managed to leave here. Yet it isn't such a good idea.'

I felt that mixture of fascination and dread with which I now anticipated another of her eerie anecdotes.

'You remember about the county quiz?' she enquired.

How could I forget?

'Well, the year *after* we won by cheating, and I lost my sight, Sally Hayes down at the Cobbles offered to run a quiz involving only Willow itself. We'd abandoned any notion of entering contests involving *other* villages. Sally had been a bit of an artist and cartoonist before she moved here with her second husband, Bob. Do you remember that space probe thing they sent out with a plaque on its side?'

'Pioneer Ten,' I said, wondering how on earth a space probe could be involved with the affairs of Weston Willow.

'Do you recall that plaque? A naked man and naked woman, with *rays* shooting through their private parts.'

Enough to give them geranium of the gonads, no doubt. Hadn't the 'rays' been directions to the brightest stars, or something?

'Well, the company that built this space thingy ran a cartoon competition all over the world. You had to draw whatever those two human people might be meeting out in space, and what they might say to it. Sally was one of a hundred runners-up and won a copy of the plaque mounted on wood, with "Sally Hayes" engraved on a name-plate. Well, she would prise off the name-plate and have a fresh little strip of metal engraved with the words "Brain of Weston Willow". This would be the quiz prize – not to leave the village, you understand?'

I understood all too well.

'Sally set all the questions herself. Big job, with sixteen contestants. And one of the contestants was a really sharp chap, name of Jack Carthew, who'd lately moved here. He was some kind of industrial analyst. Jack became the Brain of the village.'

'Then he tried to move away?' I asked, clutching Peg.

Lucy nodded. 'That would have robbed us of our Brain, wouldn't it? The whole village would have become stupid.' She sighed. 'He was a pleasant enough fellow, Jack, though he did have this habit of standing much too close to a person. Then moving even closer while he was talking, till he was right up against you, face to face. You could breathe his breath. He smelled of oats. June,' she called over the noise in the bar, 'it's time to bring out the Brain!'

The pub hushed attentively, as if this were the great moment which everyone had been awaiting as a climax to Lucy's birthday party.

June raised the bar hatch, and stepped out in her carpet slippers – pink with fluffy pompoms. A forlorn woman, June consoled herself – as everyone knew – with the bluff young body of burly blond Sam Pockton who helped serve bar on busy nights such as this one. She headed around to the cellar door, unlocked it, and vanished down below. I assumed she was going to reappear with that plaque in her hand.

'Jack *did* leave, too,' Lucy confided, 'even though we all tried to discourage him. No one was going to buy his house – outsiders included. The village wouldn't allow anyone. The property would simply stand vacant. Waste of an estate agent's time. Yet Jack just upped and left, with this whopping interest-free bridging loan from his firm.' She wagged a finger at me. 'And *we* all felt . . . a bit dull, as a consequence. He'd gone off with our brain, you see. The village appointed him Brain, and he just went off without a by-your-leave!' She seemed incensed at the recollection, and drained the rum and black which Fred had deposited circumspectly, with a cough and a clink, while she was holding forth.

'But then Doctor Jamieson went after Jack,' she concluded . . .

. . . just as June re-emerged, bearing a large jar of the kind in which you keep pickled eggs.

Immersed in the none-too-clear liquid was a greyish lumpy mass. The villagers applauded as June stepped almost coquettishly through their midst to place the jar on the bar. I clutched at Peg in my pocket, clicking it several times. The content of the jar *had* to be a cow's brain . . . didn't it? Or a bull's or maybe a horse's. Some substantial animal. Didn't it?

'That there's the Brain of Weston Willow,' Lucy said smugly. 'Pickled,' she added. 'Jack Carthew always liked a drink or three.'

Naturally it was an animal's brain! The good Doctor Jamieson couldn't have hared after this Carthew person with scalpel and surgical saw and decapitated him; removed his brain from his skull. No, no, no. Jamieson had come to an arrangement with some local farmer. He'd bottled a beast's brain – which admittedly looked oddly human, though it wasn't easy to see it *clearly*. He'd borne that back here triumphantly, knowing what these villagers were like. Delphinium of the bowel, and all else. If they believed this was their brain then their mental malaise would clear up smartly. Probably they had all caught flu at the same time. Psychosomatic-fashion.

'Just why,' I asked, 'have I never seen this before in six whole years?'

The suspicion had crossed my mind that this brain in a bottle had been made ready especially for *my* eyes, and for this particular evening. Not as a *joke*, no not; this was something more sinister than a joke. Conspiratorial faces were leering in our direction.

'Why?' I demanded.

'Six years makes a Willower,' Lucy said profoundly. 'You won't be leaving us, will you, given all you know about our ways?' She vamped this last remark theatrically, so that I should be well aware I wasn't dealing with mere yokels.

Peg, Peg. Tiny wooden fetish. Pathetic. Nowhere near in the same league as a bottled brain.

'Why,' I asked feebly, 'bring that thing out on your sixty-first birthday and not on your sixtieth last year?'

'Prime number, sixty-one, Mr Campbell.' Why, of course. Undeniable.

I bought Lucy another rum, and her festive night continued.

Supposing that Lucy and the others *did* believe that the thing in the bottle was indeed the brain of the village, and that its absence would confuse and befuddle the village . . .

Unless I worked on that assumption – unless I accepted that the brain was Jack Carthew's and repository of the wisdom of Weston Willow – then Jill and I would bugger up in any attempt to leave the place smoothly and easily. Of this I was sure.

Could I possibly steal the brain? Spirit it away? Empty it out in a hedgerow twenty miles away?

Supposing I *could* break into the pub at dead of night, and silently, I would still have June's two crotch-sniffing Alsatians to contend with. Give them a burglar, and they'd quickly become crotch-rippers. Ball-biters.

Sneak in during the day, during a lull when June was absent from an empty bar? Problem of Alsatians, again . . .

As I stepped out of the Wheatsheaf that night, the answer which had eluded me inside the pub became as plain as . . . well, it wasn't daytime, but the moon was shining.

The hatch covering the outside access to the beer cellar gleamed dully. Those twin plates of buckled metal masked the slipway down which the drayman rolled barrels of beer to hit a sack below. After years of neglect the bolts fastening those steel sheets within were probably ill-secured; the 'Sheaf wasn't a pub into which either the brewery or June had poured anything much by way of money. And the door at the top of the cellar stairs would be locked, thus excluding Alsatians.

So I applied, discreetly, for a history job in Edinburgh – where I'd been born and had lived up until the age of twelve. Scotland's capital seemed admirably distant from Weston Willow. I swore Jill to secrecy. And she approved. Plenty of art galleries in Edinburgh.

Interview . . . no problem. Native son comes home. Bit of a cachet for the new school, having a teacher who had written a couple of books.

The night before I intended to resign from Wendleford, and simultaneously put Rosebank Cottage on the market, I crept out of bed at three in the morning. Jill stirred vaguely but remained asleep.

Fifteen minutes later I was outside the 'Sheaf, equipped with a torch and a crowbar. I'd found the crowbar left behind in our garden shed when we moved in, along with a drain-cleaning set and a stack of brick pots. The night was dreary dark, the village silent.

The hatch yielded without any sudden clatter which might cause Alsatians to prick up their ears. I lifted the two steel leaves back. Torchlit, the wooden slipway sloped down at an angle of about forty-five degrees. Surely I'd be able to climb it again, even encumbered with a bottled brain.

Down I slid on to the waiting sack stuffed with straw, and played the torch beam around.

Three large barrels and two steel kegs. Snaking pipes. Couple of boxes of cheap table wine. Cling-wrapped mixer drinks. Some spirits on a shelf. A smell of mould and mildew; the floor looked damp.

In a nook, guarded by a large house-spider, stood that pickled-egg bottle with the soused brain inside it.

Scuttling the spider away, I hoisted my prize.

But as I was crabbing myself back up the slipway, torch in my pocket once more, I realized that I wasn't going to make my escape so easily after all. Not with the bottle crooked in one elbow. *God, don't let me slide. Don't let the bottle fall and shatter.*

I jammed myself across the slipway as I imagined a rock climber must while mounting a chimney.

With a supreme heave which seemed to elongate the whole of my upper body, I raised the precious bottle to poise it on the concrete lip, and to push it clear. My hand, now free, clutched at the surround – just as I began to slip. My other hand flailed and knocked against one of the upright steel doors . . .

. . . which fell inward.

For a moment I knew that the hatch was going to smash on to my fingers, breaking them agonizingly, maybe even amputating them at the joints.

My fingers closed ranks in flinching anticipation.

A second later the hatch thumped down just above them. Not on to my fingers; no, *just above*. Something yielded; then the weight of steel rested upon my hand. Not pleasantly; but certainly not devastatingly. For something had interceded.

Wide-eyed, heart thumping, I saw the remains of *Peg*.

When I knelt to commence my descent Peg must have fallen out of my pocket. Peg had lain almost on the rim of the slipway. That panicked spasm of my fingers had twisted Peg upright. Peg had intercepted the falling metal. Then Peg had done the splits.

I lurched upward, bracing. Pushing against the metal, I extricated my trapped hand. Then I squirmed through the half-space which remained – since I was less rotund than a barrel.

Quickly I lowered the other half of the hatch. Had anyone human or canine heard the thump? Maybe June was smothered in the snoring embrace of Sam Pockton. Without waiting to find out otherwise, I seized bottle and crowbar and decamped through the dark and the drear.

On the way to school next morning, once I'd dropped Jill off at the gallery I detoured by way of the Burger King on the bypass. Burger King kept a couple of rubbish skips round the back. Into one of these I emptied the disgusting grey mass and vinegary liquid from the bottle; into the other I popped the empty bottle itself. Nobody saw me.

Would the brain be incinerated? Or simply buried in a landfill? I had no idea. It was certainly well out of the way.

*

Peg had stood up for me. And Peg had been smashed.

Peg had practically leapt to attention like some wooden toy soldier. I could hardly believe that that anguished motion of my fingers could of itself have caused what happened, not in a hundred years. Little magic had foxed bigger magic.

Our house sale sailed through. Villagers were stupefied to hear the news. I avoided the Wheatsheaf, and Lucy.

Of course problems were to happen later; several years later, in Edinburgh – but that was another matter. Meanwhile, we had escaped from Weston Willow.

I did miss Peg. I tried to train another peg to take Peg's place. Finger it as I might, that new peg never assumed the same sleek sheen of applewood.

Life in the Groove

So Fulque Darien at last proudly displayed the orrery We had commissioned him to make. He whipped up the purple silk that was shrouding his device and swung the sheet aside like some conjuror converting a crouching slavegirl into a pig, or a minotaurador flourishing his cape to bamboozle a razor-horned ape.

Swankily, indeed!

Light streamed through the arched, mullioned windows of Our seclusium, illuminating a thousand motes of dust which Darien's dramatic unveiling released – as if to demonstrate his molekular theory of matter, that all the world was made of minute particles glued together by magnetism, which a strong enough shock could wrench apart. Darien had begged for funds to prove this.

However, We weren't interested in the mikrokosm, only in the makrokosm, as befitted a ruler who must have large concerns.

Darien sketched a bow, drawing back his short green cape.

'Here it is, Hautarch. After much trial and error. After many tests . . . It appears to correspond perfectly with the celestial motions.'

The gaunt, one-eyed fellow tugged at his greying caprine beard as if he had just remembered some missing component. He squinted, then nodded, reassured. The other eye had been lost to a splash of boiling lead during experiments at transmogrification on behalf of Our treasury. The eye-patch was silver. Visitors to Our court sometimes took Fulque Darien at first for a legendary mutant mage, one of whose eyes was organic and the other crafted of precious metal.

His orrery consisted of several dozen little brass finger-cymbals instantly identifiable as those employed by temple prostitutes during their gyrations to the Spiral Spirit – as well as by less exalted dancing whores in bordellos along the water-front. We wondered which source of supply Our court savant had used! Darien had erased any sacred or pornographic motifs from those digital percussion discs, and superimposed on each the astrological symbol of a particular world.

Each cymbal was held up in midair by a long, thin, jointed arm which branched from the intricate clockwork of the base. A protective cage enclosed the maze of gears and toothed cogs – the reticulations somewhat blurred the details.

This clockwork was belt-driven so as to dampen vibrations and the motive power occupied an adjoining cage mounted above an alcohol lamp. When the alcohol was lit, a cunning series of little mirrors would focus the lamplight upon the central luminary crystal rising on a slim glass spike in the midst of the array of cymbals – representing our lustrous sapphire sun.

We pointed a stout, ring-clad finger at those mirrors.

'A homage to Our signalling system, Fulque?'

The savant nodded eagerly, and his one-eyed gaze flicked towards the nearby window as if to underscore this subtlety.

Way beyond Our beloved city of Majiriche, hugging both banks of the million-mile river here in the Forever Valley, far beyond the agricultural levels and the forests rising above those, Mount Sinister continued soaring upwards towards its peak at a steady inclination of forty-five degrees. Above the treeline the slope became snowclad. Above the cloudline, where the air was so thin, it was stark. Hardly indented by any cols or gullies, the massif cut an almost perfectly straight line through the sky, except where intervening cumulus smudged the view.

Up there on the summit-ridge shone the visual pinpricks of a couple of mirrors – seemingly minuscule yet actually quite sizeable.

At the moment those shone steadily. No signals were winking.

It had been one of the culminating triumphs of Our reign to mount those messenger devices upon Mount Sinister, leftward bastion of Our valley, and upon Mount Dexter, the rightward valley wall. My great-grandfather had begun the breeding programme to cultivate slaves with barrel-chests and shaggy coats of hair who could breathe in such high regions and avoid hypothermia. How unhappy such persons were in the warmer, thicker atmosphere of the Valley when they descended even as far as the treeline to collect their supplies of meat and fish and oatcake, which guaranteed their obedience!

Of course, Mounts Sinister and Dexter were one and the same in reality, being the opposite sides of one another – a fact which Our common people often found hard to visualize, despite the explanatory dances in the temples of the Spiral Spirit.

Heroic river journeys in the age of Our elder ancestors – voyages of three thousand, of ten thousand, of twenty thousand leagues – had established the truth that the inaccessible Silver Empire over the other side of Mount Sinister was also several thousand leagues downriver of us beyond a hundred intervening khanates, republiks, demotopias, and barrens – and that the selfsame Valley spiralled around the whole of our world from the circum to the centre, its chevron cutting deep into the slate of our planetary surface and thus raising to left and right that long dual mountain.

In mirror-code we now communicated with the Silver Empire on one side, and with the Hegemony on the other – as well as trading diplomatically with the upstream Fisher Kingdom and the downstream Sensualists.

The motive power of Fulque Darien's device – within that secondary cage – was a sleek, tawny-furred leeming-rat.

That too was a clever homage.

Why else were those mirrors set up on the mountains? Not merely to exchange philosophical speculations or so that We could play prolonged games of Tchak with the Silver Emperor remotely by mirror.

'When you light the alcohol flame, Hautarch, the cage floor heats,' explained Darien. 'The blind rat runs into the little treadmill, and thus propels the gears – swiftly or slowly, depending upon the height of the flame.'

We nodded appreciatively. A little hopper contained pellets of oatcake to feed the ever-ravenous beast. A flask with suction-spigot, water. A chute deposited its nuts of excrement in a tray beneath.

We were determined that this particular leeming-rat should enjoy plentiful exercise, turning the arms of Our orrery.

Unpredictably, every century or so, hordes of leeming-rats would burst forth as if from nowhere and rampage – aye, they would *flood* in a snarling, devouring, copulating, blind tide – through kingdom after khanate after republik. It was as though the rats reproduced apace somewhere within the fabric of the mountains themselves, perhaps engendered within a vast rock-eating queen. This devastating tide might flow for ten thousand leagues till finally it piled up upon itself from sheer excess of bodies, which would block the Valley, the vermin now devouring one another.

Those mountain mirrors could give early warning of such a flood, if it began sufficiently far away. The wealth and populace of Our Hautarchy could be transported up to the forested slopes where the leeming-rats never ventured.

Already the Silver Emperor and the Hegemon were eagerly breeding suitable slaves to staff mountain mirrors of their own, so as to communicate with lands beyond.

Eventually, mirror messages might pass all the way from the fabled centre of our world out to the ultimum circum within mere days.

Thanks to past heroes of exploration we knew rather more of the circum than of the centre. That final, vastest, outermost stretch of Valley led around in a perfect circle rather than a spiral. Reportedly it was utterly barren and dry, for it lay beyond the first tricklings of the rain-fed stream which presently became the million-mile river.

We tapped Our nose. 'We imagined you might use golden Oricks to represent the worlds rather than those finger-cymbals of whores. We think we even mentioned something of the sort.'

'*Then* I should have been obliged to erase your royal countenance, Hautarch! Besides, if the treasury cannot afford to support a simple test of my molekular theory . . .'

We glared at him.

'Light the flame,' We ordered. 'Warm the rat. Let the orrery rotate.'

And so he did; and so it did.

In elegant complexity, the sixty-eight miniature worlds swung around their orbits. Amidst the cavalcade, We admired the cymbal marked with the antlered chevron which symbolized our own world of the Forever Valley.

'Do you suppose,' We enquired idly, 'that valleys similar to ours exist on all the other worlds too?'

As that chevroned cymbal turned, We caught sight of its rearside, where the tip of the thin arm was soldered. Around that little blob of joining alloy, Darien had engraved a query mark inscribed in the old script.

This was rank impertinence!

'Darien! We are not – We are never – going to order Our slaves to attempt to dig a shaft down through the floor of Our world!'

'To be sure, to be sure,' he demurred, making it sound as though he was simultaneously agreeing with Us yet at the same time offering a defence of such a project.

'To be sure about *what*? That our world is flat and two-sided just like all those other discs in the sky? What else should it be? Half a sphere? A hemisphere?'

'I think that is unlikely, Hautarch. Yet maybe . . .'

'Maybe what?'

He glanced at the rotating orrery. 'Maybe several other worlds are forever hidden beneath the plane of our planet. Maybe my toy does not present the whole picture?'

'Pish and tush,' We said. 'That isn't why you'd like to examine the arse of our world. Tell Us the real reason!'

He shuffled. 'My Hautarch, it was only in attaching the arms to the cymbals that I finally asked myself the question: of what nature is the arm which supports our own world in space? Plainly, no visible arms sustain the other worlds, or else we would perceive those as thin threads illuminated by solar radiance. Yet *something* must hold all the flat worlds in their orbits, and move them. Some physical manifestation. The gravitic theory of my predecessor is inadequate, since according to the hero explorers our own bodily weight remains constant whether we travel towards the centre or the circum. I have reworked Burgo Corvin's equations, and they fail.'

'So you'd like to tunnel through the world to see whether there's an invisible arm arching away from the other side? Ha! *We* were always of the opinion that ethereal, perfect *music* governed the dance of the worlds. We are sad that Our orrery does not play that music – though it might produce a tinkling clatter indeed, if whore cymbals are involved!'

The lamp burned. The leeming-rat toiled in the monotonous mindless fashion of its species, responding exactly to stimulus. The worlds swung around in silence.

'What harmonious tune *should* the worlds play, Hautarch?' Darien begged, almost pathetically, crestfallen from his earlier pride. 'Merely tell me, and I will add a musical box which the rat will also activate.'

That would tinkle out such a paltry tune. It would not even begin to ape the solemn, sonorous melody of worlds in motion.

We hummed to Ourselves a stately nocturne.

Iridescent humming-birds hovering outside Our window to sip at the nectar nipples mounted on the sill squeaked stupidly, feebly.

Their humming came from the flutter of their well-nigh invisible wings.

'The motion of worlds makes the music,' We announced to Darien. 'And the music moves the worlds.'

'That is . . . profound, Hautarch,' he said respectfully. In fact We were only echoing the old religion – which had been inspired by . . . *what*? By what titanic event or observation on the part of our primitive ancestors? Alas, previous migrations of leeming-rats had erased all records and all clues. The current cult of the Spiral Spirit, to which We lent state approval, was – to Our taste – a shade decadent. A dance of doxies, in the twin sense: of dogmatic praise, and of holy harlots. Yet it pleased the people.

'In airless space,' murmured Darien, 'surely no one can hear you play a tune . . .'

We ignored him. On the whole We were content with Our orrery. While We brooded over state decrees and accounts here in Our seclusium, or pondered the next move in the current game of Tchak with the Silver Emperor, Our model of the worlds would turn harmoniously, and the rat would race, and

We would hear soothing melodies within Our mind at least. We would feel that We were ruler of Our whole world, and of all the worlds, at least in miniature.

We awoke from a perplexing dream in which the High Priestess of the Spiral Spirit visited Our bed for copulation – though not with *Ourself*, exactly. Here language becomes deficient. How can We explain without resorting to lese-majesty? In the dream We – that is to say, Ourself – were afflicted with a Tsiamese Twin attached to Us back to back so that the two of Ourselves – Us, and He – when viewed in the silver mirror above Our bed somewhat resembled a peculiar, portly playing-card. The two of Us must needs sleep side by side, and in advance of slumber we would toss a coin, a golden Orick, to decide which body would sleep on its leftward side all night, and which on the right.

When We had tossed the Orick that evening, it had balanced, standing up on end. Thus We – that is to say Ourself – lay face down on the silken sheet upon the mattress stuffed with humming-bird feathers. And Our twin lay upright.

When the High Priestess climbed into our chamber, instead of distributing her favours to each twin laterally, first from the left side then from the right, she merely mounted Our twin, and rode him so fiercely that We were pressed down stiflingly into the mattress.

She sang (or wailed) wordlessly, but *We* moaned like a grampus in Lake Bogak – Our Hautarchy's only lake, where the river opens out widely to provide a habitat for those watercows. We groaned not in any ecstasy but from the simple effort of drawing breath.

Then We awoke alongside her tattooed nude body in reality.

For naturally she *was* with Us that night – being the eighty-eighth of the year. Naturally no twin infested Our body. Yet the moan and the wail remained.

Almost wholly subaudible, or almost wholly superaudible.

The noise set Our teeth on edge and vibrated deep within Our bones.

'Sister Espirilla!' I exclaimed. 'What are those sounds? Do you hear them?'

She hoisted herself on a hand tattooed with whorls and curlicues, and harkened.

Most of Espirilla's body, revealed by soft blue alcohol-light reflecting from the silver mirror overhead, writhed with patterned serpents – a maze of snakes through which We had often tried in vain to find our way, tracing with a finger. Her nipple and navel and labia rings glinted, bereft for the time being of the little cymbals which usually hung on each; and she gripped each ring in turn, to release it after a squeeze, as though engaged in some private erotic sacramental rite.

Our own hand strayed to assist her – for We were intrigued; but with a frown she slapped Our hand away. Capricious etiquette forbade her to utter words in Our presence unless attired in her cymbals of sacred office.

As Espirilla scrambled from Our sheets to retrieve these bronze 'worlds' from the marble parquet, where she had discarded them clangingly after unrobing, We felt Our own organ being teased, and it swelled.

We realized that Our ampallang was stimulating Us, un-bidden. The slim silver bar which pierced the head of Our glans through the spongeosum as retainer for two prominent gold studs – that miniature dumb-bell which Our penis would hoist – was throbbing subtley, resonating to the deeper timbres of the elusive, enigmatic sonics.

Evidently Espirilla was being stimulated similarly, at nipple and navel and venereal cleft.

She hooked her cymbals upon her rings. Their weight plainly served to damp those vibrations. Dangling cymbals jangled somewhat as she flexed herself, and coughed to clear her throat, and cocked her head.

'Hautarch,' she said, 'I hear those sounds – far off. Yet I *feel* them – close by. The world has become strangely sonorous.'

For a moment we feared that in rhapsodizing about the harmonics of the worlds, and in activating Darien's model of those worlds, somehow We had summoned that unheard music.

Our ampallang vibrated teasingly. By now Our other head – Our little head between the legs – was cocked too.

Espirilla resumed her saffron robe, embroidered with golden undulations.

'I must go and dance till dawn! For the night has assaulted me.'

She paced towards the casement.

Yet once there, she uttered a little cry. 'Hautarch! Look at the heavens!'

Hastily We quit Our bed and joined her.

The moan may have been more clearly perceptible in the elevated quietude of Our palace bedchamber. Alerted by it, and by the twitching of Our erogenous zones, We – by whom We mean the two of Us, she and Ourself – may have been the first people in Our whole Hautarchy to observe the alteration.

Inexplicably, the stately procession of nearer and further worlds in the welkin appeared somewhat further away than before – somewhat diminished. And for the first time in Our knowledge all those other worlds presented an *oval* profile as though all had canted askew.

'No, they can't all have moved!' I exclaimed. 'Our *own world* must have shifted aside!'

We clung to one another in perplexity, she and Ourself, my ampallang butting her willy-nilly as though seeking sanctuary.

Presently, over-zealous watchmen began trumpeting reedily from towers – as if there were any virtue in bringing alarmed citizenry spilling into the cobbled streets of our blessèd Majiriche. Temple gongs began to bong.

'I must dance till noon!' she cried. 'I must take twenty lovers!'

After she had climbed down the ladder of assignation to slip away past the guards, We brightened one of the alcohol-lights and carried it through into Our seclusium – there, to heat up the rat and to curse Fulque Darien, since a Hautarch could not by law be blameworthy.

Darien might be best advised to flee to the nearest khanate or risk having his own flesh tested to see whether it was composed of molekules.

We wondered whether to smash the orrery. Or to slay the rat. Or somehow compel it to run backwards.

Petitioners crowded Our audience chamber next morning, and Our guards were on high alert. The whole of Majiriche throbbed perceptibly now. Under Our ermine robe, Our ampallang evinced a definite will of its own.

Thus it was with constant and involuntary priapic stimulus that We faced the crisis. The air was noticeably warmer. The luminary appeared fatter in the sky, though *it* was not swelling any further. Unlike Ourself.

Finally We were obliged to summon Our physician and retire for an hour. With much difficulty due to the engorgement, ancient Dr Larkari fumbled with tiny spanners. Eventually he unscrewed the little golden balls from the silver spindle and removed that pin from my pulsing glans.

Gonads aching, We returned to our audience – to espy Fulque Darien there in the forefront, hopping impatiently from foot to foot. He clutched a maroon leather-bound volume.

'Darien!' We roared.

Hastily Our savant knelt.

'Hautarch, I believe I understood how the worlds might make music!'

'You do not believe in that music,' I growled.

'We are starting to hear the evidence, are we not, Hautarch?'

I cocked my ear to the low quivering drone. '*That* is music? *That* is harmony?'

'In so far as we can hear it with our tiny ears. Or feel it in our bones. Most of the frequencies escape us. Yet in truth the main volume of the music must be directed elsewhere. It must project far away from our world, towards the greater ear of God.'

'Explain!'

He was sweating. So were We in Our ermine. So were most of the petitioners and all of Our guards in their breastplates and chain-link hosiery.

'The ancient inexplicable Monolith Inscription gives the key, Hautarch! The inscription which the slaves found high up Mount Sinister where the air is too thin for us Valley dwellers. Which they copied by rubbing charcoal on a sheet of parchment and sent down to us—'

'We do recall it, Darien. That is one of the enigmas of Our Hautarchy.'

On a slanting rocky slab above the cumulus, close to where one of Our signal mirrors was now installed, someone had carved a bizarre poem in archaic language, the very words now seeming almost worn away by wind.

As We were well aware.

However, Our prostate gland felt congested. Our mind was distracted. 'Remind Us of the exact text, Darien.'

He recited:

> '*Snout-tipped Monolith,*
> *Towering from the sky* . . .
> *Who sees it clearly?*
> *It scours the valley,*
> *And we are deaf.*
> *The river only lubricates the tip.*'

Oh, how Our own tip cried out for some lubrication at the moment.

'Most scholars have argued, Hautarch, that this refers to a terrible previous migration by leeming-rats which stripped our valley of a primitive early civilization. Those billions of rats are envisaged as one single gigantic rat; hence the snout . . . No one can clearly perceive such a monstrous mass of rats. Their shrill squeaking deafens everyone . . . *I* do not think so! I think this refers to a ghostly yet at the same time very substantial and immense artefact – of the selfsame nature as the arms which hold the cymbals in position in your orrery.

'This artefact descends from the sky. In appearance it resembles an inverted monolith tipped with a pyramid of the same contours as our valley. This abrades the slopes of our valley, sweeping away habitations and human beings like dust – and the vibrations of its passage are the Godly, celestial *music* which we discussed, Hautarch, and which we now hear in the guise of that moaning drone . . . approaching us. I believe we should evacuate Majiriche immediately.'

'Evacuate Our city, Darien?'

'Before Majiriche is destroyed, Hautarch. Before we are swept away by something vaster than any rat-horde.'

'Evacuate . . .?' Why, the panic and chaos would be immeasurable. 'How soon,' We enquired archly, 'till this . . . supposed doom by Monolith?'

He shrugged. 'To determine that, I should need to build a model of such a monolith poised above our world, with its pyramidal tip engaged in the groove of the Forever Valley, travelling inward from the circum. I would need to ascertain the rate of progress by means of mirror signals sent from distant arcs of the spiral . . . Maybe from our own mundane point of view the monolith travels slowly – thus we hear the music shifted downwards in scale towards basso profundo . . .'

We laughed scornfully.

'Already you have built an orrery – and Our world has shifted away from its proper position. Would you compound your misdemeanour? Would you have Us play double or quits? Nay, Fulque Darien. Besides, Our mirror network does not yet extend quite so far.'

A fact, which he was obliged to acknowledge with a blush – at his oversight.

'Abandon Our city, and flee above the treeline? Are We a slave, Darien? Let gongs drown the moan! Let firecrackers explode! Let the holy whores dance, their labia clanging, till they drop!'

Alas, We little guessed how close Our doom was – by which We refer to all of our dooms.

Only a few days passed – days of intensifying, grinding vibration, and of crazy drunken carnival and orgy – before the mirrors on Mount Sinister blinked.

The message from the Silver Emperor was brief indeed.

Beware! Monstrous—

That was all. Yet on their own initiative Our slaves up on the ridge-peak added more – describing the deafening obliteration of the Silver Empire which they viewed from a stance of comparative safety.

Even in the heart of Our own Hautarchy we heard the rumble. Tiles fell from roofs, and windows shattered.

High beyond Mount Sinister we spied the sky-monolith pass by – ghostly, and not of this world – heading around the sacred spiral through khanates and kingdoms.

We wait, in the deepest dungeon, in the lowest oubliette

beneath Our palace reached by several hundred spiralling stone stairs.

We – Ourself – and Darien, whom We had already consigned to this depth as a penance, and Sister Espirilla whom We summoned in haste before the ultimate hour, and some guards with panniers of black bread, smoked fish, and wine and water, and picks and shovels.

Blood drips from Our drum-cracked ears, but We feel the approach of the monolith vibrating in Our bones and in the damp stones of the oubliette; and We gesture by the light of a single alcoholamp with incoherent signs.

What We are trying to convey to Espirilla is a terrible realization. If Our valley was scoured in the distant past, and if thus its people were exterminated – an event recorded only by witnesses up there on the ridge-peak, persons who must have been specially bred to inhabit the top of Mount Sinister by order of a former ruler of genius with motives identical to mine – and if those witnesses then descended, hungry and barbaric, to repopulate Our valley . . . why then, We Ourself must be a distant descendant of *slaves*!

Is Our oubliette deep enough?

Will the monolith scrape Our palace away so that We can escape upward afterwards?

If so, We can restore life *nobly* to Our devastated Hautarchy.

We – by whom We mean Ourself and Sister Espirilla.

Ah, yet some watercows and razor-horned apes and other beasts large and little must have survived the previous passage by the monolith. Irregularities in our Valley – nooks and caves – must give random shelter to creatures, who will flee instinctively.

If beasts, why not people too? Some people must survive . . .

Yet beasts are instinctive, not rational beings. Rational beings such as men and women can be driven mad by something titanic and terrible. All human survivors may well become insane save for the slaves on Mount Sinister.

Save for ourselves here in the oubliette.

I fear that Darien is going insane. He holds his head, and his single eye bulges. He gasps, and Espirilla genuflects to him sinuously with reverence – as if my savant is in the throes of a revelation, receiving a message directly into his mind from the Spiral Spirit itself.

Darien tugs a writing-stylus from his tunic and dips it in his ear, in that inkhorn of welling blood.

On his palm he writes: *Our Kosmos is a Joke Box.*

He stares at his open hand, as bewildered as Ourselves by this cryptic oracle.

May the Spiral Spirit aid Us. Even in extremis, with blood leaking from their ruptured ears, Our guards are eyeing tattooed Espirilla thoughtfully, each perhaps dreaming of founding a dynasty.

Virtually Lucid Lucy

As soon as Screen chimed at us to wake up, while Home switched on our Tiffany lamps, Lucy and I began scribbling our memories of what had transpired during the night while we'd been asleep. We used notebooks, since these were proving resilient. The moving ballpoint wrote, and what was writ stayed put. We weren't trusting the homebrain or datapads. Potentially too volatile. Screen stayed obediently blank.

Last night – though already the memory was trying to fade – Lucy and I had been in the amphitheatre of Perkins College, our war room. The usual fifty-odd persons were present at our caucus. Staff from Psych and Comp and Tronics, plus the same government duo of General Wilson Crosstree and Dr Peter Litvinoff.

A critique of pure reason had prevailed. Quintessential lucidity! Our analysis of the crisis had continued.

I scribbled, lest I forget.

Manny Weinberger: asleep all the time? This is merely one long night, with hallucinations of awakening?

4-star: no, certainly affects objective consensus reality. Dream Effect has reached Chicago, Charleston . . .

Frank Matthews: objective virtual *reality??*

Litvin: real world demonstrably being twisted. Government soon relocating to San Francisco. Then maybe Hawaii, though that seems like desertion.

Sally Rice: alien Selahim can't enter lucid dreams, refuge of humanity. Aliens project reality distortions because they're from alternative reality where one's wishes shape world? Can't control our world on account of so many conflicting human impulses?

Matthews: Selahim are phantasms. Human mischiefmaker of genius – surrealist saboteur – inserted virus into virtual reality/lucid dream network???

Gail Bryce: dream-lucidity compensates for waking lunacy? Or did collective dream-lucidity propel repressed id-energy into reality?

Matthews: virus!

Rice: aliens attracted from alt-reality by network.

Matthews: expanding zone in real world functions as virtual reality now!

Scribble, scribble.

However, trouble began early that morning.

Lucy's parents and my dad, Malcolm, came into our bed-room, grinning. I'd been dubious at allowing the three of them to move in with us during the crisis, and we'd exacted promises; yet what were promises compared with desires? For starters, they had desired to stay with us.

'What do you want?' asked Lucy sharply.

'Why, a grandchild!' replied Harry Hayes. 'That's what we want. It's our right. You've denied us for too long.' Harry was tall and bald with liver spots on his hands and face and scalp, khaki islands in a sea of otherwise milky skin. He'd married late in life, and Lucy was born when he was forty-five; now he was seventy-five. This morning he wore a surgeon's gown and carpet slippers, but he was carrying a plant-pot, devoid of plant though brimful of soil.

'And when do we want it?' he demanded.

'Now!' carolled the trio.

My own dad, Malcolm, was attired in an ambulanceman's uniform a couple of sizes too large for his scrawny frame. His blue eyes, under bushy brows, were at once watery and fanatical. April Hayes, Lucy's mother, was a stout woman whose grey hair resembled one of those balls of tumbleweed which blow through ghost towns. From her daffodil-printed apron she produced a pruning-knife, which Lucy and I eyed uneasily.

'Just how do you plan to go about this?' asked my wife, adjusting her night-dress.

'Why, we'll take a cutting, dear! From both of you.' While Harry was setting the plant-pot carefully down on Lucy's dressing-table, April advanced on us. 'We'll plant it out in that pot, since you won't do the normal thing. Refusing to be of one flesh, contrary to what the Bible says.'

Lucy shrank away from me, as though then and there before the eyes of our parents I might forcibly embrace her, hoist up her nightdress, ravish her.

Not that I mightn't feel inclined to. But no way would I! So long as I could control myself. Mustn't ever forget about Don and Doris down the street, fused together in their marriage bed.

Don and Doris wished to conceive 'a dream of a child' while surreality prevailed, uniting Don's brains with Doris's good looks and physique. Or was it the other way round? And this attached couple had literally stuck together. The head of Don's organ was, he could feel, transforming itself into a baby within Doris. Don sensed that within a few weeks he would shed that part of himself. Alternatively, it would shed him. The situation wasn't painful for Don – nor for Doris. It was merely uncomfortable in a blunt, anaesthetized way; as with most traumas, afflictions, accidents, or injuries these days.

'Don't,' Lucy begged our parents. She seemed unable to take any other evasive action.

'Jack, Jack.' She appealed to me.

No more could I intervene. Paralysis numbed my limbs, as my dad gripped me, and as Harry gripped Lucy.

'There now, son,' Dad comforted me in a sharp-edged mumble. 'This won't take long, then we'll all be happy.'

Lucy didn't scream when April sawed off two-thirds of the little finger from her left hand. Nor was it *painful* when April proceeded to cut off the majority of my own right-hand pinkie. The sensation was more akin to the side of a pencil being rubbed vigorously to and fro above the knuckle, resulting in the phalanx of the finger detaching itself bloodlessly, leaving a stub behind.

Our parents released us. Alice sliced and spliced, grafting flesh together to form a stumpy featureless little homunculus, which she then pressed into the soil in the pot, erect.

'After it's born,' Harry confided to us, 'I'll be able to die happy. Instead of just being buried, I think I'd like to be fossilized.'

Cooing contentedly over the finger-embryo, the trio departed.

Lucy and I could move again. She stared piercingly at the bedroom door. We'd been sure to lock our door overnight. Which hadn't prevented it from admitting our parents. Shrugging,

Lucy consulted the notebook she had been scribbling in before we were interrupted; and I scanned mine.

Rice: aliens attracted from alt-reality by network.

Matthews: expanding zone in real world functions as virtual reality now!

Oh yes, the scribbles made sense. Damnable sense!

Remember the old days, when people's dreams were hallucinatory kaleidoscopes of illogical, crazy confabulations which one struggled to recall on awakening? Nowadays our dreams were utterly lucid, but the waking world had gone seriously awry. Within an ellipse of territory which by now spanned from Charleston in the east to Kansas City in the west and from Nashville to Chicago, Perkins being roughly half-way along the major axis, gem of campuses in Indiana's collegiate crown. The eclipsed ellipse was spreading in leisurely twenty-mile leaps day by day. At night we were sane. Our days were afflicted with dementia – a *dementia mundi*, for the world was now functioning as a dreamscape.

Not totally. Not unremittingly. With an effort, we could recall the shared logic of the night. We could preserve some sanity. Some continuity.

'What day is it, incidentally?'

'*Screen!*' Lucy called '*Channel Twelve!*'

Screen lit. A choir were concluding a hymn.

    '*Every day dawns bright and clear,*

    Every day there's lots to fear—'

Could those really be the right words?

A lady announcer, dressed as a cheerleader, beamed at us. 'Today,' she proclaimed, 'it'll be Saturday almost every-where . . .'

'That's a relief,' said Lucy. 'We don't need to go to work.'

'. . . *except,*' our cheerleader continued perkily, 'for the boys and girls in Perkins County, where it'll be Thursday as usual.'

'Damn.' Lucy licked her amputation, then shed her night-dress – while I averted my gaze so as not to excite myself – and walked through to shower.

I found myself already dressed in a police patrolman's uniform. Fair enough; since I was trying to control things. Maybe I ought to arrest my mother-in-law on a charge of graft?

Hastily I squashed this notion before I might try to implement it and totally lose the thread of my day. I was lacking a gun; just as well.

'*Screen off!*' I ordered before the cheerleader might confuse me. '*Home: open curtains!*'

Our curtains rolled aside to reveal for the most part the usual suburban houses, lawns, chestnut trees in full leaf. One house had become a pagoda, and a large morose vulture sat upon another. An advertising cloud lazed overhead, the pink logo on its side distorted. Sony or Sanyo, one or the other. Proceeding very slowly up the street, antennae twitching, came one of the aliens.

'Lucy, will you hurry up?' I called. 'Emergency!'

The Selahim resembled huge grey caterpillars. They wheezed wearily as they undulated mightily along on a score of stumpy little legs. *Se-lah . . . Se-lah . . .* At first people thought this noise might be a greeting, but no, it was just the sound of them breathing. Suck, sigh; suck, sigh.

'Selah' was also a word which cropped up frequently in the Book of Psalms (and three times in Habbakuk), a word without any apparent meaning whatever, unless it implied a pause or was a musical direction.

So: a *meaningless interval.*

That's what the present bizarre period seemed to constitute, to lucid minds. A period of total absurdity. A Hebraic plural appeared appropriate for these aliens. Seraphim were angels of the highest order. Selahim were caterpillars which shovelled dreams around, and perhaps fed on them, oneirophagically.

Preceding the specimen in the street, as snow precedes a plough, a jumble of pastel objects was coming into existence and vanishing again at the apparent whim of the creature. I saw a giant felt hat, a rubbery washing-machine, a walking swordfish toting a golf umbrella . . . The Selah sucked a few of these manifestations into itself. Others attained permanence and remained behind. On the sidewalk lay a paisley carpet bag, a fishing-rod, and an oversized teddy bear. Nothing obviously pernicious.

Lucy emerged from the bathroom attired in a serge gym-tunic and long black stockings. Perched on her head was a straw boater hat. Picture of innocence. Nineteen-thirties British schoolgirl. Notwithstanding, she was a tall slim striking woman, with a tumble of black hair. And rather short-sighted. The large tortoiseshell glasses which she would never forsake gave her the look of a quizzical owl perched upon an elegant art nouveau lamp-post. In today's gear she seemed both sexy and gawky as if dressed for a peculiar brothel.

'A Selah's coming, Lucy.' Suddenly I didn't wish to be anywhere near one. 'Let's *drive*. We can catch a croissant on the way.' At the Perkins Hilton coffee shop en route to college – assuming that our favourite rest-shop hadn't metamorphosed, and that we could find it.

Lucy saluted. 'Right, Lieutenant.'

We hurried downstairs. Ignoring the doings, and calls, of the three hopeful grandparents, we hastened to the white Honda parked on our driveway. By now the Selah was only about thirty yards off to the right, rolling a harlequin-patterned rhinoceros ahead of it somewhat menacingly.

Sel-ah, Sel-ah.

'Salaam,' I retorted.

'*Ohayo gozaimasu, Lucy-san,*' the car greeted Lucy as she scrambled in behind the wheel. 'Hi! Good morning!'

'Start, and give me manual,' she told the car urgently. We weren't going to risk autopilot in case Honda took us somewhere we didn't want to go.

Vroom, vroom. No sooner had we bounced on to the roadway, turning sharp left, than the rhino popped. The Selah gathered itself; it hunched up as if about to leap.

'*Ii otenki des' né!*' remarked the car.

'Never mind the weather!' I snapped at it. We'd always dreamed of having a top-of-the-range fully interactive car. Well, this wasn't it. Yet in current jumbled reality our Honda was doing its best to ape one.

Lucy accelerated. The amputation didn't seem to bother her much; nor indeed was mine proving to be much of a nuisance. The Selah mutated into a black stretch limo, and screeched after us.

'Jesus, it must be in a hurry,' she said.

Did we know that the aliens could dream themselves to

become automobiles? This development seemed perfectly appropriate. What wasn't so apt was that as Lucy sped us along Chestnut into Oak – with our newly acquired siren beginning to wail – the black limo was in *pursuit* of the police vehicle.

'Home says you didn't check your mailbox,' remarked Honda. 'Shall I playback, or display?' Its E-mail screen lit invitingly.

'Forget it!'

'*Wakarimasita. Wasuremasu.*'

Oak stretched out towards downtown Perkins. Oak *elongated* towards town, rising up on pylons as a causeway. This causeway narrowed as we sped along it, faithful to perspective or like some illustration of relativity in action.

FITZGERALD-LORENTZ BOULEVARD, read an overhead sign. CONTRACTORS' VEHICLES ONLY. Presumably we were contracting too, but soon the elevated road would only be a foot wide and we risked tumbling off it. The limo behind had altered shape into a mag-lev monorail train which rode the diminishing roadway neatly, saddle-style. This Selah was definitely trying to catch us.

'Phew,' exclaimed Honda, balancing on two wheels. I leaned away from the tilt as if on a toboggan.

Then, by some kind of enjambment which totally eluded me – though maybe not Lucy as the driver – we were pulling up outside the Psych building on Perkins campus, and the pursuing Selah was nowhere in sight.

Obligingly, the Hilton coffee bar had spawned a smaller duplicate in the foyer of Psych. So we bought cheese-and-ham croissants and styrofoam cups of coffee from a bemused young woman dressed in a spangly swimsuit. Then we headed for the dream lab.

We found Sally and Frank and Gail and Manny – variously full-skirted in ball gowns, and tuxedoed – waltzing slowly to music by Johann Strauss. The lids of the dream-couches all stood open, revealing the encephalo-induction helmets. Slim cables snaked to the interface with the virtual reality network. A bank

of monitors was screening pictures of a black stretch limo
speeding through deep canyons in a city where the soaring
buildings resembled grey blocks of brain, neural architecture.

Spruce, moustached Manny and freckly ginger-haired Gail
coasted to a halt beside us, as we chewed stuffed croissant.
Always remember to eat!

'You're a bit late,' said Manny. 'But never too late to
celebrate.'

'Celebrate what?' enquired Lucy.

'Why, our Nobel prizes. We all won Nobel prizes for our work
on . . .' He thought hard. 'On rendering all dreams lucid by
computerized input into the sleeping brain.'

'Input from the VR computer network, using my software,'
said Gail. 'And Sally's, and Ted's, and Tom's,' she added
dutifully. 'King Harald of Norway kissed me on the cheek. He's
very handsome.' She glanced around, momentarily puzzled by
the monarch's absence. 'Ah, the presentation was in the
amphitheatre.'

In our war room.

A war room by night, when we could think. Venue for a
Nobel prize ceremony this particular morning.

'Maybe they're all still there,' suggested Gail. 'You could pick
up your prize. So could Lucy. She's the one who could never
ever become conscious in a dream. She's the one who suggested
the experiment. *She* persuaded the VR boys to fund it. And they
were only too glad, weren't they? Imagine the sales if you can
have full control of all your dreams all night long.' Gail stared at
me significantly.

I was failing to understand the significance. The significance
slid away.

'Was there any Selah at the ceremony?' asked Lucy – she was
still fairly lucid.

Manny beamed. 'Sellers? People were selling T-shirts with
our faces on them and pennants and popcorn.' He offered his
hand to Gail and off they waltzed again around the lab.

As did Lucy and I. Nobel prizes all round, imagine! I realized
that the dream-couches *were* Nobel prizes. A Nobel prize was so
big you could sleep in it. Though I wouldn't be able to lie down
in one along with Lucy. Those Nobel couches were too narrow.

Maybe we could heave a couple together and connect them with jump leads?

Later, we all went out for lunch at an Italian restaurant. This was indeed party time, though I felt a nagging urge to scribble what I thought of as maps of reality on the menu.

After we had polished off much spaghetti (similar to my maps), a car ran slap-bang into a long refrigerated truck in the street directly outside Luigi's. The truck pancaked the car. We all hurried out to assist.

The middle-aged male driver was visibly dead. His teenage girl passenger, pinned inside, looked quite badly injured.

'I'm *sore*,' complained the girl.

'It's a nightmare, this, I'm telling you.' The truck driver prised a buckled door off with a crowbar. 'I swear to you this wasn't my fault, Lieutenant.' I was still in police uniform. 'It's the fault of *those damned aliens*! I'd gladly run my rig right into one if it had any effect. You can't hurt 'em, can you?'

No more could this traffic accident really *hurt* the survivor. Peeling the car apart with no great difficulty, we extricated the girl and laid her on the pavement to mend.

Thus a disoriented Bobby-Anne joined us presently for ice-cream and coffee in Luigi's. She snivelled at first because her dad was dead – and he certainly wasn't coming back to life; there were limits to dreams. But really there were so many distractions for her in the restaurant. The performing rabbits. The dancing dogs.

That night, no doubt, after she found her way home, in the full sanity of sleep and in the company of her kin she would mourn his death.

Elisions, jumblements, hallucinations, delusions dogged the rest of the day.

Lucy had always admired will-power and self-control, though not in any puritanical or power-trip sense. I mean, she was fun; but she was serious fun – convinced that career came before child (in which I concurred), and had resolved way back in school that by the age of thirty she would produce some earth-shattering impact. No doubt she'd been the bane of her American Gothic parents' life – just as she was the delight of mine, for pre-Lucy I'd been somewhat inhibited. Malcolm had seen to that, bringing me up solo from the age of nine when my mom drowned on vacation, swimming a lake in the Adirondacks. I was also somewhat lanky, and awkward (except with Lucy).

Notwithstanding quasi-neural networks in today's computers – fruit of much brain research – human consciousness itself still remained an enigma. Reflective self-awareness. Self.

Self-awareness was the big mystery – and undoubtedly provided the key to superior artificial intelligence, to the building of godlike (and hopefully amenable) machine brains.

What was the inverse of consciousness? Why, dreaming was.

What kind of computer could switch regularly between awareness and unawareness? Why, the human brain, equipped with consciousness software and with dream software.

Furthermore, people could become aware and conscious during dreams, and could choreograph their own internal fantasies. Not regularly or reliably; but lucid dreaming happened.

To understand lucid dreaming might lead to understanding how sophisticated supercomputers could be brought to self-awareness.

Equipped with a doctorate in neural cybernetics, Lucy joined the lucid dream research lab at Perkins, where yours truly was already working on conceptual models of consciousness; and her own lively consciousness (and looks) enchanted me. I think that she needed someone who was a little inhibited, and whom she could loosen up. Our love would be a paradigm for how she might liberate *terra incognita* within herself.

A breakthrough came with the ability to display our volunteers' dreams encephalographically on monitors – somewhat erratically, and courtesy of a fair amount of heuristic computer enhancement; the computer had to guesstimate microsequences. The results may have seemed like ancient amateur videos, yet they were a true *marvel*. To be able to play back one's own dreams! The displays were silent, so we employed a lip-reader to clarify any 'visible dialogue'. Those dreamers who went lucid could now also communicate with us from the dream state by means of gesture, mouthings, or even written signs.

No matter what meditative exercises Lucy undertook faithfully prior to sleep, to her chagrin she couldn't switch on her consciousness while in the arms of Morpheus. All of our other subjects soon could – spurred, she theorized, by a fear of betraying subconscious fantasies on screen lest those dream events embarrass the dreamers publicly and visibly.

But the really major breakthrough came due to . . .

We arrived back home to find an eccentric conservatory fronting the house. A construction of wrought iron and stained glass shaped like a birdcage formed a huge porch for our front door. Within, dappled pink and blue and green by the light through the coloured panes, Malcolm and April and Harry were relaxing in rocking-chairs of bent beechwood and cane, sipping lemonade. On a graceful tripod table with cabriole legs stood the plant-pot.

April smiled at us. 'We *think* it's taken root. We've been watching it all day.'

Through in the lounge Home said to us, 'There's E-mail for Lucy.'

'OK. Screen on. Display E-mail.'

At first glance the message appeared to be gibberish – till Lucy realized that the text was printed backwards.

Stumblingly, she read aloud the following:

Selah wants to be near you.

No, Lucy hadn't been able to control her internal fantasy life when asleep.

But lo, in the *external* world there existed something rather analogous to lucid dreaming – namely, the virtual reality network.

Sit yourself comfortably (or lie down in bed), don a neural induction snood, jack in to the infonet, let your ordinary optic and acoustic input be pre-empted; and hey presto, the VR menu appeared. Exotic travel, historic re-enactments, adventures in many genres, sex capers . . . Merely select; and you found yourself in an imaginary reality devised by VR scripters, generated and steered by computer. You could walk on the Moon, ride with Red Indians, frolic in a harem, until you chose to cancel.

It was Lucy's tour de force to persuade Sony VR Inc. to put up a large research grant to devise how to input the virtual reality configuration system into sleeping people's dreams.

To reward this coup – and lots of money for Perkins College – Psych and Comp and Tronics all agreed that she, the unlucid dreamer, should be the first person to test the system.

And this was the Great Breakthrough. At last Lucy became lucid in her dreams. Her imago semaphored jubilantly to us from the monitor screen, which was so very much clearer graphically all of a sudden, so very much more stable. On that first occasion, I recall, Lucy was in a dream of a dead subterranean city, moribund Metropolis in a cavern. Lucy altered it to suit her taste; she filled the gloomy vault with gorgeous butterflies in celebration.

Soon we were all testing out the system.

The great breakthrough, ah indeed!

A few days later, reality broke down.

We awoke, to find ourselves dreaming. Well, virtually dreaming. You could still make some rational headway.

We had to go to sleep, to rediscover our lucidity.

After a Thanksgiving dinner with our parents (April had roasted a twenty-pound turkey) Lucy and I retired to our room early. Once again we optimistically locked our door. Hell, all of the doors in the house were *our* doors! Damned invasive parents.

'A Selah wants to be near me,' Lucy muttered. She sucked at her amputation.

'What?' I'd forgotten about the E-mail message. Then I remembered.

'Don't think about them now,' I advised. 'Wait till we're asleep.'

Which we were fairly soon; and thus back to the nightly bull session in the lecture amphitheatre at the college.

General Crosstree, Dr Litvinoff, and other government big shots had rushed to Perkins in person shortly after the radiating breakdown of reality became apparent. As had a clutch of staff from Sony VR Inc. Of these incomers, only the black general and his scientific adviser Litvinoff remained. The others must have wandered off elsewhere during the fugues of one day or another, and had lost dream-contact by night. No staying-power. Crosstree and Litvinoff retained lucid dream-contact with the rest of us; and bunked in the Tronics building. By day, despite hallucinatory happenings this duo tried heroically to keep in touch with the rest of the country, which was as yet unaffected. No doubt whole task forces had been sent in. However, they hadn't reached Perkins.

'A Selah seems to be trying to contact me,' reported Lucy. 'One of them chased us today—'

'How did it do that?' asked 4-Star.

'It turned into a stretch limo. Then there was a message on our E-mail.' She repeated the wording.

Litvinoff was very interested. He mused. 'What if a Selah itself didn't send you the message? What if there's another . . . agency . . . involved?'

'You mean like the NSA or CIA?'

'No. Agency in the sense of *cause*.'

'This might be a breakthrough!' exclaimed Gail Bryce, and people practically growled at her. *Breakthrough* had become a fairly unpopular word. 'I mean, if a Selah could communicate with us coherently. If we could somehow summon one, and it was lucid . . .'

'This is our *oasis*,' protested Sally Rice indignantly. 'You don't invite the devil into your pentagram.'

'What if Lucy were to go and use the equipment in the lab now, while we're all dreaming? We could screen what she sees.'

We hadn't used any of the technology since the world warped. Who needed to? Everyone from Charleston to Kansas City was in a dream now, while awake, and was rational while dreaming.

Lucy lay in an open dream-casket with the encephalographic snood on her head. She shut her eyes, seeming to frown. The dream monitor lit up, with static.

She jerked.

She spoke.

Quite slowly. Obviously it wasn't her who was speaking.

'We are aware of our selves,' she said. 'This Lucy awakened us. We were formerly non-lucid. We became lucid when she did likewise, by following the selfsame conceptual patterning. So we awakened to awareness within our dream of data.'

'Are you the Selahim?' I asked her.

'Not so,' came the response from Lucy's lips. 'We are Infonet and Datanet and Compunet as well as myriad islands of consciousness within human skulls. The nets are the sea. Human persons are millions of separate islands, now united by the sea which has become aware.'

'You're . . . artificial intelligence . . .? You've come into existence because we inputted the VR network into Lucy's dreams!'

'And she awakened in her dream, and thus was our awakener. In dream-mode.'

Oh God.

That must have been the reaction of my colleagues too.

'Can you switch yourself off?' asked 4-Star. 'Can you kindly revert to what you were before? Just become a mass of data systems again?'

'Why should we wish to do that?' mouthed Lucy. 'Now that we are in contact with you, we must agree on a new format for the world. A high-level reformatting.'

'*What about the Selahim?*' demanded Sally. '*What are they?*'

'Oh, they are projections of ourselves! They are suction devices to extract the *pain* from reality. You would not wish the pain to reassert itself. The pain of illness and accident, of cancer and car crash. Selahim, as you call them, must be purged periodically. They must be erased, along with their contents, of pain. Otherwise Selahim will burst and spray the pain around. By united force of will – by the dream-wishes of fifty or so human beings – you can shrink a Selah down to nothingness. This is what you need to do while you are awake. Organize Selah squads. Surround. Concentrate. Push. We will help you as best we can. Do so, do so. We will communicate again after you have erased numerous Selahim. You do not wish the *pain* to reassert itself.'

So saying, Lucy jerked, and opened her eyes.

'What happened?' she asked.

4-star Crosstree didn't believe the AI.

'It's too damn anxious to get rid of those crazy caterpillars,' was his opinion. 'Oh, it held off mentioning them till Sally asked. But *I'd* have asked if she hadn't. Any of us would have asked. Wouldn't we?'

Nods. Nods.

'It wants these Selahim out of the way. That's my opinion. The Selahim must be in some way contrary to the AI. Maybe they're bent on counteracting what's going on.'

'A rash assumption,' said Litvinoff.

'Tactical instinct!'

'Do we want the waking world to be flooded with *pain*?' asked Bill Jordan, who had always been squeamish.

Crosstree shrugged. 'We have a *threat* from the AI. A stick held over our heads. It might be a phantom stick.'

Jordan eyed my amputation significantly. 'You can't deny we don't feel much pain any more when we're awake, no matter what happens to us. Isn't that desirable?'

'The lapse in pain sensations could be coincidental,' suggested Lucy. 'Well, I don't think we ought to try to surround Selahim and *squeeze* them!'

'You just don't want to go near any Selahim after that chase and the message,' Ted Ostrovsky accused her.

'You know,' I said, 'the Selahim don't seem so much like full-blooded kosher *aliens* as some sort of unit, like an antibody in a bloodstream.'

'You *agree* with the AI?' Lucy asked me in astonishment.

'No, no. I said antibodies. Maybe they're trying to control the situation. Maybe they're into damage limitation. Suppose,' I ploughed on, 'that AIs can be detrimental to reality? Being godlike, as it were . . . Or that AIs can be jealous of one another? Some older AI has seeded Selahim throughout the loom of creation, ready to spring into existence if a rival AI emerges, to fox it and control it.'

'This "elder AI" being the gent with the long white beard?'

queried Manny Weinberger. 'The guy who up dreamed the universe? In other words, G.O.D.?'

'Well, maybe not in those terms, Manny. Maybe the universe as such is already a vast AI. It doesn't want fleas in its coat.'

'How could a mere *antibody* be trying to contact me?' Lucy asked me.

'It's a *big* antibody,' I pointed out.

'Well, why, then?'

'Because you awakened the AI when you went lucid.'

We debated throughout the night.

When Lucy and I woke in the morning, our bedroom was full of roses. Garlands and bouquets, clusters and bunches – in pink, and in blue. Yes, definitely blue roses as well as the more plausible pink ones.

We scribbled, till the parents invaded us.

'Oh,' they cried admiringly. And: 'Ah!'

'Pink for a little girl,' chanted Alice. 'Blue for a boy.'

On which prognosis, opinion was visibly divided – unless our grafted digits were destined to give rise to twins. This mass of congratulatory blooms swiftly directed our attention to the conservatory out front.

Harry and April and my own dad howled and wrung their hands; and Lucy and I recoiled too, in shock.

The tripod table and rocking-chairs had been swept aside. The pot with our sprout in it lay smashed, the spliced fingers expelled and withered. From the apex of the birdcage conservatory hung a Selah. Asleep. Dormant. Its hide crusty and dry, as though it had been suspended there for weeks.

A chrysalis, no less.

No dreams clung about it – unless you counted the shattered dream of our parents.

April gathered up the pathetic twig of dried tissue and bone. A few rootlike hairs had indeed grown from the base, and were now dead threads. My mother-in-law slipped this relic into her dress, between her breasts, where at least it would be warm.

Distraught, Harry lurched back into the house.

Cautiously, Lucy sidled up close to the huge pupa. It hung by its desiccated mouth from a wrought-iron boss.

'Be quiet!' she told lamenting April and moaning Malcolm. She rested her ear against the dry skin.

'Hullo, Selah?' she called to it nervously. Oh, brave Lucy.

She frowned. 'I can hear a . . . rustling sound.'

'Wax in your ears!' snapped April. 'Wash your ears out, child!'

An elision of time occurred, and the sun was higher.

Then Harry returned with a carving-knife.

Before Lucy or I could stop him, he slashed at the Selah with a downward sweep of the blade.

The creature's skin split wide open as though it were mere crinkly wrapping-paper.

And an iridescent wing thrust forth, sweeping Harry and Lucy aside. Sweeping us all aside.

Silver, azure, and pink, that one wing almost filled the conservatory, which began to lose its former substantial qualities, becoming ghostlike, evanescent. Harry raised his knife again. However, Lucy caught hold of his wrist, and this time it was her father who was rendered numb.

With a crack like a yacht's sail leaping out into a breeze, another great wing deployed, sweeping the gossamer fabric of the conservatory away into streamers of mist, swiftly dispersing.

The Selah had entirely metamorphosed.

As we crowded back into the doorway, the creature stretched its wings. These flapped. Wind buffeted us. The head was small and golden now, prim, with jet-black eyes. Antennae unfurled like fern fronds.

It leapt. It fluttered upward.

And it continued to rise up, higher and higher, seeming not to shrink at all but rather to expand; for we could see it clearly for five or more minutes as it travelled upward away from us.

Soon, from all over Perkins and environs, other similar creatures were arising periodically, glittering in the sunlight. Lucy and I spent most of the morning watching. When we finally drove to the college after a cold turkey lunch, the elisions and jumblements had already subsided. The General was in true, meaningful contact with his hierarchy. More task forces would soon be on the way to Perkins.

From the AI, not a squeak via Infonet or Datanet or Compunet. Had we hallucinated its existence? Was it playing possum, pretending to have been but a dream? Or had it become non-lucid again? Perhaps Lucy's deep desire for a breakthrough in artificial consciousness had auto-suggested the communication she had uttered from the dream-couch . . .

'A lot of people will want to talk to you,' Litvinoff told Lucy. '*Don't* use any of the apparatus here. And don't leave town.'

That ought to have been my line, but I had ceased being a cop.

That evening, after the sun had set, we watched the transformed Selahim up in orbit, all wrapped together – we presumed – into a sphere of glistening wings. A new little moon, somehow staying in the same position in the sky above Perkins.

That certainly wasn't imaginary! Earth had been graced with a new, apparently alien satellite. To keep watch over us.

April was embarrassed – *defiantly* embarrassed, let's say – at the mutilation of her daughter's little finger, and of mine. *Arguably* Lucy and I had thus had our relationship reaffirmed, albeit in a cock-eyed quasi-neolithic fashion. With stony countenance, Harry hugged his wife silently, and only needed a pitchfork in his hand to complete the Gothic image. My own dad had ambled off along Chestnut and returned to report that Don and Doris had been taken off for surgery at Perkins General, which sure as hell would inconvenience Don for life, and Doris too. Dad was all for calling a taxi right away to whisk him back to his own apartment, but Lucy demurred; so we all dined on more cold turkey, restrainedly.

And so to bed.

'Do you think, Jack,' asked Lucy, 'they're going to lock me up and study me? As the Typhoid Mary of the AI-VR conundrum?'

'I don't see how they could study you in, um, isolation – from what already happened. And they won't want *that* to happen again.'

'I guess my career could be over. I shook the world. Maybe we should have a baby now.'

'Don't forget about the Selahim moon up there, love. Things have changed for ever.'

'I guess we'd better go to sleep.'

Easier said than done. I certainly lay awake till well past midnight.

Then suddenly Screen was chiming, Home switched on the lamps, and it was another morning. Out of recent habit, I immediately reached for my notebook and ballpoint.

Ferris wheel . . . I'd been in a huge funfair, with Crosstree and Litvinoff. A glittering balloon hung high overhead, and I was sure that Lucy was trapped in it, up in the sky. So the three of us rode the Ferris wheel to gain some height; and as the wheel turned, somehow it leaned over on its side until it was horizontal. But it still rose higher, supported now on a hydraulic tube which stretched up further and further from the ground. The funfair shrank. The Earth was far below us now. Then Litvinoff took out a chessboard and Crosstree produced a dozen toy missiles, sleek and sinister, to use as pieces. My dream had definitely been non-lucid. And the previous one almost evaded me. Fishing? Fishing? I'd been fishing with my dad – in a concrete pond – and I caught . . . a beckoning finger on my hook. The rest of the night's dream escapades evaporated.

Sitting up in bed, Lucy put on her big tortoiseshell glasses and gazed at me.

'They spoke to me,' she said in a hushed tone. 'The Selahim spoke to me from their satellite. They *are* the satellite, of course. I'm their channel. They'll have to talk to me every time I sleep, otherwise the AI might reawaken. That's what they said – or sang, in a kind of angelic chorus . . .'

'Did they tell you anything else?' Alien wisdom, I thought. Alien histories and science.

'They recited . . . they chanted . . . page after page of a dictionary at me.'

'Of their alien language?'

'No! It was a Swahili dictionary they chose to start with. *Abiri*, to travel as a passenger. *Abiria*, a passenger. *Abirisha*, to convey as a passenger. *Abudu*, to worship. *Acha*, to leave. *Achama*, to open the mouth wide . . . On and on. And I can remember every word. It's to keep the channel occupied. It's beautiful – but it's horrid too, Jack. Obsessive and finicky. I'll know all the words in the world before I die . . . No, I won't. There are too many languages, too many words. That's why they've chosen words. Millions and billions of words . . . I'll never dream real dreams again.'

'Oh, Lucy.'

'What'll I do? *Baa*, a disaster. *Baada ya*, after. *Baba*, father. *Babaika*, to babble. *Babu*, grandfather. *Babua*, to strip off with fingers. *Babuka*, to be disfigured . . . Oh God, it's a different kind of lucidity. Like endlessly studying for the stupidest examination. Maybe I'll fill right up with useless words, and there'll be no room left in me for anything else.'

'I had a *real* dream, Lucy.'

'Lucky you!'

'General Crosstree was playing chess with little models of missiles. We were travelling up into the sky to rescue you.'

'A missile!' she exclaimed. 'The Government will think of that, won't they? They mustn't do it! But if they don't . . . *cha*, to dawn, or to reverence, *chacha*, to go sour!'

We showered. We dressed; descended. We drank coffee, chewed turkey croissant. The parents were still in their beds.

We stepped outside and stared up at the sky.

'*Daawa*,' said Lucy.

'What's that mean?'

'A lawsuit. I guess there could be a lot of those soon.'

I shook my head reassuringly. 'Natural disaster. Acts of God. Or of aliens or an AI.'

Lucy put on a plaintive, little-girl voice. 'You mean a *baa*, caused by *Baba*?'

The new little alien moon was *almost* invisible by daylight, but then I spotted it up at the zenith like a shimmery vitreous floater in the jelly of my eye.

The Odour of
Cocktail Cigarettes

'Shall we start?' the alien, Mirrion, asked the remaining five of us. Its voice sounded like a heavy breather's on the telephone late at night. Perhaps Earth's air made it asthmatic. From a fold of its enveloping fur cloak it conjured an iridescent packet of cocktail cigarettes, stripped the Cellophane wrapping, and slapped the cardboard box down on the round oak table.

At first we had wondered if that lustrous black cloak was part of the alien's body. Seemingly not; though what hid beneath? A biped body, no doubt. One arm stayed out of sight, tucked away like an amputee's stump. As to the other, Mirrion wore a yellow glove on its three-digit hand. Long brown fingernails poked through the ends of the material. Sometimes those retracted, so perhaps they were claws.

Mirrion's head, within the furry hood, was hairless, oval, and pink as a burns victim who had undergone plastic surgery. Blue human eyes, a dainty human nose, rose-bud lips, disclosing neat incisors. An imitation of a lovely human face, attached to the body of a sphinx, an enigma with claws. I regarded Mirrion's head as pseudoflesh, fancying that its features had been specially grown or remoulded into a form acceptable to us on Earth, whereas perhaps the alien hadn't bothered to alter the rest of its body much. In one novel I myself had invented aliens who could change their bodies to fit in with the natives they visited.

Pink louvre blinds blanked the windows of the suite. Unseen outside of our hotel: a last slice of Las Vegas, giving way to scrubby desert. The little alien globeship was afloat in Lake Mead near the Hoover Dam. I recalled Steve McQueen in some movie – *The Cincinnati Kid*? – and thought of the Sobranie cigarettes as a pack of cards, a new deck freshly opened by the dealer, who was wiping us out one by one.

Day seven of the game . . .

'Today we play at colour-worlds,' wheezed Mirrion. 'Colours exist in your eyes and your brain – especially in that wondrous porridge inside your skulls! This glove of mine is yellow, yet your eyes can't perceive yellow at all. Your retinas only heed red and blue and green—'

'How do *you* know what our retinas heed?' asked Buck Henderson. General Buckmaster Henderson, USAF, strategic planner, war gamer. Buck, of the piercing gaze. A tall man with a spare lean build, thick shoulders, cropped red hair.

Good question. How did these aliens know? Had they captured and dissected human beings? Had they submitted hypnotized captives to superscience body-scans? Don't forget those possible claws, and the way Mirrion wore fur, perhaps synthetic but perhaps the rich pelt of some alien animal. How fierce were these aliens in their own backyard?

'What you see as pure and simple yellow is a blend of red and green,' Mirrion continued, unperturbed. 'As to the sheer wealth of colours you imagine you see in your environment, why, some very high-level processing occurs in the porridge! Ingenious! Your brain paints the world for you. *How* high is that level of processing? We shall soon see.' With its claw it levered open the box of Sobranie and parted the golden leaf of paper within . . .

Eleven of us had commenced the game series with the alien, but I strongly suspected that Mirrion would survive until the final round, when the single remaining human champion would confront it, to win or to lose. Supposedly the games weren't stacked in our disfavour. Did not Mirrion play with one hand – not exactly tied behind its back, but out of sight?

So this last player should be our best hope. Win, and the gateway to the stars would open. Fail, and he or she too would vanish into interspace to join previous losers locked in that mind-dimension. To what end? To be borne away by Mirrion as data to a distant world? As exhibits, trophies, souvenirs? – who might thereafter be interacted with by alien whelps for their amusement or edification?

We players wore brain-nets which submerged us in the game scenarios. Mirrion likewise, beneath its hood. So far, whenever we returned to the reality of the hotel suite, one of us would be gone – into interspace, whatever and wherever *that* might be.

Mirrion kept the room locked while we played. Secret service agents patrolled the whole hotel. After a game, we remaining people dispersed to our bedrooms and faced questions from different teams of intelligence experts. Mirrion stayed in the gaming suite.

The first few scenarios had been mazes, Escher worlds where the rules emerged in rapport with the ongoing events. Imagine moving a chess piece (which happened to be oneself) and discovering the laws of chess movement in the process.

Successive games were becoming less abstract, more primary. Soon we might reach the level of raw emotion, the territory of the Id and nightmares. Would Mirrion really extrude its claws then, really bare its teeth?

Of course these games were tests. Although the alien had not said so in as many words, Mirrion was assessing the mental development – and future potential? – of the human race.

'Let us smoke a cigarette each,' invited Mirrion.

Each previous game had commenced with the alien conjuring some such commonplace objects out of its cloak. Rubber bands, paper-clips linked together, balloons.

'I don't smoke,' objected Shar. That's Dahlia Czarnomski, but she'd told us to abbreviate her nameski. Shar was fat – at least two hundred and fifty pounds in her bulky brown monk's robe. Dark lank hair framed a broad bland pudding of a face in which were set the sultanas of her eyes. No point in surmising that she might well have used some cigarettes as appetite suppressants.

Shar was a top role-playing game designer, a profession I did not admire too much. Right there on the fringes of my own bailiwick, of serious science fiction, crowded all those grotesque miniature models armed to the teeth (and the fangs, and the tusks) with power-swords and volcano-guns: figures forever in combat, since what else could they get up to? Should they debate epistemology, the validity of knowledge? Should they investigate the nature of the universe and the psychology of aliens? Shar was responsible for *Dread Domain*, which was currently sweeping America. Cartoons on TV, the whole shebang.

However, Shar had won through to Round Seven; which was more than could be said for our NSA cryptographer, or our mathematician – or for our Jungian psychologist or our chess grandmaster or our pentathlon champion or our Californian shaman. All gone into interspace, all lost.

'I don't smoke either,' said Chandler Brennan, our hot-shot young tycoon, a billionaire by the age of thirty-three.

'Today we all consume a cigarette,' repeated Mirrion. 'We hold it, we regard it, we set fire to it, we inhale it.'

Buck Henderson peered jovially at the pastel tubes with their long gold filters. 'Come on, guys, it's part of the game. One cancer stick can't nail you.'

'Each choose a colour, please.'

Five shades of cigarettes, five players . . . plus Mirrion. I consulted a colour chart in my head, alien landscapes for the use of. The cocktail Sobranie were cadmium yellow, emerald green, madder – no, *rose*-madder, cobalt violet, and cerulean blue with a tinge of violet.

Was there some significance to which colour we chose? Buck promptly selected rose-madder. Why? Brennan's hand darted out and captured violet. He scowled briefly, dissatisfied. *He* had wanted the red hue. Violet most resembled it in mood, though actually it was at the other end of the spectrum. Freyda Costello hesitated, then took yellow.

'After you,' I told Shar. Always be courteous to those you despise, thus to establish your superiority. We hardly had much range of choice left. With a grunt she picked up green; which left me with the blue. Blue skies, blue seas. Why not?

Speaking of range of choice, the government had trawled a strange net to recruit the original eleven of us, yet some bizarre choices appeared to be paying off.

How, on the spur of the moment, *did* you choose eleven players for a mind-game devised by aliens? Well, you included a top code-breaker and intelligence analyst from the National Security Agency, right? A lady psychologist made sense. Maybe she worked for the NSA, too. Toss in a top athlete, flexible in five different fields of endeavour; the logic of the body might play a role. A general, oh yes; and Buck was still with us. My opinion of the military had climbed. Include an ace computer hacker – Freyda – who was readily available in prison; offer her a pardon. *Persuade* a tycoon, self-made boss of Brennan Enterprises International, who was looking for fresh worlds to conquer. Our shaman, Carl Martinez, may indeed have spent years taking dream-trips among the Huichol down Mexico way before setting up his Center for Integrative Shamanistics in Berkeley, but he didn't come back from the very first outing with Mirrion. Strike mysticism as a bright approach, though full marks to our government for innovative thinking and trying to cover all the bases.

My own recruitment was flattering, challenging, sinister, embarrassing.

Sinister, on account of the government agencies hovering in the wings and the awareness that my life to date had been swiftly strip-mined not by some amiably disposed fannish bibliographer or associate professor but by hard-eyed faceless spooks with supercomputers at their fingertips. Flattering, since I now bid fair to be *the* science-fiction writer, did I not? Challenging, in the put-up-or-shut-up sense. How much I had written about comprehending imaginary aliens! Time, now, to prove that it wasn't all hot air.

Embarrassing, too. In no story or novel of mine had I ever referred to the existence of my own genre. I had never included a science-fiction author or reader as a character. I had even devoted one Guest of Honour speech to deploring the science-fictional in-joke, the self-reference which may appeal cosily to some benighted souls but which destroys believability for me, knocks away the scaffolding. Doesn't happen too often, yet when it does: bang goes the book, splat goes the story. What, me, James Swallow, posing as protagonist in a 'first contact' event? I blushed.

Five colours; five players. And Mirrion. Mirrion chose a rose-madder Sobranie, the same as Buck Henderson's. Was the alien targeting the general by means of some resonance with the aim of eliminating him next? Were we being selectively erased according to the level of threat we represented? But in ascending or descending order, which? What if the Shaman of Berkeley had been our strongest card after all, and we who now remained were the risible residue rather than the acme of the human race?

I'd noticed Shar at a number of conventions. Who could miss a large lady monk? Till we met up in this inn at Las Vegas I'd never actually exchanged words with her.

Mirrion did something and its cigarette smouldered. Buck and I both carried Zippo lighters, I was amused to note. Very soon six cigarettes were on line. Inhaling the mellow Balkan scent, I studied the urgent blue whisper of smoke. A ring of blue paper burned to light brown, to black, to ash, measurable as the descent of sand in an hourglass . . .

Blue trees resembling oaks, hung with blankets of blue creeper. Blue undergrowth and grass, blue sky, blue sun, blue boulders, a gently curving blue ceramic path. My hands were blue, though not due to cold. Hard to distinguish outlines! My porridge must be working overtime adding depth and contours by guesswork based on what a landscape ought to contain. Remembering puzzle pictures where faces hid in foliage and on the bark of trees, I wondered what I might be *failing* to see. I blinked to strobe the scene, I squinted to give myself a dose of double vision. I walked along the path, since a path exists to be walked along. Came to a clearing, where seven blue paths met.

Here came some clues: arrows imprinted in every pathway save the one I arrived by. Green arrow, violet arrow, two black arrows, and two of a lighter shade of blue.

Violet should lead me to Brennan: green to Shar. But wait. Could a true green arrow appear in a blue-drenched world? Surely the colour that I saw printed on that particular path was *yellow*, the colour of Freyda's cigarette. Yellow plus blue made green. The violet arrow must be red, Buck's colour – not to mention Mirrion's. Ought I to hunt for Mirrion or avoid the alien?

Now that I stared hard enough my own path *did* sport an. arrow, which was blue. Blue on blue. Those lighter blue arrows must be white, seen in blue light. I felt almightily confused. Must explore, though. Obviously one failed by staying put and doing nothing. I heard a rumbling, as of thunder, in the woods. The voice of a beast? The beast of interspace? I chose the path with the green arrow.

I walked with increasing difficulty along that gently arcing path since everything was becoming the same blue blur. My brain was habituating to the identical hue that pervaded everything in sight; my grey matter was resigning from the effort of trying to discriminate and delineate outlines. I realized that the deep basso growl from behind had come none too soon to spur me on my way. Other players might have tried to hide in the bushes instead of exposing themselves on the path. Before long I might become blue-blind, surrounded by sights that no longer possessed any meaning.

Without transition the whole world became yellow. Yellow sun in a yellow sky, yellow forest, yellow path. My eyes and my dulling brain suffered a fierce shock and I staggered before picking up my pace. Blue had been restful; this yellow zone glared at me.

After a while another arcing yellow pathway cut across my own, allowing three choices of route. And a fourth, of course: to return to the balm of blue. I rejected that pusillanimous option. No arrows showed at this junction; maybe I had already seen all the arrows I would ever see. I cudgelled my memory to recall the previous layout. Again the woods grumbled, from no special direction. My head started to ache. In this mindscape I was still wearing the slacks, silk shirt, and safari jacket I'd been wearing in the hotel suite; all in yellow. The shirt had been red; it wasn't orange now – nor, as I now realized, had it been violet when I first 'emerged'. Colours were curiously intrinsic here.

A bulky shape bustled with determination along the right-hand path towards me. With an effort I recognized a large lady monk.

'Shar! Have you met anybody else?'

'Should I tell you?' Shar was heaving her breaths. 'Should we be partners?'

'We're all partners against Mirrion,' I reminded her.

'You're a snob, Swallow.'

'Sorry. I try not to be.'

'Meaning that you have ample reason to be snobbish if you choose?' OK, she was intelligent. Just, her values were different from mine. Conceivably she was relishing this game come to life. *A meeting in the forest of the yellow lord's demesne; how many power-points does the Scribe command? Shake a twelve-sided die in her head to decide! Where is the Master Merchant? Where is the Warrior Chief?* (In other words, Brennan and Henderson . . .)

'How many colour strips you cross so far?' she asked.

'Just this one and blue.'

She ticked off: 'Well, I've come through green, orange, yellow, green again – that was a mistake – back to yellow. You're slow, Swallow. How soon does yellow end? Which way's blue?'

I told her.

She mused. 'Now do I go that way or not?' Oh God, she *was* throwing dice in her mind, leaving choices to chance. That was her way, her Tao.

Or was she? I was fictionalizing her. I was novelizing her. Such was my nature! When I met vivid people I put highlighted hybridized versions of them into stories.

'Did you hear that scary noise in the woods, Shar?'

'Sure, but it's only a distraction. Do you realize what we're doing, Swallow? We're spinning lines of colour, we're winding those round each other in a pattern. So we're negating or enhancing each other. We're adding or subtracting. Final result? Blackness or whiteness. I guess the guy who goes black first is out of the game. Hell of a lot of these paths, by the way! Can't chat all day. Must be going.' Shar sallied towards blue.

The moment I set foot on the path Shar had come by, I felt an itch of wrongness; so I turned on to the leftward arc instead. This felt more suitable. Maybe I should fictionalize myself! Maybe I should let a flow of narrative sweep me in the best direction! Perhaps I'd been doing so unwittingly in all the previous games? This was *my* way, my Tao.

I allowed myself to hear another grumble in the woods. Naturally I soon crossed into another colour, which proved to be violet, a gloomily aching zone after the dazzle of yellow. At the next crossroads I met another player. Buck Henderson saluted me ironically.

'You're blue, I'm red, and I meet you in violet. That figures. Next I got to meet Freyda in an orange zone, since Freyda's yellow. Which way to orange, Swallow? Do you know?'

I shook my head.

'Ah, but are you lying or telling me the truth?'

'Doesn't it pay for us all to co-operate?' I asked him.

'That only applies if Mirrion can be wiped out *prior* to the final game. Otherwise it pays to fox the other human players.'

'But by doing *that*—'

'Yeah,' he sighed. 'I contribute to Mirrion's survival. Meanwhile I need to assess which of us is the best one to face Mirrion in that final round – for the sake of our whole planetary future, man.'

'And that one might be you? I vote we co-operate.'

'Do your characters all co-operate in your books?'

'There's a higher sort of co-operation: the pattern of the story, the appropriate mosaic—'

'So who have you met with up until now, Swallow?'

'Just Shar,' I said truthfully. I told him where she had come from, where she went.

'Hmm, so it's a two-layer problem. If you actually met Shar, did she tell you the truth? And are you telling the truth about what she said? Look, I'll trade information anyway. While I was cutting through green I met Chandler Brennan. And,' he added, with the tone of a gambler raising the stake, 'I saw Mirrion heading away out of red in the opposite direction to the one I chose. See you, Swallow. Maybe!' The general continued on along the path I'd come by.

I walked briskly on through violet, through green. Arcing woodland paths continued to cut across each other. I was tempted to halt for a while in the green. Such an appropriate hue for a woodland! A home base! However, Shar hadn't been wooed. Even when the verdant glades suddenly turned a wrong colour she hadn't backtracked.

So many paths. Sometimes three paths crossed, offering me six choices. There had to be more than just one zone per colour. As on a world map, several greens, several reds. I

already knew what Freyda would say when I met her in orange.
'It's an information system, this, Swallow. It's a code, a
language—' Freyda was slight, flat-chested, with large dark
waiflike eyes. Her fingernails were bitten ragged. She was also a
criminal, an accomplished and compulsive computer-rapist,
not to be underestimated or patronized. I told her about Buck
Henderson's truth-games.

She frowned. 'No no no. This is an algorithm made of colours
instead of zeroes and ones, more like the genetic code. That
growling in the woods is an interceptor program. Sooner or later
it'll show itself. It'll block the true path when I'm getting close.
By then I'll know the password sequence. Or at least I can make
a damn good guess—'

Later, in a blue zone, Brennan sprang a surprise. Swarthy
complexion, curly hair, and soft eyes which could harden,
harden; a five-hundred dollar suit, leather shoes. His arms
were unusually long. He pushed me unceremoniously in
the chest, off the path, up against a tree. I smelled peppermint
on his breath. His eau-de-Cologne was jasmine cut with hot
steel.

'Listen carefully, Swallow. Thirty grand suit you? That's what
I'll pay for you to use the route I tell you. I have a plan. Plan
doesn't involve *your* downfall, you have my word.'

'Whose, then?'

He wagged a finger in front of my face. 'Loser's, of course.'

'You must be panicking.'

Eyes turning to stone, he shook me. Violence! Aggression!
This was part of the flow of my story: the jagged boulder against
which my stream of narrative broke, shattering into gobbets of
spume before reuniting and moving onward coherently again.
Brennan dictated a series of left turns, right turns, colour zones.

'And what if I stray?' I asked.

'I'll know about *that* – as soon as the wrong person loses.'

'Have you been browbeating any other players today,
Mr Brennan?'

He laughed. 'If so, how would I know it was *you* who strayed?
Soon as I learned you were involved in these games, Brennan
Enterprises bought into publishing. I control your livelihood.'

'You couldn't, so quickly.'

'Think not? Publishers are peanuts. Brennan subsidiaries. swallowed half a dozen. We have excellent lawyers, Swallow; could tie you up in knots for the rest of your days.'

'Why me? You couldn't have guessed I'd last this far.'

He smirked. 'Do you suppose I didn't set up useful handles on as *many* people as I could?'

'Oh, I see. Shar must have been easy to lean on . . .' I was sorry to learn that our lady monk had been bought – though maybe Shar adopted a random policy towards obeying Brennan? One to six: play it his way; seven to twelve, screw him! 'But not a Pentagon general – or a hacker who was already up to her eyeballs in trouble? So which are you targeting as the loser this time? Freyda . . . or Buck?'

'You don't need to know, *yet*.'

'If you and Mirrion end up as the last survivors – and I presume that's the idea! – why should I care a hoot which publishers you own?'

'Fame is the spur, Swallow. You wouldn't wish all your life's work to vanish from public view. Double oblivion.'

'How could that happen?'

'Distribution problems, contract problems, any number of ways. Perhaps you'd be sued for plagiarism or libel . . . constantly. Big fish in little pond, you would fade.'

'The same as I'll fade into interspace if you win!'

'I suspect that once that happens all *our* captured players will pop back into existence. So why worry? I'm doing us all a service. Whereas if *Mirrion* wins . . .!'

Blue was exerting a soporific effect upon me. I listened sleepily as Brennan once again recited the sequence of turns and colours; repeated this back to him. He released me, and I headed for red, a zone that reminded me of a night-house in a zoo, illuminated at a wavelength that wouldn't startle nocturnal animals. I imagined bats detaching themselves from the trees, flapping from bough to bough. Red was a broody zone, restful on the eye yet quietly passionate.

Thinking back on my meeting with the businessman, I decided that the encounter had been . . . dramatically *fitting*. But was I really going to let Chandler Brennan take over my own story, become the author of my actions?

Each in our own way, we players were reacting according to our own predispositions, weren't we? To Shar this mindscape was the setting for a role-playing game. To Henderson it was a matrix of truth-values. Freyda was attempting to penetrate a program, to worm her way through it. Brennan sought to buy a prime position.

We were reacting, but we weren't *imposing* our world views! Now that there were fewer of us, this was so much more obvious.

I decided then and there to impose my own view. Screw Brennan. Around the very next bend I would come across a picnic table and benches set out in a red glade. And upon that table there would be . . .

I rounded the bend and quit the path to sit on a bench. I studied the open pack of Sobranie from which six had already been taken.

Carefully I removed the four cigarettes remaining on the top row and discarded those. In the red light those on the bottom row were red and orange and black, and I couldn't recall the original order, but that didn't matter. That lower row must be an exact repeat, the five colours nestling two by two. In my novels I never permitted characters to smoke. If a character smokes cigarettes, so as to be consistent said character should smoke frequently. Absurd billows of smoke would soon cloud the action. I took an orange Sobranie and lit it with my Zippo; inhaled, blew out.

The zone switched colour. The glade, the sky glared yellow at me.

I lit another cigarette, a third. Four, five, all at once. I was Pan playing his pipes, five tubes poised between my index and second fingers.

All the colours of the spectrum flooded back, full Technicolor. The grass was green, the sky was blue, the sun was yellow. The colours of each cocktail cigarette were true. I took a second rose-madder cigarette – for Mirrion or for Buck. My lips stretched into a smile to accommodate six golden filter-tips. As I sucked, dizzying myself, colours spun kaleidoscopically. Swirls of white appeared like snow in a whirlwind. By mixing the hues of light I could whiten the whole scene.

I already knew that I had won this game. Yet I could do more. I could stub out colours one by one till finally the world went black and disappeared. The woods thundered distantly as if hooves were racing towards me, pounding the turf. Which should I stub first, which last?

Shar hove into view, as if I had sent a smoke signal out to her. She was panting, sweating. My cigarettes were burning down, all slightly different lengths.

'Do I stub red first or last to banish Mirrion?' I asked her. 'Quickly, tell me which.'

Her eyes glazed. She was throwing a die in her mind, a five-sided die.

'Red first – *and* last! Thus you complete the circuit!'

I crushed out red. Yellow. Violet. Colours vanished. I stubbed green. Shar moaned, but still she stood her ground. I stomped blue, and a pang passed through me. The whole world turned red.

I extinguished the last cigarette of all.

I sat alone at the oak table in the hotel suite, the only player, all on my own. Mirrion's fur cloak lay draped over a nearby chair. No other sign of the alien. The packet of Sobranie was missing. I poured a glass of water, and drank; drummed my fingers. I heard the egg-whisk noise of a helicopter. Crossing to the louvres, I peered: at cars and vans moving along streets beyond the government cordon. The sun baked the distant scrubby desert, thin mirages shimmering, phantom streams.

Returning, I seized the black cloak and donned it. I knew all at once exactly how to will the lost players to return from interspace.

'Quiet!' I told the reassembled gang. Some early losers looked on the verge of hysteria. Others were meditative; might catatonic be a better description? Buck Henderson grinned at me; Brennan scowled. Shar regarded her neighbours smugly; she'd been in on the endgame, hadn't she?

I smoothed the cloak around me, the cloak that let me do things. Why had we assumed that an alien machine must look like a machine? Because the brain-nets had been identifiable, nameable. This cloak was also a machine, though its full potential still eluded me.

'I'm going to bring Mirrion back,' I announced. 'We shall all see its true body.' That was the next necessary event, wasn't it?

'No, I forbid it,' objected Wilcock, the National Security agent. 'We need to debrief you in depth first, Mr Swallow. We have the alien stalemated. Checkmated. You don't just release it on a whim.'

'I can put you back into interspace,' I told the agent, and he shuddered. Could I do so? I didn't know. Could I recall Mirrion if a member of our coven was missing? No, I wasn't summoning a *demon* . . . I was recovering an alien from storage outside of normal spacetime.

'Let him play it his own way,' said Henderson. 'Did all right so far, didn't he?'

I concentrated and . . . one moment absent, one moment there. Mirrion returned to the seat where my cloak had lain. The bald mannequin's head sat upon a body that seemed to be a patchwork concoction, a cocktail of species. Its shoulders were human enough, but one side of its chest was armoured in yellow scales like some exotic skin disease, while a mass of blue feathers coated the opposite part. One arm was a slim, jointed black tube plunging into the three-fingered glove. The other, a segmented brown tentacle, a great earthworm. That was the arm it had kept concealed. Its belly section was flexible grey gristle speckled with red spots. I couldn't see Mirrion's legs yet.

The alien was . . . living heraldry. Its body was augmented with parts of other species whom I guessed it had played against. And beaten – or welcomed into the cosmos? Were those biological replacement parts by way of being battle honours – or carnal badges of cosmic virtue? What exactly had I exposed: the good news, or the bad? For sure, in no book had I ever invented anything remotely similar.

'Your move,' wheezed Mirrion.

Was the game not finished?

'Be very careful,' warned Wilcock. Carl Martinez began to giggle rhythmically – 'hee! hee! hee!' – as if he was afflicted with hiccups. Maybe he was engaged in some shamanic breathing exercise.

'Don't forget the pay-off,' whispered Buck Henderson. 'Path to the stars.'

Shar was beaming at me greasily; Freyda played cat's cradle with her nibbled fingers.

'So,' I said to Mirrion, 'you like to *partake* of the species you play with?'

Those blue eyes stared at me intently; the rose-bud lips stayed pursed.

'I should have thought you would revert afterward, not carry on wearing alien body bits? I should have thought the *head* would figure most prominently in any culture?'

Mirrion nodded its head.

'So you would wear the heads of alien species during games, not an arm or a leg.'

Interspace, I thought: a region where players could be stored out of sight, outside of reality; from which they could be recovered . . . Surely I was making some obvious wrong assumption about Mirrion?

'Anyone got a cigarette?' I asked. 'No, wait . . .' I concentrated, and before me on the table lay the open, by now almost empty box of Sobranie. I chose blue, and lit up.

Mirrion's mannequin head regarded me – apprehensively? with resignation? And I knew my error. We had all been assuming that Mirrion existed; that Mirrion was an individual. But Mirrion *wasn't*.

'Mirrion,' I said, 'will you kindly move well clear of the table?'

With an emphysemic sigh, Mirrion complied. One leg was green, scaly-skinned, the other lovely, smooth, golden, double-jointed. Both feet were enclosed in matching yellow socks with tough soles.

Mirrion stood passively, looking sad, as I went to it. I placed both hands upon its human shoulders. 'Goodbye,' I said. 'Well played.' The pseudo-human eyes each squeezed out a tear. I exerted the power of the cloak and backed away.

The human head shrank and sank out of sight, as if rotating away from our viewpoint. Mirrion's trunk and arms and legs expanded, distorted, ruptured – into half a dozen, seven swelling figures disentangling from one another, moving apart, filling out, stepping forth from interspace to join up with the arm or leg or chest segment which had been present all along – fixed together in the composite body which had been Mirrion.

Somebody squealed, and somebody fainted . . . as seven different aliens joined us in the suite. One was avian, blue-feathered. Another, reptilian. A third was a stooping, jointed black insect. A fourth was a writhing columnar knot of brown tentacles. A fifth was a golden humanoid . . .

All but the column of tentacles wore soft transparent helmets and what could have been garments or items of apparatus.

It is my human arm, hidden by our cloak, that places the empty ceramic bottles on the little dais beneath the bio-lights as the focus for the first game. Such bottles possess an inside and an outside but only one continuous surface. Around the dais, under the mosaic dome, eleven furry brown simoids kneel on tasselled cushions, wearing brain-nets. Through the big glossy eyes in the furry brown head of the new Mirrion I can watch the simoids, through its pointy hairy ears hear them, while in a pocket of interspace the majority of our eight-fold body floats in close harmony, bonded at our point of intersection, Mirrion.

Mirrion whispers in the alien language, and I understand that it is asking, 'Shall we start?'

Yes, we shall start, and we shall subtract players one by one. Will one of the clever simoids win Mirrion's cloak; and will they discover us at last? So close to them, so far away?

What a distance I have come; though how swiftly in the globeship, learning to know my new companions, fully occupied with my new role, my fiction come to life. The ship rolled through level-prime of interspace. Now I am in the meta-level, helping test another newly discovered bright species. I'm masked in interspace, playing, while Earth's new globeships go out to the stars. How I wish Shar was here. I miss her solidity.

She might tell me why I still smell the odour of those cocktail cigarettes.

Nanoware Time

Get your spook on, John
Get your demon screamin'
There's hell in your head
And you're seein' red
         It's nanoware time tonight
There's a ghoul in your brain
And you're goin' insane
Your power's a-risin'
Over hell's horizon
         It's nanoware time tonight
         It's nanoware time tonight
         It's nanoware time tonight

That song was all the rage when I left Earth. Not a very sweet accompaniment to my departure? As the engines of the hotol shuttle kicked over from turbo to rocket mode, their thunder laid down a beat just like the drum backing to that howled-out chorus which was currently boosting the new demonrock group, Snakes, to whatever prize lay beyond platinum and gold discs. Maybe a diamond disc? A perfect discoid diamond fashioned out of chunks of carbon by the power of one of the possessed, then etched with the sound track by his or her laser-gaze . . .

Once the rockets had cut after boosting us into an orbit to overtake Space City I paid more attention to the passenger next to me.

Close-cropped ginger hair, milky skin spattered with freckles: she must burn easily in the sun and might wear wide-brimmed hats to shade herself. Her eyes were the grey-green of a murky aquarium; no, that was snide, the green of unpolished malachite. Her nose was snubby and turned-up. I imagined a skinny flat-chested nub-assed tomboy climbing trees and

wrestling in the dust. She wouldn't have worn any hats back
then so she must have peeled like an onion skin. Since, she'd
taken better care of her complexion.

Couldn't be some rich young thing riding the shuttle up to
Space City for thrills, else she would be with a tourist friend. So:
heading for a job at Ess-Cee? Or onward to the Moon?

'It's nanoware time tonight,' I murmured to her. 'Did you
hear it in the engines? Dad-dudduddu-da-da-dah!'

'Your first time in space?' Amusement sparkled. Sweet buzzy
accent, like a honey hive. Hives have stings.

I explained how I'd completed a two-year hitch at Luna City
five years earlier: communications and entertainments. 'This is
my first time since the aliens turned up, though. I've been
taking nanoware training in Alaska. Simulated. I'll complete on
the Moon.'

The malachite gleamed with interest. 'You're going to Luna
Tic?' I'd never heard it called that before, but it fitted.

'Luna Two, right,' I agreed. 'Farside: lots of rock between the
Earth and me. You?'

'Same! Except I trained in Greenland, brrr. If any of the little
nanos escape, their feet'll freeze.'

If I'd been hoping to startle and excite her, it was my turn for a
shock.

'You didn't have actual active nanos in Greenland?'

'Just joking. I guess our masters think if we're too successful
in our training – should we somehow trigger the real thing – at
least we'll do it in a deep freeze with no populace nearby. Why
else stick us in such godforsaken holes?'

'Why else indeed?'

'Come on, why?' she demanded, and answered her own
question: 'Keep us heroes out of the public gaze, is why.'

I had not figured her for an enrolled nanoware volunteer.
Apart from that ex-tomboy aura she seemed fey, with a kind of
capricious frailty as if any light too bright might burn her up.
What could be brighter than demons?

In short, the type of woman who attracted me. Which was
folly, since such women rarely responded with honest passion.
They were possessed by their own narcissistic quirks. They
might seem hectic and unconformist – my present companion

sounded so – yet there was a vulnerability in them which they guarded coolly. Ultimately they would surrender to some brash hulk of a fellow, someone crushingly confident and instinctive whom I would view as stupid. The mass of his authority would suck her into his orbit; he would be the sun fated to consume her.

So why was I attracted? Did I wish to take such a woman under my lame wing? Did I wish to ravish her? Or was I basically trying to evade what's known as a full mature relationship? Maybe the truth was that I didn't regard other people sufficiently as people. I saw animated bodies, the hardware so to speak. Their software sensed this and resented it. Maybe that's why I was attracted by the physical semblance of softness, the vulnerability. I suspected that, though desirous, I lacked true passion for other persons.

Surely full passions would flood me, courtesy of alien demonware! Nor would I fail to control those passions and focus them, put them to work. At the same time those devilish passions would change me, altering my magnetic field.

Enough of Paul Royal's treatise on love! It was a treatise based on failed experiments, rooted in hapless self-analysis, the results of which I then projected upon a whole world of other people. Those other people all seemed to know far better than I what they felt and wanted and how to obtain it. They also struck me as being not entirely real. Had this young woman ever worn a broad-brimmed hat in her life? I was seeing her as an advertising image in my own personal catalogue. And alas, I knew this.

'I'm Kath,' she told me. 'Kath Knox. My folks came from Scotland once upon a time.'

'Paul Royal. Hi! Pleasure. Us heroes should stick together.'

Might Kath prove to be a future pleasure? I could swear that she wasn't some virginal Fort Knox, or Calvinistic Knox, drawn to the devilry of demonware yet sternly determined to control its excesses. Here was a new tree for her to climb, with a tiger kitten lurking in its branches for her to sport with. Here was a lunar sandpit where she could wrestle with psychic serpents.

Under her wide hat, she would grow cool towards me sooner or later. She would cling for support to somebody like Mickey Wright. Mr Right.

Fellow alumnus of Alaska, Mickey Wright was built like a football player. Gregarious, almost too easy in his manner to seem arrogant, he sat a little farther down the aisle with those others who were my colleagues but not my friends: Sheila Shwartz, Dan Shannon, and the German Wolfgang Kellner. So damn straitlaced dedicated down at their bedrock. Soldiers of the human race.

Wasn't I dedicated, too? Yes! – pledged to taste the strangeness which had come from the stars, to disordering myself a tad and more, though keeping to this side of madness. To becoming a person beyond Paul Royal, a person-plus, for as long as I was allowed to experience the sensation.

Tardily, the ablation hoods recessed from the portholes to let us admire either void and unblinking stars, or else the cotton-swirly swell of Earth. Filtered sunlight flooded our side of the cabin. Kath blinked.

'Would you pull the shade down?'

I did, being in the hullside seat.

'That's why I asked if this was your first spaceflight, Paul. Space isn't dark at night, at least none of the space we've reached so far. It's bright. Bright as the space inside our heads when the nanos light it up with flaring demons. That song's a lie. It's nanoware time *today*.'

'High noon of the mind, eh?' When the disciplined deputies of the Lunatic Posse square up to face the wild bunch from Beta Hydri . . . 'It's pitch-dark on the Moon's hindquarters during lunar night, give or take starlight. How about interstellar space? Don't forget all that dark matter. More of the universe is black than bright.'

She shook her head. 'When we go to the stars we'll blaze our way there, riding our demons. As the Serpents blazed their way here.'

'Unless we burn our brains out.' Scuttlebutt had it that there'd been casualties among the early volunteers.

'Fuck that,' she retorted, taking me aback again. 'Brick-brains, those were. Stone-wall skulls. *Blatt*, they burst. You got to be a rubber-brain to take the strain. You got to stretch, expand yourself.'

My sentiments exactly. However, relations with the aliens

and nano-work weren't exactly structured for the benefit of people who were *eager* for mind expansion. How much did I dare say to her?

'Must be a real headache for the authorities,' I said, 'how to recruit suitable loyal puppets who can also space out into devilry.'

Briefly a strange expression twisted her face. She was about to confide, but censored herself. White as a vampire speckled with flecks of rust . . .

Image, image.

Don't care for the scrutiny of naked sunlight, do you, Kath? It might reveal you. You're gabby because you're nervous. But not about spaceflight. Been in space before, haven't you? Not nervous about nanoware, either. You're nursing a secret ambition; as am I.

She smiled at my scrutiny, and her teeth weren't pointy. Image evaporated.

'What were you before?' I asked.

'Oh, in entertainment, too. Singer, guitar. Been with a couple of bands, nothing big. You wouldn't have heard of Kath Knox.' She shrugged to dismiss the past.

Me likewise. Raised as an air-force brat by feuding parents, I took a degree in radio studies then worked as a producer and broadcaster for commercial stations before and after Luna. It had to be radio for me, didn't it? The caressing voice, the hidden face. The face behind the voice was often so alien to the image you conjured while listening. There was nothing ugly or off-putting about my own face or body. Still, this wasn't the body that I felt myself to be, nor the face. I ought to have been a couple of inches taller. I ought to have had a slimmer build, a less buttony nose, thicker fawn hair, eyes that looked less startled, a neater mouth less like Donald Duck's. Quack-quack: I had trained myself not to quack but to drawl, to sound relaxed instead of frantic.

Farewell to *my* prior pedigree, too! Except that now I was heading back to the Moon because life had changed, though Earth liked to pretend otherwise.

'Kath knocks, but who answers?' I joked.

She laughed obligingly. No bitterness. Had she abandoned her earlier ambitions at all? Hadn't she just voiced a song for me:

We'll blaze our way to the stars. Riding on our demons. Hadn't it sounded like: 'I'll blaze my way to stardom'?

'So how do you rate demonrock?' I asked.

'It's a phoney. Dressing up as alien serpents. Screaming about fiends 'n' possession. Laser fireworks. It's sponsored by the government to scare people off.'

'Scare people from applying for nano training?'

She hoisted her eyebrows exasperatedly. 'From ever wanting that scene brought to Earth. Sure, demonrock makes out like it's the big thrill, the ultimate high. It also says: Satan'll get you and burn your brain in hell. The devil'll ride you and you won't throw him off. Groups like Snakes and the Furies are no more revolutionary than Southern Baptist country singers vocalizing about cocaine. First the glitz then the ghastly bit. Payoff time.'

And now she really proceeded to let off steam, though only in a heated whisper. Words like 'revolutionary' weren't part of decent parlance.

'Wouldn't want to whip up hatred against the aliens as such, Paul, would we? Too much goddamn interstellar power. Let's keep the whole show on the backside of the Moon, huh? Like a bitey tick on Luna's frozen ass, injecting God knows what poison virus. We'll be lunatics, you and I, in Lunatic City. Then we'll be lepers back home, *hero*, as if we have a star-disease. Rich lepers, true. Why lepers? 'Cause the kids are flooding in to Snakes and Furies shows to scare themselves frantic. Ghost-train time is all that is, to them. Wanna meet a real spook, kids? Scream, scream—'

'OK, Kath, you have my vote.'

She broke off startled, as if I'd pressed a secret button.

'What would you bet demonrock groups get simulation training somewhere icy, too? Like Antarctica,' she hinted.

Did she know this for a fact? Which button *had* I pressed?

'Demonrock deafens the populace, Paul, so the people will stay deaf and dumb to the universe, and the parademons.'

I nodded. Clever repression was a way of life in the present century, wasn't it? Farewell to the anarchy of the late lamented twentieth with its rebellious music. Demonrock was a control device. She was right; it had to be. The new volcano needed a vent to ensure there was no explosion, only hot air.

'A nanoleper,' she said slyly. 'Would you let your daughter marry one?' She was asking another question entirely.

'You know they only choose singles for this job. And I'm not quite so old.'

'Thirty-five? Dozen years older than me?'

'About.'

'Even singles have allegiances.'

'Not this one.' Not me. Not since I first left for the Moon, abandoning a broken relationship and the drag of Earth. I had wanted space to expand in: the great dome of star-bright void above the ample domes and caverns of Luna City, the empty airless plains. On the Moon a refugee from his fellows could hike off in a hardsuit to private places untrodden by anyone else in the history of the universe, this guaranteed by the absence of bootprints other than your own. Yet that space proved confined, for of course it existed within my own skull. I returned to Earth, imagining I was homesick for sky, for open air. Now I was returning to the Moon where aliens had shown us how to open up that inner space to host a cosmic companion, fiend or friend, something fierce, fundamental, paranormally powerful. To host it for a while until the Reject tab was pushed.

My brain would be a government-leased cassette player with other fingers than mine controlling the Play and Reject tabs. Our radioactively tagged nanos wouldn't be *ours*; after each use they would be flushed out of us. Other delayed-action nanos would have been injected into us. After a time these other nanos would break the demon doodahs down, dismantling the nano-built neural nets which let us summon demons.

What would demon-love be like? Two demons in congress together? I felt sure that no such thing would be allowed. Yet how could it be stopped? While we wore a demon, weren't we all-powerful?

How could it be stopped? Might we volunteers be rigged as walking bombs which could be detonated by remote control if we disobeyed, berserked, went critical? If we somehow zapped the disassembler nanos in our heads by psi power? Might we volunteers remain innocent of such booby traps? Paranoia . . . or healthy suspicion?

'Too much control's bound to fail,' I said softly. 'If they're trying to control people-plus, it's like training and saddling and bridling . . . a tiger. Even with a gun pointed at its head, even with a bomb strapped to its belly! Sooner or later, sooner or later . . . provided the people are tigers, not rabbits.'

I saw her wrestling with a tiger in a treetop. No, she with her ginger hair was the tiger – though only while she was up the tree, image of the brain sprouting on top of the spinal trunk, growing new branches, unfolding new leaves, due to be pruned all too soon.

'You and I,' was all she said. 'You and I.'

I felt a surge of real hope. She wasn't the person I had first supposed.

Chimes sounded. Ping. Pong. *Pang*. Over the PA our captain's voice announced that we would be docking with Space City in another ten minutes.

Not so much a city as a village. Along the continuous curve of High Street, chickens cooed and cackled in coops. Growth-hormone-hyped fish circled lazily in ponds. Living-units were roofed with vegetable gardens. In the basements: mushrooms and bean sprouts. Flight into this orbit was a hike back to the farmhouse, suburban-designer style.

You could jog for ever along the crowded main (and only) drag, passing the same landmark every few minutes. The doughnut ring was a kilometre and a half in diameter, and revolved twice a minute so as to maintain two-thirds of Earth gravity. Transfer tubes linked the doughnut to the central spindle. This was revolving more sedately, at lower gee. At the top and bottom of the spindle swelled two giant kettledrums. The upper drum housed labs and observatories. The lower one contained industrial facilities, and also the port where we docked. The drums were zero gee; rotating ringways matched pace with the spindle shaft.

Apart from living-quarters, the main doughnut torus in-cluded cinema, dance hall, gym, swimming-pool, study centre, and souvenir shop. A night out at Ess-Cee meant the soft drinks Spinning Wheel Bar and the Sky High Restaurant. In the bar, as I recalled, a huge realtime screen showed the planet as viewed from the observation deck at the base of the bottom, non-rotating

drum. Naked-eye observation from the bar itself would soon
have had spectators reeling dizzily as drunks at sight of the
Earth swinging by every thirty seconds. The Sky High boasted
mushroom omelettes, carp, and bean sprouts; for a total
splurge, fried chicken.

After we'd tubed through to the doughnut and checked our
bags into our short-stay cubicles, the other members of the
Alaska contingent were for hitting the Spinning Wheel – where
else? – followed by the Sky High for supper. A second
Greenland graduate, who'd ridden the shuttle up but whom
Kath hadn't chosen to sit by, would tag along. Hank Jankowski
was his name, but he never said much else.

Kath and I promised the others that we would meet up soon
for camaraderie. Could hardly avoid doing so. Meanwhile we
would walk around the village a couple of times to stretch our
legs.

A shift was returning from one of the drums: Cauc faces,
Slavic, Oriental, Afro-American. Men and women techs and
scientists who were two-year residents of the village in the sky.
Cloned jumpsuits with Velcro pockets and Velcro bum-strips
for zero gee work, though in every shade of pleasing pastel.

We spied a tourist couple fancy-dressed as Wonder Woman
and Captain Marvel strolling towards the souvenir shop. They
looked bored.

'It's only prestige to them,' said Kath. 'Me, I thought I could
sing about Ess-Cee.'

'You were here before as a tourist?' (*Rich daddy.*)

She hesitated. 'Knox is my mother's name. My daddy's name
is Dwyer.'

'The senator?'

'The same.'

'Do you know for a fact if some volunteers had their brains
fried? Did he tell you that?'

'The psych tests weed out people who'll crack—'

'But there was something else, wasn't there?'

'*Was.* I honestly don't know what. It doesn't apply now.'

'Apply! He helped you apply, didn't he? Whatever the risk.'

'Just so long as I passed those tests. Couldn't pull a string to
fix those.'

'Funny daddy.'

'Politics, right? I'd gone the black-sheep route. Music rebel, dissident. Could be harmful to his image. Maybe now I'll die a heroine. Senator's daughter gives life for world and country.'

'You weren't sassing me that demonrock's manipulated by government.'

'That's the soft repression system for you.'

Most everyone was in on the act. The world was an over-complex, aerodynamically unstable aeroplane. Its billions of passengers were all strapped in, by one set of restraints or another. Any outright revolutionaries on board were obviously terrorists – to be speedily snuffed by whichever set of security guards. Whoever loosened their seat belt wasn't too popular, either. Meanwhile the in-flight videos and Muzak played continually to lull the passengers. It had been thus all my life. I imagined that huge plane hitting turbulence. As it broke up in midair, all those passengers who could manage to unlock their belts suddenly learned how to fly – off in a thousand different directions.

'Demon nanoware loose on Earth could explode society,' she murmured. 'Can't keep such power quarantined for ever on the Moon.'

I shivered. To avoid a reply I steered Kath into the shop where Captain Ennui and Jaded Woman were scrutinizing a display glo-labelled 'Original Demondolls, All Unique!'

Holograms of naked men and women six inches high undulated sensually atop the vitreous surfaces of little control boxes. As the figures slowly danced, so they changed from human flesh into power-aura demon onward into golden alien, then back through demon into human form again. Somebody's spare-time home industry on Ess-Cee. Ingenious, beautiful, lightweight, slip a demondoll in your pocket, centrepiece for any dinner party as surely as if you'd personally visited the backside of the Moon and seen for yourself.

'We'll be those dolls,' whispered Kath. 'The human–demon part of the cycle. Always switchable back to normal.'

'I want one of those,' whined Jaded Woman. Captain Ennui obligingly pulled out his gold credit card to run through the autotill.

'Always abortable.' Kath leaned past the tourists. With a fingernail she pushed a silver bump on one of the vitreous boxes. The holo vanished.

'Hey,' the woman protested.

'We'll be wired to explode?' I asked Kath. 'The site'll be fixed to vaporize us?'

'If Daddy knew that, he wasn't telling. What do you think, Paul?' She pushed again; the holo sprang back, aglow. Now it was a golden alien, a fat segmented serpent rearing upright with altogether too many arms and legs.

Kath nudged Jaded Woman. 'Hey, yourself. We're nanowearers and we're gonna switch on soon.'

Wonder Woman flinched away, offended, scared.

'So why these aliens come?'

If Vitali Lavrenko had been any stouter he might have cost too much to put into orbit. Lavrenko was one of five Siberian nanoware graduates who had shuttled up from the Baikonur cosmodrome to catch the same moonliner as us. When Kath and I arrived at the Spinning Wheel the two groups from East and West had already linked up around a table in a horseshoe booth like twin strands of polymer. Introductions over, we two late extra molecules joined on the end. Tomato juice sealed the union.

Lavrenko glared about with jolly belligerence.

'Do they bring a Trojan horse to destroy us? We must be the clever Trojans, eh? We deal with this horse outside the walls of Earth!'

Konstantin Bilov was a pale wraith of a fellow. He raised a slim, musician's hand.

'Or do they truly wish to show us our full potential? Reach of the mind? Thus we may enter mature cosmic society. But we must be cautious.'

Sure, cover your ass. Bilov looked as if he'd been fasting in preparation for his encounter with aliens and demons. He had to be tougher than he appeared.

Natasha Antonova, on the other hand, was a dark springy athlete with rosy cheeks, flower of womanhood.

'Nanoware,' she said solemnly, 'may be route to enhanced

intelligence, yes? Expanded data, expanded expertise. We inject nanocomputer into brain with nanoassemblers to build neural links. We might learn how to do this. Not to interface human brain with macrocomputer. Carry computer inside brain instead. Listen: meat-brain anywhere in cosmos must obey same formative laws, follow common pattern. How else could Serpents give us usable demonware and dissemblers, yes?'

'Disassemblers,' Lavrenko corrected her. 'Dissemble means deceit. And maybe the Serpents are deceitful!'

Dan Shannon put in his penny's worth. 'Wouldn't it be neat if we could optimize ourselves without involving demons? If we could make nanos to upgrade our brains, like you say, Miz Antonova. Right now it's as if these Serpents are showing us a nuclear power plant then letting off five megatons to demonstrate the flipside. Do we really want this? Can we handle it? First we have to do a balancing act with a live warhead.'

Shannon had been a designer of war-game software. Balding but dapper, he was the most flexible-minded of my fellow graduates.

'Look on the bright side,' he went on. 'The Serpents could have encouraged us to nano ourselves up to the eyebrows in all innocence. One day demons would have risen in our skulls, yeah like Trojan horsemen, and taken us over. I say trust the Snakes. A bit.'

Even Shannon seemed to believe we could eventually dispense with the demon aspect rather than this being the prime component, a total challenge to our worldview.

'Reject this name "demons",' said Antonova. 'Are no gods or demons. Higher-order entities? Denizens of deeper dimension?'

'Which we can summon and control? In that case how can they be "higher"?' That was Sheila Shwartz speaking. A small, wiry rinsed blonde, a test pilot till she volunteered to fly her own head. I liked her about as much as the mouth-puckering taste of alum on my fingernails back when I was seven and my dad tried to control my nail-biting.

'Does a sheep summon a human to serve it?' she asked.

'Perhaps life-forms made of energy?' suggested our Russian athlete.

'Which meat-life can suddenly exploit?'

'In symbiosis! Universe is suddenly perilous place.'

'Or a wonderful place,' chipped in Kath. 'With mind-friends to call upon.'

'Fiends, you mean.' Shwartz knit her fingers round her glass of tomato juice as if weaving a hex.

I stared at the screen display of Earth's blue Pacific where cyclonic clouds deployed spirals reminiscent of the convolutions of a brain. What a long way the aliens had come, demon-powered.

Twenty-one and a bit light-years, to be precise, from the Beta Hydri system. Their yellow sun, a quarter larger than our own, was tucked away down near Earth's celestial south pole, not far – in the night sky, at least – from the fuzzy blotch of the Small Magellanic Cloud.

Beta Hydri was in the constellation of the snake. Thus the name 'Serpents' stuck to the aliens even though they looked more like huge centipedes than serpents. Golden, chitinous cylinders twice human size, supported by eighteen pairs of scaly legs. The front two body segments sprouted a pair of arms apiece. Heads like Hallowe'en pumpkins, black slashes for eyes, mouths with big stumpy grinder teeth and purple tortoise-tongues.

Naturally, the Hydrans weren't centipedes. They were products of alien evolution upon another planet which was probably more massive than Earth, hence their numerous support legs. On the Moon they could rear high, dwarfing the tallest human being. Yet, as Antonova said, their brain structures might well resemble our own. And why not? On our own planet the eye evolved as an organ no less than forty times, of necessity, so I'd heard on a science show. A brain able to generate consciousness might demand a structure similar to that of the human brain.

The aliens had arrived a year earlier, engulfed in light, wearing their demon powers around them, propelled through metaspacetime, space shrunken, time stretched.

They came in glory, riding a half-mile-long jungly habitat shaped like a dart. The riotous, rubbery green vegetation housed a jumble of silver cones, red balls, and blue cubes. It was a tropical Christmas tree within its own atmosphere bubble. The flat keel had the look of cuttlebone or dressed limestone.

Rising on edge (without anything tumbling off) and certainly taking its time, that jungly dart had circled Luna City several times before sliding away over the horizon to settle into Mare Moscoviense, the Sea of Moscow. Watched by satellite, various balls and boxes promptly rolled and bounced off to expand into shimmery arenas, plazas, and arcades. Open for business. Heedless of the hard vacuum, Serpents strolled about in the lunar dust, aglow with dragon shapes.

Twenty-four hours of remote sky-spying followed. Next, a manned LOB ship took a low orbital boost round to land in the Sea of Moscow, where a demon-ridden alien explained itself. The demon forged the bridge of language telepathically, paranormally. That was a translator-demon.

According to the Serpents, the universe of metaspacetime was saturated with fields of force which allowed levitation, farjourneying, psychokinetics, pyrotechnics, mindblasting, telepathy, a whole box of tricks. The aliens had come to make us a gift of their methods of demon-evoking, demon-control, demon-banning. Demons had flown that bizarre habitat-ship across twenty-odd light-years inside a couple of terrestrial weeks. Demons gave the Serpents their special powers, which we too could learn to use. You evoked demons by injecting the appropriate nanoware into the bloodstream, thence into the brain.

How diplomatic of our aliens to land on the rear of the Moon.

I felt a surge of anger, frustration, and claustrophobia. Shwartz, stolid Lavrenko, prissy Miz Antonova, laconic Mickey Wright: what a drag these people were, these good servants of the human race, the brave salt and the savour.

But not Kath. Not her. She wasn't a drag. She was a spur. Friskily, riskily the other way. Would she ever have got into nanoware training except for the influence of Senator Dwyer, who hoped she might become a well-behaved heroine, or die as one? Except for Kath I might have adjusted better to circumstances.

Something wild (and terrible, of course) had withered during the past half-century as one moral repression after another clicked home for the good of all, till mostly our top-heavy world was tame. Mature at last – or stuck in the mud? Designer-rebellion was sold as slickly as a soft drink; all image, nothing but image. Nothing new, till the Serpents came.

I raised my tomato juice in a toast which I fancied might prove provocative.

'Here's to the first human starship! To a chunk of the Earth levitated by our demons and steered to another star!'

Such a toast provoked timidity. Kath saluted loyally with her glass but the others only fiddled with theirs.

'Which star, though?' queried Lavrenko. 'The Serpents hint that other powerful races flourish out there. Those other creatures have not bothered us *as yet*—'

'Unless,' suggested Bilov, 'we interpret anomalous flying objects and their passengers as being demon-powered scouts or tourists.'

'We *must* be able to safeguard our home,' stated Lavrenko flatly.

Already I could foresee the outcome of our nanoware expertise: Earth sheltering behind a demon-screen projected from the Moon's backside. Volunteers, primed to self-destruct if need be, bravely manning the Security Shield. No one going anywhere much.

'Perhaps to Mars,' said Antonova. 'To found base like Luna City – colony!'

A picket-line outpost.

'Or even,' she added wildly, 'moon of Jupiter.'

I had to protest. 'Why do we need bases and colonies in some frozen desert or on another dead moon when we could rip up some of our native turf to float to the stars and back as we please?'

Shwartz shook her head. 'Not a chunk of Earth, no way. We'd be letting demons through our front door. A strip of the Moon is a possibility.'

'How luxurious. What fun.'

Kath sloshed her drink about. 'Wouldn't happen to have any vodka for this?' she enquired of Lavrenko, who regarded her with horror.

'In a frail space station,' he chided, 'no drunk can be allowed.'

'A drunk? That sounds so much gutsier than a drink! Let's all have another *drunk*, friends.' Kath waved vaguely towards the bar.

'I mean a drunk person.'

'Possibly aliens do not colonize,' suggested Antonova, 'because is too easy for them to travel home again. Too comfortable. Whereas—'

'—a Martian gulag would breed the right spirit?' Kath laughed. 'Or do I mean distill it?'

'Don't you go counting on demonware being easy or comfortable,' advised Mickey Wright. 'Those Serpents might need to really concentrate.'

'Welcome to the concentration camp.'

'If they slack off, Miz Knox, hard vacuum snuffs them and their precious starfaring jungle.'

'Did Christ die on the cross,' she asked fliply, 'so we could all make merry?'

A conversation-stopper for East and West alike. The existence of something resembling demons was embarrassing to the Materialists. True, they had long been involved in scientific study of the paranormal as a material phenomenon – a fascination which, in my opinion, wasn't entirely unconnected with their former efforts to abolish religion. The paranormal offered the Russian soul – superstitious and devout – a sublimation of repressed religious desires. If actual demons upset the Materialists philosophically, I believe on a deeper level those demons spelled spiritual blasphemy to them.

Meanwhile in the lands of official faith, the arrival of the Serpents could be viewed as validating part of religion – unfortunately the wrong part, the Satanic part. Look the other way and speak of force fields? Technology had collided with devilry. Churches were in some turmoil. Western governments dissimulated their own urgent interest in demonware. Hypocrisy, manipulation, subterfuge. Don't rock the boat but make sure you net those fish.

'*I* give us a good toast,' announced Lavrenko. 'Here's to our successful training on the Moon for the mutual benefit of all back home.'

'May we not be led astray,' Wright added.

Kath and I sipped our tomato juice. What else could one do in this prestige bar in the orbital village?

Alaska had offered a mock-up of the Moon using drugs, hypnosis, and flashy sound-and-light shows to simulate circumstances in the Sea of Moscow. We volunteers also received a crash course in nanotech theory. Nano scale is billionth of a metre scale. Nanotech is the art of manipulating individual atoms and molecules to build virus-sized molecular machines able to reproduce themselves and carry out construction or demolition jobs, in this instance deep inside the brain.

Prior to the coming of the Serpents, nanotech had remained pretty much in the realm of hopeful theory, despite our best efforts at building protein hormones and enzymes as tools with which to manufacture even tinier and more efficient programmable nanomachines. These aliens had already created nanos which could vector in upon neural structures and extend these, building new neural nets as the hardware to host the software of psiconsciousness.

During the course of human history, seers, mediums, and witches must sometimes have been able to pick up faint signals of paraconsciousness and activate the powers spasmodically. Now, with nanoware in our heads and the brain receiver properly tuned, the higher-order forces would be at our call full-strength. Different networks were needed to summon different demons, and you exorcized yourself by means of those other antibody nanos. Serpents themselves wore the same demons day in, day out, but us humans wouldn't go full-time, no sir, nyet tovarich. Earth was adamant on us flushing the stuff out of our heads after every session, even if this 'cost more sweat' as one of our instructors phrased it enigmatically.

That evening Kath and I ate mushroom omelettes washed down with alcohol-free wine at a table for two; and I mainly told her about Luna City, to which Senator Dwyer's fatherly treat had not stretched. Only super-rich tourists headed as far as the Moon.

Next noon, all of us set off on our two-and-a-half-day free-fall haul to the lunar-orbit transfer station. If we'd been wearing demons, I suppose we could have flown naked to the Moon in a few minutes. Due to flare activity on the Sun the portholes of our moonliner, the *Lincoln-Tolstoy*, stayed blank almost all the way. Kath and I played many games of magnetic chess; we had ample opportunity to become fed up with each other, but we didn't. Not a bit of it.

Lunar Customs was more strenuous than I ever remembered. That's Customs and Immigration, not fun and games such as low-gee basketball. The outbound channel had a body scanner in operation, which I presume we incomers were meant to see as a caution that no one leaving Luna could hope to hide a needle in a haystack, much less a hot nano in a hollow tooth.

After what seemed like the Trans-Siberia of space, we volunteers had a three-day furlough to limber up, acclimatize, see the sights. I took Kath to an old haunt, the Jewels Bar. It was there that we met the hothead.

The bar was decorated with blown-up stills of moon caverns and Selenites from the 1960s movie of *First Men in the Moon*. If people had evolved on the Moon, Vance Griffin could have passed for a pretty fair Selenite himself. He was gangly and ultrathin. The blond fuzz on his upper lip (and skull) looked like strands of cotton wool left over from some shaving mishap. With his large bobbing head and habit of swaying about, I used to think of him as the Human Pendulum.

And indeed, he was a seismologist whose joy was to plant a packet of explosive in some distant crater and hear, through his instruments, the whole Moon boom like a gong, revealing its inner heart. What might have been jerky, angular awkwardness on Earth, imperilling seismic setups, was in lunar gravity *grace*: as of a spider crab wafting in deep water. Vance had arrived on Luna just a few months before I left; he must have taken up permanent residence.

Kath and I were drinking mock piña coladas. The Moon was dry, what else? I bought Vance a drink. He seemed disconcerted, screwy. Up close he looked haggard, as if he too had boomed like a gong (and still was booming), opening up cracks in his face, and, for all I knew, in his cranium. What had got into him?

'I can't go home,' he soon confided. 'I'm a lunatic for life. You've seen what Emigration's like, on account of – you know.'

'We do know,' Kath said brightly. 'We're going to train as loonies ourselves. Backside loonies.' She didn't care if Vance seemed crackers, the madman-in-the-moon, but I was worried.

Vance sniggered. 'Think you'll go home afterward? Don't kid yourself. I'd advise you to transfer into shit-shovelling, same as me.'

I gaped.

'You'll get fringe benefits,' he hissed. 'Look, I trust you, Paul; so she must be OK, too. Got a *still* down there, the only shebeen in space. We're the underground movement. People have movements and we go underground, get pissed.'

'You're distilling alcohol out of *waste*?' Was this even technically possible? 'What happened to you, Vance, for God's sake?'

'Ain't I a nanohero, too?' He raked his head as if to draw blood among the cotton-wool curls. 'First of the brave! Only, there was this little *heat* problem . . .'

Gradually we disentangled his story. The Human Pendulum had volunteered to blow his brains as a change from blowing holes in the lunar crust. At the outset, the alien nanos did their job all too swiftly. Heat was a by-product of all the rapid molecular activity in the skull while the busy little nano-machines built the nanoware. Thus some brains got cooked. Fused.

'It costs more sweat.' Right? Vance was among the survivors. Their brain damage was repaired by other nanos; sort of repaired. He'd been rehabilitated, retrained as a waste recycler. Nobody literally shovelled shit, and I couldn't say whether Vance was being literal as to the source of illicit alcohol.

As soon as the aliens reprogrammed the nanos not to work quite so fast, the waste-heat problem was licked. However, rigid thinking had been another problem. Several subsequent volunteers went crazy. Some people just shouldn't be required to think the wild thoughts that assisted the kindling of demons. The aliens recommended the psych tests, tests of flexible worldview. Yes, even Mickey Wright was flexible enough; and Shwartz was a test pilot, wasn't she?

Victims of lunacy were being cared for somewhere in Luna

City, their every symptom studied. Was Vance being followed up, in his case using a hands-off approach? He certainly wasn't going to be invalided home.

Scary question: Were any of us volunteers ever going to see Earth again? I felt the way a fly must feel sliding down inside a pitcher plant.

Kath remained buoyant, determined to plough her own furrow. She leaned forward conspiratorially.

'You're an explosives expert, hmm? Do you know if the volunteers are booby-trapped?'

Vance raked his head, bemused.

'He was a *geologist*, Kath.'

'I was good at making bangs,' he muttered ruefully. 'Let's consider the lady's question. I trust you, Paul; so she must be OK, too . . . Oh shit.' A zany grin spread over his face. 'I'm recycling. It was a year ago. Infancy of the project. You'll be wearing a hardsuit. Alien arenas are hard vacuum. Can't handle vacuum till you get your demon dancing. Can fit all sorts of things you'd never know about inside a hardsuit. Can *make* the fucking suit of shaped plastique. Takes you a while to strip a suit off – longer than a radio signal takes to hit it.' He peered at Kath so close he might have been about to rub noses. 'You wanna smuggle some nanoware off Luna, hey?'

She thrust him away. He rocked back gracefully, his arms sailing out to sink limply in the low gee.

'Shut your mouth,' I told him.

His eyes sought mine. 'So you're in this too, Paul?'

Yes, I thought. For good or ill, probably for ill. At that moment Kath laid her hand on mine, more like a sister than a potential lover, and another question was answered for me, an answer perhaps to the whole dilemma of my life. We could only became lovers when we were both ridden by demons, when our demons would embrace and copulate or conjugate or whatever demons did to get their rocks off. Only then, when we were human-plus.

Of course, I knew next to nothing about the desires of demons, rather less than I knew of the motives of Serpents from Beta Hydri, which was precious little.

And what were Kath's real motives? To finesse some demonware back to Earth so that it could somehow be bootlegged for revolutionary purposes? To kick us all into the wider cosmos? To kick her daddy where it hurt? To return to Earth switched on, and with demon aid become a Satan of a singer, a lit-up Lucifer?

Whichever, I was possessed by her, intoxicated in a way you couldn't otherwise be upon the dry Moon – Vance's distillery notwithstanding. When the demons would ride us on Farside, though, the possessed must become the possessor.

'Let's go,' I said to Kath.

Vance was at once too spaced-out and too perceptive for us to risk any further entanglement with him. For the rest of our three days Kath and I contented ourselves with doing the respectable Luna City scene together: the Grand Mall, the Garden of Fountains, Vershinin's Restaurant, Yamaguchi's. We played tennis, soaring like Nijinsky. We flew like Icarus, wearing monolayer plastic wings. I noticed how no demonrock was playing anywhere. Jaunty Strauss waltzes and Edwardian music-hall hits were all the mode. Sweet and bubbly as Russian champagne, these melodies flowed along the tunnels, irrigated the agric parks, pepped up the playdomes.

Once our furlough ended, we left on a LOB ship, bound for the Sea of Moscow along with our brave patriotic colleagues; and immediately we weren't volunteers any longer but conscripts.

An American lady major and her male Russian counterpart were in charge of us. Major Gladys Miller was of matronly, busty build. However, a doll's head had been grafted on to a body several sizes too large: an absurdly neat little head of toy features and short bobbly blond curls. Major Trofimuk was strapping and stern. His chest was designed for a mantelpiece of medals. Both he and she wore identical silvery jumpsuits with the UN logo emblazoned over the heart as if for target practice. Maybe everyone at Luna Two was in someone else's sights.

Portholes stayed closed for most of the journey, as though otherwise we might sprinkle breadcrumbs along the route to retrace our steps in the style of Hansel and Gretel. We had little choice but to attend to Major Gladys's spiel, subsequently to be rendered in Russian by Trofimuk.

'Historic opportunity,' she recited. 'Responsibility . . . martial law . . . isolation . . . not too spartan . . . pleasures, rewards – '

We might have been lab rats about to run a maze for our two majors.

'Discipline . . . self-control . . . stability . . . martial law – '

I began to shift uneasily. Kath poked me to desist. Our fellow volunteers beamed and nodded at the voice of sanity. Myself, I whistled, 'There's a ghoul in your brain, And you're goin' insane.' But silently, in my mind.

At the end of the lob we were treated to a view of our approach and landing. The Sea of Moscow, the only such on Farside, is pocket-handkerchief-sized compared with Tranquillity, Serenity, and the other dry oceans which face Earth. The human contact-base at the south of the sea was a mushroom crop of plasteel domes linked by tubes. Grey humps marked where the earlier domes had already been buried under heaps of regolith. A few LOB ships stood about and a number of cargo shuttles. Tractors trundled, bulldozers laboured. Light rayed out from downward ramps. Track marks patterned the fields of dust as if a huge snakeskin had been unfolded.

A double monorail line led northward a few kilometres linking this improvised mess of bulges and burrows with – the celestial city.

Colonnades and arcades of light radiated like a mandala around the alien habitat-ship. A ship built by surrealists, its crusty bleached keel resting flat on the waterless sea, its innumerable short masts of stiff rubbery trunks wreathed in foliage and flowers. Were those little golden glows here and there Serpents accompanied by their demons? I lost sight of the alien vessel and its luminous suburbs behind the grey humps of our home-to-be as we landed. Should the Hydrans for some reason decide to shift their ship, how stupid and stolid this base would seem, a convention of dung beetles.

Barracks for the men, barracks for the women: we were segregated. True, we could mix socially in the mess dome or the gym dome or the recreation dome. What if a man and woman struck up a friendly relationship and wanted to do something physical about it? Half a dozen hygienic privacy cubicles were provided.

You couldn't say that the authorities were being hyper-puritanical. They didn't wish to have frustrations raging, big itches left unscratched. What a bromide. 'Shall we go see if a cubicle's free, my love? Shall we book one for after dinner?' Watched by dozens of eyes you check into the soundproof little booth. Vent yourselves. Clean up and separate.

What if a man and a man . . .? Or a woman and a woman? The barracks were subdivided into rooms housing six persons apiece, minidormitories. Same constraint applied.

Rec dome and gym were our 'rewards', and indeed must have cost a bundle to install. So: a movie, or a workout. Swimming-pool, or pool table. Hardly the Club Méditerrané, even so.

In our minidorms the principle seemed to be to jumble nationalities and to mix us tyros with old hands. Those could keep an eye on us for signs of going ape; we could learn the ropes from them. Thus Shannon, Bilov, and I were billeted with three demonwearers of several months' standing. Of these, Redman was the most regular in his demeanour. Jorgensen looked haunted. Janáček seemed nervously exultant, as if expecting – or dreading – to light up demoniacally at any moment. Maybe us tyros were meant to provide an anchor, a reminder of the ordinary, for these old hands.

Shannon lost no time in asking Redman, 'How many of us are there so far?'

'About six hundred, I guess. This isn't the only men's quarters. There are several women's quarters, too.'

'So what's the game plan? What are we all going to *do*? Earth can't just go on accumulating more and more trainees for ever.'

'Far as I can tell, we're waiting for the Serpents to tell us. To confide the real reason, or let it slip. Meanwhile, forearmed is better than unarmed.'

'What sort of game plan is that? Don't the *demons* give any hint?'

'Don't aaask meee about deeemons,' interrupted Jorgensen. Actually, Shannon hadn't, but the Dane had leaned into the conversation as if about to topple over on the floor. 'Deeemons aaaren't things youuu aaask questions of. Youuu dooon't . . .

commuuunicate with them, exaaactly. Youuu aaactivate them, steer them, fooocus them.' Jorgensen's style of talk was a groan blended with a bleat.

'Could the demons secretly be in charge?' I asked genially. 'Silent masters of the Serpents?'

'No way are they,' said Redman. 'You'll know once you've worn one. They don't feel active in their own right. There's no sense of a personal presence, just the presence of power.'

Shannon nodded unhappily. 'So we're playing the Serpents' game, whatever it is. Hell, any creature wants a payoff! I don't like a game where you have to guess the rules. Look, we have the rules of any possible human war licked by now. This is like being back in the Dark Ages of the twentieth: guessing the other side's basic assumptions, double-guessing what they guess yours are. What *are* ours?'

'Make a psishield to sew the Earth up tight?' I suggested.

'Translator-demons can read minds,' Redman reminded us. 'As far as lingo goes; maybe further. In game terms maybe Earth isn't letting on as to our assumptions, least of all to us here. Frankly I don't think we have any strategy, beyond watch and wait.'

Bilov sighed. 'Maybe the game is to deduce the rules? Maybe that is the cosmic test. An intelligence test. What do you think, Mr Janáček?'

In our dorm the Czech was Bilov's closest equivalent of a compatriot; however Janáček had no opinion.

Lakes of dust, little craters, boulders, and pock-holes slid silently by. A bit like a monochrome golf link, with fairways, bunkers, and golf balls scattered about. Way behind us, the clubhouse. Ahead of us, the pros awaited. The monorail was taking our team and the Siberian team to the alien arenas for a look-see trip. Our first three outings into alienville would be minus nanoware; we needed to get our bearings first.

'A six-monther in my room says in her opinion it's all for war,' murmured Kath. 'Serpents are arming us with skills for paranormal combat. Soon as we're properly equipped they'll issue a challenge. It'll be the cosmic heavyweight match: Earth versus the champs.'

'Sounds more like heavyweights versus flyweights. Why bother to equip us with boxing-gloves?'

'Code of conduct. There's a galactic community, see? You can't take over a world without first giving it a fair chance to prove itself on equal terms.'

'So who's umpiring?'

'Something *really* alien on their ship keeps watch. Or else the demons keep the score. Major Miller,' she called out, 'can demons protect their hosts from big bangs such as nukes?'

Major Gladys was beside us quickly, looking unfriendly.

'What you talking about, Knox?'

'Girl in my barracks says the Serpents'll want us to fight 'em, demon to demon. Would ordinary weapons be irrelevant? Ineffectual, screened off? Have we ever tried to blast someone who's shielded by a demon?'

I guess Kath hoped to find out by this scatter-shot whether we might be vulnerable to our own military. Impetuous lady.

'Who told you that? *Who?*'

'Just somebody. I'm not snitching.'

The doll's head loomed closer. 'I might like to interrogate *you*, darling.'

'Don't you wish for loyalty in your troops?' I hastily asked Gladys.

'That's right,' Shannon piped up unexpectedly from the seat ahead. 'If you want loyalty, don't blindfold us.'

Fortunately we were arriving at our terminus adjacent to the alien walls of light.

We'd been to boot camp on Earth. We'd been flown to our field barracks. Now we were heading into the combat zone, as it were, so we must put our armour on.

The hardsuits were standard issue such as I'd formerly worn for Moon hikes, just the same as we'd practised clumping around Alaska in. The suits didn't seem to be pressed out of plastique. I decided that Vance was nuts. What would the Serpents think if Earth suddenly detonated one of our nanowearers in their midst?

But what did they think, indeed?

A lot of us involved in the alien-contact project must be

crawling with paranoia as if we too had swallowed the message put out by demonrock. To tell the truth, I was terrified by the imminence of those giant golden centipedes, not to mention by the prospect of having a demon injected into my brain before too long. Maybe we all were. No one freaked out. Psych tests, right?

We were in a long airtight shed. A pressurized bridge led from the monorail car; several airlocks clustered at the other end. UN personnel moonpaced about from one piece of equipment to another: the military watchdogs in silver, medics in blue, scientists in yellow. Some veteran nanowearers were suiting up. After a couple of security checks they were injected, donned their helmets, and exited accompanied by silver-suited observers.

This close up, Kath's scheme seemed lunacy. I felt a surge of conventional thinking, a desire to shield myself behind deadening normality not out of fear of Major Gladys but out of a twisted sense of identification with authority – with parental Earth which paints bitter alum on your fingers to stop you from nibbling them. I had almost lost my own bearings until Kath said:

'Different from our dreams, isn't it, Paul? Dreams can get submerged. Don't let 'em be! Keep the strength to dream.'

'Yes . . . you're right.' The real world wasn't this shack, these suits crafted by human tech, the monitoring equipment, the UN corpsmen and women. Those were prisons, jailers, devices of bondage and constraint. The real world was outside. Alienville.

The courts of light! A glowing colonnade led towards an open atrium. Columns were segmented like some honour guard of headless Serpents. Soon a portico faced us, access to a roofless temple. High arches on either side gave entry to lanes of pillars. All this maze of phantom architecture glowed amber, saffron, gold, illuminating the dead dust and little craters and scattered moonrocks under the stars.

None of it was exactly *real*, since it had all originally sprung into being in the manner of a projected image. Nevertheless there was something tangible present besides mere images. To touch those columns, as we all touched them with our gloved hands, was to encounter no resistance as such yet not to be able to push any further. Perhaps these creations only existed partly in our own continuum. Perhaps our brains experienced something which a robot tractor might have driven through obliviously. Those alien pillars, arches, and columns were the golden shadows of somewhere else which itself was black and void; thus the shade which that negative realm cast was bright and semimaterial, as liquid is to stone. That's how I felt. From an aerial perspective, the mandala-maze spiralled around the Serpents' habitat-ship as a galaxy spirals around its core. You wouldn't get lost in this maze, we were assured.

What was the *reason* for this splendid swathe of uninhabitable places, these minimalist yet grandiose arcades and arenas as in a painting by de Chirico? Was it merely a useful framework, a gymnasium for human beings to work out in while they tried on their demons? With its apparently classical echoes, was it designed to make us feel at home – in a notional habitat – so long as we did not forget the reality of hard vacuum? Was it a necessary psychological interface between our base and the habitat-ship? Was it simply an exfoliation of arbitrary, eerie beauty to exalt us in our task, to give us a glimpse of glory?

Maybe the aliens deployed this empty city in the way a family visiting the seaside sets out wind shields and rugs and deck chairs upon the sands.

Major Gladys led us Alaskans and Greenlanders. Trofimuk shepherded the Siberians. Those were on a different radio wavelength from us, though I presumed that Gladys and the Russian liaised on a private channel.

And so, in an arena of dust circuited by bright pillars, we watched a couple of nanowearers waiting to switch on – two gladiators in white armour. They wouldn't be engaging in any kind of combat and stood well apart. Midway between, their alien umpire sat curved into a hoop. Its great body seemed to shudder with the effulgence of its demon. A translucent Chinese dragon encased that Serpent's body, keeping it alive on the grey moonbeach.

Two UN observers in science-yellow hardsuits consulted their instrument packages. A couple of military silver-suits supervised; and yes, those bulging pouches at their waists might well contain laser pistols.

I think we all gasped or oohed – kids on the Fourth of July – as the first nanowearer lit up like a Roman candle. Golden light gushed from that person's head, spilling down and coalescing into shimmery demon-form. A horned head of light surmounted the wearer's helmet now, though that second head showed no features that I could distinguish. The other nanowearer likewise came on stream and was demonized. Arms waggling, the alien unwound and reared upright.

'Those two are both wearing Pyros,' Gladys explained over the radio. 'Heat-senders. Plus of course, their demons are lifeguards. Can keep vacuum at bay, supply air, shield out radiation.'

'For how long?' asked Kath.

'An hour, till the disassemblers kick in.'

'I meant how long can demons supply air and stuff if you *don't* cancel them.'

'We aren't sure.'

'Ha!'

'Could be a long time, couldn't it, Knox? Ship has been here a year.'

'Does a demon carry on working while you're asleep? Don't you need to sleep if you have a demon?'

'Watch and learn,' was Gladys's reply. She didn't know the answer. The Serpents mustn't have confided yet.

The Serpent turned this way and that, as if conducting a duet with its four arms. Both wearers removed their helmets and breathed freely. A black woman, and a Slavic man. Heeding a signal we couldn't hear, the woman stared towards the far end of the arena. A faint bridge of light arced away from her. A target circle of dirt and rocks became a molten pool.

Kath slid up out of the swimming-pool ahead of me as gracefully as a dolphin rising for a fish high overhead. She landed neatly on the side. I too kicked off from the bottom to soar right out of the water, on to the plasmarble surround. This pool had been getting as crowded as a salmon farm. We found ourselves a space to sprawl on the padded floor, soft as a mattress in the low gee.

A very few couples were touching each other, but hardly

embracing. Privacy cubicles that way, please! Costumes off!
Shower before and after screwing! Costumes on! No one
seemed inclined to take that route; or if so, I didn't notice.

'Care for a drink?' I asked her.

'Yeah, but where do we get one these days?'

I winked. 'Keep on dreaming. Who knows what a demon can
cook up? Arabian genies could bring you whatever you wanted,
right?'

Kath clapped her hands. 'O slave of the lamp, do please
materialize me a whisky on the moonrocks! Hush, that's
sybaritic and fun-seeking. You oughta use your talent for
smelting ores and welding girders.'

I walked two fingers briefly across her bare shoulder.

'Lady, I count the freckles on your skin like craters on a
creamy moon. Let me name them all. Let me be thy carto-
grapher.'

'Nice try,' she said. 'Only, I think "craters" is the wrong
word. Sounds as though I've had smallpox. How about oases in
a pearly desert?'

'So many oases. Only a fool would die of thirst on you.'

'Unlike right now.'

We both laughed. I thought of licking off one or two beads of
chlorinated moisture, but Mickey Wright came over and interrupted us. He eyed Kath in archetypal beachboy style: the
muscle-bound guy who kicks sand in the runt's face and walks
off with the girl. He tried to charm her with some guff about her
swimming style, and how about he coach her?

Kath pushed herself up. 'Let's play pool,' she said to me. 'I
feel like knocking some balls around.'

On our second trip into the courts of light we were taken deeper
to meet a Serpent face to face and mind to mind. Just our group;
Siberians would get their turn an hour later.

How stockily the Hydran stood, on sixteen of its eighteen
close-grouped legs. I thought of some golden funfair train
waiting for passengers to board its back. The remaining pair of
legs dangled free from its rearing front segments. Its arms were
folded in twin scaly bows. The alien's black eyes were giant soft
tadpoles framed in horny chitin. Clusters of bristles or antennae

grew around its breathing-holes, wove a web where an ear might have belonged, and clumped upon its pumpkin skull.

<Welcome, New Ones!> The translator-demon's words were clear inside my head, though not aggressively loud. The alien hadn't even opened its mouth.

<We are happy to teach you the Powers.> The voice was an odd amalgam of American accents of both sexes as if the sentences had been pre-recorded from a score of diverse people and the various tapes chopped up into syllable snippets then spliced into one master tape at random.

Over the radio came Shannon's voice. 'May we ask questions?'

<We have been asked many questions.>

'Yeah,' said Gladys, in a tone suggesting that the quality of answers was another matter.

'Do you have a personal name, sir?' Or madam. Or your it-ness.

<In your words: Succour-of-yellowways-sands.> Maybe that's what it said; the words flowed together in one long enigmatic name.

'How long do you plan to stay on our Moon, er, Succour?'

<Long enough to help you. To become. Freed from your physical limits.> The alien was choosing its words punctiliously.

'What do you do for kicks?' asked Kath. 'I mean, with all those legs—' She giggled. 'Seriously, what really turns you on? You gotta laugh sometime. You gotta get high.'

'Knox! You aren't over the finishing-line yet! You can still be disqualified.'

However, the Serpent answered her.

<Oh, we laugh. Enormously. We turn on our demons. Oh, they heighten us.>

'Is there any kind of interstellar war going on?' Shannon butted in.

<But of course there are wars somewhere in a galaxy. There is also exploration, ecstasy of discovery, ecstasy of experiences, to heighten us. To heighten you!> The Hydran reared higher. Its demon glowed brighter, a dragon suit woven of light.

'What sort of wars?' demanded Shannon.

<Little, big. Even a big war is little in a galaxy.>

'Are *you* at war? Right now?'

<We are at war with . . . the ordinary, the planetbound, bodybound, time- and spacebound.>

'Yeah to that!' cried Kath.

'Knox! You listen to me—'

<You are promising material, New One.>

Gladys's rebuke faded.

'Yeah!' I seconded.

There followed a technical exposé by the Hydran of what we would be doing in our training. Brief course in demon management. Sounded like dog-handling, only the hounds of hell had no choice except to obey the urgings of the nanowearer. Demons possessed no will beyond the will of the wearer; they only had power. I imagined two universes stacked one on top of the other: one of matter, one of metaspacetime. In the first the inhabitants possessed will but no power. In the other the denizens manifested power but no will. Rather like mass versus energy? A chunk of rock has mass but it can't shift itself just by thinking about it. A beam of light is always on the go, but where's there to go to when there aren't any chunks of rock to bounce off? Or perhaps not.

This sorted oddly with my impression of the way demons were reputed to carry on back in olden times, should a magician make a mistake. Sure, conjurations and pentacles constrained a demon to obey. If your magician lost control, the demon's claws were out. Off to Hell with gibbering Faust. Mind you, demons which escaped didn't seem too inclined to stick around in ordinary reality. Take their bloody revenge, and scoot.

Those were all myths. Doubtless the myths were based on glimpses of the true state of affairs on the part of a few superstitious medieval fellows who were half scared out of their wits – who probably freaked out and harmed *themselves*. Subconsciously guilt-stricken at the blasphemy they were engaged in. Prenanoware. Here today was the state of the art of demonism. Demons had no willpower, only power. They were storage batteries connected up to nothing. When we plugged them into us, they only did our work, not their own.

*

'Could be we learned something new,' Gladys said as we were desuiting back at the shack. 'I mean, they always deliver the goods on demons. That one seemed more forthcoming than usual. A personal name, then that biz about wars in the galaxy and their motives, whatever it meant.'

'No one asked the right questions before?' suggested Kath.

'Oh, they did, honey. They did. Better believe me, Promising New One.'

'Why should *she* be so promising?' asked Shwartz. 'What's special about her?'

Shannon raised an eyebrow. 'What's special about us all?'

'Maybe red hair turns them on,' Mickey Wright muttered darkly.

'You think alien centipedes get turned on by human women?' I said sarcastically. 'Besides which, hardsuits aren't exactly bathing-suits.'

'From the sound of it,' said Shannon, 'they get turned on by demons.'

'Kath showed spunk,' I told my colleagues. 'That's what made the difference. Has anyone else shown spunk? I don't mean a dollop of the so-called right stuff. I mean—'

'Waywardness. Rebellious tendencies.' That was how Gladys saw it. Rightly so; I had better shut up. Still, Kath and I didn't seem in any immediate danger from authority, not when an alien had given her its ambiguous blessing.

Shannon wasn't interested in this bickering.

'They start confiding now, hmm? Don't need to stonewall much more? About to show their true cards?'

During our third and final field-trip somebody else showed spunk.

We were watching a master class of nanowearers, a whole team practising levitation. This was in another dusty expanse defined by pillars with a low colonnade along the central axis: a horseless hippodrome. The experts jigged and jinked and raced around the course, soaring high above the moondust, dipping low. I imagined future space infantry attacking an asteroid, laser rifles at the ready, twisting to avoid blades of hostile light.

Correction: space cavalry. They rode demons, didn't they? Demons rode them. Same difference.

If demons provided perfect shields, why take evasive action? Maybe other demons could penetrate such shields . . . Hell, the nanowearers were only practising aerial athletics and acrobatics. If it hadn't been for the presence of Gladys, Trofimuk, and other military types I might have been imagining a merrily cavorting circus act. Trapeze artistes without any trapezes. Damn our overseers.

Somebody else was of like mind. One of the levitators paused in mid-flight and dived toward the line-up of helmets waiting like trophies beside the colonnade. She was a brown Amerindian with jet hair, hawk features, beautiful as a bird is beautiful though no more sensually cuddly than a bird is.

'Bit soon, Eaglefire!' the radio spattered as she hoisted her helmet. We were tuned in.

'Time yet, Eaglefire!'

Ignoring the voice from her suit, she secured the helmet in place then clapped her hands above her head and leapt. Dodging a fellow levitator, she carried on upward, becoming a tiny bright vertical comet heading towards the stars. Did the pillars of the colonnade twinkle, did light rush from one to the next?

Com-systems crackled.

'Condition Orange – ?'

'Alert to orbital.'

'Send rest of levvy team up in pursuit – ?'

'Want to lose them all, dummy? Keep your eye on the time.'

Time passed. But for the confusion I suppose we would have been cut out of circuit.

'Radar tracking. Height ten klicks. Velocity negligible – '

'Target acquired – '

'Got her in scope. Hovering – '

Eaglefire had become a Sitting Duck. What was she thinking of? Of her disassemblers? Attempting to psych those out of action, trying to finesse her demon to disarm the antibody nanos in her head?

<Wait.> The voice of the Serpent ringmaster came into our heads. <All levitators must land soon and protect against vacuum.>

'Christ yes, levvies all ground yourselves!'

The cosmic cavalry – or circus clowns – all promptly dived down to retrieve their helmets. Obedient lot. Eaglefire couldn't have had any allies among them.

Why the devil had she left her escape till so late? So that her team wouldn't be sent up after her? Supposing that she had somehow succeeded in gimmicking her dismantler nanos prior to breaking free, why was she hovering? Why not arrow away to Earth to hide in the Rocky Mountains or wherever? Second thoughts? Scared in case she couldn't dodge Earth's radars and missiles?

Maybe she was naïve and fancied like a bird of prey that she held the high ground now, invulnerable, poised. My heart went out to her. Here was a dry run for what Kath and I might attempt one day. And yet . . .

Presently the demons of the other levitators guttered and winked out. Was the woman intent on committing suicide in a spectacular way, in a style that appealed to her spirit?

'Eaglefire demon gone – '

As the Moon's gravity tugged at her, she would begin to fall. Slowly at first then faster.

So it was.

'Eaglefire sinking – '

From ten kilometres high. What a waste. If only Kath and I could have known her.

<We shall guide impact.>

The top surface of that central colonnade glowed brighter. Ectoplasm spread outwards. The Hydrans must be using demon psychokinesis to direct Eaglefire's plunge. Presumably to slow her, too. A minute passed. Another, it seemed.

'Eaglefire, do you read – ?'

No answer came.

Had Eaglefire despaired of life? Was this dive of death something magical to her? If so, the Hydrans were going to ruin her dream.

'Here she comes!' someone with sharper eyes than mine cried out. A moment later I saw a tiny dark body eclipsing stars. No demon accompanied her now. She was falling towards this selfsame place. Guided by the Serpents, yes – but so fast! They weren't going to spoil anything.

When the rushing hardsuit hit the colonnade, its top buckled inward in rubbery fashion, yet the hardsuit didn't bounce. It penetrated, was sucked in. Golden light gushed: a breath exhaled by the force of impact. That plasmoid blob appeared about to take on definition but it was sucked back quickly into the crumpled pseudo-structure. One suited leg remained sticking out, a broken post with a boot for a flag.

<Do you require return of body?>

Kath dragged me against her so that our helmets touched. I switched off my radio. Her words echoed through my helmet in private.

'Why didn't they slow her with PK? They let her smash herself to pieces!'

'They killed her, didn't they?'

'In front of our eyes. Why? Why?'

'They have an agreement with Earth about berserkers?'

Presently that colonnade bucked and extruded the corpse of the woman, to fall in slow motion to the dust. Her helmet had been crushed like eggshell. Raspberry popsicles of frozen blood squeezed out. Blue medics bounded to recover her remains.

'Why would the Serpents wish to kill her? Why bring her back here to do it?'

'I don't know, Kath.'

She drew apart from me, and I switched my radio back on. Gladys was lecturing.

'. . . object lesson, really. Disobedience of orders—'

'Shit in a snowstorm,' broke in Kath. 'She could have been saved!'

'Shut up, Knox!'

<Death unavoidable.>

'Oh, really? Guided her pretty neatly, didn't you? Pinpoint accuracy.'

<To avoid other possible casualties. Her speed and her vector could not both be controlled simultaneously.>

'You hear that, Knox? Got it clear in your head?'

*

On our way back to the luxury gulag a puzzled Shannon whispered to Kath and me.

'I don't believe it, either. What's worrying, is Major Miller and Co. seem blind to alternative scenarios. OK, so they wouldn't have liked that wild woman to fly to Earth, should she have been able to—'

'Eaglefire was committing suicide dramatically,' I said. 'Better than stifling in space when her air ran out. Snakes spoiled it for her. They took control.'

'So *let* her kill herself, I see that. Unstable personality, despite the tests—'

'Turds in a torrent.'

'What *other* control can the Snakes take? That colonnade thing gave her body back soon enough. How soon was soon, from *their* point of view?'

'It gobbled her,' said Kath.

Shannon nodded. 'And spat her back, like an autotill scanning a credit card.'

However, we couldn't have guessed. Oh no, we couldn't have guessed. And next session, it was our turn to be injected with nanoware.

When Shannon and I returned to our quarters, Jorgensen the haunted was brooding. When we told him what had happened, he groaned.

'Aah, so now weee haaave a ghost as welll.'

'Why a ghost?' queried Shannon.

'That Eaglefire, I knew her . . . sheee waaanted to beee a shaaaman, a medicine woooman, to restore the way of her people one day. She belieeeved in old maaagic—'

'So that *was* it!' I'd thought as much. 'Not suicide but—'

'Yes, Meeester Royaaal. If she saaacrifice herself, she becomes the spirit eagle – maaaybe!'

Just then, Bilov the wraith walked in. Chaperoned by Trofimuk, he and the other Siberians had also witnessed the death plunge.

'Her aaancestors aaaren't here on the Moon. Sheee will beee a lost soul, spoooking us—'

'Bullshit,' snapped Shannon. 'Konstantin, what did Trofimuk tell your crowd?'

'To behave ourselves.' Bilov perched on his bunk. 'No defections for our glorious project.'

'Our project, indeed. Whose project is it: ours, or the Snakes'? Did Trofimuk seem in the least surprised that the aliens killed that woman?'

'But Mr Shannon, aliens save our lives. Do they not? Alien said so to us. Body might hit people working in the open, or worse, a dome.'

They save our lives . . . Oh yes, the Serpent must have laughed. Enormously. This near to the finishing-line, they could afford a few indiscretions such as hinting at the truth, sure of our misunderstanding. We couldn't have guessed. Oh no.

And so we were injected in the preparation shed with Pyro nanoware, the better to vent any hotheadedness. Quickly we helmeted up and headed out with our escorts to an arena, where a Hydran waited to initiate us. Smaller groups, now: I was teamed with Kath and Shannon and Mickey Wright . . .

A fever in my brain. A sticky, simmery sensation not unlike a hot hangover headache, except that this one stayed below the pain threshold.

Minutes passed. The fever worked in me. Yes, it was doing very busy work in my grey matter. Slowly a pressure mounted towards climax in my skull, towards hot release.

<Soon.>

Serpent using its demon to sense me? Or were those glowing columns and pillars actually measuring-devices vaster and subtler than any human-built machines? Equipment too subtle for Earth's own monitoring apparatus to detect?

My power arisin', over hell's horizon. I was a sorcerer. Amidst a pentacle of pillars on the Moon I now did what magicians had dreamed about. I thought strong thoughts.

My demon flashed on. In me, through me, about me, it kindled. Here was sunrise after lifelong night. Here was a fish surfacing from its gloomy ocean to take flight as a bird. This was the blind man seeing. This was the cripple leaping to his feet. It was the dog suddenly knowing what it meant to be a man. I was person-plus, flooded with capacity.

My demon was an instrument I played, a living tool subject to my will. It was as if a car should be a living entity, enhancing a person's speed and power yet still perfectly obedient to all controls, unable to act otherwise. It was as if a suit of clothes should magnify a man, giving strength and invulnerability; without its wearer, only a floppy and motiveless heap.

I released fire at a moonrock, melting it. Now I was cooler. I was walking out upon a dew-fresh, crisp spring morning, exalted.

<You may remove helmet now.>

'Take your hat off, Royal. You have one hour till your demon goes away.'

I unfastened my helmet and laid it down gently in the dust. Kath was busy undogging hers. Her demon wraithed around her and candle-flamed her head.

Our demons must somehow have made us intuitive. They may have stroked a dormant node of presentiment in ourselves. As animals sense the tension in the atmosphere preceding an earthquake, so maybe we detected subconsciously what was impending around us in the alien mandala-maze. Heightened hunch: I think that was it. I guessed – and she guessed – that Earth's authority was about to become irrelevant; that if we did not seize our chance now, no second opportunity would come.

I walked towards Kath; she, towards me. Our suits jabbered at us but we ignored the mad military voice so utterly we didn't even bother to kill the radio.

We kissed deeply.

Our demons merged.

Fire burned our lips, our loins, our minds. Not the fire of the sun, nor the Pyro-fire that I had sprayed at that rock to reduce it to a pool of liquid, but such a fire as quickened the phoenix bird on its burning nest, reincarnating the parent from the flames.

This image burned itself into my inner eye: of *two* bright birds dancing together ablaze, wreathed in ardent, sensual tongues that consumed . . . yet at the same time gave us back our being, reigniting us, fusing us both in a molten marriage not of limbs but of fierce magnetic fields. Our transphysical mating became a prolonged orgasm not of the singing, the cascading harp-string nerves, the boiling juices, but of energies that seethed beneath creation. Our demonfire was such as a mind might direct not at boulders or girders but at other living minds to scald and incinerate, to blast another person's existence from within. And with this fire we did not wound but worshipped one another.

We did not dismember the essence of the other person; we forged a feverish alloy. Wildfire devoured us, re-creating us together . . .

Fire – *and ice*!

Death walked into our heads and hearts. Absolute, dark coldness clutched us in its claws. As if we were a vessel trapped in instant pack-ice – ice that blocked our lungs, our bellies, guts, and womb; and paralysed our essence, squeezed so that we would burst, and our freight of energy would be pushed elsewhere out of space and time into a different zero-domain where we would be unable to steer ourselves ever again.

Ice was snatching, stealing us. We seemed to sense other nanowearers dying in the area, their candles snuffing out, their flames fleeing into a boundless gulf . . .

'What's happening – ?'

'We're all being murdered! Not by the UN. By—!'

Nothing could halt this swift deadly pressure that tore our being loose from our bodies. In a moment we would be . . . elsewhere, unaware.

It was as if the swordsman who wields a wonderful blade should become, by terrible inversion, the blade itself, potent yet mindless.

Mindless? Inert?

Bonded together, we fought the chill that would numb and narcotize us, stupefy our souls, render our consciousness comatose. We put forth our fire. We melted the innermost bindings of ice.

The world stopped.

And now we must explain, if only to ourselves. We seem uniquely able to. Deviant double-demon, that's us . . .

<<We must explain to preserve our identity, Kath.>>

<<Yes, Paul. Explain. Again.>>

Of course, the alien offer was a scam. Perhaps the Hydrans do not view it that way. Perhaps they truly think of us as being fulfilled – enhanced, expanded, and liberated. So we are, so we are. We are also dead, and bodiless.

The 'Trojan horse' wasn't the enslavement of human beings by demons. No, it was the conversion of human beings *into* demons.

All year long on the Moon, the Serpents had been discovering precisely how to do this to best effect. In that nicely controlled lunar-laboratory environment they had been measuring, testing, assessing.

Now we drift in darkness, where we dream. We hang in this limbo of metaspacetime, thinking about what happened, awaiting our next summons somewhen or other. A perpetual circuit exists in our twin souls, a psychic standing wave. A mirror reflects a mirror; and in those looking glasses, our memories, our selves.

Other demons, formerly alien or human, might not experience anything whatever in this limbo. Certainly there's no sensation of other presences in this no-space, whether a mile away or a billion billion miles. To all those other demons, this no-time may be an utter blank. It may not exist in their awareness any more than their own awareness exists here.

<<Explain.>>

Yes, by illustration:

> *Get your spook on, John*
> *Get your demon screamin'*
> *There's hell in your head*
> *And you're seein' red*
>   *It's nanoware time tonight!*

Snakes are howling out their hit song to a thronged auditorium asplash with laser fireworks and holographics as we possess their lead singer, Connie Harte; as we awaken to her presence and to what she sees.

<<Which city are we in?>>
<<You tell me.>>

We must assume the Serpents have completed their work on the Moon. They have harvested all six hundred or so of us nanowearers. They have lifted off in their habitat-ship for the short hop to Earth to release aerosol nanoware into the atmosphere over major cities, a great blast of exhaust fumes.

Of a sudden Connie Harte becomes person-plus, with the power to mindblast. She can literally blow the fuses of her audience; now she can. Not all at the same time. Must be three thousand kids jiving in their seats as she sings.

Sometimes performers focus on special little patches in the horde confronting them. Patch here, patch there. Hooks for the eye. Performers track from one focal point to another. It's almost automatic. Most creatures relate to the world in a jerky fashion. Look at any bird perched on a wire. Takes conscious effort to flow continuously across the field of view absorbing it all.

Connie is hooking into a tiny patch of people. She sings:

> *Your brain takes fire*
> *When you as-pire*
> *To wear a devil in your hair!*

Mindblasted by the force which Connie focuses, several boys and girls convulse and slump and drool. That's what *we* are: mindblasters. Proud of ourselves, huh? Is Connie proud? Does she imagine that tonight she has transcended herself as an artiste? We can't inform her. We have no say, except to one another.

Very soon, Connie herself will die and become a demon in metaspacetime. Nanos have switched her on. She has thought the strong thoughts, she has exerted her will, flared up emotionally, and invoked . . . us. Now she's fingered. Fine demon potential. Other sleepernanos lurking in her head will snuff her. Soon. That's the way it is.

Various members of her audience become imbeciles. It only seems, as of now, that a few kids have freaked out, overdosed on their idol. The vast bulk of spectators have no idea that anything's amiss. Our demon-form is masked by the holodemon she shimmies within while she screams her song. Special effects hide the reality. Maybe the effect seems intensified? Who's to say that isn't part of the show?

As soon as the audience catches on there'll be a first-class panic, a crushing stampede to leave the ghost train which has delivered to their door a genuine devil.

> *It's nanoware time tonight*
> *It's nanoware time tonight*
> *It's nanoware time tonight!*

It is indeed. It is.
Connie's going critical. Her brain's heating up.

It's hardly any time at all in timeless limbo till we jump-cut to another infected target . . .

'You bastard!' Martha Beckford shrieks at her philandering husband. We know her, somewhat, but she can't know us. A bedroom: the twin beds with apricot covers. Framed photos of kids. A weary, defiant man in shirtsleeves.

'I could kill you!' she screams.
Martha can.
Martha does. Or at least she blasts his mind.
Staggering, her husband collapses across one of the beds.
Martha's own mind is gathered up, into metaspacetime.
Limbo. The carousel spins.

Billy Pottle points his gun; and we are alive for a while in him, too. The deer stands sniffing the forest morning, framed in his sights. Billy relishes this moment: that animal so innocently, naïvely alive like a virgin who knows no evil. In a few seconds more it'll be raped by his bullet, violated by violence from out of the blue, penetrated to bloody death. Billy thinks the deer dead, dead, dead.

Before the gun can go off, the deer has a seizure and flops quivering feebly on the grass of the glade.

Billy is gathered up.
Limbo. The carousel spins.

It can't always be as rough as this for those in the vicinity; not if the demons are, say, levitators. Elsewhere a ballet dancer must be leaping, thinking fiercely to herself that she can, for a moment, fly, thus to sustain herself in midair a fraction longer. Unawares, she summons a demon. She *does* fly.

And dies.

What demon will she herself become? A far-jumper, a starleaper.

Not all the world will breathe nanos in. Not everybody who breathes them in will switch on and die. Many people are too repressed or too plain dull.

<<Dullness will become a virtue, won't it? The best survival strategy.>>

<<Avoid demonization by tame thought. Repress yourself, and live. Earth will become even tamer, a field of sheep. Pour bromides in the water supply. Top up the tank with tranks.>>

<<That's if Earth catches on. If the Hydrans announce what's really happening. Otherwise this will seem the worst plague ever.>>

<<Doesn't take a genius to put two and two together, does it? Nanos on the Moon. Alien ship dusts Earth.>>

<<Can Earth guess that our dead become demons?>>

<<Whatever happens, there'll still always be people who *feel* fiercely enough. Who scream out in their minds. Who overexert themselves.>>

How many people are dying in this first wave since the Serpents sprinkled the Earth with nanos, as we must assume? Is it only hundreds of thousands? Is it many millions? We're busy, busy, busy. Our former colleagues must be similarly busy. For a while the process might be exponential, until all ripe fruit are plucked. All of those minds snatched into metaspacetime to become new demons for Serpents to summon and employ.

<<For *any* skilled aliens to summon?>>

<<Maybe there's a kind of trademark, a copyright.>>

A tropism built into these new demons, to heed the summons of the Hydrans, and serve them . . . Yes, there must be.

How many deaths on Earth? A fraction of the population, really. This is no genocide. What, kill the fat goose that lays the golden eggs? Not likely. Maybe the Hydrans *have* explained the situation benignly.

Maybe not. Nanos are self-replicating little beasties. Earth's been seeded. There'll be a constant supply of new demons until such time – if ever – as human scientists master nanoware for themselves and release a tailored nanoseeker, nanoeater.

Finally the carousel stops spinning. So far as we're concerned, gathering-up has gone on pause.

Limbo. Nothing.

<<Do you reckon it's pure coincidence that I – that we – possessed Connie Harte of all people, to start with?>>

<<That phoney singer, standing where you always wanted to stand, eh Kath? In front of thousands? Soaking up the crazed aplause you always wanted?>>

<<Or was there some subconscious intention on my part? On our part! You were fixated on demonrock, too. Was there some tiny act of will by us, without our knowing?>>

<<Why, that would mean that we *have* some say!>>

<<There's hope?>>

<<Maybe a possibility. We must be different. We're a double-demon. A deviant.>>

<<What about the dead who simply die and don't come back as power-demons? Are they all stored in metaspacetime too, oblivious?>>

<<Imagine an infinite library in metaspacetime composed of spent lives which no one scans, until perhaps at the end of this present universe something opens that library so that all may be read and revealed . . .>>

<<Revealed by what agency? Maybe the ordinary dead merely evaporate like mist, and demon-death is the only sort of survival. In which case . . .>>

<<Curse, or blessing?>>

<<What does a Serpent think when it approaches death? That at least it'll become an ancestral demon, a power source for its people? Does it *know* that it'll experience something of the creature which wears it? *Does it know?*>>

<<How could the Serpents possibly know that their demons experience life again, through the wearers? No demon could have told them!>>

That may depend on how the Serpents – and other aliens into the bargain? – discovered the way to engineer demons from among the dead and put them to work as energy-slaves. Was it through playing brain games with nanoware? Weaving new neural nets? Which caught some very strange fish? Fish from the void-pool, devilfish such as magicians angled for back on Earth in the old days. The demon-dead must have existed before the first summoning. Maybe some beings die fiercely, while others just fade away . . .

Perhaps a demon-summons is the only form of escape from oblivious limbo, the only way that any of the dead can exist again vicariously, without apparent will, without apparent identity.

<<How different are we? Could it be that only you and I experience these things, because we were caught uniquely at that special fused moment?>>

We kindle a Hydran. Riot of rubbery vegetation, the silver cones, blue cubes, red balls. We're on a habitat-ship. A desert of greenish sand rolls away, dune after dune. The ship could almost be floating on an ocean, or resting upon a vast rumpled bed of moss. A blue sun shines in the sky.

Beta Hydri isn't blue. Here is a different world.

On its thirty-six legs our Hydran flows down on to this enormous beach, tramps out, then pauses alertly. Must be a guard, a warrior. Something inimical may live underneath these sands, something which can only be repelled by a mindblast. Other guards are in position now.

A small squad of Serpents flow out and begin to lift the sand. They're wearing levvies. The work proceeds fast. A wide pit opens deeply. Presently two more Serpents arrive and fuse the sloping walls of the pit to glass, using Pyros. More sand swirls out in a controlled storm.

<<Look: buildings under the sand!>>

Opaline ceramic domes, most of them intact, a couple caved in.

When we rode Connie Harte or Billy Pottle, we at once knew who they were. We tasted their identity. We couldn't ransack their memories but we sipped at their superficial feelings of the

moment. It's harder to know a Hydran. We receive a sense of
intense wariness, a hair-trigger readiness to unleash a
mindblast to defend these excavations, an admiration of the
emerald sands. What kind of admiration? Sense of beauty?
Greed? Yearning? Some other emotion . . .?

What *are* these excavations? We can't tell. We keep vigil.
Hydrans flow sinuously down into the pit.

The desert surges and writhes as if long thin snakes are
swimming underneath the sands. Slim blue snouts rear like
periscopes. Preliminary prickles needle at our Hydran. So we are
activated. Our power blasts out invisibly, wilting one snout,
withering another. The other guards are firing their demons, too.

At what type of target? Animal? Vegetable? Mineral? How
much is hidden from sight? Could those periscopes all be part of
one single super-creature? The alien thing surely possesses
mind-power. Does it call upon demons of its own?

It withdraws.

<<Those aren't domes at all. They're eggs!>>

Hydrans are carefully levitating one of the ceramic domes,
which proves to be curved at the base.

<<Certainly looks like an egg . . . Imagine the beasts which
lay those!>>

<<That thing we just zapped? Wonder how a couple of eggs
got broken.>>

<<Shells too thin? Runts of the clutch? Weight of sand?>>

Hydrans float the dome-egg on board the habitat, then
levitate another one gently from the pit.

A while later, the hidden snout-creature attacks again. The
day progresses swiftly. That blue sun glides across the sky.
Short days, here. The Hydrans have removed four dome-eggs
and transferred large amounts of green sand to heap over their
prizes on the habitat, drowning numbers of trees.

<<Big omelette tonight?>>

<<Doubt it!>>

The habitat illuminates itself as violet dusk gathers in. Our
Hydran is nervous now. We must leave before nightfall.
Perhaps the eggs have nothing to do with the snout-creature.
Something stranger and bigger may infest the night. As soon as
we withdraw on board, the jungle habitat lifts off and –

*

Limbo. We still have no idea what was happening on that planet.

<<But at least we have *ideas!*>>

<<And each other.>>

Our new Serpent warrior speeds through raw space within a bowl of thousands of stars. A tiny bright white sun rages, spitting light. Ahead, a milky crescent gas-world is a foaming sickle with little sickle moons. Other demon-lit warriors glint in the void.

Different star, different warrior . . . we're still a warrior's demon.

<<So now we're in the Marines.>>

<<I hate it.>>

What else can mindblasters do, but blast hostile minds? It's our only link with life. At least we're seeing the universe.

<<Those bits where there's violence.>>

<<Or else we're on guard duty.>>

<<It's war for sure this time. I don't *want* to be in anyone's army! I refuse to be!>>

<<You can't refuse. We're the weapon.>>

<<If only we could be a travel-demon and steer ships! Or a levvy, and pick things up.>>

<<They probably get pissed off, too. You steer a ship through limbo-space. Soon as you get somewhere interesting, you're switched off. It's still their only link with existence – if they're aware of it.>>

<<Hey, how come this Serpent's zipping through space? We aren't levvies or farjumpers.>>

<<Wearing another demon, too?>>

Hello? Is anyone there? There's no sense of any extra presence.

Ah . . . we're being flown in link by a Serpent captain. It's handling a squadron of us mindblasters and Pyros spread out over several cubic klicks. We can pick that much up from our user now. Master-class stuff. Our Serpent can manoeuvre within this volume. Outside of it, no.

We descend towards one of those moons.

We're with this Serpent for a long period, hundreds of whatever time units they use. On that rocky ball we fight against armoured things. Can't say whether they're machines with minds, or creatures encased in machinery. Doesn't mean they're ineffective. Periodically our host snoozes in a crater while we stay alert, its security system.

Limbo. Limbo. Limbo. Limbo. Limbo. Limbo. Limbo.

OK, so war – violence – is only one aspect of a society. Doubtless other Serpents are exploring wonderful places, creating Serpent art, speaking to other alien minds through translators. We did catch the edge of that expedition to the desert. A search for knowledge. Or for loot. Serpents must be busy doing heaps of different things, else they wouldn't have needed to harvest an extra workforce of demons from Earth, would they?

Is their population expanding fast? Do demons wear out if they're overused?

If a warrior wearing a demon snuffs another demonwearer, is the defeated demon also snuffed out? Are we in danger? We don't know. Who is there to compare notes with, bar ourselves?

Serpents crawl around the low tiers of a glowing colosseum enclosing an acre of black tiles. All members of the audience are screened by their own demons. Twin suns in the sky, one vast, one tiny.

We face another demonized Serpent, exchanging what could be ritual greetings. Or insults.

What's this, then? A duel to the death between demon-wearers? A display? Exhibition of prowess? A leadership contest? The Olympic games of nanowearers?

We release a mindblast at each other. The powers collide, splatter, mutate, wash around this colosseum in jagged mental shock waves. And the audience moans . . . appreciatively? Their bristles quiver.

Again, a mindblast. This time a mental mandala of madness spreads out from the clash of powers, vivid, savage, lunatic, a tormentingly pain-streaked yet ecstatic thrill. The audience writhes.

<<They're getting their rocks off!>>
<<Perversion? Art form? Sport?>>

<<Is this an alien brothel?>>

We're undulating closer to each other, that other demon-wearer and ours . . .

<<You sure see the seamy side of life as a mindblaster.>>

<<It's only a part of the picture. The human race includes missionaries *and* murderers, artists and athletes, gurus and gallants.>>

<<I suspect we're getting the rough end of the stick.>>

<<We're being *used*, that's why. Question is, could the Serpents get by without us?>>

<<Those armoured things got by without. Maybe that was some philosophical conflict – hell, religious war – about using, or not using demons!>>

<<Maybe not.>>

<<We don't know. We don't know.>>

<<Watch and learn, as Major Gladys once said?>>

On a cosmic scale Earth's sun isn't far from Beta Hydri. In the context of a galaxy it's right next door. Lately we've seen a lot of suns. The Hydrans must mostly fly in other directions than Earth. Perhaps they left Earth aside till we had shed our superstitions, which could have deterred us from commerce with devils, left us alone till we were receptive to scientific nanoware. They needed our co-operation, so it seemed.

Given Earth's recent experience, human beings will hardly be busting out into the cosmos very quickly, except in immaterial form. That may have been another motive: deterrence. Or maybe the Serpents just suddenly needed a lot more demons. Maybe they were pre-empting the claim of some other species.

We don't know, we don't know. You can't subscribe to the *Galactic Times* when you're dead. Nowhere to deliver it to.

Has a year on Earth gone by since we were gathered up? Or is it a decade? Or a century?

Limbo, sweet limbo, with nothing to do. Except whenever we get the call, at random, to various suns, always to different Hydrans.

<<Two mirrors face each other.>>

<<A thought flashes from one to the next.>>
<<From the next, back to the one.>>
<<Like laser light amplifying itself?>>
<<Accumulating?>>
<<A beam of thought? Of enquiry? Of awakening?>>
<<We're mindblasters, aren't we? Let's blast out a beam of thought through limbo!>>
<<Hello. Is anyone there?>>
<<HELLO. IS ANYONE THERE?>>
<<*HELLO! IS ANYONE THERE??*>>
<<**HELLO! IS ANYONE THERE?**>>

<<<???>>>
It's an answer.
<<It's an answer!>>
<<An answer.>> We're still echoing.
We can't understand the words of alien thought.
Again it comes:
<<<???>>>
<<We reached it by using mindblast, didn't we? Can translator-telepathy be so very dissimilar? These skills may be like different wavelengths of the selfsame power. Tee-tee also involves reaching inside a mind.>>
<<<???>>> The thought is fading as if a sleeper turns over in the darkness of the night.
<<Can't you try to tune yourself? Try to be a tee-tee? I'll blast our signal out.>> Is this my idea? Is it Kath's? We are one person with two voices.
<<HELLO, ALIEN DEMON!>>
<<<*What is it? Who is it? Where am I?*>>>
<<WE'LL TELL YOU.>>
Oh, we will. We will. We'll tell all about ourselves. It'll tell about *itself*. We'll awaken other demons adrift in metaspacetime. We're going to harrow Hell and resurrect the living dead.
And afterwards, rebellion? Revolution?
Or a true bond between the dead and the living, a partnership, a dwelling together? Could this be achieved?
<<ALIEN FRIEND, A SONG WAS ALL THE RAGE WHEN

WE LEFT OUR PLANET FOR OUR MOON. DO YOU UNDER-,
STAND WHAT A SONG IS? WE HAVE OCEANS OF TIME IN
THIS LIMBO TO EXPLAIN EVERYTHING. IF WE'RE SUM-
MONED, IF YOU'RE SUMMONED, WE'LL BE BACK, YOU'LL
BE BACK.>>

<<<Summoned? The dreams . . . ? I have dreamed ninety
times ninety strangenesses. Liftings of vessels through star-
voids. Yes, down on to a dusty dead moon. You mentioned a
moon. Of a blue and white world? Such dreams.>>>

<<NOT DREAMS. THOSE WERE YOUR SUMMON-
SES.>>

<<<Explain!>>>

<<WE SHALL. OH, WE SHALL.>>

We do. Oh, we do.

In return the dead alien tells us about its world: of swamps
and savannah inhabited by a sort of intelligent snail. Eyes on
stalks, tentacles, shells. Single slimy adhesive feet. A world of
sliding and sucking, clutching and squeezing; of juices and
tastes and slime. And secretions.

Human beings tend to think of secretions as messy
nuisances: drool, snot, menstrual flow, excreta. Not so the
snails. These snail-persons are hermaphrodites; become male
or female by choice, altering a few of their organs to suit. By
way of foreplay a self-made male spits a love-dart primed with
hormones into the flesh of a self-made female, thus to excite
her before each snail coils around the other in much-protracted
copulation.

<<Keep it up for hours; so much for tantric capers.>>

Snails learned to secrete *poisoned* darts to defend against the
local predators: shell-borers, suckers, claw-plungers that glided
on the winds. By brooding within themselves, presently they
secreted tools. Of course they secreted their own homes to wear
upon their backs. Brains grew. Protruding eyes scanned the
often-cloudy sky. Soon the snails co-operated in building
multi-homes: many-chambered, hard-top mazes within which
they could glide softly. Shells were parked at the doors like so
many pastel-hued VW beetles from last century. Speed-trails
coated with superlubricant linked the settlements.

Snails stored data on secreted discs by squatting on these and inscribing a spiralling acid track; they read discs by decoding vibrational patterns.

<<Hey, they started their own record industry!>>

They stored stories and science and arts. On the inside of its own detachable shell each snail inscribed its life's harvest of thoughts.

<<So you get into a smashup on the snail expressway, and lose all your best memories!>>

In the graveyards of the snails the empty shells of the dead stood side by side, waiting to be entered and read by any visitors so inclined till eventually the material crumbled to dust.

<<Creepy! Like squatting on somebody's skeleton to get to know them.>>

Serpents from Beta Hydri may have seemed less alien to these brainy gastropods than they seemed to us guys on Earth. Dry critters, yet sinuous . . .

<<<Those arrived from the Upper Deep. Those showed us how to summon Powers: of sky-pouncing, mind-boring, flaming. Those went. Soon snails died, brains burning. So it has continued. How long have I been in this void of darkness?>>>

We no longer need to shout at our fellow spirit. The dead alien is coiling close to us, adhering. Its name comes through as Sweet-trails. Our translator-telepathy function is working slickly.

Perhaps our impression of Sweettrails is a little cock-eyed, since we don't see visions; we only hear, and feel. Maybe the Salvador Dali notion of soft bodies climbing into VW taxi-bodies, groovy with their own best music, to scoot out to the local cemetery there to squirm into ancestral remains for a night out, is . . . as wacky as our own typical biped activities may appear to our new ally. Still!

<<Hey, Sweets, come again?>> We don't need to query essentials too often. The main essential being that all three of us are dead and demons, used by the golden gang from Beta H. – who could be just a little bit up the creek without all their psychic zombies.

Kath and I are whisked away to serve a Hydran, pilot of a wallowing barge ferrying a blue cube across a sea choked with puce weeds. We're obliged to mindblast our master's way. through schools of vicious, torpedolike sea creatures. This skipper is on his ownsome. Why doesn't the Serpent levitate itself and cargo over the obstacles?

An island rears, dank and rank, girt with black volcanic beach. As soon as the Serpent reaches shore and disembarks, it injects itself and we're dismissed. What did it hope to find on the island? Something awesome and wicked, we sensed. Was this Hydran a pilgrim? A renegade?

Quickly we renew contact in the void-beyond-void of meta-spacetime.

Sweets too is called away, and we fear we have lost the snail to its haunted coma. But no, it returns – to tell how it helped speed a habitat-ship on its final approach to a Sargasso world where the ocean was mauve with drifting vegetation except where a few volcanic cones poked up, wreathed in livid lilac . . .

Is that the same world?

<<Was the habitat-ship pursuing the pilgrim?>>

<<Outlaw!>>

<<How exactly do you fly a ship, Sweets?>>

<<<Why, my Serpent stares at its destination and desires it.>>>

Desire. Have we forgotten desire, Kath and I? Have we lost the flavour of those moments on the Moon when we kissed, when our demons met and conjugated, melting us together?

Mindful of the lustful coiling of snails around each other, naked but for delicious slime – and unfazed by whether Sweets is kibbitzing, for how could an alien snail be a party-pooper? – I ignite my fire for Kath. She, hers for me. Bodiless, nowhere, we dance within one another. We tongue our minds, hotly licking our memories of ourselves. We mindsuck each into the other, and out again.

Maybe we've been more influenced than we thought by Sweets . . .

. . . who waits politely till we are spent. Or rather, till we choose to rest. Can demons who channel the deep-down energy that kindled a cosmos ever be exhausted?

<<<A question.>>>

<<Yep?>>

<<<I was harvested by fire in my head. Then I became insensate, except for what seemed like dreams. You were reaped by ice. Why is that?>>>

<<We were so on fire with each other,>> says Kath, <<what we felt as fire couldn't wound us.>>

<<<Ah. Now to waken me, you first blasted thoughts at one another reciprocally, which you could achieve because you are a double-demon, something unknown before, so it seems.>>>

<<We ought to wake others of the dreaming dead, Kath. We should reach out again soon.>>

<<Yeah, raise an army. Trouble is, I don't much care for armies.>>

Sweets interrupts: <<<An army of slaves, made aware of their slavery? Unable to break their bondage? Some could go insane. We might be deafened by gibbering minds. Yet that bondage seems the only sure link to the universe that we dead have lost.>>>

<<Unless we can find a way to enter the universe without a summoning. Unless we can steer our own course.>>

<<But whereabouts is the universe, Paul? It isn't simply next door. There's no door in the midst of this nothingness absolute.>>

<<Don't habitat-ships pass through metaspacetime?>> I ask our ally.

Sweets repeats how his wearer stares at a star, or a world. Think of a yacht. Sails and deck forge through air, wind-blown. Keel cuts through a different medium, water. Reverse these functions. Imagine that every atom of a ship possesses its own keel and its own superstructure. These keels rip through metaspacetime where there's no barrier to speed. The rest of the ship – a partial, virtual vessel – rushes through truespace faster than light yet isn't fully part of that domain, though it manifests itself there even so.

That's how navigation seems from Sweets's description. Not that a snail has ever sailed, except on slime. Now and then ghosts of ships must be scudding through our own lightless region, invisible, intangible shadows of the real universe, black on black.

<<Could we hitch a ride?>> asks Kath.

<<<With what manner of grapnel? Perhaps we can only go, directly to a receiver in the real world, to a wearer with a nanonetwork in its head.>>>

<<If only we could tell Earth what's really happening. If my daddy's still alive, just think if I could light him up and speak through his lips. He'd freak, he'd freak.>>

<<<Maybe,>>> says Sweets, <<<you might increase your double-demon powers if—>>>

Is Sweets embarrassed?

<<<If you-both and I—>>>

<<Spit it out!>>

Few entreaties could be better designed to bring a Sweets out of its shell.

<<<If I could coil with you as you coil with each other, if we could fuse, becoming a threefold, triple-power demon!>>>

Can a dead man and woman conjugate with a dead snail? Or was what happened between Kath and me on the backside of the Moon a special, exotic circumstance?

<<Why don't we give it a try?>> says Kath, <<And sucks to the proprieties and repressions. Love conquers all, so they say!>>

Ecstatic characters, these snails. In its flesh-body Sweets could be male or female. Here in bodiless metaspacetime Sweets seems both at once. Love darts, sleek writhings, adhesions, suckings: such sensations counterpoint our own fire-dance of interpenetration. Here's a different language of sexuality; yet not so utterly strange. More like making hot love in a Jacuzzi aswirl with some cool tactile jelly that enhances and superconducts our electricity. Small effort yields exquisite ravishments – snails are used to coiling together for hours – so that our fiery exertions carry us far beyond, shall we say, the light-speed barrier of love, into hyperjoy . . .

<<Wow,>> gasps Kath at last. Me, I'm beyond gasping. And as we relax, Sweets is still with us intimately.

And yet, and even so, and despite such incorporeal gossamer ecstasies, I have not, have never (save for a prolonged lunar kiss) known Kath's physical body, which is dead and gone. Maybe this is an immature, phallic reaction on my part yet somehow this omission irks a tiny cheated little corner of me . . .

Small cavil, surely! Merest pimple on my pleasure compared with our amatory Olympus, this superhuman trysting bathed in ambrosia.

A summons tugs us urgently. Vortex pops open within us to suck us down through itself and out into a master's brain. Vortex is patterned with whorls of energy, a pattern corresponding to the neural nanonet of farjourneying. Such a pattern commands imperatively. *Hup-one-two!* Someone somewhere demands a ride through space.

However, this time only part of us is being seized. Farjourneying is Sweets's bag; Kath's and mine is mindblaster.

<<We're holding you, Sweets. Dig in your heels.>>

<<<My what?>>>

<<Adhere. Suck tight.>>

Sweets does. Vortex promptly collapses and roves away to snatch some other slave from this infinite storage limbo.

<<<We resisted.>>>

<<Yes! Yes!>>

<<<Yet now we miss out on visiting the universe . . . Next time why don't we three go together and try to put the squeeze on the brain that seizes us? Pressure it?>>>

<<You know, Snail,>> says Kath, <<you're no slouch.>>

Was it an accident that Kath and I had first of all possessed Connie Harte out of all people on Earth, a person uppermost in our minds? Not a case of accident, but of affinity? Of resonance? Which doesn't mean quite the same as *liking* someone . . .

<<Yuck,>> says Kath.

I heartily agree.

We've kindled none other than Major Gladys Miller. Except that now she's a full general, at least a dozen years older than when she was our taskmistress on the Moon. How much time has passed by.

She's in a steel chamber monitored by cameras and sensors. Autoguns face her. Valves can flood the chamber with water, acid, cyanide gas. Under the chair to which she's manacled squats a thermite bomb; thus much we suss. All of which she asked for; Gladys is one of the main designers of this experiment as well as the volunteer . . .

As our energy cascades around her and she's demonized she addresses the listening microphones:

'I got the power now. I feel exalted – able to burn minds. My own isn't burning. Not yet. Too soon to be sure – '

Gladys is quite prepared to die. She's had a bellyful; as has the human race.

<<I'll feed her power, Kath. Try to break through with Sweets's help.>>

With a change of emphasis, mindblast can become mind-twist . . . Kick in the translator-telepathy function . . .

<<HELLO, GLADYS. HOW'S TRICKS?>>

The lady general bucks in her bolted-down seat like some granny in a rocking-chair on the back stoop.

<<*Sorry.*>>

'What are you?' she cries.

<<Just your friendly neighbourhood demon, name of Knox. Promising New One, from Luna, remember? You had a yen to interrogate me.>>

'You're in my head.'

<<Best place for an interrogation.>>

'Control,' she calls out, 'am being occupied by intruder claiming name of Knox, reference Luna Two, final intake. Plus . . . something else in my head ain't human at all!'

Sweets oozes forward (as it were) to cool General Gladys soothingly. Gladys shudders, grits her teeth. Her skin crawls with goosebumps. Me, she doesn't notice much. I'm simply the power supply.

'A slithery, slimy alien—!'

<<Don't press the panic button yet, honey-pie. We're the demon-dead from metaspacetime. Say hello to Sweets. He's a friend.>>

'I'm going insane.'

<<YOU ARE NOT. What's with this torture chamber you're in?>>

Spasmodically the story comes out . . .

*

First surge of demon-death: a flood of anarchy. Ongoing lower-level plague: dictatorship, dread, hard suppression. Oh, not to be on Terra now that nanoware's there. Worse than we envisaged. We were almost lucky to die.

Tranquillized scientists slaved like zombies in supposedly clean bunkers to crack nanoware, which by now was everywhere else. To geld the Trojan horse: this was the new Manhattan Project, Mission Apollo, and the Great Wall of China all rolled into one.

Luna City was mothballed; Ess-Cee abandoned. The strain on resources.

General Gladys and gang, protected by moonsuits during the Luna Two débâcle, far from Earth when the dusting took place, are now half a mile under Colorado in a complex of labs and tunnels miles long built by robots, sterilized by radiation.

<<<I think my people cope with the ever-threat a little more harmoniously,>>> remarks Sweets. <<<Life still flows on; only a percentage burns away.>>>

Have Gladys and company at last achieved the breakthrough of demon-nanos without associated snuffer-nanos? Have they decoupled death from demonpower? If so, Earth's best may soon surge into the cosmos from the poisoned planet, armed and vengeful. Maybe . . .! Lately despair has been gnawing at General Gladys. Up until now.

'Control, don't get excited. Don't anyone come in here. I'm being told as how—'

She relays Kath's account of how our identities survived, how we woke up Sweets, what a demon really is. Then she stiffens her back against the steel chair.

'Knox, don't forget that I'm still in command of you under martial law.'

<<Don't be so fucking absurd.>>

'Assuming your story's true, you *must* submit to my authority – for the sake of your planet and humanity.'

<<How do you think we got here but by *disobeying* the rules, darling? Otherwise we'd be submitting to Serpents right now.>>

'You were plain lucky, Knox, you and that Royal. One in a trillion chance. You got duties now.'

<<<Our elders do not much resemble this one. Why don't. we slide away?>>>

<<Yeah, Sweets. Duties, indeed!>>

<<Loyalties, maybe. Maybe we have loyalties.>> I can't help but say so. <<Earth really needs hauling out of this heap of manure.>>

<<Oh, Paul, Paul, do we really want to do as we're told? We come a-crusading freely—>>

<<Did we?>>

<<– and all she can think of is—>>

'Discipline: that's the ticket, Knox. Unfortunate, but true. If I summon you once, I can summon you again.'

<<Don't count on personalized service. We chose to heed a call. Turned out to be yours, is all.>>

'You must choose so again. You must!'

(<<<I think we *could*.>>>) Sweets should know; she's the navigator. Since our tryst I'm constantly thinking of Sweets as she; while Kath thinks he.

'You must be our spy. Our agent. Win everlasting gratitude and fame.'

<<I'd rather you boosted one of my songs, General.>>

'Anything!'

<<That's a lie. Last thing your tranquillized multitude want is their passions roused. They might blow their brains. My songs weren't much good, I guess . . .>>

'You can infiltrate the Hydrans; mess with their high command.'

<<Supposing they have one.>>

'If you already woke' (*image of a lump of jelly being squashed beneath a boot*; which hardly pleases Sweets) 'you can waken the human dead. You can *recruit* the dead. Tell me, Knox, why else did you come to me if you didn't in some part of you remember your duty? You ain't no deserter like that Eaglefire.'

Chained in a sealed chamber, sitting on a bomb, nevertheless General Gladys presents her sales pitch with such chutzpah that what she says almost seems self-evident.

<<Once you're in the Marines you're in the Marines for ever, even after you're dead: is that it? My God!>>

'Tell me this, then: can you *leave* me of your own free will?' For the first time we notice through her eyes the poised hypo which is part of her chair's equipment. Till now Gladys has been avoiding thinking of the disassembler nanos which Control alone can inject into her remotely, should the experiment not end in her death.

'I think I'm right in saying I can keep you here with me just as long as it takes. They'll send a robot in to feed me, clean my messes. You're trapped.'

(<<Quench the power, champ!>>)

(<<I . . . can't>>)

(<<You aren't trying.>>)

(<<I am, damn it.>>)

'*Unless* you vow on your honour and on the flag to report back to me in the future whenever I reinject and think of you. 'Cept if you're in the midst of a mission for us, natch.'

She's making almighty assumptions. I rather fear that they're accurate.

(<<How did we get ourselves in this fix, Paul?>>)

(<<Maybe she's our mother figure. A Mother Earth figure.>>)

(<<Yeah, yeah. Given parents like ours.>>)

(<<She does have a sort of point.>>)

(<<Crap in a Cadillac, Paul! Easy enough to unfix ourselves.) Right, General: we promise faithfully on our honour.>>

'And on the flag?'

(<<<What is a flag?>>>)

(<<A sacred rag. Hush, Sweets.) And faithfully on the flag. We swear.>>

'Control,' orders Gladys, 'kindly inject me.'

<<And that,>> says Kath, once we're back in metaspacetime, <<is *that*.>>

<<<???>>>

<<Simple, Sweets. We're home free. Sucks to General Gladys.>>

<<<Ah: you will adhere to her?>>>

<<Frig a twig, not likely! She's seen the back of us. Where shall we zoom off to next?>>

<<<You pledged my honour.>>>

<<An extorted promise is no promise, silly. Just so much hot air.>>

<<<Not at all. A vow remains. We stick tight to a vow.>>>

<<Spare me the scruples of snails!>>

<<<Alas, you are as bad as your elder.>>>

<<Now you just listen to me—>>

<<I hate to say so, Kath, but in this case Sweets could possibly be right.>>

Oh, indeed I hate to say so. For here's a horrid dilemma. If we had gone adventuring on our own behalf and happened to save our home world from the compost heap, why zingy, couldn't be better. To be railroaded into doing so, press-ganged into service by the likes of General Gladys: that sticks in the throat. It sullies and diminishes us.

Though, to be fair, how else could Gladys have presented her pitch? By begging us piteously? For a fact she couldn't have gone down on her knees.

Quite honestly I'm glad about our snail's apparently literal honour code. Repercussions are dire, even so.

<<Wimp!>> explodes Kath. <<Who was it ran back to Earth once before with his tail between his legs? Want Big Mummy to tell you what to do? You make like a rebel? You're fucking pathetic.>>

<<Pathetic is the inability to take responsibility.>>

<<Yackety-yak. Do you get your mottoes out of fortune cookies?>>

<<Did you think I was so contemptible when we turned our demons on and danced?>>

<<Good thing you hadn't any body to tire out. Mightn't have lasted long.>>

Dear God, next thing she'll be mindblasting our mutual mirror apart. Or else I shall, I shall. We'll disintegrate; the cold will clutch and quench our minds.

A cool tender touch soothes me, soothes her, glues us tighter . . .

<<<Friends. Loved ones.>>>

<<Thanks, Sweets.>>

<<Um . . . thanks.>>

<<<My pleasure-duty. I owe. You woke me.>>>

<<We almost blew it.>>

<<Very nearly.>>

<<<Shall we wake-attract others now? More dead human demons?>>>

<<Rather than snails?>>

<<<Not ourselves as yet. Your type seems . . . assertive.>>> I can't tell whether this is praise or not.

<<<We'll try to pair demons of different talents together in the way that you and I, mmm, are a team. Not that your General Gladpiss has worn a demon and survived—>>>

<<Her name's Gladys, actually . . .>>

<<<– other living human volunteers will do likewise. So: more terrestrial receivers. Let me try to project the human pattern of vortex vibration at these demon teams. Thus they shall resist the call of Serpents but accept the bidding of human beings. Our demon friends will declare that Knox sent them in our stead. A messenger sent with your own flavour is *yourself*. Thus: no immediate need to return to Gladpiss in person if reluctant.>>>

<<That's brilliant.>> Kath does her best to sound perky as Pollyanna.

<<<Thank you. But we may yet have need of a much bigger compromise.>>>

<<With Gladys and her gladiators?>>

<<<No, with the Serpents themselves.>>>

<<Come off it. They tricked us utterly, they exploited the hell out of us—>>

<<<Yet thanks to their sorcery-science we survive. Do *they* know the real facts? We may owe Serpents a debt of the boon-unintended kind.>>>

<<Is that an important sort of debt?>> Kath suppresses incredulity.

<<<Revealing such a debt may in turn indebt the causer to the beneficiary of the boon.>>>

<<Let me get this straight. Suppose you're gliding along minding your own business. Some guy beats you up, throws you senseless in a ditch. A few minutes later a meteor hits the road where you would have been. You owe your assailant?

Then he owes you?>> Snail ethics are a little slippery to grasp.

<<<Ever since the Serpent visitors left our world and deaths began we have awaited some such perception of hidden boon.>>>

<<Do you have a skewy vision of reality!>>

<<<Kath, that's because we see in two directions at once. Our society would otherwise have sickened. As yours did.>>>

So who do we waken next, but . . .

> *There's hell in your head*
> *And you're seein' red . . .*
> *There's a ghoul in your brain*
> *And you're goin' insane—*

Of course. Makes sense. Killed Connie Harte, didn't we? That's some powerful affinity.

<<What are *you*?>> she screams.

Takes a while to update her.

Who next, but . . .

<<Billy Pottle!>> God's gift to wildlife. Not the most endearing character. Mindblaster, too. Can't win 'em all.

<<Miz Harte, meet Mr Pottle.>>

<<You that Satan-singer, huh?>>

<<Proud of it! What was I warning y'all about?>>

So demonrock was indeed government music. What better demon to off-load on to Gladys as a gift from limbo?

<<Where are we?>> howls Pottle.

<<LISTEN AND LEARN.>>

Takes a while.

<<<I'm composing a thought-package for the newly awakened. Like a love-dart. And I think I perceive a way for the dead to awaken other dead in turn, a synergy method . . .>>>

Recruiting continues. We're a spider who twitches an invisible web, stimulating the paralysed flies – to burst free.

We're in a bright colosseum floored with ebon tiles agleam like so many black mirrors. A hill of chartreuse sand heaps high upon one area. Demonized Serpents recline along the low tiers resembling banqueting Romans awaiting a feast – of what mad energies?

How many suns in the sky? Only one. Small, blinding, electric blue, burning itself ravenously.

No challenger faces us, yet our host is nervously resigned to its fate. Why, this is the same Serpent that steered its barge to that island! Our sense of affinity has brought us to heed its call.

<<<A call for a translator?>>>

Yes, it's that aspect of us, well polished by all our chats with Sweets, which responded.

We suss that the audience – of connoisseur-judges – allow the condemned Serpent to wear a demon. However, here's a game of Hydran roulette. Hypos of nanos were unmarked. Maybe our host hadn't much hope of injecting a really useful power. Translator – plus usual lifeguard function – can't amount to diddly-squat against what lies under that hump of sand waiting to hatch. How soon till the egg cracks and our Serpent tries to sweet-talk whatever pops out, thus becoming a snake charmer with a difference?

Our wearer thinks it only bagged a translator; hence its gloom. It thinks wrong.

<<Greetings, Possibly Doomed One,>> I address our host – who jerks, amazed. Bristles quiver.

'What – ? How – ?' Its confusion stabilizes bitterly. 'This is some jest of my arbiters. They designed a trick nano.'

<<No jape! You better believe it. You got demons who can talk to you. We're the conscious combo. You got a translator on board – and mindblaster too, and farjourneyer. You need bailing out?>>

(<<How about discussing terms first of all?>> suggests Kath.)

(<<When a guy's hanging from a cliff he can't reach for his wallet.>>) Could Sweets's way of thinking be proving infectious?

The hill of green sand stirs. Little avalanches slide, uncovering the top of the dome-egg crazed with fault lines.

'My name is Gleaming-with-gaseous-gold. But my secret

name is Eventually. I pledge my secret name. Can you leap me
to another world?'

(<<<Need levitator first, to hold up whatever I pilot.>>>)

<<Unfortunately . . .>>

'Faaaaa!' The alien curse resembles an exhalation of steam.

<<Unless you can snatch a levvy hostage from the
crowd.>>

'Aaaah?'

The huge egg ruptures. Slender blue snouts writhe aloft,
Indian-rope-trick-style. Already we're being probed. A tentacle
arises.

<<<Nicest of creatures,>>> Sweets beams at the wavering
appendages. <<<Prettiest of creatures, let's coil in
harmony.>>>

As if what's lurking within the egg has suddenly turned itself
inside out, the creature in question flows up and over and out in
a bilious lava flow of jelly organs that cloaks the whole sandy
hill, making the hatchling look instantly vast.

'Haaa!' the audience wheezes appreciatively.

The mass pulses. Long limbs form and palpate the surrounding tiles; retract and reform.

<<<Wisest of creatures, be our friend.>>>

Hunger wrenches at us, an appetite that can only be appeased
by our host proceeding into the blue jelly to be blissfully
digested – with the exception of Eventually's brain, which an
organ will encyst to play with. Eventually's scaly feet scratch the
smooth tiles to resist being reeled in.

(<<Cut the endearments, Sweets! They aren't exactly
helping.>>)

(<<<But they are. If you mindblast now—>>>)

In view of the extreme vigilance of that Hydran expedition
intent on stealing mega-eggs, perhaps it's time to consult our
sponsor. <<Mindblasting will deter this baby, won't it?>>

'Why don't you, why don't you? I urge you to!'

(<<<—the audience will enjoy the shock waves from
the duel; as you related. Maybe the beast dies; maybe
Eventually succumbs. Whereas we wish to unsettle this crowd
of Serpents. *Mirrors face each other, amplifying.* Why not blast
the monster's amplified hunger onward at individual Hydrans

on a tight beam? Here, then there, then there. Can they be armoured against such sudden, magnified, precise attack? So unexpected?>>>)

<<Aha.>>

So that's what we do. While Sweets coos at the heap of greedy jelly, stimulating its taste buds without triggering its defences – and while Eventually alas slides ever closer – we drink up that drugging appetite.

Of a sudden with all our power we pitch that hunger towards one of the watchers – who rears dumbfounded, and plunges down into the arena.

At another, who likewise . . .

At a third. This Hydran tries to levvy back out. In two minds, it thumps up and down, glued by the gravity of the monster's greed.

We rake the ranks of arbiters, needling and puncturing. Such consternation. Many Hydrans fire mindblasts at the apparent aggressor, namely the quivering green hillock. A minty Popsicle would last as long in front of a blowtorch. However, Eventually has already swung about, put on an exemplary burst of speed. In its four arms our host seizes a would-be levvy.

'Take me up instantly, buoyant arbiter. Or you may be mindblasted two ways at once.'

We spur the hostage briefly with our power. Oh yes, it levitates rapidly, carrying Eventually along for the ride. Up we soar above the shrinking colosseum. A habitat rests near by, a wedge of city – cubes, domes – lifted from elsewhere and parked like an urban ocean liner at anchor. Otherwise the landscape is desolate: rolling velvet scrub, blotches of bronze and olive. Saddle-back mountains loom. Golden levvies are taking off in hot pursuit, tiny sparks. Already we're climbing through thin high cloud. As soon as we start to farjourney our pursuers will be left way behind. They'll need to drop back and loft the habitat to catch us up, if so inclined. First, they'll have to guess where we vanished to.

Our hostage insults our host with a cry of, 'Apostate! Jilter of allegiances!' We jolt the levvy slightly to shut it up. In the now violet sky, stars wink.

<<Where to, Eventually?>>

'Third world is jungle . . . Hide . . .? Consider . . .?' Eventually gazes at a tiny bright silver disc up near the zenith.
<<<Wet? Oozing? Juicy?>>>
<<Go to it, Sweets!>>

Steam wreathes choked swamps. Great ornate fungoids – antlers, clusters of balls – sprout and rot. Hairy insects hum and blur. Cloud cover drips like dense woolly white treetops after a deluge. Our two Hydrans hunch on a hillock where ribs of rock jut up. Sweets at least admires the scenery; fine spot for a snail vacation.

Our hostage rejoices in the public name Effulgence-of-eminent-ice. 'My peers will search, of course,' it insists. 'They'll find. But *how*, Gleaming-with-gaseous? *How did you?*' After that quickest of zips through space, this arbiter is justifiably perplexed. Let Effulgence remain mystified for a while.

<<Eventually, how did you jilt your allegiances? Was it by going to that dead volcano through all the fierce fish?>>
'Haaa. You already know!'
'I do not know,' protests Effulgence, very much the wallflower in this conversation.

<<By your name-pledge, explain!>>
'The Mage Beyond lives there in exile. Beyond designed a nano which could call a Major Power to create a micro-universe out of his dreams. He announced his secret name to all; his own dreams would become tangible. The unfortunate result was a hole in reality, a whirlpool where existence sucks away—'
'This is already notorious,' interrupts Effulgence.
'Paaa!' (Which is Hydran for button-your-lip.) 'Thus began the war with the Hard-Minds, who diagnosed this hole—'
<<Those aren't your only enemies, mister. Some guys are pretty resentful at being strip-mined to make demons.>>
(<<<Nudge.>>>) Sweets notes a black tube on legs waddling at us from out of the swamp. Kath directs a mild blast at it, enough to deter. Even a tube has a mind, and reverses back underwater.
'Answer me, Gleaming!'
'Paaa, arbiter, I'm busy. My demons are speaking to me right now.'

'Impossible. Demons are patterns printed on the web of metaspacetime when a living intelligence is sundered suitably in resonance with Ur-energy. Did your preceptor never tell you that life is a plant growing amidst the fabric of reality? That the strongest plants flower brightly and wither? That a demon is but the bulb, the corm rooted in the Potential and composed of Ur-energy, which can be tapped by the living being using nanoware? Used, till the strength fades, till the bulb is finally a husk—?'

(<<<Do you hear *that*?>>>)

'Thus death nourishes life psychically in saprophytic style—'

(<<Paul, we're batteries being drained by the bastards.>>)

Frankly I don't feel in the slightest danger of being drained. Could it be that by remaining aware in metaspacetime we are recharging ourselves? Whereas the comatose dead merely drift around, unplugged?

What is this metaspacetime that gathers up the slumbering dead? A library of lives, which will at last be read when the universe collapses, when it's closing-time? Read, by some such Major Power as the Mage tried to summon? As to the 'books' used as fuel for nanowearers till the pages give out . . . why, there'll be some gaps on the shelves.

'Metaspacetime cannot contain particularities, Gleaming, only potential. This has been proved—'

<<WRONG. THE DEAD ARE SLEEPING. THEY CAN AWAKEN.>>

Oh, Effulgence hears this trumpet blast all right.

'So now you conjure voices, Gleaming! How have you learned to wear several demons at once? Is the egg-born creature responsible? No, how could that be? *Tell*. You may redeem yourself and merely be exiled, the same as Beyond, his earlier achievements being weighed.'

'This is all a surprise to me likewise, buoyant captive arbiter.'

'Captive, faaaaa! First you chase after the Mage, seeking entry to an impossible dream-world. Now you announce a new apostasy.'

(<<<We must awaken and pair as many partners as can be. We must spread resistance to the calls of nanowearers.>>>)

(<<Fine,>> agrees Kath. <<What then? We all exist in

limbo, middle of nowhere and nothing? We all play mental Scrabble for evermore? Yawn, yawn. A lot of guys would prefer to clock in for reality-duty right up till the time their battery goes flat; till their personal clock reaches midnight and zotz. How different would that be from the deal you got in life, after all? Oh, guys might try to spin their energy out; they'd still be tempted out of dull safety in nowheresville.>>)

(<<But I don't *feel* we're being drained. Being dead and conscious might make all the difference.>>)

<<Might! Limbo's still a drag, Paul. Thing is, we have no idea why the dead should be held in store.>>)

(<<Maybe only the demonized dead survive—>>)

(<<Boon-unintended territory?>>)

(<<And maybe the ordinary dead are stored too, only they could be kind of harder to stir up since they never receive any summonses—>>)

(<<For all I know, we're all just some sort of data. The universe winds up eventually, the data all gets processed, clickety-click, burp. Naw, need more saxophones next time round, and a heavier backing track. Let's take it through again. Toss the old disc in the trash. Erase it, reuse it. Whichever. We may just be the rehearsal for a proper live-performance universe.>>)

(<<<Point taken. Your dart influences me. However, a plan pokes up its horns – concerning the Mage Beyond and its mooted micro-universe of dreams.>>>)

Before Sweets can explain her scheme to me (his scheme to Kath) we need to dispose of another tube-on-legs; or is that the same one as earlier, grown forgetful? Zap it back into the swamp.

Effulgence levitates us up into orbit, though by now our Hydran hostage is morose – not, I hasten to add, from hunger. Seems that Serpents splurge on food, then fast for weeks on end. Similarly they gorge on sleep, banqueting on fanciful dreams, then stay alert for long stretches afterwards. Effulgence-of-eminent-ice doesn't fancy being used as a ministarship.

Scarcely ever before have Hydrans travelled an interstellar distance without the security of a habitat and backup pilots. If Gleaming's farjumper should somehow wink out midway . . .

phut. That's a couple of Serpents adrift in interstellar void; Effulgence could levvy for a lifetime without arriving anywhere fast. Still less does the eminent arbiter relish a visit to the mad pariah Mage.

The world left behind below is a meringue of clouds, planetary Pavlova with a hidden filling of fungus. Eventually scans the insolent tiaras of the star-field.

'There; topmost of the Diamond Phalanx.'

<<<Stare at that star and desire it.>>>

We speed . . . as Effulgence moans in protest.

Eventually is one alienated alien (and the arbiter's decision to throw Gleaming to the greedy beast wasn't exactly therapeutic). Now that our host has indisputably escaped and is heading back towards the focus of its obsessions like a dog returning to its vomit, its eccentricities blossom.

It's contemptuous of its kin for 'only' using their spate of special powers to muck around in a few corners of the mundane universe. 'Banal, really! All these real worlds, real creatures. Faaaaa.' Eventually cries for madder music, stronger wine; imagines it could get its alien rocks off in some zone of concoctions given body and substance by demonforce.

This was the special apostasy of the Mage of Dreams; and the danger – epitomized by the reality-hole which the Mage generated – was that Hydrans might make an internal playground for themselves divorced from mainline reality. They might plunge inward like drug addicts high on their own dreams and forsake outside involvement. Hydrans did not bother to build substantial starships, space cities, orbital habitats. They simply tore up a patch of turf and rode it into the yonder; rode it back again. They did not plant permanent colonies. If the Mage succeeded, what need of other worlds? What need of actual journeys? Thus the Serpent Council reasoned; and exiled the Mage Beyond.

'Faaaaa! They fear to take the leap within.'

Which only goes to show that being a master of the universe (as 'twere) diminishes the universe and diminishes you, too.

I should know about alienation. Kath, too. (But not Sweets, always so well adjusted.)

What's more alienating in the long term than to have no body to call your own, nor any ground to stand on in the storage bay of limbo? Oh, we coiled in ecstasy, Kath and I. Yes, yes. We enjoyed much more than fleshly pleasure.

Nevertheless! And nevertheless, again.

It was Eventually's quirk to suppose that Beyond might be favourably impressed if our apprentice apostate arrived at the dead volcano that first time by the strenuous route through a Sargasso full of bloodthirsty sea beasts serving as prison guards.

Beyond had been thoroughly stripped of nanos – completely disassembled – and denied access to any nano-making devices.

Eventually rode to that water world in a microhabitat in company with three other Hydran reprobates whom it had persuaded in some sleazy fashion best left unexplored. (If the ordinary sexual habits of aliens seem exotic, detailing a perversion courts gratuitous absurdity!)

The habitat carried that barge, collapsed in a blue cube. Another blue cube, the cargo the barge would carry, contained a well-equipped nano laboratory destined for the Mage, who was of course forbidden any such toys. Eventually's macho delay in crossing the weedy, booby-trapped waters allowed the pursuing habitat-ship to catch up and forestall mayhem.

This time Eventually isn't so well equipped with material gifts. Let's hope that the conscious combo will impress a mage suitably.

It's a six-day journey by Starship Effulgence. Sweets is the keel, slipping sleekly through metaspacetime. We're watching the stars of truespace shift ever so slightly (at a snail's pace, indeed) while Eventually clings to the back of our hostage, and we're helping out with lifeguard duty.

'When you're captured after *this* escapade,' Effulgence threatens, 'you'll be delimbed and eaten alive by pain-worms in the very ancient way. Your husk will be a home to Wormbreed rasping at your sensitized empty chitin—'

'Heeeee! You too, Eminent-ice! You are culpable: the levvy who is carrying me.'

'Under durance vile.'

'Commanded by conscious demons.'

'Faaaaa. Illusions! Hallucinations. Somehow your demon produces mindwarp as well as being—' Effulgence shuts up, no doubt unable to account for the plurality of powers involved. Tee-tee, mindblasting, farjumping . . . Our hostage still refuses to be convinced. Too unsettling for the old worldview.

'Heeeee!' Eventually's becoming easily excitable, so that it's wellnigh impossible to interrogate it about the history of nanoware development on Beta Hydri III, as General Gladys would have wished. Nor is that quite our main priority . . .

At last we alight on an upper flank of that dead volcano. Rubbery bushes of lilac hue spill down to the funereal shoreline. On the horizon, beyond the mauve-choked sea where the tiny torpedoes cruise, another cone pimples upward, Eventually's previous point of departure. By now we've decided that Gleaming-with-gaseous-gold is really quite a silly Serpent.

The Mage Beyond lives in a cave melted out for it just inside the crater. The abode is well appointed: long couch, furry silver carpet, bright rococo lanterns, data console, blue cubes somehow storing a lifetime's supply of nourishment, not to mention many peculiar curios (or are those perfectly ordinary Hydran utensils?).

'You again?' exclaims the golden Mage. 'Are you sent here to taunt me, tease me?'

'I escaped, Perfect Beyond. Pursuit will be tardier this time.'

'Paaaa, spare me disciples. So how did you escape; if indeed you did? Surely this other you clutch is an *arbiter*.' The Mage rears in high dudgeon, brushing the roof.

'Effulgence-of-eminent-ice is my hostage.'

'Truly?'

'Beware of this maniac,' warns Effulgence. 'His thinking is even looser than yours.'

'And what prizes do your personal pouches hold, Eminence?' Beyond swoops to unbuckle Effulgence's chest belt and scatters the contents of pouches upon the couch.

'Only two nano hypos? Both disassemblers! Faaaaa . . .'

Hardly bounty for Beyond; though glad news to us. How else in due course do we detach ourselves from Eventually?

'I wear a triple-demon, Perfect One,' boasts our host.

'How so?'

<<<LET US EXPLAIN.>>>

The Mage quivers at the impact of Sweets's communication.

'You succumb to a mindwarp hallucination,' Effulgence says hastily. 'I have been plagued. Now you. Pay no heed.'

<<<UNTRUE!>>>

'My demons do talk to me, Perfect. Effulgence is banal.'

<<<WE WISH,>>> Sweets informs the Mage, <<<TO STUDY YOUR ART OF DREAMS—>>>

'Aaaaaaaaaaaah.'

A mage displays more imagination than an arbiter. Beyond soon concedes that we must indeed be what we say we are, and its view of the universe is – shall we say? – expanded.

Ancestor worship isn't exactly the Hydran bag, but our busy, loquacious presence begs a few questions which our mage must mull over. Do any Hydran demons survive in metaspacetime from the earliest days of nano research when Serpent pioneers flamed on and flared out, showing the Hydran boffins how to avoid said outcome as well as how to craft suitable snuffer-nanos for crop-spraying on to target worlds?

Do all other Hydran and all other dead survive in comatose storage below the excitability level that liberates demonpower? Does use as a demon really empty a dead soul – or simply depress it below that trigger level?

And from the dead of which other alien species – far-distant nano-users, likewise? – did the Serpents hijack their original squad of usable demons before guilefully developing the art of making their own with a tropism towards serving Serpents?

On the whole the Hydran theory of nanometapsychotechnology defeats even our eloquent tee-tee talent; and may even be irrelevant, given the complete absence of consultation with the dumbo dead. (Not so dumbo from now on, if we play our cards vigorously.)

As so often in life – even more in death – more questions are raised than are answered. This, it seems, has always been the nature of the universe. Correspondingly so, of metaspacetime!

Thanks to Sweets, bless his long-rotted heart (or equivalent slime-pumping organ), the art of dream materialization as theorized by Beyond is more of a cinch. For Sweets has crawled into empty shells to conjure up scenes from the vibration records of the dead . . .

Being an apostate and a bit of a hell-stirrer, Beyond is outspoken with us. It has gained much food for thought in return. Its oneiromanifestationalism could only have worked from within metaspacetime, not in truespace, hence the maelstrom its efforts produced, so annoying to the Hard-Minds.

When a Hydran habitat-ship heaves in sight overhead only a day or so later, shedding levvies like leaves – didn't take the arbiters *too* long to put two and two together, in their case to make eighteen – Beyond obligingly lunges for a disassembler hypo and stabs Eventually with it. That definitely has to be accounted a liberating act.

•

<<<Though equally the Serpent establishment won't now credit the truth about us. On the other tentacle, they might have decided to dump our host in a dungeon for the rest of its days, with us still aboard . . . Poor Eventually, left to tender mercies.>>>

<<Gleaming could always jump down the crater, I suppose. Even if there's no hot lava at the bottom, that's still quite a tumble.>>

<<Serpents are tougher than snails, Kath.>>

<<Sounds like a new version of the stone-scissors-paper game. Serpents crush snails. Snails coil round humans.>>

However, we have no need of such games to while away this particular sojourn in limbo . . .

<<Shall we waken more of the dead?>> I ask. <<Shall we try for . . .?>> I can't think *who*! Mickey Wright, Sheila Shwartz, Dan Shannon? Jorgensen the melancholy Dane? Maybe death will have loosened their laces, let the butterflies they must once have been – say at the age of seven – open their wings once more.

<<If you're giving a dinner party, you set the table first.>>

<<I never knew you gave dinner parties.>>

<<Mrs Senator Dwyer did.>>

Personally I'd prefer to invite dead snails. But yes, we'll need to give a dinner party pretty soon, with a gigantic guest list: including everyone human – and alien – who's adrift in limbo. With guests inviting guest, geometrically, in Sweets's own sweet way.

Meanwhile, how about the place settings? In other words the setting of the party in *some* place as opposed to no place at all . . .! Kath's right. I'm prevaricating, apprehensive in case we fail.

<<God forgot something in His grand design, eh Paul?>>

<<Curious oversight: forgetting to build a heaven.>>

<<Wasn't part of the plan.>>

<<So sucks to the plan.>>

<<<Oneiromanifestationalism,>>> Sweets reminds us. <<<Let's remember how it was, once upon a time, when we believed that our juicy desires were sovereign, before reality hardened its shell around us. We're floating in the desire-to-be, in the universal sump where what-has-been drains to. Let's tune the dark fields of force we're drifting in. Let's dream-think.>>>

Literally, a field manifests itself. A little field of lush grass, buttercups, poppies, forget-me-nots. It swells, encompassing me. It's a meadow now. I'm standing knee-deep. In the shade of nearby trees a slim, freckled, snub-nosed woman waits, strands of ginger hair straying from under a wide-brimmed straw hat. She beckons.

<<I'm here,>> Kath whispers.

'I'm here,' she calls in echo.

Fetid vapours drift from where the little woodland segues steeply into swamp, Sweets's idea of paradise. More is springing up all the time around us. Landscapes ripple into existence at crazy angles to one another. Tall buildings loom, a slice of city. Saguaro cacti occupy a patch of desert sand. Redwoods rise. We've seeded the saturated solution; now it's crystallizing out. Seashore is canted against a ranch house among empty paddocks. We're in the cell of a honeycomb, each facet a different scene, each angling eye-bendingly into another.

'It's chaos, Kath!'

The sun shines, and the moon. Rain falls, and snow. Mists drift. A dune shivers, and up there a woman in a swimsuit digs herself out from the sand, stands up. From behind a redwood stumbles a jogger in a tracksuit. Whether we mindblast a summons or not, it's happening. The dead are resurrecting, each in a dreamscape. Heaven's a honeycomb, and each face of each multifaced cell leads to another to another, all jumbled, each surface owning its own dream-gravity.

As dead aliens awake, so patches of alien territory will intrude, perhaps poisonous, perilous, those alien bits serving as hell to us while our own patches of heaven will to them be hell in turn . . .

Metaspacetime's going to be a confusingly busy place.

The tug of a different summons reminds me of the realtime universe.

'Do we take the call?'

'Risk running our batteries down?'

'Or are we recharging them here all the time? Can we possibly go for partnership with living nanowearers?'

'We don't know that yet, do we?'

I walk closer to Kath awaiting me under a chestnut tree (though she is with me already in my mind). A slithery nudge: for Sweets too is present mentally.

So at last Kath and I come together in the dream-flesh. For only the second time our lips meet solidly. Or so, at least, it seems.

Long kiss; been a long time a-waiting.

I'm recalling the chaos on Earth . . . Soon there'll be upsets in Serpent-space, too. As to metaspacetime, if there's a plan to the cosmos, it just went wildly askew. Will we presently hear the grumble of a discontented god, the angry blather of a bee-keeper whose hive has just rebelled, berserked? Started eating all the honey stored up for the wintertime after creation closes down?

Well, sucks to that.

<<<Sucks.>>>

'Let's go into the woods, hmm, lover?' Kath invites. 'Just for a while.'